EDEN
INTERRUPTED

EDEN
INTERRUPTED

BY

BEVERLEY HARVEY

Beverley Harvey

First published in Great Britain in 2019 by Urbane Publications Ltd
Suite 3, Brown Europe House, 33/34 Gleaming Wood Drive, Chatham,
Kent ME5 8RZ
Copyright © Beverley Harvey, 2019

A CIP catalogue record for this book is available from
the British Library.

ISBN 978-1-912666-38-6
MOBI 978-1-912666-39-3

Design and Typeset by Julie Martin
Cover by Michelle Morgan

Printed and bound by 4edge UK

urbanepublications.com

SUMMER

CHAPTER 1

The Wildes

Feeling more fifteen than fifty-four, Ben took a last drag of his Marlboro Light before stuffing the tip into Lisa's petunias. She'd go ape if she knew he was smoking again, he thought, hearing the distinctive throb of her car as it pulled onto the drive.

After a quick spritz of breath freshener, Ben went inside, inhaling the smell of freshly ground coffee mixed with the tang of lemon cleaning fluid. He'd joked once that he wouldn't recognise Lisa without a cloth in her hand and was just considering whether being house proud was a good or bad thing when a delighted yap from Nellie confirmed his wife's return.

'I'm back,' Lisa called as the little Chihuahua trotted at her heels.

With her blonde hair slightly mussed and her face glowing from exercise, Ben thought she looked beautiful. He preferred it when she looked a little undone – too much grooming was less of a turn-on.

'Hello Mrs Wilde, you're early.' Ben kissed her, careful not to exhale.

'Yes, well I did my spin class, but Tanya couldn't stay for a coffee afterwards, so here I am. Good session though – I'm knackered. What have you been up to?' Lisa kicked off her shoes.

'Nothing,' Ben answered too quickly.

'I just meant have you had a good morning? Have you heard from anyone?'

It was becoming a loaded question.

Ben shook his head. 'Coffee?' he said, busying himself with the shiny Italian machine that Lisa had installed before they'd met.

He hadn't *heard from anyone* for several months; Greg Lyons, his manager, and the team at Electra, his publisher-cum-record label, had fallen ominously silent. *No Surrender* had gently tumbled down and out of the album charts and the phone had simply stopped ringing. It gave Ben a sickening sense of déjà vu that took him right back to the 90s.

'You look fed up, hon,' Lisa said, wrapping toned arms around him. 'I know you're worried, but something'll turn up soon – I just know it.'

The telephone warbled.

'You see?' she said smiling, 'Bet that's Greg now.'

Ben smiled weakly knowing it couldn't possibly be; all business calls came to his mobile phone.

'Oh, hi Mum.' Lisa put her hand over the mouthpiece. 'It's Mum,' she said unnecessarily.

'You're where? Oh my god! Really? Oh no … what happened? Oh no! Bless you.'

Ben's heart sank; one OMG, two *oh no's* and a blessing did not bode well.

Pacing, with the phone crooked against her shoulder, Lisa listened a while longer. 'Alright, I'm on my way,' she said, before turning to Ben, her blue-green eyes wide.

'Guess what? Rita's fallen off her platforms and she's broken her ankle,' Lisa said. 'Babe, she'll have to stay here for a while – at least until we sort something else out.'

Ben managed to arrange his face into a mask of sympathy but inside he was dismayed. Having Rita in the house would almost certainly burst the post honeymoon love-bubble they'd been floating in.

He raked a hand through long salt and pepper curls and mused how only six weeks earlier they'd said their vows on a windy beach in the Algarve, before partying all night at *Andrea's Bar & Grill* with around thirty close friends and family.

Relieved and happy for her kid sister, Andrea had thrown the lavish party free of charge, saying it was her wedding gift to them; Lisa had been deeply touched.

Then they'd hung around for another ten days, taking a secluded villa in the hills which had its own spa, maid service, and an infinity pool that Ben was only out of when he was either eating, sleeping, or making love to his new wife; frequent occurrences on all counts.

He marvelled at how rarely Lisa knocked him back. To Ben's delight, their love-in continued once they were back in Eden Hill, and with neither of them working much, there was plenty of opportunity.

Now that dynamic looked set to change.

Feeling glum at the prospect, but determined not to sulk, Ben drove them to Maidstone Hospital where they liberated Rita from a waiting area filled with patched-up old ladies.

'Give us a song, Ben, lovely,' a woman called to him as they passed by, pushing Rita's wheelchair and looking for signs to the nearest exit.

A fan! Ben rewarded the septuagenarian with his sexiest grin. 'Not today, gorgeous – on a mission,' he said. 'But I'll sign your magazine if you like.'

The woman clasped her hands and beamed.

It was good to know he could still make someone's day.

•

While Lisa settled Rita in the guest room, with its pretty floral eiderdown, matching drapes and immaculate en-suite, Ben made tea, keen to escape.

He'd always found Rita difficult and harsh – now she was meek with gratitude. But how long would that last? How long did broken ankles take to mend? Falling off her platforms – daft old bird!

Lisa joined Ben in the kitchen. 'Thank you,' she said, putting her arms around him and nuzzling his neck.

'For what?'

'For not making a big deal about Mum staying for a while. I know she's not the easiest, but it'll only be for a week or two, until she gets used to being on crutches.

'Anything for you, Princess,' Ben said.

'Oh, but darling – can you not smoke while she's here, please? It slows the recovery.'

Ben gaped, unsure whether to come clean or deny everything.

'Leese, it's just the occasional … shit! How did you know?'

Lisa laughed and patted Ben's curls.

'Because, my darling, with that mop, no amount of breath freshener can hide the smell. I know you'll stop again when you're ready.'

•

'You are daft, Mum,' Lisa said, refilling Rita's glass with orange squash. 'I don't know why you can't wear comfy shoes like everyone else your age; you're seventy-two next year.'

Rita pursed her lips. 'Precisely. *Seventy*-two, not *ninety*-two! What's wrong with making an effort? Don't you go writing me off just yet, young lady. This,' Rita pointed to her bound ankle, 'is just a setback.'

'Well I'm glad to hear it, Mother. Right, everything is within reach; water jug, wine gums, your magazines, your book and the TV remote. When you need the loo, you'll have to ring this little bell and I'll help you.'

'I can manage,' Rita said.

'Not yet you can't – it's just until you get used to your crutches.'

Lisa went back downstairs where Ben was in the kitchen opening a bottle of Merlot. He poured Lisa a large glass and pushed it towards her.

'I've just phoned for pizzas – let's not cook tonight,' he said.

'Yeah, sod it.' Lisa put the TV on and surfed for a while, stopping at a crime drama that looked familiar.

When the pizzas arrived, Lisa cut several large slices and took a tray upstairs. Rita, who had been talking animatedly on the phone, ended the call abruptly when Lisa entered the room.

'Here you go, Mum. You've got a choice of Hawaiian or green pepper and onion. Who was that?'

'Oh no, I can't eat green pepper; it gives me terrible wind,' Rita said, ignoring Lisa's question. Lisa returned to the kitchen and swapped the offending pizza for the sweeter variety and went back upstairs.

'You got a bottle open?' Rita asked, a note of hope in her voice.

'Yes, but I don't think you should mix red wine with painkillers … that's not a good idea, is it Mum?'

'Oh, all that nonsense about alcohol and medication – a small one won't hurt.'

Lisa jogged downstairs, poured Rita a glass of wine and took it up to her.

'Thank you, love,' Rita said, staring at the television.

Lisa had barely finished eating when the little bell tinkled from above.

'I'll go,' Ben said, getting up and wiping greasy fingers on kitchen paper.

'Bless you, babe. Better not – she probably needs the loo.'

The demands continued until ten o'clock, when Rita announced grandly that she needed her beauty sleep.

After settling her, Lisa collapsed gratefully on the sofa. 'I'm knackered,' she said.

Ben removed her suede pumps and began massaging her feet.

'Mmm, that's lovely. Thank you darling. We'll get into a routine, won't we ... it's only the first night.'

Ben nodded. 'Yeah, of course we will.'

It could have been worse, thought Lisa. At least Rita was accepting of Ben, she'd never knowingly said a kind word to (or about) Justin during all their years of marriage. Even after he'd died, Rita still couldn't find a charitable word for him.

'You had your pick of all the boys, beautiful girl like you ... you get that from me of course ... and you chose a footballer – with a *drink* problem. My god, girl, you've picked some corkers,' Rita was fond of saying.

By contrast, Ben had charmed her. Not that she approved of him being a 'bloody pop-star' as she'd put it, but because he'd had the good sense to flatter her from the outset.

Nevertheless, it would be a strain having a cuckoo in the nest. But options were limited. Andrea was in Portugal with Molly, Rita's only grandchild, and showed no signs of returning. And why would she? The restaurant had started to make money, and had become the go-to haunt of the Algarve sailing set, and things were finally good between Andrea and Molly's dad, Carl. As for Lisa's father – or the "invisible man" as she and Andrea had referred to him when they were teenagers – he'd last been seen living in Cornwall with a woman half his age who bred Yorkshire Terriers and owned a crystal shop. Lisa wouldn't be holding her breath for help from either her sister or her dad any time soon.

She said a silent prayer of thanks for Ben.

'Shall we go up, my darling?' Lisa said. 'I am absolutely shattered.'

For the first time since they'd met, Lisa got into bed beside Ben without brushing her teeth, or changing into a pretty slip, sliding between the sheets in the vest she'd had on all day.

She was asleep in minutes.

CHAPTER 2

The Mortons

When she looked in the mirror, Chloe Morton could see disappointment etched in the bones of her face. No wonder so many women resorted to Botox, she thought, pulling her olive skin taut at the temples and forcing a smile.

The last nine months had weighed heavy with disappointment. Top of her let-down list was the café she'd dreamed of opening for years. Her vision of *Chloe's Coffee* had been that of a bohemian community hub, where people could get their daily caffeine fix with a triple-shot of wit, wisdom and irony on the side; a place where book clubs would mushroom, community debates would evolve, and romances would bloom. And in addition, a great many delicious, organic, locally-sourced cakes would be consumed by artists, writers and musicians – anyone in fact, who fitted Chloe's idea of 'interesting'.

But the reality was that most days, her customers consisted of harassed mothers towing toddlers who would pulverise and scatter Chloe's tray-bakes all over her faux-oak floor boards, pensioners who could make one cup of tea last an hour, teenagers taking refuge from prying parents after school, and office workers, grateful to escape the grind for ten minutes.

At eight A.M. Chloe already felt exhausted.

Donning her apron and twisting up her long ash brown hair, she flipped the *Closed* sign to *Open* and steeled herself for the day ahead.

Usually she had reinforcements in the stunning form of Lillian who helped between nine and four. This morning however, Lillian would be at the dentist until eleven, so she'd be on her own until then; it was less than ideal.

Customers straggled in, two or three at a time, seeking solace from the summer rain in the form of baked goods. Chloe always sold more cake when it rained. Today, she recognised a few faces, noting the usual suspects who came in for pre-work caffeine.

It had taken Chloe a couple of months to realise that good looking, mature, single men were in short supply in Eden Hill. At forty-two, she already felt the odds were stacked against her, despite protestations to the contrary from Bryony and other stalwart friends left behind in South London.

At least Jake had made friends – dozens of them by all accounts. Hundreds even, if Facebook was anything to go by, which Chloe suspected it probably wasn't.

Perhaps that was the problem – too much time spent online in an effort to be popular – and not enough focus on maths, sciences and geography, subjects he'd loved and excelled in at his old school. Chloe consoled herself that at least he was involved in a number of after school clubs, including gymnastics and street dancing, although the jury was out on the latter; it seemed an odd choice for someone so un-streetwise.

She'd pushed hard to get Jake into Kenilworth Grammar and he'd wanted to go. Even William, his flaky father, had managed to instil the value of education in their only son. But now, in his second term at Kenilworth, Jake was screwing up wholesale.

Chloe had tried to explain why fifteen was exactly the wrong age to stop working hard: Jake had listened but, if anything, his grades had been more erratic since her pep-talk.

'You know you can tell me anything, don't you, darling?' Chloe had ventured over shepherd's pie one evening, adding 'about drugs … sex … anything, just shoot.'

'Oh god, Mother – gross!' Jake spluttered, 'Please … don't even …' Then he'd picked up his plate and gone to his room.

Feeling foolish and desperate, Chloe had phoned William, but her call went straight to voicemail. There seemed no point in leaving a message, so she did what she always did in a crisis.

Bryony answered after two rings.

'B, it's me. Can you talk for a bit?' Chloe's voice wavered.

'Hey, what's up? You sound upset. Talk to me.'

'Oh god, sorry ... I know I'm being silly ... are you eating, love?' Chloe asked, feeling guilty that she was about to unload on her best friend – again.

'No ... and it wouldn't matter if I was – how long have we been mates? What's on your mind, honey-bun?'

It was such a relief to talk that Chloe found herself unburdening a ton of angst on her best friend; Jake's falling grades and his hostile attitude at home, the daily grind of her lacklustre coffee shop (she'd laughed at her own pun), and the total absence of any decent adult company.

'Darling, I'm sorry. Look, it'll get easier when you've made friends – it's less than a year since you moved. As for Jake acting up, it's probably for exactly the same reason. He's just missing his pals and overcompensating. Tell you what though; William needn't think he can just bog off with his new girlfriend and leave you to it! You two might be halfway through a divorce, but he needs to know what's going on and take responsibility,' Bryony said crossly.

'To be fair,' Chloe refilled her glass with Sauvignon Blanc and slipped lower down the sofa, 'I don't know if William even realises what's going on with Jake – he never answers his bloody phone.'

'Well how fucking lame is that?' snapped Bryony, 'How dare he? Send him an email – keep it business-like, no whining – suggesting that *he* has Jake for at least a fortnight in the summer holidays.'

Chloe sighed. 'God, B – I'd feel even worse here on my own. A fortnight is bloody ages.'

'A week then ... or three days ... I'm just saying you need a break and William needs to man up and be a proper dad. Okay, lecture over. How's the café doing?'

'It's alright ... just not the way I imagined. It's a hard slog and well, *boring*.'

'Really? It's because you don't know anyone yet – and that'll change. Chloe, you're great with people, warm and kind and ... feisty.' Bryony was pulling out all the stops.

Chloe laughed. 'Bless you, B. I don't feel very feisty at the moment ... just old.'

They'd talked a while longer but the conversation had done little to lift Chloe's mood. Instead it made her want to 'go home', as she still thought of London.

The plain fact was that as a soon-to-be-divorced mother, she could never have afforded to rent a coffee shop in London; and as for buying a decent-sized property for her and Jake, that ship had sailed. So she'd moved 'out' to a new town in the heart of Kent, and at first it had felt pioneering, brave and hopeful, buying a modern four-bedroomed detached house, where she and Jake had their own bathrooms, plenty of storage, and a pretty back garden to dream in.

The unit she'd leased for the coffee shop was a cheerful space; bright and airy, painted in shades of white and cream. It should have been perfect, but then one day Chloe woke up and it felt all wrong.

Whatever had possessed her to move miles from her friends, and a *world* away from her beloved shops, cafés and galleries? Ah, but on the other hand, she was also miles from William and his gormless girlfriend with her big white teeth and the blonde mane she tossed incessantly.

Every cloud thought Chloe bitterly.

•

The following morning, Lillian arrived early in a cloud of copper curls and high spirits.

'Morning! How are you Chloe?' she trilled, turning the music up a notch as she wiggled her narrow hips behind the counter. Chloe had already begun brewing up and dusting cakes and pastries with icing sugar.

'Hi, Lilly – you're incredibly cheerful this morning.'

Lillian beamed.

'Oh, you know, just glad the sun's out. It's my birthday on Sunday and my mum's taking me late night shopping tonight. Ooh, I love a good splurge on clothes – and shoes of course. She's brilliant like that, my mum. Might have a look at handbags as well …'

She continued babbling happily about her potential new wardrobe and the outfits she'd earmarked online.

Perhaps that was the answer; to take Jake clothes shopping. Get him some cool new stuff – trainers and hoodies or whatever he was into these days. It would be a lift for both of them and a real bonding session.

'Can't you just give me the cash,' Jake said, when Chloe mooted the idea that evening.

'Darling, that's not really the point, is it? I thought it would be nice for us to do something together. We can go to Burger Meister afterwards – get some of those curly fries you like,' Chloe said, trying to sound upbeat.

'Whatever.'

The word was a slap in the face. When had her handsome, kind, articulate son started using words like *whatever*?

'Great,' she managed, determined to win him round.

•

The following week, despite his best efforts to affect indifference, Jake cheered up considerably once they hit the vast indoor shopping emporium that was Lakeview, and after netting new jeans and trainers, two T-shirts and a zippered hoodie, Chloe saw a glimpse of the old Jake.

'Mum, can we like, actually *afford* this stuff? I mean,

it's not my birthday and clothes are bloody expensive, aren't they?' he said, earnestly.

'Sweetheart, don't you worry about that. I've set a budget and there's a bit left. Come on, let's eat,' Chloe beamed.

Laden with carrier bags, and lured by the smell of fast food, they walked in the direction of the restaurant zone which was buzzing with hungry, shopped-out families.

Chloe tucked her arm into her son's and snuck a sideways look at him. At five feet nine, he was already two inches taller than her, and she loved that except for Jake's brown-eyed gaze – which was unmistakably his father's – it was her DNA that shone out of his lean frame and olive skin.

A queue snaked outside Burger Meister; as they approached Jake pulled his arm away and hissed that he didn't fancy burgers after all.

'Really? I've been fantasising about a lovely organic cheeseburger for the last hour. What would you like? They've got plenty of other–'

'Mum! Can we just go, now – please?' Jake said, clearly agitated.

'Alright darling – what's the rush?'

And then Chloe spotted her; a beautiful doe-eyed girl, with coltish limbs and a tangle of brunette hair almost to her tiny waist. Cool and edgy in a charcoal T-shirt and ripped jeans, she looked like a teen-model in a magazine. Buttressed by two similarly dressed young women, the girl held up her slender hands and made a heart with her thumbs and index fingers – right in Jake's direction.

'Oh Christ!' Jake yelped, before stalking off, leaving Chloe to scuttle after him.

Later, seated in a nearby tapas restaurant, Chloe waited until several terracotta bowls of food had arrived before digging for information.

'I've no idea who she is,' Jake said, attacking cheese croquettes and chorizo.

'Well she seemed to know you – she made you a heart sign! She's very beautiful Jakey. Does she go to your school?'

'Er … yeah, I think so, but she's not in my class. Mum, can we change the subject?'

'Ah, so you *do* know her then.'

'Oh god, Mum. Why do you have to be so bloody painful?' Jake said.

Chloe smiled. 'It's my job.

CHAPTER 3

The Bevans

Mindful of his reddening torso, Martin reached for the sun cream and tried not to stare at the young woman parading semi-naked before him. She couldn't be English, he decided – not with such a flawless tan and that abundant nut-brown mane. He wondered if she had matching collars and cuffs. Then again, none of them did these days; it was all Brazilians and Hollywoods – his daughter Hayley had regaled him with the ways of modern pubic styling.

'They'd only got Fanta or lemonade,' Jan said, as she sank down on the lounger beside him.

'I'll have either, my love,' Martin said holding out his right hand. It was thirsty work, sunbathing.

'You want to be careful,' Martin said, noticing the rosy hue on his wife's shoulders and passing her the sticky plastic tube. 'Put plenty of this on … better still, you should move into the shade.'

'What, so you can get a better view?' Jan said, indicating the bikini-clad girl, with a roll of her blue eyes.

'I hadn't noticed,' Martin lied, before turning onto his stomach. 'I just meant be careful – English roses can soon wither under a Spanish sun.'

'Ooh, get you. That was poetic, Mart,' Jan said, adding, 'Is she getting in that pool, or what?'

Then to Martin's amazement, Jan got up, flatfooted past the hesitant young women and jumped into the pool with a shriek and an extravagant splash.

'D'you mind?' the woman scowled and blotted her face with a towel.

Martin grinned. English then, he thought, noting her estuary dialect. He watched Jan who'd stopped spluttering and was pulling long strokes in the rippling water.

It was good to see her so relaxed, although she'd taken some convincing.

'But what if my customers desert me?' she'd said.

Martin had been quick to reassure her. 'Love, even dog walkers go on holiday – you're entitled to a life, you know.'

He'd not been without reservations himself. Martin had never closed the shop for a whole week before. Not that he provided an emergency or life-enhancing service; people could always wait a week or two for new carpets and flooring.

Jan had stopped swimming and was treading water. With her light brown hair slicked back she looked like a bright-eyed pink seal.

'Come on, Mart!' she beckoned, but Martin shook his head and held up his paperback – a murder mystery he could have sworn he'd read before but couldn't remember the ending.

•

'Give us a hand with this zip, Mart,' Jan said, stepping into high-heeled sandals. 'Will I do?'

'You look lovely,' Martin answered, noting how her face glowed from sunshine and her mascaraed eyes shone.

'You don't look so bad yourself,' Jan beamed, adding, 'for an old git!'

'Ooh, you cheeky mare!' Martin mimed smacking her behind, then caught himself. 'I love you, you know, Mrs Bevan,' he said, kissing Jan on her sunburned cheek.

'Soppy sod,' Jan said, taking Martin's arm as they walked to the lift.

The restaurant was heaving. Dozens of British, German and Dutch holidaymakers vied for tables with a view of the pool, while others were content to sit at the bar enjoying pre-dinner drinks.

Jan surveyed the chaos, 'Looks like we've all come down at once.'

Martin nodded. 'We could get a taxi into the square and eat with the locals,' he suggested.

'Ooh no, Mart – I wouldn't know what to order. Anyway, there's a show later; an Abba tribute band, followed by a proper flamenco duo,' Jan said.

Hearing this, a man in his sixties with a creosote tan nudged Jan so hard that she wobbled on her heels. 'That's tomorrow, love,' he said.

'Careful!' Martin said, annoyed.

'Sorry darlin'. Don't know me own strength!' the man rasped. 'Nah, tonight's karaoke … and I'm going on as Tom Jones.'

Jan's face fell.

'Come on,' Martin said, taking Jan's arm, 'let's take a cab into town.'

Twenty minutes later, upon the taxi driver's recommendation that his brother worked in the best restaurant in the region, they were speeding round hairpin bends bound for *La Finca*.

'Well, that's more like it!' Martin said, impressed by the rustic white-washed villa, lit by dozens of Moorish lamps and candles. Open floor-to-ceiling shutters revealed a stunning view of the bay below, inky in the fading light. Gentle laughter bubbled from a few tables of exquisitely dressed diners and Martin saw a different island from the one he and Jan had inhabited all week.

'Can we afford this, Martin?' Jan said, peering round, 'This holiday has already cost us a fortune.'

'You worry too much, my love.' Martin patted Jan's arm. 'It's high time we started enjoying life and treating ourselves more often.' He lowered his voice: 'Love, I hardly recognise us compared to two years ago, when you were housebound with depression, and I was … well, I was a fool – having daft ideas … anyway, the point is we're on the up. Hayley seems settled now, the shop's doing well, and – hats off to you, Jan – you've built a good little business out of dog-walking. What are you up to now? Eight regulars?'

Jan puffed out her lips. 'More like a dozen. I don't know how I'll cope if I get any more, although they're not all every day, thank goodness.'

A raven-haired waiter set down two large gin and tonics before Martin decisively ordered the seafood salad for both of them.

'I'm proud of you, my love – incredible achievement,' he said, 'but maybe it's time to take someone on … you're not getting any younger.'

'Oh, charming!' Jan said, 'although you're right of course. I'm knackered some days and before we know it, we'll be sixty.'

'So get some help. There must be plenty of youngsters in Crabton and Eden Hill who'd like a bit of pocket money.'

'It's not that easy, Martin,' Jan said, mildly affronted. 'There's a lot responsibility. It's not just about looking after other people's dogs … there are keys … and blummin' alarm codes to consider; that side of things can be a nightmare.'

Saved by the arrival of a heaped seafood platter, Martin let the subject drop.

Jan's eyes widened. 'Oh, Mart – we'll never eat all this.'

'Of course we will – half of it's shell,' he said,

snapping the head off a king prawn and popping it into his mouth.

•

'I've loved all this, but I'm not sorry to be going home,' Jan said as they boarded the airport shuttle bus two days later. 'This heat gets on your wick after a while.'

Martin agreed. 'I could do with a proper cuppa, too. Why they all serve bloody Liptons, I'll never know.'

The flight to Gatwick was uneventful. Subdued by the prospect of returning to work and real life, most passengers read, dozed or listened to music.

Martin's thoughts turned to the shop and the summer sale he'd be gearing up for. He'd knock thirty per cent off carpets, and twenty-five per cent off hard flooring. Laminates were always bestsellers, especially during the summer months, thanks to the house-proud residents of Eden Hill.

Young Trina had been pleased with her pay rise – not to mention a week's paid leave while Martin shut up shop. Despite appearances, with the nose ring and ever-changing hair colour, Trina was a practical soul and the customers loved her. During the last sale, she'd been a real asset, working late regularly and without a word of complaint.

'Well that was painless,' Jan said, as the *Fasten Seatbelts* sign lit up ready for descent.

'Now all we've got to do is remember where we parked the car,' Martin said, rooting in his wallet for the ticket.

•

Just outside Crabton, Martin felt a prickle of unease that he couldn't put his finger on. By the time they drove into the little market town, it had swelled to a wave of apprehension. Something was off, but what?

Jan sniffed the air like a terrier. 'What's that funny smell, Mart?'

Martin's mind spun, his palms becoming damp on the wheel.

He could smell it, too. Chemical, acrid, sour.

The early evening sky was muddied with filthy black plumes and as they rounded into the old high street, they were met by searing blue lights, and a wall of scarlet as fire engines blocked the road, and firefighters swarmed the rapidly blackening building.

'My shop!' Martin tried to cry out, but the words died in his throat and no sound came.

'Oh my god, no!' Jan shrieked, her hands flying to her open mouth.

Then Martin was out of the car, stumbling towards the scene of carnage. Frozen by shock, Jan watched at a distance, her heart breaking from the expression on Martin's face; it was a look she would never forget.

CHAPTER 4

The Bradshaws

With a jolt Rosemary realised that an hour had slipped by and she was running late to collect Iris from school. Grabbing her bag and car keys she started up the Volvo which smelt faintly of rotting apples due to the browning core that her daughter had pushed into a side-pocket that morning.

Driving out of Eden Hill and joining the bypass, Rosemary was irritated to find herself in the wake of a large farm truck that was belching out fumes and bouncing along at barely twenty miles an hour.

'Come on!' Rosemary drummed the wheel with frustration. She hated to be late for Iris. Two weeks earlier, she'd arrived at the school gates twenty minutes late, to find her daughter clinging to Miss Devonshire's hand, tearstained and breathless. It had taken chocolate milk and three back-to-back princess cartoons to sooth her. Now Rosemary was in danger of creating another meltdown.

Hazard lights flashing after parking in someone's private space, Rosemary's statuesque form strode through the school gates, bleating apologies.

'There's Mummy,' said Iris's teacher, relief evident on her face.

'I thought you weren't coming,' hiccupped Iris, her

wide brown eyes blurred by tears that spilled down golden cheeks.

'Silly! As if that would ever happen. Mummy will *always* come, sweetpea.'

Not for the first time, Rosemary wondered at the wisdom of privately educating her daughter outside of Eden Hill – particularly when the local primary schools were so well regarded, not to mention walkable.

But Nigel had been adamant. 'What can be more important than giving our daughter the best start in life? Private education is a privilege – and for as long as we can afford it, there's no question in my mind that Iris should go to South View.'

Even at six years old, Iris showed considerable academic promise, but it broke her parents' hearts that she seemed unable to make lasting friendships.

'It's hard for her to fit in,' reasoned Rosemary over dinner one evening. 'We're still relatively new here, and Iris is the only child in her class with a black mum and a white dad. Can you imagine what that's like for her? Kids just want to be like everyone else at her age.'

Nigel sighed and put his knife and fork together.

'If we take Iris out of South View, she'll be new all over again – how does that help?'

'Yes, but at least Eden Hill is more ethnically diverse … I mean, not compared to where we used to live in South London, but short of moving back there …' Rosemary trailed off, tired of repeating herself.

What was the use? Nigel had always been the breadwinner and as such, the decision-maker. Sometimes Rosemary felt swept along, like a twig in a stream.

'Let's try and get to bed early,' she said, beginning to clear the table. 'You've got a long drive tomorrow, and I'll be with Joyce in the morning.'

Wednesdays filled Rosemary with utter dread. No sooner had she left Iris at the school gates, she would turn the car around and drive for forty-five minutes in the opposite direction, to spend an hour or so with a woman who barely knew she was there. Well, better that than being mistaken for Joyce's cheerful Zimbabwean nurse, Thelma, which had happened a fortnight earlier. Rosemary had spent the first fifteen minutes of her visit explaining why she wouldn't be giving Joyce an enema.

There seemed little chance of Nigel visiting his mother. Six months had passed since he'd last been to the care home.

'It's easier for her to talk to a woman,' he'd said when Rosemary challenged him.

'Nigel, that's not true. She has dementia; you're her son – if *anyone* can get through to her, it's you. Some weeks, Mum doesn't know who I am.'

Later, as Rosemary performed her bedtime ritual

of applying scented creams to her hands and face, she contemplated how it had come to this.

Some days she was so tired she could weep. The house, which Nigel had chosen, was far bigger than they needed and just cleaning it sapped her energy. Then there was the laundry, the cooking, the food shopping, the school run – as well as attending events and meetings at South View – driving Iris to her Saturday morning dance club, *and* the weekly visits to her mother-in-law at Glen Heights. No wonder she was exhausted.

Most of her neighbours used local cleaning firms; she'd see the little squadron of liveried vans parked within the gates of Regents Square on Thursdays and Fridays, so that everything sparkled for the weekend. It was hard to imagine the couple next door, Ben and Lisa, expending energy on cleaning four lavatories, or endlessly washing floors and windows.

Seeing Lisa move lightly between house and car, often toting her Chihuahua – and always immaculate – made Rosemary feel old, although she guessed Lisa was probably a few years her senior. Most mornings, as Rosemary cajoled Iris into the car, Lisa would emerge dressed for the gym, blonde hair in a ponytail. The two women would wave from their respective driveways and call out a cheerful greeting.

Sometimes Ben would follow Lisa out of the house, and they'd share a lingering kiss before she got into her convertible. Such displays of affection between Rosemary and Nigel were unthinkable – which was a relief. She had quite enough on her plate without an amorous husband to contend with.

•

'Is that son of mine ever coming back?' Joyce said in a rare moment of lucidity.

'Of course, Mum. He's away for work … in Huddersfield. He seems to be up there more and more these days. Anyway, how are you feeling today? What have you been up to?'

'Oh, I've been out dancing most days – haven't you heard?'

Rosemary patted the old woman's hand. 'Good to see you joking and smiling for a change, Mum.'

'What – you calling me a liar? I'm in *The Final* – against that bloomin' Susanna Reid, with her daft face-pulling and all that hair.'

Rosemary supressed a smile; the fog had returned. On another occasion Joyce had been convinced that a fellow resident, Mr Baldini – eighty-six years old and hard of hearing – had stolen her watch. She'd been most vociferous about calling the police, until her gold-plated Rotary had turned up inside a tin of the Highland Shortbread she was partial to.

'Mum, I think you're getting mixed up again – with

Strictly Come Dancing, on the television,' Rosemary said.

'You'd be good at that,' Joyce continued, taking no notice. 'You've got natural rhythm – what with you being black. Not like my Nigel; two left feet.'

Rosemary sighed. 'I'll get us both some tea, shall I Mum?' she said patiently.

•

The Bertram Hotel had seen better days. Even the manager knew it – which was why he felt able to turn a blind eye to the occasional escort who teetered in on a weekday evening. Lone business men were the Bertram's bread and butter. Without them the hotel would almost certainly have closed down, leaving Jacob and his staff of twenty-two locals unemployed.

Nigel Bradshaw had his own reasons for frequenting The Bertram. It was exactly one hour from the Huddersfield head office – making it just the wrong side of convenient for meetings conducted over drinks with subordinates trying to suck up, or other senior managers wanting to pick his brain. It was also the only independent hotel in the area, which afforded it a more homely feel than the myriad corporates nearby; and with this homespun shabbiness, came a degree of discretion which had proved useful.

Sticky and drowsy, Nigel yawned. He felt as though he'd been driving all day. The sheer volume of traffic had meant cruising at around sixty miles an hour for great swathes of the M1, adding a good hour to his journey. Passing a sign for Junction 32, Nigel sighed with relief; he could almost taste the gin and tonic he'd be ordering from Marion or Julie in the guests' bar within the next fifteen minutes.

It was his cue to call home.

'Rose, it's me. How are my girls?' he shouted into the hands-free system that glowed from the dash.

'We're okay, love.' Rosemary sounded tired.

'How was Mum today?' Nigel felt his features tense into a grimace ... god, he felt guilty about Joyce; he felt guilty about a lot of things.

'Oh, you know ... it's funny ... some weeks she's sleepy and doesn't say much, but today she was chatty. She told me she's in the Strictly Come Dancing final.' Rosemary's warm, low laughter filled the car. 'Hey, Iris came top in a spelling test today *and* she's been invited to a classmate's for tea next week.'

'Fantastic! She's a clever girl – like her mum. Love, I've got to go. I'm just stopping for petrol, then I've got another hour's drive, and tonight will be a directors' dinner. Bloody boring if you ask me, but it's a warm up for tomorrow, so I need to be there. I won't get a chance to call later, but I'll ring you tomorrow when I'm on my way home. Kiss Iris for me. Bye.'

Nigel hung up, manoeuvring smoothly into the Bertram Hotel's car park.

CHAPTER 5

The Mortons

With a stomach full of tapas and cola, Jake lay on his bed, his cheeks burning as he reflected on the evening's events. Picking up his mobile, he swiped photos of Amber in a pale pink bra. Not that he needed his phone to picture Amber in her underwear; every freckle was etched on his memory. Anyway, he'd deleted most of them – there was always the possibility of private stuff like that getting into the wrong hands; like his Mum's.

Jesus, she went on at him. It wasn't her fault – she was his mother after all – and he got that. But it was so bloody embarrassing; the way she always wanted to *talk* about everything. Even if his dad hadn't been so crap, and shacked up with bloody Jodie, Jake wouldn't have talked to *him* either. It was private stuff – feelings that made him feel hungry and sick and alive.

It was happening again. Every time he thought about Amber, he got hard – which felt fantastic and terrible at the same time, especially with his mum downstairs. She'd never get off his case now – not after the Burger Meister queue horror.

What had Amber been *thinking*? She was beautiful and clever too, consistently coming top in maths and chemistry. But honestly, where was her common sense? Attracting his mum's attention like that! Fuck. They'd made a pact to keep things secret.

Obviously, if he'd known she'd be there with her sister Jade, and Megan from school, he'd have swerved Burger Meister by a million miles. She'd never mentioned she was going, but to be fair, neither had he. Far too embarrassing to fess up to clothes shopping with his mum – *and* she'd been hanging onto his arm like he was eight years old when Amber clocked them arriving at the restaurant together. Could anything *be* more cringe-worthy than that?

He'd probably never get to have sex with Amber now. But please god, as long as he could keep looking at her. Oh god – it was happening again. Maybe it was time to take a shower, at least then he could lock the bathroom door and deal with his discomfort.

The one good thing about living in this dead zone dump (apart from Amber) was that he had his own space; he had his own bathroom, and his bedroom was bigger than in London, with tons of cupboards for all his stuff, and space for both his guitars. In London he'd had lessons every Saturday morning with Mr Loveday – who was a weird fucker, with stale smelling ash-coloured hair down to his man-boobs. But when he played, it was awesome. Now he relied on YouTube for tuition, which just wasn't the same.

Jake's mobile shivered on the night-stand.

'Your mum looks nice,' said Amber's text 'you could have introd us?!'

The phone buzzed a second time. A selfie emerged of Amber, hair in a ponytail, wearing a blue and white gingham bra. Jake wondered what she had on the bottom half. Oh god, that really was too much to bear.

'Mum, I'm taking a shower before bed,' he called over the banisters.

•

At one o'clock, Jake looked for Amber in the lunch queue. He couldn't see her, and it wasn't cool to go staring around the cafeteria, like you were so obviously looking for someone. So after bagging a pretty stingy portion of lasagne, he sat down with Matt and Dylan, and kept his eyes on his plate, still cringing inside from the heart experience the night before.

Supposing Amber was in love with him? He didn't love *her* … at least, he didn't think he did. But how would he know? He wanted to kiss and touch her all the time – and she was the only girl who didn't annoy him. Most girls had awful voices and talked utter bollocks, but Amber was different. She spoke softly and knew about cool stuff – like how they killed animals for food, because her Dad was a farmer – she'd helped lambs to be born when she was little. Jake liked that she didn't make a fuss about things when there was no need. About some tiny random spider, for instance – she could even pick them up, he'd seen her do it once. He supposed it was because Amber didn't have a mum. She'd been ill and died years ago, so nothing would be a big deal after that.

The thing was, she looked like a model but she was cool and not at all vain. By contrast, Jake couldn't imagine spending more than ten minutes with her best friend, Megan, without wanting to yell at her. Megan was a shrieker, no doubt about it.

Perhaps he *did* love Amber. He looked across at Matt and Dylan, who were arguing about which was healthier; green or white pasta (idiots – green, obvs!). There was no way he'd talk to either of them about Amber. Not for the first time, Jake wished he was back in South London with his old buddies, where he'd been able to tell Jeremy and Ryan anything. Once, they'd even compared (his cheeks flushed at the memory). Oh, never mind – in hindsight maybe that hadn't been such a great idea.

Jake felt a hand on the back of his neck and ducked.

'S'okay – only me!' Amber was standing behind him, smiling into his eyes; beside her, Megan grinned gormlessly.

Jake glanced at Dylan, then at Matt; both were staring in awe, quite possibly because the girls had even acknowledged him.

'Follow me,' Amber mouthed before gliding off in step with her friend.

'I need the bog,' Jake said, getting up with as much nonchalance as he could muster.

As usual, there was much milling around by the toilets where Amber was leaning against the wall, checking her phone.

'Hey. Alright Jakey?' she beamed. 'Can we walk home together?

'Er … yeah, cool,' Jake said, feeling anything but.

It was Friday; they didn't normally see each other on Fridays. So far, their contact had been limited to gymnastics on Monday evenings (which is where they'd met properly); walking home together afterwards and sitting on Jake's blazer, in one of her Dad's orchards talking and kissing (although obvs that would have to stop in the winter); then on Wednesdays, they *pretended* to go to Street Dancing, and instead went for coffee in Crabton, making their flat whites last an hour or so.

'But your Mum owns the coffee-bar in Eden Hill. We should go there. It'd be cheaper … free even,' Amber had said the last time.

'Mum just rents it. Yeah, cheaper maybe – but you don't know what she's like. Since she split up with my dad, everything is about me and she'd want to know all about you … about us. What we talk about, if we've … you know – and it's none of her business, is it?'

'Right. Are you ashamed of me, Jakey?' Amber's

eyebrows knitted above the bridge of her delicate nose.

'God, no! You're like, too gorgeous for words ... I don't even know what you see in me.'

Then under the table, she'd run her hand up his thigh, briefly grazing his crotch, and he'd held it together pretty well considering he felt as though his school trousers could detonate at any moment.

She was looking at him expectantly now.

'Yes, okay. I'll meet you by the small gate at chucking out time,' he said, feeling a shudder of excitement. Third time this week; maybe it *was* love.

CHAPTER 6

The Wildes

'My mother is up to something,' Lisa said, as she and Ben prepared dinner together in the shaker style kitchen where they'd spent most of their evenings since Rita's arrival.

Ben looked bemused: 'How do you work that one out? There's not much she can do with a broken ankle, babe.'

'Pfff, don't you believe it!' Lisa said. 'She chats away on that mobile of hers and I've no idea who she's talking to. Three times I've walked in on her and she ends the conversation – just like that,' Lisa snapped her fingers. 'It's not as though she has many friends.'

'Well perhaps she's ringing your sister,' Ben offered.

Lisa shook her head, 'Andrea's not really into cosy chats – she's got a family and a restaurant to run.'

'When Rita's on the phone, is the telly on?'

'Sometimes, why?'

'Ah, that's it then,' Ben said, sounding pleased with his detective work. 'She's on the bloody shopping channel – buying all that old lady shit … you know, scarves and handbags and so on.'

Lisa laughed. 'Where is it then? All that 'old lady shit'? Nothing's been delivered, has it? She's been here two weeks.'

'Don't remind me,' Ben rolled his eyes 'Leese, babe – I know she's your mum and everything, but I want you all to myself.' He kissed Lisa and pulled her to him, grabbing her pert behind and growling softly.

'Sshh, don't! Mum might hear. Look, the doctor said it'll be at least another fortnight before she's strong enough to use crutches properly. Short of putting her in a nursing home, what else can I do?'

Ben smiled wickedly, 'Now there's an idea,' he said.

•

The following morning from the study window, Lisa watched Rosemary shepherd Iris into the Volvo. As if aware of being watched, Rosemary looked up and waved. Lisa waved back, embarrassed to have been caught.

Lisa was fascinated by the mismatch between her neighbours. Rosemary was a fine-looking woman; long-legged and athletically built, she possessed a ready smile that reached almond eyes usually unadorned by make-up. Her wardrobe was that of a harassed mother – dark colours chosen to hide spills and jeans and loafers for ease of movement.

By contrast, Nigel, who had a soft, putty-coloured face and thinning sandy hair, was given to wearing well-cut suits and the occasional vibrant tie. Even at weekends he favoured chinos and polo tops over jeans and sweats. He carried himself with a whiff of arrogance that neither Ben nor Lisa had warmed to.

'They never go out together – have you noticed?' Lisa said to Ben one Saturday morning when Rosemary and Iris had left home in one car and Nigel had pulled away in the other. 'I don't think I've ever seen them touching – not so much as a peck on the cheek. Don't you think that's sad?' Lisa said.

'Not really. For all we know they might be hot and heavy behind closed doors. Like us,' Ben grinned.

'Yeah, maybe. They just strike me as an odd couple. She seems lovely … smiley and sweet … but he's so stiff and boring! He must be at least ten years older than her, too.'

Ben harrumphed: 'Like us then. Leese, I don't think age has got anything to do with it. You can be a boring git at any age!'

Lisa giggled. 'Perhaps we should make more of an effort,' she said, 'try and get to know them a bit.'

Ben nodded. 'Alright. Good idea. Invite them round for dinner and we'll loosen 'em up with a few sherbets and a bit of the old Wilde charm.'

So Lisa had waited until Rosemary's car reappeared before knocking on her door.

'Yes? Oh, it's you, Lisa – I thought it was somebody selling something … how are you?'

'I'm well, thanks – and I wanted to ask you

something. Would you and your husband be free for dinner at ours one Saturday in August?'

Rosemary laughed softly. 'We're free *most* Saturday evenings – the joy of being parents. That's very kind of you, we'd love that.'

'Oh, and bring Iris, of course,' Lisa added hurriedly.

'Thanks, but I'll try and get a babysitter – more relaxing for all of us. It's really nice of you to ask, Lisa – thank you. What shall I bring?'

They'd made a date, before Lisa had factored in Rita's presence.

'Oh no, what an idiot! I wasn't thinking,' she complained to Ben. 'What about Mum? I can't cancel them now, I've only just fixed it up.'

'Rita will just have to be on best behaviour. I'm sure she can be civil for one night. Either that or we can lock her up and slide a bowl of gruel under her door.'

To Lisa's surprise, when she mentioned having dinner with the Bradshaws, Rita glowed with approval.

'So important to get on with your neighbours,' she said, adding, 'I'd love to meet them – they look like such an *interesting* family. Can I invite a friend though, love? What with me being the only gooseberry.'

'Yes, of course, Mum. Who do you want to ask?'

But Rita had changed the subject, before turning her attention back to her favourite TV show.

•

As much as Ben enjoyed pottering around and playing house with Lisa, it irked him that his music career appeared to have stalled. Again. Twelve months earlier *No Surrender* had stubbornly bubbled around the bottom of the top fifty album chart, its persistence buoyed up by not one, but two ad campaigns: First *Benton's* ('the nation's go-to store for food and frillies' as he liked to describe it) had used a dance remix of his 90s hit, Seagull – and that had seemed fluke enough. But then the following year, he was blown away after being commissioned to write the soundtrack for a three-ad campaign for *Helium*, an energy drink from the US that had arrived in a whirlwind of PR and hyperbole.

The fact that he'd begun dating Lisa, the former wife of deceased footballing ace Justin Dixon, had added another layer of intrigue, and the gossip mags had come knocking. For the second time in his career, Ben Wilde had become a media darling.

Now, it felt as though his star was fading faster than daylight in December. Swallowing his pride, he'd done a ring-around of his record company, his manager and his agent; the consensus was that the summer months were dead, but that during September, 'things were bound to pick up'.

'Maybe this is it, Leese,' Ben said, leaning on the breakfast bar while Lisa polished her beloved Italian coffee machine, still wearing her gym gear. 'Perhaps

I'm done with all that … I'll be fifty-five next year. Fuck! I'll be part of the Saga generation. Not very rock n roll, is it?'

'Try telling Mick Jagger that … or Iggy Pop. Babe, you're still hot. Your voice is amazing … and as I'm always telling you, you look better with age. You're slimmer and fitter now than when I met you.'

Ben patted his flat stomach. 'I've got you to thank for that, forcing me to the gym regularly and all that bloody rabbit food we eat. Yeah, maybe there's life in the old dog yet.'

Lisa beamed. 'That's the spirit – you shouldn't be moping around here, hon. You need to do what you do best. Get back in the studio with the boys and work your magic.'

Ben looked resigned. 'Studio time costs money, Leese.'

'I know, but what's that saying … speculate to accumulate? It's not as if we're on our uppers, is it? You need to get writing again; it's what you're about … what makes you tick. Ben, you owe it to your fans, they'll be wondering where you are.'

Ben laughed. 'Yeah, all five of 'em. Maybe you're right, babe – I'll give Rick and Steve a call later, see what they're up to.'

Ben grimaced as a toilet flushed overhead. 'Hello – the Kraken awakes. You'd better take your mum her morning arsenic. God, Leese. I can't wait to have you all to myself again.'

'Patience, my love. It'll only be for a few more weeks – and I promise to make it up to you,' Lisa said, grazing a manicured hand over Ben's crotch.

CHAPTER 7

The Bevans

According to the Fire Investigation Unit a single smouldering cigarette, dropped in a wheelie bin at the back of Bevan's Flooring, was the probable cause of the fire.

Martin had never smoked a cigarette in his life.

'Not only is it a filthy and expensive habit, but smoking kills! Well, no daughter of mine …' He'd thrown the book at Hayley when he'd caught her smoking in a neighbour's ginnel, two days after her fifteenth birthday. Hayley hadn't pursued a smoking career after that – not because her parents were livid, but because it hurt her throat and made her feel spinney and sick.

Trina on the other hand was a habitual smoker, routinely puffing on up to twenty a day. She wept when Martin telephoned to break the news.

'Oh god, Martin, I can't believe it … that's awful! Your lovely shop … all those years. What are you going to do? What am *I* going to do? That's me out of a job, isn't it?' she'd wailed, as the penny dropped that she was now unemployed.

'I don't know Trina, love. I've got some serious thinking to do. Thank goodness for insurance.'

It was Saturday morning when Martin had gone

round to his young employee's parents' cottage; he needed Trina to look him in the eyes.

After buying two large cappuccinos and finding a table at the back of the café on Crabton High Street, Martin put the typed report on the table between them.

'You okay, boss? Trina pointed to the document: 'What's that?'

'It's a report, Trina … about how the fire started. The Investigations Unit says it was due to a discarded cigarette.'

Trina's gaze was unflinching as he continued. 'And I have to ask, Trina – do you know anything about this?'

Trina was indignant. 'No way! For one thing, I'm dead careful about things like that, and for another, I was nowhere near the place. What, you think I'd bother to go round the shop on my week off – then pop out the back for a ciggie? Well, that's bloody charmin' that is, boss!'

'Don't get upset,' Martin shifted in his seat, 'it was a question, not an accusation … but I had to ask, with you being a smoker.'

'Not guilty – so you can buy me a bloody cake for that, an' all!' Trina pouted.

•

'Oh, Martin! Tell me you didn't accuse that poor girl

of starting the fire?' Jan hid her face in her hands. 'Of course she wasn't involved; you gave her the week off! She'd have been in the park with her mates, or out buying clothes like youngsters do. For goodness sake ... how long has Trina worked for you?'

Martin was sheepish. 'Yes, alright – I just needed to know. If she says she wasn't there, she wasn't there. End of. It doesn't matter now. Could have been anyone – and whoever it was, it was an accident. What I've got to decide, as soon as the insurance company pays up, is where we go from here.'

•

A dated little shop in an unremarkable market town; it was hardly the stuff of dreams. Yet Bevan's Flooring had been a landmark of Crabton High Street for almost fifteen years and the locals were outraged by its demise.

'I can't believe how many people have told me they're sorry,' Martin said, after he'd been stopped in the street for the third time, just in the course of buying milk and a newspaper.

'You were gone ages,' Jan moaned, leaning over to tie her laces, 'I thought we were having a cuppa. I've got to go now; I'm walking Poppet and Spike at eleven o'clock.'

'Well *they* sound like a match made in heaven,' Martin muttered.

'They're both sweethearts actually; a spaniel and a pug.' Jan felt for their respective keys in the pocket of her cotton jacket. 'You should come with us, Mart. It's such a lovely day – less sticky than last week – and the exercise will do you good.'

'Don't you worry about that, my love – I get plenty of exercise with my badminton … I did mention I've got a match with Jeremy on Thursday evening, didn't I?'

Jan nodded.

'Anyway, I need to chase the insurance company – that shop's an eyesore, and it drags down the whole high street.' Martin opened his paper, in no hurry to make the call.

'Suit yourself. I've got a German shepherd after this pair, so I'll be a couple of hours. Perhaps we can have a sandwich in the garden later. Bye, love.'

Revelling in the unfamiliar luxury of time spent home alone, Martin made a cup of tea and took it outside. The garden looked tired with its sun-baked grass dotted by dandelions, its dated crazy paving and weathered mis-matched flower pots. He unfolded a padded chair and with a deep sigh, angled it towards the sun.

It amazed Martin just how relaxed he felt. Only three weeks earlier, they'd returned from holiday to find the shop ablaze and his heart had all but broken to see flames licking up the building, as acrid smoke filled the air. Yet now he felt content, philosophical. Free.

'What if it was a sign?' Martin said that evening as the dishwasher whirred, and Jan watched one of her soaps.

'Hmm?'

'What if the fire was meant as a sign ... that things needed to change around here?'

'Don't be daft, Mart. It was a terrible accident – someone could have been killed,' Jan said.

'Yes, but they weren't, were they? Nobody was even injured – thank god. So what if it was meant to happen?' Martin's eyes were bright. 'I'd never even considered early retirement before, but perhaps this is the push we needed.'

Jan muted the television and looked at him, her blue eyes expectant.

'Love, I've been doing a few sums and we're better off than I thought. Property prices have shot up around here, and unlike most traders in the high street, I own the freehold. As for this house, it might only be a semi, but people go mad for period homes these days. It's tempting to get a valuation on both and sell up.'

Jan was incredulous: 'But where would we live? And what would you *do* all day, Martin? You'd go out of your mind with boredom without that shop – I can't imagine you doing anything else.'

'I could take up golf ... or hiking or–'

'Hiking? Martin, you won't even walk the dogs with me – hiking indeed! What's brought this on? I thought you were happy.'

Martin hesitated. 'Well, I was ... to a point. I just fancy a *change* – is that so peculiar? I can just picture us, living in a nice modern, low-maintenance house ... spending more time together. What if I invested in your dog walking – turned it into a proper little business? Or we started another business together – doing something we both enjoy?'

'My dog walking *is* proper, Martin. I like things the way they are. And this house ... it's full of memories – Hayley was born here.'

'Yes, but it's not been plain sailing, has it? A couple of years ago, you were so depressed you didn't know night from day. That was a terrible time for us.' Martin shook his head, remembering.

'Oh, thanks for bringing that up, Mart. Look, if you really need a change, I suppose there's no harm in getting valuations done is there?'

'None at all, my sweet. The insurance company should pay out in the next couple of weeks and then the world's our oyster.'

Martin beamed. Perhaps it was time for a new chapter – other people reinvented themselves, why shouldn't they?

CHAPTER 8

The Mortons

Jake prowled the high-ceilinged drawing room of his father's South London flat. What a crappy start to the summer holidays. He hadn't asked to stay at his dad's for a week – and his dad didn't seem to want him there either, but somehow, his mum had made it happen.

Her face had been set and stubborn, like before the divorce, when they used to row – a lot. God, he didn't miss that. He didn't miss his dad much, either. And bloody Jodie was a pain; always trying too hard, talking to him about music and girls. She'd given him some really 'icky speech, about not wanting to be his mum – and that he should think of her as more of a big sister. Gross.

She wasn't even good looking. He'd only met her once before, but she looked different now. Her face, which was shiny with make-up, was all puffed up, especially her lips. Even her blonde hair seemed bigger – and suspiciously like a wig.

A couple of girls in sixth form had hair extensions, which they flipped around and played with all the time. Amber didn't need them. Her hair fell almost to her waist and smelled like flowers in the rain – not that Jake had ever told her.

He looked at the clock on the marble mantel

piece; one fifteen. They'd said they were popping to Sainsbury's, but that had been two hours ago. It was boring enough staying in at home, but here, with hardly any of his stuff, it was even crappier.

He heard the street door slam, then footfall as keys jangled at the flat door.

'Hi Jakey.' Jodie came in first, a plastic shopping bag in each hand – didn't she care about the environment? His father struggled through the door behind her, breathless with the effort of carrying another three bags, sweat visible on his big pale forehead.

'It's a gorgeous day,' William called from the kitchen as he and Jodie began to unpack groceries. 'How about we take a picnic to the park?'

'Sure, whatever,' Jake said. He couldn't be bought with a few sandwiches and an hour spent feeding the ducks – he wasn't five! But it was a better option than being stuck inside the flat.

'Great!' His father sounded genuinely pleased – or relieved.

'Can I er … help?' Jake asked, watching Jodie butter practically a whole loaf of granary bread, while William sliced tomatoes, grated cheese, and chopped sticks of raw veg.

'No son – but thanks for offering. We'll just throw this lot in a bag and then head over to Brightling. Can you grab a rug, please? Should be one in your room.'

His room; little more than a box room, it had floor to ceiling book shelves against one wall, and a folding – although remarkably comfy – bed against another. It was painted in what his mum would call *baby blue* and had spriggy curtains at the windows which Jodie said she'd put up especially for his visit.

'We want you to be happy here, Jakey – this room is yours whenever you need it,' she said, giving him the benefit of her big white teeth.

'Er, thanks … that's nice.' Jake said without meaning it. It would take more than bloody curtains! If she'd *really* wanted him to be happy, he thought grimly, she wouldn't have shagged his dad and caused his parents to divorce. But it was done now, and somehow, they'd all have to get along, at least that was what his mum said.

It would be even worse when his mum got herself a boyfriend, he thought, as they walked the few blocks to Brightling Park – and it would happen, eventually. Because even though she was really old (he knew that because he could remember her celebrating her 40th a couple of years earlier – like it was anything to be proud of!) she didn't deserve to be alone, like some sad spinster in a Dickens novel.

It took *an age* to get to the park, thanks to Jodie's stupid shoes, with their thin straps and high heels – she'd have been better off in a pair of trainers, or even those awful Hush-Puppy things that his dad wore.

They were both staring at him now – and then he realised: he'd said it out loud! Oh god, he'd dissed her shoes, right to her face, with his dad listening.

'Jake, that's a bit rude, actually ... making personal remarks about someone's clothes,' his dad was saying in an even voice.

Feeling his face redden Jake apologised, adding: 'They look lovely though, just ... um, not brilliant for walking.'

To his relief Jodie laughed. 'Yeah, Jakey – you're right, they are soo painful,' she said with a grimace.

Lured outside by the searing heat, droves of people littered Brightling Park's lawns. William scowled: 'I wasn't expecting it to be quite this crowded. Oh well, we're here now – and I'm starving. Hey, look – over there, there's a space by that willow tree – we can pitch camp there, right Jakey?'

Jake nodded. He was too hungry to care where they sat – breakfast seemed an awfully long time ago. He and his mum always ate lunch between twelve-thirty and one o'clock and it was at least two now.

Jodie made an elaborate business of smoothing out the rug and handing out paper napkins before producing a bottle of white wine.

'Dad, can I have some, please?' Jake said watching Jodie pour two glasses.

'Best not, Jake. You're fifteen ... your mother

would have a fit! There's lemonade for you – or fizzy water.'

Jake made a face. 'Mum's not here, how would she even know?'

'He has a point,' Jodie said. 'How about I make him a spritzer? Go on Will – just one.'

William sighed and nodded. 'Okay. Slowly though, Jake,' he said, through a mouthful of cheese and tomato sandwich.

Jake had drunk alcohol before of course. In fact he'd shared a whole bottle of cider with Amber in her father's field only two weeks earlier. He'd felt sick afterwards – and grateful that his mother had been working late at the café that evening; she'd have rumbled him for certain if he hadn't showered, brushed his teeth twice and pretended to revise in his room until bedtime. Studying had been out of the question, the words in his chemistry book had turned fuzzy and even more confusing than usual. Amber on the other hand had seemed unaffected – except that her cheeks shone pinker than usual and she giggled more at his jokes.

Now, as Jake watched little kids playing on bikes and scooters, and people walking their dogs, he felt the same fuzziness wash over him, only this time, he didn't feel as though he might puke.

•

Standing before a full-length mirror, Chloe appraised her reflection; kohl-ringed eyes that glittered darkly looked back at her. Turning sideways she saw how her new skinny jeans accentuated her waist and the daring wedge heels she'd dug out from the back of her wardrobe made her legs look even longer than usual.

Not bad, she thought, grabbing a scarlet pashmina and slouchy bag.

Moments later, she watched Bryony's car pull up outside, and ran downstairs to greet her best friend, who was laden with wine, flowers and an overnight bag.

'B! You're really here!' Chloe squealed as her friend pressed a bunch of scented stocks and roses into her arms.

'Oh they're beautiful, you shouldn't have – you didn't need to bring anything. I'm so pleased to see you. Hey, come inside and let's have a glass of wine before we go out. The table's booked for eight and the restaurant is only five minutes away. I've called a cab so we can both drink,' Chloe said with a wink.

•

The Speckled Hen Bar & Grill was heaving with well-dressed diners, keen to let their hair down on a Saturday night.

'Ooh, I like this,' breathed Bryony, admiring

pewter walls, rich teal curtains and huge vases of white hydrangeas on every available surface. Following the elegant maître d', the women passed the bar area and wove their way to a table overlooking the candle-lit patio garden.

'So, how are you ... really?' Bryony said once their wine and a platter of mixed mezze starters had arrived. 'I mean, you look bloody amazing. My god, Chloe, your body! You're skinnier than ever.'

'That'll be the stress and exhaustion diet then.' Chloe took a large swallow of Pinot Grigio. 'I'm okay, B. I just feel ...' she paused, groping for the right words, 'discombobulated, you know?'

Bryony waited for her to go on.

'I just can't seem to *grip* anything. Okay, so when Will and I were married, I knew my priorities. I was Will's wife, Jake's mother ... I had the big house in Streatham to run. And yeah, I was knackered and didn't get a minute to myself, but I knew what to *do* – I had a routine. And even after things went wrong, when Will ... well, it was a mess, but it was *my* mess.'

'God, Chloe. I know you miss London, but I thought you were enjoying your freedom – and don't knock it. Look at what you've achieved. You run your own business now for god's sake! That's incredible and I'm so proud of you.'

'But that's just it,' Chloe half whispered, 'I thought I'd love it. But I don't. I hate getting up so bloody early and the drudgery of it all. Being at the coffee shop six days a week is like spending all week in the kitchen. And when I close at five o'clock, I am so relieved. And you know what? And this is the worst part, B … I thought I might meet some interesting, sparky people. But I don't … I haven't made a single friend. When did I become so … *invisible?*'

Bryony shook her head vigorously. 'You're not. Eden Hill obviously isn't a very friendly place. I know you, Chloe – you chat to everyone.'

'It is actually … it's very neighbourly. It must be me, putting out the wrong signals.'

'Well *he* doesn't think so,' Bryony jerked her head towards the bar, where a dark-haired man with a lived-in face north of forty had been watching them. Caught out, he began studying the front page of his magazine with great concentration.

'Sshh! Keep your voice down!' Chloe said, unable to resist a second look. 'Poor man's only come in for a drink and a read. Men can do that, can't they? Can you imagine either of us propping up the bar all alone?'

'No, not really – I wouldn't dream of going to a bar by myself,' agreed Bryony.

'Well, you're lucky, you don't have to – you live with a total studmuffin.' Chloe topped up Bryony's wine glass and added a splash to her own. 'Whoops! That bottle disappeared quickly. Shall we order another when the mains come?'

Bryony nodded. 'Paul's not really a studmuffin, you know … not after eight years. But I do love him, and I know I'm lucky because above all else, he's kind.'

Chloe sighed. 'You see? That's all I want – a kind man to put his arms around me,' she said, a note of self-pity creeping into her voice.

'You've got one. I wish I had a gorgeous son like Jake. Whatever else happens, that boy is yours for life. He's a total credit to you and nobody can take that away.' They clinked glasses and drank deeply.

'You're right … ooh, I need to slow down … I'm feeling a bit giddy to be honest, and I'd forgotten how much you can drink,' Chloe said.

Briony raised a quizzical eyebrow. 'None taken!' she said.

Chloe slumped in her seat. 'I hope Jake's okay at William's. I bet *she's* there, he was very vague on the phone … *bitch*.'

'Yeah, bitch!' Bryony echoed as they both dissolved into laughter.

They swerved dessert and were sipping americanos and nibbling tiny almond biscotti in an effort to sober up before leaving.

'Think I'll fall over in these heels if I get up now,' Chloe sniggered. 'I do need the loo though.'

'I'll come with.' Bryony rose, and they tottered

towards the cloakroom together, passing the bar where all that remained of the dark-haired man was a copy of Farmer's Weekly studded with rings from a wine glass.

'Oh, so he's a farmer, is he?' Bryony said as they joined the short queue for the ladies. 'Shame he's gone, he was hot! Sad eyes though … sensitive looking. We could have had a drink with him.'

Chloe groaned. 'No way! We've had enough. Let's get reception to call us a taxi.' She stifled a yawn and leant her head on Bryony's shoulder. 'My bed is calling.'

CHAPTER 9

The Bradshaws

As July melted into August, Rosemary found herself in a state of near contentment. Without the tyranny of the school run, and with her visits to the care home halved for the summer, the days became long and languid.

'Mummy, I wish it could be school holidays forever,' Iris said, echoing her thoughts.

'Me too, sweetpea.'

Rosemary watched her daughter take a packet of biscuits from the larder and carefully pour a glass of pink lemonade before carrying them out to the garden.

'Do you want to draw with me, Mummy?' she asked, her face a picture of hope as she settled into a makeshift camp of blankets and cushions, scattered with colouring pens, a notebook and Gloria, her favourite doll.

Rosemary sighed. 'I'd love to, sweetpea, but I've got chores to do. I've Daddy's shirts to iron for one thing.'

'Can't he do them himself?'

Iris looked so serious that Rosemary laughed aloud. 'My baby feminist!' she said, clearing a space on the blanket and squatting beside her. 'It sounds like a good idea, doesn't it? But Daddy has to work, so he doesn't have time. My work is here, looking after our house, and you and Daddy.'

'And Grandma ... don't forget Grandma Joyce.'

'I don't look after her, do I? I just visit her in the care home.'

'What's a care home?' Iris said, pulling apart her third Jammie Dodger.

'Iris, that's the last one, okay? A care home is where people go when they are too old to look after themselves properly, so they all live together in a big house, where they can make new friends and somebody can cook for them and help them with getting dressed and ... other things ...' she concluded vaguely.

'Oh, that sounds lovely,' Iris said, dusting crumbs from her fingers.

'Not everybody thinks so,' Rosemary said, realising that a change of subject was in order. 'So, how about a trip to the seaside this week? We could drive to the beach, have a paddle and get ice creams. What do you think sweetpea?'

'Yaay! I'd love that! Can we go tomorrow?' Iris was on her feet, bouncing up and down, eyes shining.

'Maybe ... or perhaps we can go with Daddy on Sunday,' Rosemary said. 'Let's ask him; I'll give him a call later.'

Her daughter's face fell.

'Okay, but I don't think he'll want to come,' Iris said.

'Hey, that's not nice. Of course Daddy wants to do fun stuff with us!'

Out of the mouths of babes, thought Rosemary, with a prickle of unease. Leaving Iris to her drawing, she went inside and made tea which she drank in the coolness of the sitting room. With its tasteful putty coloured walls and thick silk drapes, the room was far more grand than necessary, particularly as nobody ever came to the house.

Rosemary thought back to the home she grew up in; to the Victorian terrace in Sydenham, with its labyrinth of narrow rooms with mismatched carpets and scuffed skirting boards. Rooms that had vibrated with the laughter of her older sister Abi, and younger brother Joseph, and with the chatter of her parents, Joan and Ade – until her father had died suddenly of a blood clot on the brain while the siblings were at school. That summer, Aunt Kiki had moved in to help – and had stayed. Somehow, over time, home became a happy haven of familial chaos again, where it was hard to find a quiet corner to study in, especially during the summer months, when the back door was permanently open and there was always a party somewhere in the street.

At nineteen, Rosemary had left home to pursue a business degree which she'd achieved with a blend of grit and natural intelligence. At her graduation, Joan and Kiki had wept with pride – before dropping the bomb that they would be returning to Nigeria's capital the following year, leaving Rosemary and her siblings to fend for themselves.

'But why, Mum? London is home and your children are *here*.'

Joan had been resolute, 'Because my darling, granny is dying. Auntie and I will come home after she's passed, but right now, she needs us.' Years later, and long after Granny's last breath, Joan and Kiki showed no sign of returning.

To her utter amazement and pleasure, Rosemary found that independence suited her. She worked hard and morphed into corporate life with ease. Working through the ranks in a marketing firm near London Bridge, she'd been promoted several times before she reached thirty, leading her own team and bagging enviable accounts.

Nigel Bradshaw had been a client and had thrown all professionalism to the wind, doggedly chasing Rosemary until one day she had allowed herself to be caught by agreeing to have dinner with him.

He'd intrigued and charmed her, taking her to art galleries and to the ballet. From self-confessed, unashamedly humble beginnings, Nigel was nevertheless well read, well-mannered and respectful. It didn't matter that he was twelve years her senior, or that nobody would ever describe him as handsome; what fatherless Rosemary saw was five-feet-eleven-inches of security. They'd been together for four months when Rosemary discovered she was pregnant. Despite their mutual shock, neither of them had ever uttered the word *abortion*.

'But you can't marry him if the love's not there, girl,' Joan had said during Rosemary's weekly call to Abuja.

'Mum, I didn't plan any of this ... but a baby ... a new life ... I've realised it's what I want, and we'll grow to love each other. He's a good man, very decent and cultured. You and Auntie would like him.'

The wedding had been a hasty affair in a south London registry office where Rosemary had counted the guests on two hands. But months later, Iris had brought real joy into their lives, welding them together, although the join was clearly visible.

When Rosemary mooted returning to work, Nigel wouldn't hear of it. 'I don't want Iris to have the kind of upbringing I had,' he said. 'No daughter of mine will need a childminder or be a latchkey kid – children need their mother.'

He had a way of ending discussions – that really weren't *discussions* at all – by holding up both hands as if stopping traffic, a gesture which Rosemary found dismissive and intimidating. Leaving their cramped London terrace for a bigger house in a Kent garden-suburb had been another of Nigel's ideas – one that had baffled Rosemary.

'Nigel, I get that we need more space, but moving further south makes no sense at all. Surely it will make work more difficult for you on the days when you have to drive up north ... which seems to be more and more these days.'

But Nigel had been adamant that living in Eden Hill would work for all of them and in the end, Rosemary had acquiesced.

Her sister Abi had been the first person to use the term 'control freak', at least to her face. 'You leave London and you'll be truly isolated. What about *your* needs?' Abi said. 'Rosie, you've got a good brain and you were great at your job. Why should you be reduced to wiping bottoms and noses?'

Rosemary hadn't the energy for a fight. 'It's what mums do ... it's family life. Abi, just think about what our relatives in Nigeria endure every day. Living in a big house in a gated community in the suburbs doesn't sound like much of a hardship to me.'

I must try harder, thought Rosemary, finishing her tea and carrying the empty cup back to the kitchen.

From the window she could see Iris chatting earnestly to Gloria. *Some women would kill for what I have,* she thought, lifting her head higher with characteristic determination.

•

The porcelain-skinned young woman had no idea if the faint whiff of semen masked by pine air freshener was actually present or merely etched on her sinuses; all hotel rooms smelled the same to her these days.

She turned to the middle-aged man propped against pillows on the bed before her. Fully dressed, except for polished shoes discarded on the floor, he was silent, watchful; the only sound was of the ice cubes that rolled around his gin and tonic.

Unbuttoning her diaphanous blouse, she let it fall to the floor and waited.

When he spoke, the man's voice was hoarse. 'Very nice. Now the rest ... slowly, please.'

'I know what to do,' the woman whispered, 'I know exactly what you like.'

CHAPTER 10

The Wildes

The studio was a converted cowshed fifty minutes' drive from Eden Hill. Facilities were basic; the kitchenette and tiny windowless loo wouldn't be appearing in House Beautiful any day soon, Ben noted, but the price was reasonable, and the owner seemed pleased to have them, greeting Ben like a fan.

'Good to meet you, man, I love your work. Me and the missus played Seagull at our wedding; first dance … ah, takes me back.'

'Yeah? Kind of you to say so, Josh. The lads should be here any minute; Ricky and Steve, on lead guitar and keyboards. We'll need a drum track … if that's cool with you? How long you been doing this?'

'I've been producing for years, but I bought this place about eighteen months ago … a few things clicked at the right time and so I went with it.'

The front door buzzed and seconds later Ben was hugging Ricky and Steve as introductions were swapped and drinks offered.

'Coffees all round, please Josh,' Ben said hurriedly. It was only ten o'clock but he'd detected a whiff of booze on Rick, who appeared to have aged overnight, and was looking decidedly unkempt, with matted hair and a T-shirt in dire need of a wash.

Steve looked the same as the last time they'd met,

except that his hairline had crept back and a modest spare tyre was just visible beneath his faded black shirt.

'It's fucking great having the old crew back together,' Ben said after a jam-style warm up which loosened wrists and inhibitions and got them all grinning from ear to ear.

Taking only brief coffee and cigarette breaks, by four o'clock The Wilde Ones had laid down three new tracks. Two were songs newly penned by Ben that he'd emailed to the boys days earlier, keen to hit the ground running. But the third was spontaneous and had mushroomed there in the room, evidence of the trio's creative chemistry.

'We've still got it – that was awesome!' Ben was pacing the studio, high on the music. 'We should start gigging again – and not fleapit pubs, but proper muso venues … I'll speak to Greg Lyons–'

'Greg's a tosser,' Rick said, fumbling for his cigarettes. 'What exactly does that man do for you, Ben?'

Ben nodded: 'Yeah, I get it. I know he comes on like a snake … I didn't say I *liked* the guy. But to be fair, it was Greg that relaunched my career – well sort of – and all those TV interviews … most of them were down to him.'

Rick smirked. 'Yeah, I remember; Loose Women! You were – *are* – the menopausal woman's crumpet,

Benny-boy.' The three of them guffawed good naturedly.

'Cheeky half, then?' Steve said as they began loading amps and instruments into Rick's van.

Ben nodded. 'Be rude not to – although it's not like the old days, is it? Seeing as though we're all driving home to our wives.'

Ben could have sworn he saw Rick's face darken, but he said nothing.

·

It was eight o'clock by the time Ben drove through the gates of Regents Square. He palmed the CD from its player, having spent the entire journey listening to it on repeat with a critical and professional ear.

From the kitchen, he heard Rita's gruff voice and Lisa's tinkling laughter; a smell of roast chicken emanated from the oven.

'Evening ladies, something smells good.' Ben kissed Lisa full on the mouth and air kissed her mother with a loud *mwah*. Nellie stirred in her bed, before pointedly burying her head under her blanket.

Lisa beamed. 'Hello sweetheart! You're back early. I thought you'd go for a drink with the lads. How was it today?'

'Yeah, we had a swift half – but as we're all driving, that was it.' With a triumphant grin, Ben waved the

CD. 'It was good thanks, babe. Knockout as it goes … we nailed three fucking ace tracks.'

Rita rolled her eyes and mimed shock.

'Sorry, Rita, excuse my French. You were right, Leese – it was exactly what I needed. Sometimes I forget what I'm about.'

'Well I never forget – and I'm so proud of you.' Lisa pressed tight against Ben's torso and kissed him.

Rita cleared her throat: 'I am here you know.'

'Oh, for god's sake, Mum – we're married!' Lisa said, taking the CD from Ben and sliding it into the player. Seconds later, the room filled with Ben's voice, soft and breathy to begin with, becoming soaring and powerful. Goosebumps lifted on Lisa's neck and arms as she began swaying rhythmically.

'Oh god, Ben! I love it. Hey, and Rick's guitar sounds bloody amazing. Oh, you have to release this, hon – it could be massive.'

Even Rita tapped her good foot. 'It's got a decent beat, I'll give you that,' she said, drumming painted fingernails on the granite worktop.

No sooner had all three tracks played out, Lisa hit the play button again and she and Ben began dancing around the kitchen, with Ben grabbing a ladle for a mic.

'I'm feeling distinctly green and hairy,' Rita grumbled, 'help me upstairs will you, love – I've got a couple of phone calls to make ... and I can see you two need your privacy!'

•

'You haven't forgotten we've got the neighbours on Saturday night, have you hon?' Lisa stroked Nellie's silky ears as she lay nestled between them while they drank a blissful first cup of tea in bed.

Ben pulled a face. 'I had, as it happens. Nigel's such a boring git ... I mean, she seems nice, but they're so *straight*, you know. Are they bringing the kid?'

'No, they're getting a babysitter for Iris. She's a sweetie, but she'd be bored out of her mind. Mum insisted on inviting her mate Jackie, too, so there'll be six of us.'

'Oh, joy! Even better; well I hope your mum behaves herself – she can be pretty caustic at times. Let's hope she doesn't offend anyone.'

Lisa was indignant: 'My mum's got many faults, but she's not a racist.'

'I never said that, I just–'

'Well that's what you were implying,' Lisa pouted, before swinging toned, tanned legs out of bed. 'Right, we'd better get this day started.'

Ben stretched and raked back his curls. 'What's she like?'

'Who, Jackie? No idea. The only thing Mum said was that they haven't known each other long. Ah, bless her. It's nice that she can still make new friends at her age.'

'Never mind about her age ... what about mine?' Ben said, as he limped stiffly to the bathroom. Moments later, Lisa heard him belting out one of his new tunes in the shower.

CHAPTER 11

The Mortons

'So what did you do in the evenings? Did Jodie cook?' Chloe despised herself for pumping Jake for information; he'd only been back a few hours.

'Only once. She made Spag-Bol ... but not like you make it.' Jake wrinkled his nose. 'It had bouncy bits in it.'

'Bouncy bits?' Chloe's heart soared; so, the younger model couldn't cook!

'Oh, I expect she's very good at *other* things,' Chloe turned away and hoped that her son wouldn't notice the edge of spite in her voice.

'She's okay, actually – I mean, her and Dad are kind of weird together and she kept on about how I should think of her as a big sister, which was gross ... but at least she didn't tell me what to do or–'

'I should bloody well think not!' Chloe snapped, flouncing out into the kitchen. Silly bitch; older sister? That was pushing it a bit!

'Well how about I make it for you properly tonight – the way you like it, hmm? It's too hot for Sunday roast.'

'Yep, whatevs. I'm going up to my room, Mum,' Jake called as he thundered up the stairs.

Chloe let out a dejected sigh. Apart from during Bryony's visit the previous weekend, her week without

Jake had crawled by. Chloe had buried herself in work, doing long, thankless shifts at the coffee shop.

'I don't know how you do it, Chloe,' Lillian had said, during a midweek lull. 'You get here before eight – you never leave before five o'clock and you only close on Sundays. I'd go round the bloody bend! Oh, no offence, I mean, I like my job and everything … but I have Thursdays off and I finish by four most days. Don't you get, like, *really* tired?'

'I do, Lilly, love – but it's different when it's your own business. The buck stops with me.'

Overhead, Jake's room began to vibrate with the sound of indie rock music and even Chloe recognised Jake's favourite band of the moment; *Baby Dogs*. It wasn't long before another sound echoed above it as Jake played along on his electric guitar.

Chloe was about to yell upstairs to tell Jake to turn his music down but caught herself in time.

When had she become such a cliché?

•

They'd texted each other dozens of times a day, but now Jake was home, all Amber wanted to know was whether he'd missed her while he'd been away.

Nobody cared what he thought or felt – everyone had their own agenda; like his mum asking about Jodie. He could tell that she'd wanted him to dish the dirt but he couldn't be bothered. The thing about the bouncy Spag-Bol was true and had made his mum feel better, but although he didn't *like* Jodie much, he didn't *dislike* her either – she simply wasn't important enough for that.

'When can I see you? It's been ages …' Amber simpered over the phone, snapping him back to the present. He'd turned his music down low to hear her better but was still holding his guitar across his lap.

'Dunno – soon,' he said, noncommittally, laying his guitar down and unconsciously rubbing his crotch.

'Did you meet someone else at your Dad's? Have you gone off me, Jakey?'

'What? Christ, you have no idea how boring it was at my old man's. Stop it with the questions, Amber – it's not fair. I think you're lovely … you're my girlfriend aren't you?' He paused, trying to figure out why the idea of seeing Amber didn't thrill him as much as it should.

'It's just different when we're not at school. Our parents don't know about us, and I hate lying and sneaking around.'

'Well don't then. Your mum looks nice, Jakey – really cool. Just tell her we're friends.'

Jake considered this strategy for the first time. 'I suppose I could do that … but she'd jump to conclusions, and think we were … doing stuff.'

'Well, she'd be right then,' Amber said, cackling with laughter.

Jake's head fizzed. 'Mum'll be back at work tomorrow. She wants me to hang around the café with her, give her a hand; but we could meet up late afternoon if you like?'

Amber paused. 'Dad's taking me and my sister to buy new jeans. He's finishing work early and afterwards we're going to the cinema. Jade wants to see–'

'Bloody hell, this is hopeless – see what I mean?'

'The day after then! Do you want to finish with me, Jakey?'

'I don't know!' Jake shouted before hanging up and turning his mobile phone off. Jesus. Women!

•

Two hours later and somewhat mollified by Chloe's delicious Spaghetti Bolognese (without bouncy bits), Jake relented and switched his mobile phone back on. He'd expected a barrage of missed calls and texts but there were none. Shit! He'd been pretty mean to Amber – perhaps it was *she* who wanted to end things with him.

Jake sent her a text: '*Sorry for bad mood just tired after being at Dad's. Hope I can see you soon xxx*'

He always put kisses – but not normally three.

'*Dad and Jade out Tuesday morning. Come to mine at 10.30 xxxx*' was Amber's reply.

Four kisses – and a date. Amber had forgiven him

for being a moody bastard. They never met at hers, apart from when they sat out in her dad's orchard, which couldn't be seen from her house.

Jake had never been inside a real farmhouse. He wondered what it would be like. Maybe there'd be straw on the kitchen floor, and animals running around the house. He giggled; of course not! It wasn't the middle ages. It would be just like his house, with a modern kitchen and sofas and TVs – and bedrooms upstairs. Amber's bedroom. Oh god. They would be alone in her bedroom. What if … oh, it was too much to bear … what if he got to see her *actually naked*? He'd had a feel of her boobs (three times!) which were small and soft, but that was with her bra still on. And as for the other … area … Jesus! He couldn't even *think* about that.

What would Amber be expecting? If he got to see her without her kit on, then she would want to see him, too.

Sprawled on the sofa, still holding his phone, Jake leapt out of his skin as Chloe dropped a saucepan which rebounded on the kitchen floor.

'Sorry!' she shouted, followed by a couple of muttered swears.

'Blimey, Mum,' Jake called, 'you nearly gave me a heart attack.'

Chloe appeared in the sitting room doorway.

'Why are you sitting down here in silence?' she

asked. 'Put the TV on if you want. Jake are you alright?'

Jake groaned ostentatiously. 'Yes! I'm fine,' he said before going upstairs and slamming his bedroom door.

•

By the time Tuesday rolled around, Jake was wired with anxiety and anticipation, having rehearsed every potential scenario with Amber in his head.

Even so, he managed to sleep through his alarm, only to be awoken by the postman banging the door-knocker for a signature just after nine o'clock.

Shit! He'd wanted to take his time getting ready, to make an effort, but he was due at Amber's at ten-thirty. It was probably just as well, he thought, shovelling in cereal and orange juice which made him feel unusually queasy; after all, he didn't want to look as though he'd tried too hard.

After showering and rifling his wardrobe for his favourite Superdry T-Shirt, Jake tackled his hair, which on some days teetered on the very cusp of cool and on others, like today, looked overly long and idiotic – sort of fluffy. Grabbing a pot of wax from the nightstand, Jake swirled a blob in his hands, then thought better of it and instead wiped it off with a tissue. He knew he was fussing like a big girl but couldn't seem to stop. He just wanted to look his best on the day that could be *the day he lost his virginity*. He gave an involuntary shudder despite the humidity.

Wondering if he needed a hoodie, Jake peered out at the sky where pendulous clouds had gathered – the first for weeks. Sod it, if it rained, he'd get wet; so what?

Grabbing his house keys, wallet and phone, Jake went out into the street. Christ, it really was sticky. Already his armpits were leaking – just what he needed when he was potentially about to get naked with his girlfriend for the first time.

Get a grip, Jake, he admonished, breaking into a jog that took him out of the close, along a tree-lined avenue and towards fields he would cut across to Amber's.

Within ten minutes, Jake was running through orchards, the scent of apples making him feel sick, giddy and elated all at once.

CHAPTER 12

The Bevans

Jeremy Hunter blotted his forehead with a clean white handkerchief. The humidity really was too much, thank goodness the Bentley had air conditioning.

'Sorry I'm late, Martin,' he said, glancing at his Rolex before shaking Martin's hand. 'There's a burst water main on the road between here and Eden Hill, the traffic's backed up for a mile or so.'

'Oh, is there? Not to worry – you're here now and I appreciate you doing the valuation personally when you could easily have sent one of your minions,' Martin said, gesturing him into the narrow hallway where he picked up a whiff of Jeremy's cologne; something green, rare – expensive.

'Always delighted to help a friend,' Jeremy said smoothly, 'especially one who recently thrashed me at badminton!'

Martin laughed. 'Now, now … it's pretty even I'd say. So, where would you like to start? In here? This is the lounge – or would you call it the drawing room?' Martin regretted the words as soon as they were out of his mouth. Drawing room! To his relief, Jeremy did not reply, remarking instead on the fireplace.

'Period features are always popular, Martin. It's fabulous that you've kept the fireplace open. The room's a good size, too – although so many people are knocking through now and opting for open plan living.' Jeremy continued to scribble notes as they moved from room to room.

Martin and Jan had spent the whole of Sunday sorting and cleaning. Then on Monday, while Jan was out walking her dogs, Martin had filled his car with dated or simply unwanted clothes, books and bric-a-brac. The Cancer Research shop on the high street had been grateful for most of it before Martin had got a cathartic buzz of skipping the rest at the local council tip. He'd always liked going to the dump, even taking Hayley along – until at fourteen she'd announced that the 'smelly old tip' held no thrall for her.

Upstairs, a look of consternation crossed Jeremy's tanned face. 'Buyers expect to have at least two bathrooms, Martin. At Eden Hill for instance, most homes have three. Have you ever sought planning permission for an en-suite?'

Martin shook his head. 'I know it's the done thing these days, but we never felt the need. Just more to clean, Jan always says.'

'Quite,' Jeremy grinned, reminding Martin of a shark.

'Alright, well I've seen enough to give you a guide price, Martin.' They were back in the sitting room – or the 'front' room, as Martin and Jan usually called it.

'I think you'll be surprised by how much value this

house has gained in the last twenty years,' Jeremy paused dramatically.

Martin felt his heart quicken. 'Go on.'

'In its current condition, I think we're looking at offers over £495,000. Unless of course you wanted to wait a while, put in say, a new kitchen and an en-suite, which could net you another twenty thousand or so.'

Martin whistled. 'Crikey. Off the top of your head, Jeremy, any thoughts on what the shop might be worth? After the refurb, of course.'

'Prime high street location … private parking at the rear … I think we're looking at the early four hundreds.'

'Well I never!' Martin said, unable to keep the smile from his face.

•

'Well I don't know why you're so surprised, Mart. Don't you ever look in Hunters' window, or have a nose on the internet? It's shocking the price of property round here. I don't know how young people are supposed to get on the ladder these days,' Jan said.

'Well they don't, do they … it's either the Bank of Mum & Dad, or they end up renting until they're forty.' Martin took a bite of his salmon filet, 'Ooh, is this from Tesco? That'll be the next thing … Hayley coming to us for a deposit so they can get their own place.'

'Best not go spending all our money then, eh love? Martin, there's no sense getting all excited about moving. We might make a bit of money on this place, but then we've got to buy somewhere decent, *and* pay all that stamp duty – it doesn't add up.'

Martin paused to chew carefully. 'Not if I sell the shop as well, my love. I've given it a lot of thought and flogging flooring just doesn't grab me anymore. I've done it to death, Jan.'

Jan looked exasperated. 'We've had this conversation – what else would you do? I don't want you under my feet all day – and if you think dog walking's a doddle, you can think again, Martin.'

'So you keep saying. Look, don't you worry – I'll think of something. Anyway, that's not the point – what I'm saying is, we've got options.'

'Options?' Jan made a face.

Martin lifted his chin. 'We'll have means, Jan – *means*. If we sell up, we could raise nearly a million – and on top of that, there's my pension. Love, I've barely had a day off in thirty-five years.'

'We've just been on holiday!'

'I mean apart from the odd week in the Med. Look, I just think it's time for a change, that's all.'

'Oh, for god's sake, Martin, is this another midlife crisis? I can't go through all that again …'

They bickered a while longer, until exhausted by

Jan's truculence, Martin turned the television on and pretended to be engrossed in a new crime drama.

'I've seen this,' Jan said. 'This is the one where she ends up finding her sister dead in the bath – it's very gory. I don't know how you can watch this.'

'You can't possibly have seen this before – it's a brand new three-parter, and this is the first one.'

'Alright! There's no need to shout!' Jan got to her feet.

Martin gritted his teeth. 'I am not *shouting*. Tell you what though, I'm going for a walk.' He went into the hall, picked up a light linen jacket and reached for his wallet as an afterthought, adding 'I might even go for a drink!'

'Please yourself,' Jan muttered, putting her feet up and changing channels.

•

Martin couldn't remember ever being in a pub on a Tuesday evening. He was surprised to find the Garden Gate actually had customers – one of whom he recognised as Ben Wilde. He gave a little nod of acknowledgment but Ben either didn't see or didn't recognise him and the nod was not returned.

It seemed an unlikely turn of events now. To think that he'd actually sat at the man's table and eaten dinner cooked by Ben's wife, Lisa; a full stop to a year of misunderstandings between Martin, Lisa and Jan.

Martin ordered a beer and found a seat. 'Evening,' he said, catching Ben's eye this time.

'Oh, hi Martin. How's it going? How's the missus?'

'We're both well, thank you, Ben – how's life treating you and Lisa?'

'Ah, you know … we've got a bloody cuckoo in the nest, mate.' Ben looked dolefully at his pint.

Martin waited.

'Lisa's old mum has broken her ankle and she's staying with us. I needed to escape for a bit. That's why I'm sitting here like Billy-no-mates.'

'It's very kind of you and Lisa to put her up,' Martin said.

'It's not kindness, it's obligation. Lisa's a good girl, but her mum drives us both round the bend. Anyway, listen to me going on when you've got *real* problems. I was sorry to see the shop go up in smoke. I must say though, you don't hang about – I see you've already got the builders in.'

'Yes, the insurers paid up pronto – can't fault them.'

Ben scoffed, 'That makes a change. When are you reopening?'

'Now there's a six million dollar question, Ben. It could be time to sell up and move on.'

'Yeah? You and Jan should think about Eden Hill. Mate, when I met Lisa, I moved there kicking and screaming but I don't mind admitting, I'm a convert.

It's more than just an estate, you know – more like a collection of villages. You've got the older part, the brand-new builds, the business park, and all that countryside right on your door-step. And you can't fault it for convenience. I can walk to everything … supermarket, gym, pub … I can even get a decent ruby. It's easy living, Martin – mother-in-law notwithstanding.'

'Yes, I know Eden Hill quite well. I've had a lot work up there in the last few years and I can see the appeal – not that we could afford a house like yours of course.'

'Yeah, well, that's Lisa's doing – even though we're married, I still think of it as her place.'

'Lisa's a lovely woman Ben; you're a lucky man.' Martin drained the last of his beer.

'And don't I know it,' Ben grinned. 'Fancy another?'

CHAPTER 13

The Mortons

Amber handed Jake a mug of instant coffee. He took a sip, scalded his tongue, and registered that it wasn't a bit like the stuff his mum served for two-pounds-fifty a cup in the shop.

'You look hot, Jakey,' Amber said, before bursting into peals of laughter. 'I mean, not like that – although you do look fit – I meant, you're red in the face … sweating a bit–'

'I know what you meant,' Jake said, going even redder. 'I jogged here, and it must be over twenty degrees already.'

Amber put out her hand, but Jake did not take it. He was too busy fighting the urge to run. His stomach felt how his gym kit looked in the washing machine, as it swished gently from side to side, before doing a whole loop around.

He distracted himself by looking around the kitchen; the whole place could do with a clean. His mum would have a fit if she could see the state of the counters. Two battered dog beds dominated the floor space but there was no sign of Ginger or Ralph, the two mutts that Amber often talked about; he said as much.

'They only come in at night when we're all home

– even in winter.' Amber was watching him, chewing her lip.

'Come upstairs. I've got something to show you, Jakey,' she giggled nervously. 'I've got this cool app on my laptop ... it can change you into any animal, with like, rabbit ears or whatever. There's another one that ages you. We can see how we'll look when we're really old, like at twenty-five or thirty.'

Jake followed Amber upstairs, watching her narrow hips in distressed jeans. There was a very real possibility that he'd be taking them off her before the day was over.

Sitting on Amber's narrow bed while she expertly tapped her keyboard, Jake looked around. On the walls, recognisable popstars' faces fought for space with puppies and horses. The room throbbed with pink.

'Why do girls always–' he shut up abruptly. He didn't feel like teasing her today.

Tapping away on her laptop, Amber began to hoot with laughter; when she angled her screen towards him, Jake began to laugh, too. There on the screen was a rather sombre photograph of Jake, now distorted to resemble a hound, with sad drooping eyes, long ears and a wet leather nose. They began to shriek hysterically and as Amber fell back against her pillows, Jake leaned forward and kissed her on lips that tasted of orange Chapstick.

•

A vein pulsed in Caleb Harper's left temple. Half
an hour spent crawling in first gear – and he'd only
driven two miles.

Beside him, Jade was swiping her tablet,
commenting on a host of friends that Caleb had never
heard of.

'And Dad, this is how I want *my* hair – like Sophie's,
see? It's called Ombre, where the last few inches
are like, a different colour to the rest. I can't decide
between pearl and copper.' Jade swiped the screen
again, before thrusting a display of lurid coloured
hairstyles under Caleb's nose.

'Hey, stop it – I'm driving. Look, you're not ruining
your hair with any of that nonsense; you're fourteen!'

'You're not driving, we're just sitting here and it's
like, sooo boring,' Jade sighed heavily. 'If Mum was
here, she'd let me dye my hair.'

'Well she isn't – and anyway, I doubt that very
much. Your Mum loved your long shiny hair – and
your sister's.'

Hoping for traffic news, Caleb put the radio on.

'Can't we just go another way, Daddy?'

'No love, we're stuck – nothing is moving in any
direction. We're going to miss your appointment at
this rate.'

'Good, I don't want the bloody brace anyway! As if

I didn't stand out already for having no mum, now I'll have bloody train tracks in my mouth!'

'That's enough of that language. Jade, we talked about it. It'll only be for a year or so and then you'll have beautiful straight teeth for the rest of your life. Believe me – you'll thank me one day.'

'Yeah, but–'

Caleb shushed his daughter as news of a burst water main between Crabton and Eden Hill came through the air waves.

'Bloody ridiculous that it can cause all this chaos,' he barked.

'No swearing, Dad,' Jade sang, wagging her finger at him.

Caleb rang the dental surgery, explaining gruffly why they were running late.

'Well, I'm sorry,' came the receptionist's nasal voice over the speaker, 'but Mr Hart's got back-to-back appointments for the rest of the day. I'll have to rebook you. When would you like to come in?'

'Oh, I don't know … I'll ring back at a more convenient time,' Caleb said, the heat only adding to his ill humour.

'Are we still going out for milkshakes afterwards? You promised, Dad,' Jade pouted.

'After *what*? We might as well just go home, love.'

'Please, Daddy – I was looking forward to it.'

Caleb agreed, conscious that yet again he was

giving in to the guerrilla demands of one of his daughters out of some vague sense of guilt. It wasn't *their* fault their mum had died of cancer – and now they were all he had.

As the traffic began to creep forward, Caleb manoeuvred into a side street and even found a parking space a few doors down from the café. He exhaled. 'Come on then, trouble, let's get a cold drink before heading back. Your sister will be pleased to see us; I said we'd be at least two or three hours.'

•

Amber didn't hear her father's car coming to a stop, or even Ginger and Ralph's excited yelps as Caleb and Jade walked across the yard and in through the kitchen door.

In Amber's left ear, Jake was breathing hard and moaning, while her right was filled with the discordant strains of Tina & The Tramps, the indie band that she secretly dreamed of joining. She gasped as a gust of air filled the new space between her and Jake as he was yanked away from her, fear and shock filling his saucer eyes.

'Dad! What the fuck?!' Amber shrieked, pulling a sheet around her near naked body.

'*She's got no self-control, she does what she likes … woah-woah*', howled Tina, surmising the situation perfectly.

'Who the hell are *you*?' Caleb roared, pinning Jake

to the wall. Jake opened his mouth but the words wouldn't come.

'Get out!' Caleb shouted above the music. 'Amber, get dressed – you've got some explaining to do.'

•

Feeling wretched, Jake jogged across the fields. It had been an ugly scene ... so much yelling and Amber wailing that they *hadn't done anything*. And they hadn't – well not much. They'd both taken their tops off and Jake had ground his crotch into Amber's while he was kissing her. But even though it felt fantastic, neither of them wanted to *DO IT*.

Amber's Dad had been furious – calling Jake a 'feral little shit' and demanding to know his address. He'd been so scared he'd blabbed it, so now his mum would have to know. It was all a big fat, fucking mess.

With his house in sight, Jake began to cry, wracking sobs that choked him as he fumbled with his door keys before being sick on the hall floor.

CHAPTER 14

The Wildes

Lisa fanned a manicured hand in front of her face: 'The meat's resting and if anyone turns out to be veggie, I've made a butternut squash tart. I'm knackered already – I could do with a lie down, never mind hosting dinner for six,' she told Ben.

She surveyed the kitchen; everything shone despite hours spent chopping, sautéing and roasting. Mrs H (as Ben and Lisa called Ivy Harris, their fastidious cleaning lady) had spent half of Friday washing down paintwork, vacuuming and deep cleaning the bathrooms – much to Ben's amusement.

'Love, it's only the neighbours – and they won't be having a bath, will they? You worry too much. Anyway, the place is always spotless … between you and Mrs H, dirt's got no chance of survival in this house.'

'Ben, I just want everything to be perfect – for Rosemary, mostly. I like her, and I think we could be good friends.'

'The pursuit of perfection is the fastest route to failure,' Ben said.

'Blimey. That's a bit deep. Oh, look at the time! We need to help Mum downstairs – I told her to be ready by seven-fifteen.'

At exactly seven forty-five, the door knocker rapped loudly.

'I do wish people would ring the bell, that thing always makes me jump,' Lisa said, untying her apron and smoothing down her new topaz dress.

'I'll get it,' Ben said, greeting Nigel and Rosemary with more warmth than he felt. 'Well, don't you both scrub up a treat?' he said, kissing Rosemary on each cheek and shaking Nigel's hand. He indicated the tied bouquet Rosemary held. 'Are they for me?' he said to a ripple of polite laughter.

'We thought this was more your style, Ben,' Nigel produced an expensive looking bottle of red wine.

'Well thank you, now you're talking!' Ben ushered them through to the kitchen where Lisa was pouring champagne into fine flutes.

'Welcome! So lovely to see you both,' she said, kissing her guests and graciously accepting the flowers. 'Have you met my mum, Rita? She's staying for a while – just until her ankle heals properly.'

'Oh, you poor thing. What did you do?' Rosemary's warmth was in stark contrast to Nigel's indifference as he barely acknowledged Rita, turning his attention back to Ben.

'So, I hear you're a musician,' he said, coolly.

'Yeah, trying to be. I'm in a bit of a lull at the moment, although I was in the studio a few days ago, laying down some new material. How about you, Nigel?'

'I'm the operations director of a security firm.'

'What, alarms and stuff?' Ben raised his eyebrows, doing his best to look interested.

'In its most basic form, yes, but we use smart technology and our key markets are B2B–'

'Excuse me, Nigel – that'll be Rita's mate ...' Ben said, grateful for an escape route.

'Ooh, that'll be for me,' Rita said, fluffing her hair and straightening her beaded cardigan.

The women smiled at each other, indulging Rita's eagerness. But when Ben re-entered the room, Lisa smothered a gasp.

'Peeps, this is Jackie,' Ben said, as everyone turned to look at the suited octogenarian.

'Hello Princess,' the old man said, presenting Rita with a single red rose and bending to kiss her cheek.

•

'Why didn't you tell me, Mother?' Lisa hissed while she and Rita were alone in the kitchen between courses.

'Tell you what? That Jackie's a bloke? Speaks volumes, that does. It never occurred to you that I might meet someone at my age, did it? You think you're the only one that can pull a fella? Well Jackie's a good man – and he thinks the world of me.'

'Is that who you're always on the phone to, Mum? I'd have been happy for you – and he could have visited sooner. Where did you meet him?'

'Online, on one of those dating sites.'

'Oh my god, I can't believe I'm hearing this!'

Ben appeared, looking for wine. 'Old Jack's a scream!' he said. 'Do you know, he got his name after Jackie Charlton? Apparently, he was quite handy on the pitch in his day. Rita shoots – and she scores!' Ben said, laughing at his own joke.

Lisa shook her head: 'Ha! Well there's a thing, mother. When I was married to a footballer, I seem to remember you saying they were all thugs and losers.'

Rosemary appeared in the doorway, diffusing the situation. 'Can I do anything?'

'Be with you in two minutes,' Lisa said, adding, 'Mum, you hobble back through – don't leave Jack on his own.'

Moments later an appreciative silence descended while everyone sampled Lisa's slow-roasted leg of lamb.

'Lisa, this meat is delicious – so tender,' Rosemary said as everyone murmured agreement.

Lisa wore a look of triumph. 'I get all our meat at the organic butchers the other side of Crabton. Hey, where's Iris tonight?' she said, remembering the little girl for the first time that evening.

'In bed, I hope. She has a babysitter that we've used before, Angela – nice girl.' Rosemary's voice was soft, thinking about her daughter asleep next door.

'Shame to resort to a stranger,' Rita sniffed. 'What about her Grandmas?'

Lisa shot her mother a warning look.

'Sadly our parents are not on hand.' Rosemary looked to Nigel for support.

'My mother has dementia and is in a care home, and Rosemary's mum went back to Nigeria a few years ago. She comes over once a year, but we're pretty much on our own regards childcare,' Nigel said evenly.

'You know, if ever you're in a real pickle, you can always give me a knock,' Lisa said. 'I might not be a mum but I'm pretty sensible.'

Ben sniggered. 'Sensible? I don't know about that!'

The light-hearted banter returned, even Nigel seemed to be loosening up and Ben and Lisa found themselves topping up glasses faster than they'd anticipated.

Rosemary covered hers. 'That's enough wine for me. I always have to keep it together … in case Iris gets sick or something.'

'Of course.' Lisa rose from the table and began to clear empty plates, returning with homemade chocolate mousse and plump raspberries for dessert.

'Ben, I hear you're a pop star,' Jackie said, picking at his yellowed teeth with his thumbnail. 'Why don't you put one of your own records on, instead of this tripe?'

'Not a *Ministry of Sound* fan, then, eh Jackie?' Ben rifled through their vast CD collection.

'I'll play you my first single. It was massive back in the day … you might even remember it.'

Everyone stopped talking as *Seagull* filled the room, and they were taken back to 1997; the only movement was the flickering of candles and the stirring of filmy drapes.

Lisa gazed lovingly at Ben – the lyrics were romantic, bordering on slushy. If only he'd written Seagull for her.

A loud rap on the door broke the spell.

'Who the bloody hell … ?' Ben said, getting up. 'Christ!' he said, throwing the door wide.

'Hello mate,' Rick said, 'I'm sorry, I didn't know where else to go.'

Taking in his friend's derelict appearance, Ben ushered Rick into the study and poured him a glass of red wine.

'We've got a few people round, mate. They'll be leaving soon … can you give me a minute?'

'Yeah, yeah … of course. Soz, Benny … whatever you need to do.' Rick was meek; he drank the wine in a couple of gulps, then with an audible sigh, slumped in Lisa's armchair, closing his eyes.

'Don't go anywhere,' Ben said, realising that his bandmate was unlikely to move far.

Rick's sudden arrival had a sobering effect and the party broke up almost at once.

'Thank you both for your hospitality,' Nigel said. 'Delicious meal Lisa, you must come to us soon.'

'Yes, you must,' Rosemary agreed. 'I had such a lovely time, thank you so much for being great hosts. Rita, Jackie, so nice to meet you both. All the best. Goodnight.'

When it was Jack's turn to leave, Ben and Lisa turned away while he kissed Rita goodnight before getting into a taxi and vanishing into the balmy night.

Lisa yawned. 'I'll make us all a hot drink and fill the dishwasher – the rest can wait until tomorrow. Babe, you'd better sort Rick out. Something's obviously gone horribly wrong.'

Ben looked at his wife, who suddenly looked terribly tired and his heart swelled.

'You did good tonight, Leese, and I'm so proud of you. Tell you what, I'll load the dishwasher and bring you a cup of tea. You go up, you look shattered.'

True to his word, Ben stacked the crockery and took Lisa a cup of Earl Grey. Then he tiptoed back downstairs to find Rick emerging from the cloakroom.

'I wouldn't go in there just now if I were you,' Rick was sheepish.

'You gonna tell me what's going on, Ricky?' Ben said.

'Oh mate, it's all gone Pete Tong,' Rick hung his head, 'Jules has thrown me out.'

'Christ, when?'

'About a month ago.'

'A month? Shit. I had a feeling something was off at the studio. Where have you been living?'

'In my van … but it got towed this afternoon and I can't afford to get it back yet. Sorry about your dinner party, man – I didn't know what else to do.'

'Oh, bugger that. Look, you can stay here for a couple of nights, sort yourself out, and tomorrow we'll go and get the van.' Ben had no wish to add to Rick's pain and besides, his bed was calling.

AUTUMN

CHAPTER 15

The Bevans

'Aerial Man', as he was known locally, used a stubby pencil to complete his invoice in triplicate, and tore off the top copy.

Martin swallowed. 'Do you take credit cards?'

'Yep, carry me reader at all times. Most people don't have that sort of cash and cheques are about as fashionable as my wife's perm,' Aerial Man grinned.

Transaction completed, Aerial Man packed his tools away and left in his liveried van, leaving Martin to gaze in awe at the wafer-thin screen now filling his new sitting room wall.

'It's *enormous*,' Jan grumbled, 'and it's not like we watch much telly, is it?'

'Ha! You're glued to your soaps most nights ... not to mention all those grisly crime dramas we like,' Martin said, pacing the room to admire the screen from all angles. 'Anyway, you won't be complaining next time you're watching a good film – the sound quality alone will be worth the price tag.'

'I suppose so ... cuppa tea?' Jan went through to the bright modern kitchen which she'd already unpacked as a matter of priority. Seeing their new granite work tops gave her a little rush of pride, and she relished the smooth action of the taps as she filled the kettle.

'I still can't believe we're here ... it's all happened

so fast, Mart,' she said. 'I feel like we're living in a magazine.'

'The beauty of a short chain,' Martin said, adding, 'We've been very lucky my love – for once, all the cards stacked up in our favour.'

Martin thought back over the last few years, of all the customers he'd served from Eden Hill, feeling envious of their homes – shiny families with shiny manners, wearing shiny clothes. He only hoped that he and Jan would fit in.

He'd wanted to trade in their Vauxhall estate for something newer and snazzier.

'What about my dogs?' Jan had asked reasonably enough.

So they'd ended up with two cars; a nippy Italian job for Martin, now that he was unfettered by carpet and tile samples in his new retirement, while Jan designated the battered estate car as the 'dog wagon', her canine charges snuffling behind the grill.

'What about a house-warming?' Martin said, twitching cheerful plum curtains left by the previous owners and peering out at the close, with its well painted houses and neat front gardens, despite the browning leaves that had come down in the wind.

'Give us a chance, Mart! We only moved in yesterday. Anyway, we don't need to go gushing all over the neighbours, do we?' Jan said.

'We should at least introduce ourselves to the people either side.'

'They could just as easy give *us* a knock – see how we're getting on.'

'Jan, people don't want to get in the way, do they? Moving can be very stressful,' Martin reflected.

Outside a door slammed, and a young man emerged from the house next door, his olive complexion framed by dyed black hair that grazed his shoulders.

'It seems we have a *goth* living next door,' Martin said, emphasising the word.

'Ooh – that's interesting.' Jan peered outside. 'Do you remember Hayley's goth phase? When she sprayed her hair black and blue and got that tattoo … which turned out to be a stick-on transfer? You went ballistic, Mart,' Jan laughed.

'Well at least it was a short phase. Just look at the lad; he looks like he needs a good meal.' Martin made a face. 'Wonder what the parents are like?'

New house, new neighbours, and a new routine – it was all going to take some getting used to.

•

On Saturday evening, after a day spent arranging furniture and emptying dozens of cardboard boxes, Martin waited until seven o'clock and opened a bottle of champagne.

'Ooh, Martin, how extravagant!' Jan's eyes sparkled.

'Let's start as we mean to go on.' Martin raised his glass, 'To the future.'

'To the future,' Jan echoed, taking a sip and gasping as the bubbles hit the back of her throat. 'Ooh, that's lovely,' she said looking as happy as Martin could ever remember.

'It suits you,' Martin said, 'all this … living here.'

He put his arms around Jan, who snuggled closer. A knock at the door made them spring apart.

'I'll go,' Martin said, setting his glass down.

The porch light flicked on to reveal a dark-haired woman whom Martin surmised was in her early forties.

'Hi, I'm Chloe – I live next door,' she smiled, 'I just wanted to welcome you. I'd have come sooner but I've been at work, I run the coffee shop in the square.'

'That's very nice of you, Chloe. I'm Martin, come in and meet my wife, Jan,' he said, stepping aside to let Chloe pass.

'Oh, well – if you're sure …'

Martin took in Chloe's slim build and the way her hair was twisted into a loose bun at the nape of her neck. She smelled of warm vanilla.

'Come through to the kitchen, Chloe.' He called ahead to Jan, 'Love – it's our new neighbour.'

The women exchanged greetings, before Chloe set down a brown paper bag on the work surface.

'Just some cakes ... brownies, muffins, that sort of thing – all locally sourced and organic, from my shop.'

'Ooh, lovely, that's very kind of you. You shouldn't have – I'm naughty enough as it is when it comes to sweet things,' Jan said, thinking the woman standing before her looked as though she'd never eaten cake in her life.

'Oh, me too – but less so, since I've been surrounded by cakes all day,' Chloe beamed.

'Glass of champagne?' Martin said, already pouring.

'So ... er ... left or right?' he said, handing Chloe a glass.

'Cheers, thank you. I live to the right of you. It's just me and my son. I'm divorced ... well nearly. We've only been here a year ourselves. We lived in South London before that; how about you?'

'Crabton,' Martin said, 'we had a shop in the high street – Bevan's Flooring – and we lived a few blocks away.'

Chloe gasped. 'Isn't that the shop that burnt down? That must have been awful for you both.'

'It happened the day we came back from holiday,' Jan said. 'It was quite a shock, I can tell you.'

Martin nodded: 'But it was time for a change – and sometimes the universe gives us a push.'

'Was that your lad we saw earlier ... long dark hair, very slim?' Jan said, keen to change the subject.

'Yes – that's Jake. He's going through a bit of a phase. He's nearly sixteen and–'

'Been there,' Jan said. 'Our daughter Hayley got into all that for a while ... but it didn't last long. She lives in Brighton with her boyfriend now ... nice lad, Simon. They're engaged.'

Martin snorted, sceptical about whether Simon would ever put a ring on Hayley's finger.

'Well ... er, thank you for the champagne – it was lovely of you both. I must get back and sort something for dinner.'

'She's good looking, isn't she, Mart?' Jan said after Chloe had left.

'I hadn't noticed,' Martin lied, topping up their glasses.

•

The following week, Jan went back to work. They'd spent every waking hour organising the house so that everything had its place; pictures were on the walls, curtains and blinds hung at windows, and internet and phone lines were connected. Friends and family had been emailed or sent change of address cards, and Jan and Martin had even walked into the square and registered with Eden Hill's doctor and dentist.

'It's been a good week – productive,' Jan said. 'But

I've missed my dogs … all their trusting little faces. I can't wait to see them all.'

With the day's schedule and respective keys on board, Jan used Martin's old car to drive around Eden Hill, picking up Rosie, Poppet and Spike from their homes. It felt different somehow; going into her customers' smart detached houses, because now she was one of *them* – with a home at least as spacious and handsome of her own.

Jan drove to the woods between Eden Hill and Crabton, parking in the lane near Regents Square. Now that really was a cut above, she thought, helping her furry charges out of the rear door, except for Spike the pug, who as usual, leapt out as soon as Jan opened the boot.

Peering through wrought iron gates, Jan wondered if Lisa Dixon still lived at No. 3, and as if conjured by telepathy, Lisa appeared, dressed elegantly in a wool coat and long boots – although neither were necessary as the weather was mild for October.

Lisa waved and started towards Jan, her heels clicking as she walked.

'Hiya!' she called, slipping through a side gate to avoid speaking through the bars. 'How are you and Martin getting on?'

'We're fine, thanks – just moved here as a matter of fact, into Constance Close, up the other end of Eden Hill.'

'Oh, that's a nice road … lovely houses,' Lisa enthused. 'Aww, look at these babies,' she said, reaching down to stroke Poppet the Spaniel, who nuzzled her hand. 'By the way, I was sorry to hear about the fire; what's Martin doing now?'

It was an innocent question, full of concern, but Jan was irritated by Lisa's interest.

'He hasn't decided yet. He's taking some time off – and it's not as though we can't afford it. Anyway, I'd better go – these dogs won't walk themselves. Bye,' Jan said, ending the conversation.

Bumping into Lisa had taken the wind out of her sails. She found herself trudging through the fallen leaves on the woodland floor, stewing on the past, rather than appreciating the present. Even now, it was excruciating to look back, to a time when she'd believed Martin was having an affair with Lisa. It stirred up unwanted feelings and made her feel utterly stupid; as if a woman like Lisa Dixon had ever had designs on Martin. It was indicative of her state of mind at the time. Jan remembered the long dark days lost to depression, existing numbly under a blanket of medication. It was a wonder she had survived at all.

Poppet interrupted Jan's thoughts with a sharp bark. The little cocker spaniel was alert, standing excitedly at the mouth of a rabbit hole, wagging not only her tail, but her whole rear end.

'Poppet, leave the bunnies! Come here, girl – let's

put you back on your lead for a bit, you walk with Auntie Jan.'

Crooning to the three dogs she walked back towards the car. In another hour, she'd pick up Barker and Basil and then she'd be done for the day. Tomorrow would be much the same. It was a soothing routine that differed only insomuch as the dogs she walked and weather she walked in. Which was just how Jan liked things.

CHAPTER 16

The Mortons

Chloe poured herself a large glass of Merlot and hoped it wouldn't curdle with the champagne she'd drunk at the Bevans'.

They'd seemed nice enough – if incredibly straight. But there was something about the woman; she'd been watchful, guarded.

But what did it matter who lived next door? Chloe curled up on the sofa and pulled a throw across her lap. It was unlikely they'd become firm friends – although not impossible.

Saturday night stretched ahead of her. Chloe thought back to her old life in Streatham, to a time when a free evening in would have been her idea of bliss and the very definition of luxury. These days, Chloe spent too much time alone to relish the solitude.

She picked up her mobile phone and sent a text to her son. 'Jake, what time RU home?'

He'd said he was going round to Dylan's to play guitar and listen to music, but both his guitars were propped on their stands upstairs. Maybe Dylan, who was a keen musician, had several guitars. Or perhaps Jake had lied about his whereabouts entirely.

Chloe topped up her glass and sighed. The unpalatable truth was that since *Ambergate*, Jake had become furtive, retreating into his shell and rarely telling her anything. Her own son, her beautiful, kind, intelligent boy had become a morose, grunting, blank-eyed stranger. She could just about cope with the dyed black hair and even the occasional smudge of guy-liner, but the silent treatment hurt like hell. Well it was obvious who was to blame for that, she thought bitterly.

She remembered the particularly muggy Tuesday in August, when she'd arrived home from work, longing for a cool shower and a glass of white wine in the garden. But as soon as she'd shut the front door, the pungent reek of vomit stopped Chloe in her tracks.

'Jake?' she called out, 'where are you? Are you okay?'

Jake slouched at the top of the stairs, pale and puffy eyed. 'Mum, sorry – I tried to clean it up, but it still stinks … I didn't know what to use.' He hung his head.

'Never mind that!' Alarmed, Chloe jogged upstairs, wine and shower forgotten. 'Darling, what's the matter? Why did you throw up?' Jake was robust; she could count the times that he'd been sick on one hand.

'I can't talk about it!' Jake said hoarsely.

'Yes, you can, Jakey. You can tell me anything – I'm your mum. What is it?'

But Jake had only gone to his room and closed the

door. Chloe listened hard, sure she could hear him crying.

It couldn't be anything to do with school, Chloe reasoned. He was on holidays, what on earth had upset him?

The doorbell rang – not once, but a stabbing, urgent jingling.

Fear gripped Chloe's heart.

'Who is it, please?' she said, wishing she'd slid the chain across on her arrival home. Through the spy hole Chloe could see a man; tall, dark-haired, good looking – and furious.

'It's Caleb Harper, Amber's Dad. Open the door!'

The name meant nothing, but even distorted by rage and the fish eye lens of the spy hole, Caleb Harper's face looked familiar.

Chloe opened the door halfway.

'I need to speak to Jake's father – is he here?' Harper blustered.

'No, he isn't. I'm Jake's mother. What's the problem?'

'The problem is your son! He's been screwing my daughter. I caught them red-handed today. He denied it of course.'

'Whoa, whoa! Slow down. I think you've made a mistake. My son doesn't know anybody called Amber.' Chloe stood her ground, her pulse racing.

'I should have known … it's usually the parents' fault,' Caleb said, contempt in his voice.

'How *dare* you? You come round here, shouting the odds – you should get your facts straight before you–'

'Mum! It was me …' Jake had crept downstairs and was now sheltering behind her.

For a nanosecond, nobody spoke.

'Caleb, you'd better come in – I'm Chloe,' she said, stepping aside. 'Jake, you need to be in this conversation, too. Now let's sit down and sort this out like adults.'

But once inside, Caleb had continued to rage; about how that morning he'd caught Jake and Amber almost naked on her bed.

'I told you! We were just kissing! I'm not stupid, you know, we're only fifteen.'

'Bollocks!' Caleb shouted. 'I didn't come down in the last fucking shower.'

'Don't you *dare* speak to my son like that!' Chloe fumed, going to Jake's side. 'If he says they were only kissing, then that's what happened. What does Amber say? Who, by the way, I had no idea even existed until now, but that's another discussion.' Jake started to protest, but Chloe held up her hand.

'They were naked – from the waist up, anyway,' Caleb insisted.

'Ah, now we're getting to it. So they were topless

– that doesn't mean that they were having sex, does it?' Chloe looked at Jake whose cheeks were burning.

'I swear Mum, me and Amber have *never* had sex – we just wouldn't.'

Chloe addressed Harper: 'I believe him. It's a shame you don't trust your daughter. What does her mother say about all this?'

Something in Caleb's expression made Chloe regret the words as soon as they were out of her mouth.

'Amber's Mum passed away ... from cancer ... so it's just me, Amber and her little sister Jade. I'm doing my best, but it's not ...' He trailed off, holding up his hands in a gesture of defeat.

'Sorry to hear that,' Chloe said softly, really looking at him for the first time and noticing how sad his eyes were. *Sad eyes*; it was all coming back to her – dinner and drinks with Bryony at The Speckled Hen Bar & Grill a couple of weeks earlier. He'd checked her out and had looked mortified to be caught. She wondered if he recognised her from that night. If he did, he did not show it.

Chloe's mobile vibrated, bringing her back to the present, her memory of Caleb's rant fading.

Jake's reply to her text was succinct. 'Late.'

No 'Hi Mum', no love, no kisses. She barely recognised her son from the bright-eyed, studious child he had been eighteen months earlier. Before leaving London and her separation from William, before Jake had changed schools, pre-Ambergate, pre-being put off having a girlfriend for life, quite possibly – thanks to Caleb Harper's Gestapo tactics.

'Come back to me Jakey,' Chloe whispered to an empty room.

Realising she'd drunk two thirds of a bottle, Chloe turned the television on hoping to escape into a drama, but instead found only talent contests and game shows.

She was about to run herself a deep scented bath when the doorbell rang.

Oh, for god's sake, she thought, heading for the front door, where she was astonished to find Caleb Harper.

'Hello,' he said, 'sorry for dropping in unannounced. I didn't know how else to get hold of you.'

'Oh … well I was just …'

'Chloe, I wanted to apologise. I know it's been ages since … that day with Jake and Amber, but I'm sorry. I got that all wrong, I know that now … and I wondered … would you have a drink with me sometime?'

CHAPTER 17

The Wildes

'I can't take much more of this,' Lisa said, rubbing vigorously at a red wine stain on her cream carpet, courtesy of Rick.

'I know what you mean, babe; this place is like a dosshouse. We should start charging rent – that'd get everybody moving.'

'Ben, you've got to do something or I can't be responsible for my actions,' Lisa said, giving up on the stain, which had merely faded from deep damson to light raspberry in colour.

'Okay, I'll have a word with Ricky, but Leese, you'll have to tackle your mum. Her ankle's fine now. All this business with the builders? It's just an excuse if you ask me – she's got too used to you waiting on her hand and foot for months on end.'

Ben had a point. Rita had announced grandly that while she was 'indisposed' as she'd put it, she was having an extension built on her three-bed semi.

Lisa had been baffled. 'But why, Mum? There's only you – and it's not like you need more space, is it?'

Then Rita had dropped the bomb. Jack was moving in – as soon as she'd 'upgraded' her fusty eighties kitchen, with its froufrou beaded cabinets and faux marble counters, as well as expanding by three metres into her neglected patch of garden.

'Mum, are you sure?' Lisa said, wide-eyed.

'Oh yes, love. I've fancied doing it for years, but now–'

'No, not that,' Lisa said 'I meant Jack … moving in. Mother, he's over eighty, and you've only known him ten minutes!'

'Nine months actually,' Rita said primly. 'My Jackie's a good man – and the fact that we're both getting on a bit is exactly why we're not hanging around. Lisa, nobody wants to die alone, with just the ticking of the clock for company.'

So against all her better instincts, Lisa had welcomed Jack into the family – but was mortified when he began staying over regularly.

'Do you think they're *at it*? I mean, old Jack's still got a twinkle in his eye,' Ben sniggered.

'Oh, please – do you have to? It's not funny. Poor old thing could have a heart attack … and I've no wish to picture my mum in the throes of passion, either!'

So work on Rita's extension had commenced – until the Lithuanian builders had found a snag; a drain shared with the house next door, which, if built over, would become inaccessible. A consultation with the council followed – but only after Rita's kitchen had been ripped out and taken back to a dusty shell.

Rita was furious, blaming the builders for their ineptitude and threatening to sue – at which point,

Lukas and his changing cast of brothers had walked off the job, never to return.

Desperate to reclaim their spare room, not to mention their privacy, Ben and Lisa had intervened, getting quotes and hiring a project manager, making it all very protracted.

'It'll be Christmas before she's back home,' Lisa wailed.

'Over my dead body! Look, we've just got to trust the builders – now all that business with the drain's been sorted, they'll zip through it – you'll see, Leese.'

•

Rick on the other hand, came and went as the mood took him, but always left his battered, and in Lisa's opinion, sour smelling possessions in her study, which he'd commandeered as a bedroom slash man cave.

'But where does he go when he's not here?' Lisa said, wishing he would just stay there.

'Beats me,' Ben said, shaking his curls. 'Jules has refused to take him back. They're hardly speaking now and I think she's even mentioned the D word.'

Lisa pursed her lips. 'Well, I'm not surprised. From what you've told me, it's obvious he's been playing away for months – why should any wife put up with that? Ben, I know he's your friend, but really–'

'Babe, I'll see what I can do. I'm fed up with him

being here, too. I know he's seeing *someone* – so why he can't move in with her, is anybody's guess.'

•

The Garden Gate was dead except for a handful of office workers on their lunch break, and a trio of fifty-something women who appeared to be celebrating a birthday. Ben had taken his bandmate there with the express intention of evicting him and had opened the subject by asking Rick about his mystery girlfriend.

Rick grimaced. 'It's complicated. Jessie's married. Her husband works on a rig in the North Sea. It's a fucking mess, man,' Rick said, staring glumly into the pint Ben had just paid for.

'Ah, right. So, have you got feelings for this woman then?'

Rick nodded mournfully. 'I love her, Ben. Me and Jules have just been going through the motions for years. Of course, she found out about me and Jessie … I got a bit careless. It was always going to happen.'

'Mate, you've been living in my house for weeks – how come you're telling me this now? Look, I sympathise, I really do. But you know … me and Leese, we need to get *our* lives back on track. We've had her whinging mother since the summer … place is like a doss-house … you can see that, can't you, Ricky?'

Rick nodded. ''course I can mate. I don't want to

cramp your style and I certainly don't want to upset your missus. Lisa's a cracking girl.'

'She is, Ricky-boy. Another pint?'

The following day, in an effort to be conciliatory, Rick bought all the local papers, and began trawling rental websites.

'I'll be out of your hair in a week or so, Ben – I'll even pay to have your carpet cleaned,' he grinned.

'No, don't worry about that – we can sort it … save your money, mate. You'll need a deposit for a flat – renting is bloody expensive these days.' Ben felt his mobile buzz in his jeans pocket.

'Hang on, my arse is ringing … Ben Wilde here,' he said into the receiver.

'Ben? It's Greg – Greg Lyons,' said a familiar voice. 'I've got some rather interesting news for you.'

•

When Lisa returned from getting her hair cut and coloured in Tunbridge Wells, Ben wasted no time in telling her about Greg's call.

'Your hair looks lovely, babe. But you might want to sit down. I've got some good news and some bad news.'

Lisa was on high alert. 'Go on,' she said.

'Ok, good news first; old Ricky is moving out and going on tour.'

'I'm sensing a but here …'

'Yeah, well … the bad news is, I'm going with him.' Ben waited for Lisa's reaction.

She paused, processing Ben's words. 'Am I going to need a drink for this?' Lisa said going to the fridge and opening a bottle of Sauvignon Blanc.

'Yeah, maybe. We'll either be celebrating or drowning our sorrows, depending on how you look at it.'

Then it had all come out – the phone call from Greg announcing fifteen dates across nine major European cities, culminating with two London gigs as part of a 90s retro tour.

'Kicking off with Hamburg in six weeks,' Ben concluded, taking a sip of wine.

'Six weeks? Why such short notice? Tours like that take years to plan. Why are you hearing about it now?'

Ben rubbed two days' stubble. 'I get the impression that we weren't first choice, Leese – that some other band must have bailed. Look, I've already checked, and I'll be here for Christmas and New Year – then we're playing Helsinki mid-Jan, which will be fucking freezing, but beggars can't be choosers.' Ben shivered at the prospect of Finland in January.

'Ben, do you actually want this?' Lisa said in a small voice.

'I do, and I don't. I hate the thought of being away, and of leaving you. But it's a great opportunity

– you won't believe some of the headline acts – and financially, it's bomb proof.'

Lisa chewed her lip.

'Babe, it's what I do. Me, Ricky and Steve … on the road … hey, thank god we've had some studio time recently and are still tight, because the next few weeks will be intense.' Ben set his glass down. 'And there'll be no more of this stuff after tonight, I'm in training. Rehearsals start tomorrow and I'll be in the gym most mornings by eight.'

Lisa squared her shoulders and attempted a brave smile.

'I'll miss you so much, darling,' she said, putting her arms around Ben's neck and leaning against him, 'but I couldn't be more proud of you. Hey, I might even come out for the last leg of the tour before London.'

'That's the spirit, girl,' Ben said, suddenly excited.

CHAPTER 18

The Bradshaws

At dusk, a dank mist settled on Eden Hill. Mindless of the chill, by five o'clock Rosemary could no longer contain her daughter's excitement.

Despite her reservations, Rosemary had caved in to Iris's pleading, and was allowing her to go Trick or Treating for Halloween.

Nigel had been furious. 'I can't have my daughter rampaging around the neighbourhood, terrorising people and blatantly begging,' he said.

'Nigel, come on. It's only a bit of fun – it's just dressing up. Can you honestly imagine Iris rampaging anywhere? I'll be with her, and we'll keep it to the Square – and anyway, I hardly think a few sweets in a plastic bucket adds up to grand scale begging. Let her be a child, Nigel, it's good for her.'

'Very well,' he said coldly, before hanging up from somewhere on the M1.

Rosemary made a face as she replaced the handset. 'And where the hell are you, anyway?'

'Mummy! Are we going now? How much *longer*?'

Dressed as a witch's cat in black leggings and leotard, and wearing plush pointy ears and a long tail, Iris looked cute as a button and not remotely scary.

Rosemary produced her smartphone. 'Okay, let Mummy take a photo for Daddy, then we'll go.'

Iris posed, raising her pink varnished claws and affecting a roar. 'Mummy, please! Come *on*,' she said, opening the front door and letting in a blast of cold air.

After a brief discussion about whether Iris needed her winter coat (Rosemary's verdict was that adrenalin would keep her warm for the fifteen or so minutes it would take to knock at five houses) they set off into the darkness. Beyond the gates of Regents Square, Rosemary could see small huddles of children in spooky costumes, carrying pumpkin buckets and lanterns as they straggled along the pavements.

Iris was beside herself, tripping over her own feet in her excitement.

'Okay,' Rosemary whispered, 'remember what I said; be polite and grateful, whatever people offer you, okay?'

Iris nodded earnestly before knocking at the house furthest from theirs. 'Trick or treat!' she yelled in her high, sweet voice.

Mrs Curtis, a retired teacher whom Rosemary had met a handful of times answered the door holding a tray of iced biscuits.

'Well don't you look marvellous?' she said. 'Do take some – they're freshly baked.'

'Oh yes, I can smell the cinnamon,' Rosemary said, 'Thank you, Hazel – that's very kind of you. What do you say, Iris?'

'Thank you,' Iris said, dropping two biscuits into her pumpkin pot.

They swerved two houses that were in complete darkness and made their way to the Robertsons, who lived to the right of Ben and Lisa.

Ray and Cathy Robertson answered the door together, smiling benignly and wearing matching sweaters.

'There was no 'trick or treat' when our boys were little,' Cathy said, offering Iris sweets from a glass bowl, 'but don't you a look a poppet?'

Ray frowned. 'Another damn Americanism we seem to have adopted.'

'Language, Ray! Take no notice … go on, Iris, have another one – look, here's a caramel.'

'My husband isn't a fan, either,' Rosemary said, adding, 'Do you have grandchildren yet?'

Cathy beamed, her blue eyes becoming merry. 'One on the way … oh, we're so excited, aren't we Ray?' she said.

'Riveted, dear,' Ray said, the corners of his mouth twitching with amusement.

They chatted a moment or two longer until Iris began to fidget. 'I need the toilet, Mummy,' she whined, stamping her little black boots.

Rosemary said goodnight to Cathy and Ray and turned towards their own house.

'Can we go to Lisa's?' Iris said.

'Of course, but you wanted–'

'Oh, the feeling's gone now – I made a mistake,' Iris said, skipping up Lisa's path. In the study window, a jack-o'-lantern flickered, and the front door was festooned in spray cobwebs.

Unbeknown to Iris, Lisa had pre-invited them in for pumpkin soup and nibbles, so after the trick or treat ritual had been played out to its brisk conclusion, Rosemary and her daughter followed Lisa into the kitchen. In the warm glow, Rita was amply filling a Lloyd Loom chair, and holding a glass of red wine.

'Well don't you look a picture?' she said, arms outstretched to hug the little girl.

Rosemary laughed. 'So people keep telling her – she'll get a big head!'

'Red or white, Rose – I've got both open,' Lisa said, giving a saucepan of soup a quick stir.

•

The Halloween decorations at the Bertram Hotel were feeble. Jacob and his team had started out well enough, carving two huge jack-o'-lanterns; one for reception and the other for the bar in the guests' lounge, but the addition of strings of fairy lights shaped like ghosts and pumpkins had lowered the collective tone considerably.

Nigel sat alone nursing a gin and tonic, his eyes on the door.

'Will you be dining with us tonight, sir?' A young waitress with a broad Yorkshire accent hovered uncertainly.

'I haven't decided yet – I'm waiting for a colleague,' Nigel lied.

He hoped that the agency had booked the red-haired woman who'd called herself Cheryl. He doubted it was her real name; he doubted that any of the young women he had sex with at the Bertram used their real names for work. It wasn't important – although if it was Cheryl tonight, it would be the third time he'd seen her, and he was going to ask.

'Hello. How are you, Nigel?' Cheryl had come through a rear door and was standing at his left shoulder.

'I'm well, thank you. Please, sit down. What would you like to drink? Let me guess – a white wine spritzer?'

The young woman nodded and sat. She seemed nervous, straightening her dress and checking her appearance in a compact she produced from her bag while Nigel spoke to the waitress.

'I'm glad it's you, Nigel,' Cheryl said quietly, adding 'you never know who you're going to get and I … oh, don't mind me, I'm talking too much. How was your day?'

'Productive. Dull. Actually, I thought we might chat for a while.'

'Yes of course,' Cheryl took a large swallow of her drink.

'You seem preoccupied,' Nigel said, looking around. As usual only a handful of guests lingered in the shabby bar area.

'Do I? No, not me; I'm happy with my wash, as my mum would say.' She laughed, a fragile giggle that was just the right side of irritating.

'Do you see your parents much?' Nigel said, anticipating the answer.

'It's just me and my mum – we live together. We moved up here from Nottingham two years ago, to be near my grandma … she's old, bless her.'

A tart with a heart, thought Nigel.

'Are you hungry?' he said, changing the subject and hoping she wasn't.

'No, I'm fine thank you. Why don't we go upstairs, so we can be alone?'

They finished their drinks then using the lift went up to the second floor.

Once inside Nigel's room Cheryl began unbuttoning his shirt.

'Why don't you get into bed,' she said, 'and let me take away all the stress of the day. I can give you a massage first if you like.'

'As I'm the one who's paying, I think I should set the agenda, don't you?' Nigel opened the mini bar, then closed it again without removing anything.

'Of course. I just thought–'

'I'm not paying you to think.' He sat down on the bed. 'Now, tell me about yourself – starting with your real name, Miss Cheryl.'

•

'But don't you get lonely with Nigel away so much?' Lisa began stacking empty bowls and plates.

Rosemary stood up. 'Here, let me help … I guess I'm used to it, Lisa. When we first met, Nigel hardly travelled at all, but since the head office moved up north, he's there most weeks.'

'Mummy, look!' Iris giggled and pointed to Nellie, who was now wearing the plush pussycat ears, and doing her best to paw them off.

'Oh, Iris no! You can tell she doesn't like it – take them off her, please,' Rosemary admonished.

Lisa was unperturbed. 'Nellie's fine, she never snaps and she's probably glad to have someone to play with. So, Iris, how was your first Trick or Treat?'

'I liked dressing up as a cat and coming to your house best,' she said, adding 'but where are *your* children? Why didn't they come for Trick or Treat?'

Rosemary and Lisa exchanged looks.

'Hey! It's rude to fire questions at adults, Iris – you know that,' Rosemary said, feeling the heat in her cheeks.

Lisa smiled. 'I don't have any children, Iris – just

Nellie … she's like my baby though. Now, how about a creepy cupcake?' Lisa produced a box of iced buns decorated with spiders.

'Gross!' Iris said, making a face and taking one anyway.

'Sweetpea, why don't you take one to Rita? She's in the sitting room watching television,' Rosemary suggested, before apologising for her daughter's candour.

Lisa shrugged it off but not before Rosemary thought she saw a fleeting sadness in her eyes.

'So, how's Ben?' Rosemary said, changing the subject.

'Excited. Can you believe he'll soon be on tour? We only heard a week ago. I'm happy for him, and god knows he needs it for his sanity, but I'll miss him, Rosie.'

'Of course you will. I envy your closeness. You've got a lovely bond, Lisa; anyone can see that.'

'Do you think?'

'I *know*. For one thing, you can hardly keep your hands off each other. Nigel and I were *never* like that … even when we first met, and the more time passes–' Rosemary stopped talking. She'd said too much already. Lisa was a new friend, to say any more would be inappropriate.

Lisa smiled encouragingly. 'You can talk to me … about anything. I'm unshockable.'

'Another time,' Rosemary said. 'We should go. I need to get Iris to bed now. Thank you for our lovely Halloween supper, it was so kind of you, Lisa.'

Outside, the temperature had fallen. Leaving Lisa's cosy kitchen was a wrench, with its aura of love and good will; feelings that were tangibly lacking in Rosemary's own home – with or without Nigel in it.

CHAPTER 19

The Bevans

Martin had spent an hour putting his CD collection into alphabetical order and was pleased with his work. He'd debated with Jan about whether to file individual artists by their first or last names. But he'd floundered with the groups. Some were a breeze; the Beach Boys for instance, but he'd dithered over whether the Rolling Stones should go under R or S, finally settling on R.

'Oh, for goodness sake Martin,' Jan said eventually through clenched teeth, 'I've never seen you like this. I think it's time you went back to work. How you can make such a pantomime out of a few records, I do not know.'

'Records … arh, there's a thing. I wish I'd hung onto mine. The excitement of seeing the cover for the first time … and of reading the lyrics on the inner sleeve. And don't start me on coloured vinyl.'

Jan curled her lip; 'I won't. Martin, I worry about you – rattling round this house all day, fiddling about with nonsense. I know the shop's gone for good, but what about a part-time job?'

'Doing what?' Martin said.

'Oh, I don't know, but something – and soon, before you drive us both round the bend. Tell you what, Mart; come out walking with me tomorrow. I've got three of my regulars at ten o'clock, then a new dog at noon. Lovely girl she is, so friendly – a staffie-cross called Paula.'

Martin shook his head in disbelief. 'Paula? What sort of name is that for a dog?'

'Her owners recently rescued her from a shelter near Ashford and that's the name she came with; poor thing's got enough problems without confusing her with a new name.'

•

The following morning, after microwaved porridge and two cups of tea each, Jan and Martin set off to collect the day's dogs.

'I'll drive and you just carry on as normal,' Martin said, daunted by blundering into empty houses where dogs waited, wild with anticipation.

'How you manage three at a time, all barking and leaping about – plus managing all these locks and alarms, I'll never know,' Martin said.

Feeling a degree of pride, Jan smiled and said nothing.

Martin drove to the woods and parked outside Lisa Dixon's development where together they unloaded Poppet, Spike and Basil, just as the heavens opened.

'Bloody marvellous, that's all we need,' grumbled Martin.

'Don't fuss, Mart. It's only water,' Jan said, pulling

up the zip on her red anorak. 'Here, stop moaning and take Basil's lead while I hold Spike and Poppet.'

Undeterred by the rain, the dogs jostled, yapped and pulled, eager to get into the woods but after a while the trio fell into a brisk rhythm.

'Bless them,' Martin said, 'It's clear how much these pups love you, Jan.'

Jan's eyes misted. 'And I love them, Martin. They've changed my life. I can hardly remember the person I was two years ago, when I rarely left the house, never mind went on lovely long walks in all weathers. All those years spent sleepwalking through life, what a waste. How you put up with me then, Martin ...' Jan fell silent.

Rain continued to fall steadily, glossing the carpet of russet leaves on the woodland floor. Martin was surprised by the number of dog walkers they encountered; Jan seemed to know them all by sight and most by name.

'You've found your niche, my love. I'm really proud of you,' Martin said, as they reloaded three wet, muddy dogs into the car.

'You soppy sod! Here, help me towel them down – they can't go home in this state!'

With less than an hour until the next walk, Jan and Martin decided against going home – instead they sat in the car, sucking Polo mints and watching the rain.

'What will you do if it snows this year?' Martin said.

'Same as last year, I suppose. Put an extra layer on and bring a flask of tea … the dogs don't care what the weather's doing. Neither do the owners. Some are lovely, but I've got a couple of right snooty cows who look down their noses at me.'

Martin started the car and they set off to collect Jan's latest recruit.

'Right Martin, you stay here. Some dogs are nervous of men and it can be tricky getting into people's houses for the first time. I've only met Paula once, and her owner was there, so there's no saying what she'll do.'

Using her shiny new key, Jan walked straight into the hallway, where Paula stood wagging her tail and smiling from ear to ear. She gave an excited yelp and began trotting in circles as Jan called her name.

'Oh, *what* a good girl,' Jan crooned, casting around for Paula's lead which had been left out for her on the hall table.

Outside, the Staffordshire bull terrier leapt willingly into the back of the estate, which was already pungent with the smell of wet dog.

'Well that was easy,' Jan said with a sigh of relief. 'Okay Martin, can you drive back to the green near us, please – then we'll give her a nice long street walk.'

Martin turned on the ignition. 'Not the woods then, love?'

'Not for the first few times. I need to get the

measure of her. She's certainly a happy girl, look at that tail wagging, bless her.' Jan turned to look at the excited terrier.

By the time Martin had parked beside Cabbage Green, the verdant scrap of land only moments' walk from their home, the rain had stopped.

In Jan's experience, few owners ventured out with their dogs around midday; it was a lull that lasted until children returned from school and most dogs were given their second walk of the day.

Today, a toffee coloured spaniel was chasing a tennis ball being thrown by a rotund woman of around sixty.

Paula sniffed the air, then lunged forward eagerly.

'No, Paula – not today, sweetheart, you can play another time,' Jan said, as the terrier strained at her lead.

They set off at a brisk pace, sticking to the edge of the green, with Paula panting hard and pulling like a train.

'Ooh, she's in a hurry – and strong, too. I might have to use a harness next time. Feel her go, Martin,' Jan said, passing him the lead for a moment. As they neared the woman with the spaniel, Jan smiled and inclined her head. She couldn't remember seeing her before, but gave her a little wave regardless, mindful of dog-walking etiquette. Neither smile nor wave were returned. Jan harrumphed under her breath, irritated at being blanked.

Martin shook his head: 'Take no notice, love – some people are just rude.'

'Silly old–' Jan began, stopping abruptly as the little spaniel began hurtling towards Paula who was now on high alert.

'Aaallffieee. Alfie, come!' shouted the woman, trotting in the wake of the spaniel as fast as her bulk would allow. By now Alfie was bouncing around Paula, keen to play.

Jan tightened her grip on the lead, winding it around her hand as Paula began to snarl and bare her teeth.

'Go away, boy – she's not playing, go on. GO!' Jan cried, as Martin tried in vain to stop the little dog coming closer.

'Aaallfiee!' called the woman, her voice soaring with panic.

But the spaniel failed to read Paula's body language and Jan watched in utter horror as the terrier bit down on Alfie's muzzle and held fast.

'Leave, Paula – *leave!*' Jan shouted, bending over the two dogs who were now locked together by the might of Paula's jaws. Alfie yelped in pain as Paula let out a low rumble, before releasing her grip.

'Bloody hell,' cried Martin 'now what? She's drawn blood!'

'Oh, my poor Alfie!' wailed the woman, examining the dog, who was now quivering and cowed.

Mortified, Jan did her best to be conciliatory. 'I'm terribly sorry,' she began, 'I suspect it's not as bad as it looks but I–'

'You stupid woman!' the other shrieked. 'Look what your vicious dog has done! Look at Alfie's face! You people ... with your ... *status* dogs,' the woman spat contemptuously.

'Now then..! There's no need for that.' Martin cut in. 'She's not even our dog. My wife is a professional dog walker and it's the first time she's–'

'I don't care whose dog it is! That Pitbull should be muzzled and kept under control.'

'Firstly, she's not a Pitbull, she's a Staffordshire-cross; secondly, *she* is on a short lead – it was *your* dog that was out of control ... coming over here, causing trouble. This is ridiculous!'

'How *dare* you. People like you ...' the woman jabbed a fat finger in Jan's direction.

'Jan, take the dog and leave this to me,' Martin said, sensing a slanging match in the offing.

Jan hesitated before marching in the opposite direction, admonishing the terrier as she went.

'Look, there's no real harm done – it was only a scratch,' Martin said, bending to look at Alfie, who had recovered surprisingly well, and was now on his feet wagging his tail and snuffling Martin's hand in search of a biscuit. The wound, which had already stopped bleeding, was indeed only a nick.

'*This*,' the woman hissed, 'is a respectable community. I suggest from now on, you and your wife walk that dog elsewhere.'

Martin began to protest, thought better of it and turned on his heels to catch Jan up.

CHAPTER 20

The Mortons

The Speckled Hen was heaving with Friday night revellers.

'Thank goodness we booked,' Chloe said as she and Caleb were shown to a corner table where they could people watch undisturbed.

Chloe waited until Caleb was engrossed in the menu before stealing a glance at his profile, drinking in his strong brow, the curve of his eyelashes and his generous straight nose.

Even on their first meeting, with Caleb shouting the odds and threatening her son, Chloe had seen how handsome he was.

Handsome and rude and arrogant!

Nobody – least of all Chloe – could have predicted that only a few months later they'd be on their third date.

'Where are the girls tonight?' Chloe said, revisiting their usual launch pad for conversation.

'They're both at home, watching Beauty and the Beast – again.' A furrow appeared in Caleb's brow. 'I left Amber in charge. I've got to start trusting them, haven't I? They're almost young women. How about Jake?'

'He's at a friend's house, listening to music and playing guitar. He's getting quite good I think –

although his taste in music leaves a lot to be desired,' Chloe said.

'No girlfriend on the scene then ... since Amber, I mean?'

'Not that I know of. I think Jake's gone off the whole idea. Then again, the first thing I knew about Amber was when you–'

Caleb groaned. 'Came bursting in like a bull in a china shop. I know, I know – I've said I'm sorry. I was just being a protective Dad – my girls are all I've got.' His face clouded over.

'Are you hungry?' Chloe asked, eager to change the subject, 'I'm starving; I think I might have the lamb shank.'

Caleb nodded. 'Yep, the lamb sounds good ... just what we need on a night like this.'

'November's grim isn't it? Dark all the time, and with the spectre of Christmas just up ahead. How on earth do you manage to get up before dawn at this time of year? I think farming must be one of the hardest ways to earn a living,' Chloe said with genuine admiration.

'You get used to it ... I've done it all my life. My parents were farmers – I've never known anything else. Anyway, it can't be much different for you; you must get up in the dark to get the shop open.'

'Ah, yes. The coffee shop; the words *be careful what you wish for* spring to mind.'

'Why do you say that?' Caleb paused as a fresh-faced waitress arrived with a bottle of Malbec and two large glasses; the warm and familiar glug-glug-glug sound made them both smile as she poured.

Caleb raised his glass. 'Cheers, Chloe – so glad you were free tonight. You were saying … about the coffee shop?'

'Oh … let's talk about something else,' Chloe said, conscious that whining about work was distinctly unsexy.

•

'Have a fabulous time, darling, only don't forget the third date rule, will you?' Bryony had said on the phone a week earlier.

Chloe had been confused. 'What do you mean? What's the third date rule?'

Bryony giggled. 'Oh, come on – don't pretend you don't know what I'm talking about, hon. Even *you* can't be that naive.' She'd then taken great pleasure in educating Chloe in the wonders of modern sexual etiquette, which in its barest form meant that she'd need to have sex with Caleb pretty sharpish if she were to avoid their burgeoning romance ending up in the *just-good-friends* zone.

Chloe had been horrified; not because Caleb wasn't attractive – she already fancied him like mad – but because she'd spent a total of six hours with him. The idea of them rolling about in his bed or hers, or given their mutual teenage family status, a king-sized bed in some nearby boutique hotel, seemed preposterous.

But Bryony's words had set a hare in motion, which by Wednesday had culminated in several hours spent in her local beauty salon while Lillian had rather sulkily held the fort.

Chloe had returned to the coffee shop tingling from the hot wax that had been slathered on her legs, bikini area and top lip, and moving her hands stiffly, thanks to nails that had been shaped and polished in a daring shade of plum. At least a recent visit to the hairdressers meant that her split ends had already been whisked away and her roots were mercifully up to date.

If only she could prepare her head and heart in the same way.

The prospect of even being alone with a potential lover was daunting. It seemed like an age since any man had touched her. Chloe could scarcely remember the sensation of intimacy with William; routine married sex, with a man who had ceased to turn her on years before they separated.

She thought of William's lanky frame, his thin arms and soft white belly. Their relationship had never been based on sexual attraction, but on lifestyle and cultural interests, like a youthful love of poetry and an obsession with The Doors, Jimi Hendrix and other American rock icons who had expired before either of them were born. Love had grown slowly, organically, and then Jake had come along and made them a family, until one day, without noticing, they had grown apart to the point where William had met and fallen for a temp receptionist at work – an appalling cliché that had taken them all by surprise.

Once the shock, anger and humiliation had worn off, Chloe's most enduring reaction was one of astonishment; that Jodie, fifteen years William's junior, with her mane of straw coloured hair and her overly large mouth, could have fallen for William in return. They made an unlikely couple.

Caleb on the other hand was dark and brooding, with a toned, muscular body; the very definition of what most women found attractive. Chloe had every intention of sleeping with him – just not tonight.

She could tell by Caleb's quizzical expression that she'd missed something.

'Sorry, miles away,' she said. 'Ooh, this looks delicious. Lovely idea to come here – the food's always amazing.'

'It is ... and, Chloe, I meant to say ... you look beautiful tonight ... and I ... I really enjoy ...'

Chloe waited, while Caleb searched for the right words. Why was he so nervous? Was he aware of the third date rule, too? Did *everyone* know about it except her?

Taking a massive leap of faith, Chloe attempted a daring rescue mission.

'Look, Caleb … I just want to say, I really enjoy your company, and I'm looking forward to getting to know you better … if that's what you want, too. But,' she paused unsure whether to carry on, *oh sod it!*

'I've heard all that third date nonsense – and, well … we're adults and we can go at our own pace. What I mean is … we don't have to *do* anything.'

'Oh god … really? I mean, I don't want you to think that I don't fancy you, or anything. It's just that–'

'You don't need to explain, Caleb. It's fine. We can just talk and get to know each other. I'm glad you're not in a desperate hurry to jump into bed, because I'm not ready to go there either.'

Caleb smiled, relief lighting up his handsome face. 'Thank you for being so honest.' He covered Chloe's hand with his. 'Now we've got that out of the way, we can relax and get to know each other. Now, tell me more about Jake.'

•

'Dylan, you're a genius! How do you *do* that, man?' Jake was awestruck as his friend reproduced his favourite Baby Dogs guitar riff perfectly.

'Because,' Dylan paused, pulling hard on the joint they were sharing 'I'm a fucking rock star.'

Jake honked with laughter. 'If you were, you

wouldn't be living in this dump,' he said, taking the weed from his friend.

'That's not cool; my parents would have a fit if they heard you say that. They've worked fucking hard for this house, so that me and my sister can–'

'Alright! I didn't mean your *actual* house, Dylan. I meant Eden Hill; who ever heard of a rock star coming from a suburban shit-hole like this? I wish we'd never left London.'

'That's where you're wrong, mate. All those old dudes like the Rolling Stones and Bowie, they came from the suburbs – yeah, Kent as it goes.'

'Decrepit old bastards. Who cares?' Jake was becoming morose.

Dylan snorted. 'You need to get over that, Jakey – they might be dinosaurs to us, but they *invented* rock and roll. Baby Dogs wouldn't even exist without them.'

Jake shrugged and took another drag of weed.

'Yeah, *and*,' Dylan said, warming to his theme, 'that's bollocks anyway … about Eden Hill. We've actually got a rock star living here, in the posh gated bit. Ben Wilde lives in Regents Square – didn't you know that?'

'Who the fuck is Ben Wilde?'

Dylan rolled his eyes, went downstairs and rifled his Mum's CD collection; he returned waving two albums. '*And* he writes all his own stuff,' Dylan said triumphantly, as the room filled with the strains of Seagull.

'Hey, I know this song,' Jake said. 'My Mum's got this album, too – she plays it all the time. Well, fuck me. So Ben Wilde lives in Eden Hill, does he?'

WINTER

CHAPTER 21

The Wildes

Mesmerised, Ben gazed out at a galaxy of electronic stars. He remembered the days when performing Seagull had meant fans holding up their cigarette lighters. On lead guitar, Rick was riding the crest of the middle eight, relishing his big solo. Ben turned to catch Steve's eye; they grinned at each other.

Man, I could stay on the road forever, Ben thought, running to the front of the stage and breaking into a final chorus shored up by Ruby Stone on backing vocals, her voice soaring as Seagull came to its crescendo before the final throw-down beat. It was over.

'Thank you, Hamburg. Goodnight!' Ben roared at the 25,000 fans on their feet before him, all applauding, screaming and vibrating with joy.

There was no time for basking in glory; five tracks and *off*! It felt like a mere moment but with a schedule as tight as Ruby's jeans and the next adrenalin-fuelled act ready burst on stage, Seagull was Ben's only encore.

Whooping and high-fiving with elation, the band jogged through a labyrinth of tunnels, back to their dressing room, where an entourage waited with champagne and adulation.

Ben hugged his bandmates, and Ruby; a shared

asset, who'd be back on stage in under an hour supporting an all-girl band.

'We only fucking nailed it!' Rick screamed. 'What an amazing first night! Did you see ...' and they were off, comparing onstage experiences, yelling over each other in their haste to relive the performance.

It didn't matter that *Ben & The Wilde Ones* languished near the bottom of the bill, or that Hamburg in December was freezing – their reception could not have been warmer; it was more than they'd dared hope for.

'I'm going back out there to watch the rest of the gig. We should support these guys ... we owe them a fucking ton,' Ben said, swigging beer from a bottle and towelling his glistening hair and face.

•

In freezing fog, Lisa had said a tearful goodbye to Ben before a gleaming SUV had whisked him away to Heathrow to join Rick, Steve and seemingly, a cast of thousands bound for Hamburg and the first leg of the tour.

'Come on, babe – don't get upset. I'll be back for Christmas before you know it,' Ben said, wiping away Lisa's tears.

'Yes, and then you'll be gone again ... for months! Ooh, sorry, take no notice, I'm okay; and Ben, I am so proud of you.' Lisa squeezed Ben hard before planting a final kiss on his lips. Then he was gone.

At least Rita was safely ensconced in her own home again. To Lisa's amazement, her mother was delighted with her new kitchen and modest extension – so much so, that it had reignited her interest in cooking and baking.

'I don't know why you're so surprised,' Rita said, 'when you and Andrea were little, I used to make cakes and puddings all the time.'

'If you say so, Mum.' Lisa couldn't for the life of her remember such childhood culinary treats.

'I suppose Jack will be moving in soon,' Lisa said, changing the subject before a row could erupt.

Rita shook her head. 'We've decided to wait a while. If things are still good between me and Jackie in the spring, we'll see about living together.'

'Good idea, Mum – that sounds very sensible.'

Nobody had mentioned the 'M' word. Still, Lisa scarcely cared whether Rita and Jack were married or not – as long as Rita was happy.

The following day, even by noon it was barely light. Already, Lisa had been to the gym, walked Nellie, put a wash on and run the vacuum around downstairs. The day yawned blankly ahead.

Conscious that she'd neglected Tanya for months, Lisa sent her friend a text.

'Been too long, T,' it said, 'fancy night out before xmas? X'

Almost immediately, her phone chirruped in reply.

'NEED night out – me and Jason finished! X'

Concerned for her friend, Lisa hit the call button.

'Tanya! What happened, darling? Are you okay?'

'Yes … no … I don't know, Leese. It was me that ended things but now I feel like shit,' came Tanya's no-frills reply.

'But why? You've been together ages … what, two years? Why didn't you ring me?'

'Hon, you're always so busy – not to mention loved up. I didn't want to get in the way of you and Ben. Anyway, I can't talk about it now, I'm at work,' Tanya said.

Lisa felt a twinge of guilt. 'I'm sorry. I've been a rubbish friend lately … much too wrapped up in myself. If you're free, let's go out tonight and you can tell me all about it.'

•

The Gallery had been 'their' place and although it had been almost a year since their last visit, the maître d remembered them.

'Ladies, you look beautiful – wonderful to see you both again. Eating, drinking or both?' he said, directing them to a window table.

'Both,' they said in unison, having arrived by taxi with the intention of letting their hair down.

'I know it's only Thursday night,' Tanya said, studying the cocktail menu, 'but I can struggle through one more day at work before the weekend – and anyway, I don't start until ten tomorrow.'

Despite Tanya looking stunning in head to toe black, her magnificent mane tossed carelessly over one shoulder, Lisa could see the stress etched in her friend's face. She waited until two Cosmopolitans and a dish of olives had arrived before digging for details.

'So, are you going to tell me what happened with Jason, or do I have to guess?' she said, as they clinked glasses and drank deeply.

Tanya sighed heavily. 'Nothing happened. Nothing at all – that's the problem. I realised I'd been treading water with Jay for two years. Everything was exactly the same as when we met … except that the sex has tailed off a bit.'

'Ah, I think I see the problem,' Lisa said, popping a stuffed olive into her mouth.

'I mean, it's not like I want to get married or anything, but two years is a long time for just dating. We weren't going anywhere … I can't believe I waited so long to be honest.' Tanya drained her glass.

'Maybe,' Lisa began carefully, 'the problem was the age difference. Most blokes are emotionally immature to begin with, so going out with someone ten years younger just ups the ante. I think you did the right thing, Tan.'

'I know, but I miss him already, he was sweet and funny ... and kind. But the thing is–' Tanya's flow was interrupted by a waiter's offer of more drinks, which she gratefully accepted.

'Darling, I know what you're thinking and you're right,' Lisa said. 'You're forty-four – even if you do look barely thirty-five – and there's a point where you have to take stock. If Jason's not the one, well then you have to be free to find the lucky bloke who is.' Lisa squeezed Tanya's hand across the table as more drinks arrived. 'Cheers, darling – here's to intelligent decisions. You'll be fine, trust me.'

Two Cosmopolitans later and with no real food consumed, the women were slow to notice two men who'd been eavesdropping from the next table.

'Ladies, I wonder if you can settle an argument between my friend and me,' a shiny-headed man sporting a modest paunch and too much cologne leant towards them.

His silent friend merely smirked.

'Try us,' Lisa said, mildly irritated by the intrusion.

'Well,' the man continued, 'Gary here thinks you're Lisa Dixon, Justin Dixon's ex missus. I, on the other hand, think you look too young to be her, although I can see a resemblance.'

Lisa was unsure how to answer. It felt like an age

since anyone had recognised her as Lisa Dixon, wife of Justin Dixon, soccer star; next they'd be speculating about Justin himself, expounding their opinions as to whether he'd died a prodigious talent or a washed up drunk.

Lisa and Tanya's eyes met.

'Why don't you just piss off – this is a private conversation,' Tanya said, the alcohol making her fractious.

Lisa's eyes widened. As much as she appreciated the sentiment, she was shocked by Tanya's candour. Fear tingled at the nape of her neck.

'What my friend means,' Lisa said softly, 'is that we're just having a quiet drink, so please excuse us.' She turned her attention to Tanya, expecting the man to back-off. Instead, the women jumped as he slammed a glass down in front of them.

'No need to get fucking lippy, girls! I was only asking.'

Tanya sat up straight. 'Sorry, no offence meant,' she said.

'I ain't your mate, you old tart,' the man snarled, mishearing her.

The Gallery had been buzzing with conversation since their arrival; now it fell silent as people zoned in, intrigued by the altercation.

Lisa got to her feet. 'I think it's time to go … we can pay at the bar.'

'Nah. You're going nowhere – not until you answer my question. Which was perfectly civil, don't you think, Gary?'

Gary looked uncomfortable. 'Let's call it a night, mate. C'mon, leave the girls alone. I've had enough of this dump anyway.' He started towards the door, but his friend stayed put, blocking the women's escape route.

'Excuse us, please,' Lisa said, clutching Tanya's arm and attempting to move closer to other customers. To her immense relief, the maître d arrived, assessing the situation instantly.

'It's time to leave, gentlemen. A car is waiting outside for you. Goodnight.'

He stood resolutely beside Lisa and Tanya and waited for the men to leave. As they reached the glass door, the bald man looked back at the women and mimed firing a gun, twice.

Tanya's hand flew to her mouth. 'Oh my god! Did you see that, Leese? What are we going to do?'

Lisa paled visibly. 'Don't worry babe – they've gone now. They won't be back tonight.'

'Sorry about that, ladies,' the maître d said, 'it's rare that we get people like that in here, but it happens, especially around the holidays. Please, stay and have another drink on the house, then I'll call you a taxi.'

Shaken, Lisa nodded. 'Thank you for stepping in. I don't know what we'd have done if you hadn't come along. I think we both need a coffee after that, hey Tanya?'

That night, alone in bed, Lisa longed for Ben to put his arms around her; the five hundred miles between them suddenly felt like five million.

CHAPTER 22

The Bradshaws

Satisfied that Iris was finally asleep, Rosemary arranged some crackers, cheese and celery on a plate before guiltily adding a handful of Twiglets. Then she poured herself a glass of white wine and carried her tray to the sitting room where the television flickered mutely with an old sitcom she recognised.

It had been a long and tiring day, but a surprisingly satisfying one.

Shortly after breakfast, she'd taken delivery of a six-foot Christmas tree from the local garden centre, then with a degree of enthusiastic hindrance from Iris, had hauled last year's decorations from an eaves cupboard, before unwrapping a dozen or so glittering new ornaments. Rosemary had then convinced Iris that it would be more exciting to decorate the tree after dark.

By mid-morning, leaving Iris under the watchful gaze of Angela, Rosemary drove for three quarters of an hour to Glen Heights for a pre-Christmas lunch with Joyce.

Full of dread at the prospect, Rosemary had barely slept the night before. Instead she'd lain awake, seething with resentment that she had to leave her daughter with a babysitter, only days before

Christmas, while Joyce's own flesh and blood had prioritised work as usual.

But to Rosemary's amazement Glen Heights had pulled out all the stops, serving a delicious three course festive lunch, to the strains of Italian light opera, performed by Mario, a Tenor from Croydon, who, to the obvious delight of the residents, sounded uncannily like Luciano Pavarotti.

'He's a good-looking boy, don't you think, Rose?' Joyce said in a loud voice, timed to a lull in the music.

'He's wearing makeup!' May, the old lady sitting opposite piped up.

'Of course, he's an *artist*!' Mr Baldini said grandly, his hearing aid beginning to whistle.

The half-dozen relatives who'd bothered to turn up exchanged amused glances, some of them stifling laughter.

'It's like being at the school gates,' whispered a blonde woman around Rosemary's own age. 'The things my mother comes out with sometimes ... it's shocking, but you've got to laugh.'

Rosemary smiled wistfully. 'I don't see my mum much – she went back to Nigeria a few years ago ... I miss her. Joyce is my husband's mother, but he works away a lot.'

'And you get lumbered, I suppose. He's a lucky man, that's all I can say. I'm Veronica, by the way. I live in Eden Hill ... it's about–'

'No way! I know exactly where it is … that's where I live. Goodness, what a coincidence!' And then they were off, swapping neighbourhood gossip, as well as joining in with the increasingly good-humoured banter as the wine and sherry slipped down.

Towards the end of the meal, pink-cheeked from sherry, Joyce squeezed Rosemary's hand. 'You're a good girl, Rose; my son's a lucky man. He's always been a cold fish, even as a boy,' she said, her eyes suddenly hard.

'Oh, you know Nigel, Mum – always busy with work. I'm used to it,' Rosemary said, amazed at how lucid Joyce seemed.

After two hours had slipped by pleasantly enough, Rosemary thanked Veronica for her company.

'Lovely to meet you, too, Rose. I was dreading today, but it was alright, wasn't it? The staff did a good job – although I suspect all the old folk will be snoring for the rest of the day.'

The women exchanged numbers, vowing to meet another time and after hugging Joyce goodbye, Rosemary was back on the road.

At home, Angela and Iris were sitting at the kitchen table drawing reindeer together, while Christmas songs played cheerfully in the background. It was a cosy tableau and Rosemary's heart swelled with gratitude.

'Thank you so much, Angela – you're a life saver.'

The younger woman smiled. 'Pleasure. We had a great time, didn't we Iris? How was it?'

'It was fine ... better than I thought it would be. It was very festive ... the food was nice ... oh, and we had opera.'

'Opera? Sounds fab! Iris has been fine. She had her lunch at around one o'clock – those chicken goujons you left in the fridge – oh, and a yogurt and two satsumas for dessert.' Angela leaned forward and lowered her voice. 'Think you might be decorating the tree next though ... she hasn't stopped going on about it, bless her.'

'I had a feeling that would be my next job. Thanks again, Angela. I've paid you a bit extra ... have a very happy Christmas, won't you?'

Now, grazing on her savoury supper, Rosemary reflected on Nigel's absence. What saddened her most was that she no longer cared whether he was home or not. Iris rarely mentioned her father anymore and when he was home, he seemed withdrawn, unreachable.

Rosemary thought back to their telephone conversation that evening. Nigel had sounded tired and beaten – but indifferent, too. He hadn't even asked about lunch at the care home and she was damned if she was going to prompt him about it.

In the corner of the room the Christmas tree twinkled, mocking her with its festive cheer. She thought wistfully of the chaotic Christmases of her childhood, of how the house in Sydenham was always bursting with relatives all through the holidays.

Seared by a sudden pang of loneliness Rosemary rang her sister.

'Abi, it's me love,' she said softly so as not to wake Iris.

'Hello my sweetheart,' Abi answered fondly, 'what are you up to? You ready for Christmas? How's my little niece – bet she's full of it.'

It was good to hear Abi's voice. 'We're fine,' Rosemary said, 'Yeah, she's excited – we decorated the tree today. It looks very pretty in here. You still coming on Boxing Day?'

'Of course. I can't wait to give Iris her presents. Is Joseph coming with that girl of his, what's-her-name? Our brother is being somewhat elusive at the moment. I'm lucky if I get a text once a month.'

'That's about as much as I hear,' Rosemary said, 'Kristal – that's her name. Last I heard, he was smitten. Abi, try and get him to come down with you … with or without Kristal. It'll be so lovely for the three of us to be together. I miss you both so much – Mum and Dad and Auntie, too.'

'What's up, Rose?' Abi picked up on her sister's tone. And then the usual question: 'How's *he*?'

'*He* has got a name. I don't know Abi,' Rosemary said 'We're ships that pass in the night. I know he works hard, but honestly, Nigel doesn't feel like part of this family anymore … it feels like me and Iris against the world. I'm always alone. But you know the worst thing? I don't care anymore. The connection has gone – if there ever was one.'

Her sister was silent for a moment. Rosemary could almost hear the cogs whirring. 'Abi?'

'I'm here. I was just thinking that things must be *really* bad for you to say that. Love, you've been so loyal to Nigel – that man is a closed book. You got married 'cos you got pregnant, end of. But why on earth do you stay? Tell him it's over. He'll have to support Iris – it's the law – and then come back to London. You, me and Iris, we can live together, buy a flat.'

'Bless you, Abi. I can't. It's not that simple.'

'You can, and it is,' Abi said.

•

Nigel stole another look at the necklace and snapped the velvet box shut. There was no need to wrap it. Watching Cheryl – he corrected himself – watching *Tiffany* tear off shiny paper, miming surprise and delight, would be trawling the very depths of tackiness. He wondered how many other velvet boxes Tiffany would get in the run up to Christmas, from other satisfied clients. Nigel shuddered at his own pun.

By contrast, he'd wrapped Rosemary's gifts

beautifully – or rather his assistant had. Thanks to Joanne, the cashmere sweater, matching scarf and discreet bangle were all in the boot of his car, ready to take home and hide somewhere before Christmas Day came around and he would be forced to act out a loving family Christmas with his wife and daughter.

Not for the first time, Nigel wondered what he'd do without Joanne. She seemed so entrenched in his life these days, sorting and scanning his correspondence, managing his chaotic diary and guarding him from middle-managers hellbent on sabotaging his time with a loyalty so fierce that someone had once joked about her being part secretary and part German Shepherd. Joanne could be trusted with secrets; which is why she was the only person who knew he stayed at the Bertram Hotel, rather than the Holiday Inn, Brighouse, where he claimed to.

'Well that's not very convenient, is it?' she'd said, her brow furrowed.

Nigel nodded. 'Which is precisely the point, Joanne. I don't want people popping in for random breakfast meetings or dropping round with documents to sign late at night. This business eats into my private time quite enough already.'

Nigel belched as the noodles he'd eaten for lunch shifted queasily in his gut, a feeling he was all too familiar with lately; a consequence perhaps of tensions at work and playacting at home. Perhaps guilt and shame were literally eroding his stomach lining.

In Huddersfield, Nigel's day had been brutal. He'd left the head office of Duggan Prust Security at five-forty, armed with the unpalatable truth that he'd be starting New Year with twenty per cent less staff. Redundancies so soon after Christmas seemed excessively ruthless.

It's all coming apart at the seams, he thought, rubbing his upset stomach.

After leaving the meeting in which the fate of fourteen members of soon to be ex-staff had been decided, he'd called Rosemary from the car.

'Guess what we're doing?' she'd sounded happy, breathless.

'I've no idea ... baking a cake for Christmas?' he'd guessed, trying to sound upbeat.

'We're decorating the tree!' She half-covered the mouth piece. 'Iris? Daddy's on the phone – come and say hello.'

And then his daughter had babbled excitedly about the tree; the glittering star on top, the red, green and gold baubles, and the fairy lights shaped like angels. He'd almost wept.

Why couldn't he be like other men, *normal* guys, who loved their wives and children, and who were excited by the prospect of spending the holidays all together.

His thoughts were interrupted by a soft knock at the door; Nigel put away the velvet box.

'Come in,' he called out.

Tiffany entered the room, muffled against the cold in an ugly beige coat with ludicrously large buttons and pom-poms dangling from the collar. Perhaps he should exchange the necklace for a decent winter coat.

In the soulless room, they embraced without words.

The young woman pulled back from him and searched his face. 'Are you alright, Nigel? You're ever so pale.'

'Of course. Why wouldn't I be? I've just had a stressful day at work, but it's over now and we can relax.'

'May I have some wine, please?' she said.

'*May I?*' he mimicked. 'Where did you learn decent manners?'

Tiffany frowned. 'From my mum, I suppose. Just because I do this for a living doesn't mean I got dragged up.'

'I, on the other hand ...' Nigel sighed heavily, 'but we needn't talk about that. I hope the agency told you that I've paid for the whole night,' he added.

This information seemed to embarrass Tiffany, who prowled the room as if inspecting its shabby décor.

Neither of them had eaten, so despite his

indigestion, Nigel rang reception and asked for club sandwiches and French fries to be sent up with the wine.

Once their food had been delivered, they took off their shoes and sat side by side on the bed. 'Do you like Christmas?' Tiffany asked, between dainty bites.

'It means nothing to me,' Nigel said.

The young woman looked shocked. 'Really? That's awful. I love Christmas; the tree, the fairy lights, Mum's turkey roast, seeing my aunties and my cousins. Oh, and Home Alone of course – I love that film; me and Mum watch it every year.'

'Are your family aware of your ... career choice?' Nigel pushed his plate away; everything he ate seemed to stick in his gullet.

'Mum knows everything – but just her. All my aunties think I'm still a hotel receptionist – 'cos I was before this.'

'Yes. I can see it would only be a small deviation from the truth. Tell me Tiffany, do you have sex with all your clients?'

'No, I bloody don't!' Offended, Tiffany turned away. 'Thing is, a lot of blokes really do just want company. Someone they can have dinner with while they're away from home. Some just want to talk. I've got one old boy, Dennis – he's nearly sixty – he just likes to–'

Nigel raised his hand: 'Spare me the details, Tiffany. I'm not interested in what Cheryl does.'

'But you just asked me!' Confused, Tiffany got up to use the bathroom.

Nigel went over to the bland standard-issue dresser and took out the velvet box. He'd give her the necklace and then they would fuck, but slowly – perhaps with Tiffany on top. He really hadn't the energy for anything more strenuous.

Emerging from the bathroom with a tight smile and her red hair newly tousled, Tiffany sat down beside him; the velvet box caught her eye at once.

'Christmas is for the young,' Nigel said, holding it towards her. 'I hope you like it, but if not, I have the receipt.'

Pink spots appeared on the young woman's cheeks.

'You didn't have to … oh, Nigel – it's beautiful. I love it. Put it on me!'

Disarmed by her obvious pleasure, Nigel did as she asked, struggling for a moment with the clasp. Then he watched as she paced to the mirror, her eyes lighting up to see it sparkle against her alabaster décolletage.

'Thank you, Nigel. It's really lovely.'

'Good, I'm glad you approve. The stones are Austrian crystal and the chain is gold.' He patted the demask bed cover. 'Now come over here and show me just how much you like it.'

CHAPTER 23

The Bevans

Fighting the urge to stay inside with a steaming pot of tea and a packet of biscuits, Jan zipped up her scarlet anorak and braced herself for the first walk of the day.

At eight o'clock, Martin had gone Christmas shopping, leaving early in the hope of getting a parking space in Tunbridge Wells.

'Don't go wasting your money on me, Mart. There's nothing I need,' Jan said, as he gave her a quick peck goodbye, before winding a woollen scarf around his neck. Martin had mumbled that *he'd* be the judge of that.

Jan knew he was up to something. The night before last, he'd played badminton with Jeremy Hunter and had returned fired up and animated.

'Take it you won, then?' Jan said, opening a can of soup for him. 'Do you want cheese on toast as well … or is it a bit late?'

'Yes please, love. And yes, I did beat Jeremy as it happens. Then we sat in the bar with a beer … he wanted a chat with me.'

But when Jan had asked what it was about, Martin only changed the subject, before devouring his soup in front of News at Ten.

Once in the car, which reeked of wet dog following three straight days of rain, Jan looked at the schedule she'd typed the night before; seven dogs needed to be walked and watered before evening fell.

'Best get on with it then,' she said aloud, setting off in the direction of Spike and Poppet's house. The dogs leapt into Jan's estate, keening, snuffling and wagging their tales all the way to her next customer's dog, Basil, a few streets away.

Despite the temperature hovering around freezing and a dampness that seemed to penetrate her bones, Jan's spirits lifted as the dogs trotted at her heels, spraying mud over her and each other as they tramped through deep puddles on the woodland floor. All three dogs were excellent off lead, sticking close to Jan and their adopted pack.

After towelling the trio down in the back of her filthy car and dropping them home, Jan collected Maggie and Dougal, adolescent retrievers, whose habit was to launch themselves into every mud hole on the route. *Well not today*, thought Jan.

'Right, it's a street walk for you two,' she said, leaving her car on their drive. 'And no pulling Auntie along, do you hear?'

The dogs heard nothing of the kind and Jan fought to keep a grip on the teenage retrievers, walking briskly in the direction of Cabbage Green, near her own home, creating a fifty-minute circuit in the process. Fewer walkers than usual were about, and those Jan spotted had their collars up and their heads down against the drizzle.

Two panting, happy retrievers later, Jan set out with her penultimate dog of the day, Paula the Staffie. Mindful of the terrier's temperament around other dogs, Jan wound the lead around her hand and stuffed her pockets full of treats should distraction tactics be needed.

Ahead a young woman with a West Highland White changed direction abruptly, diving into a lane between two houses. A few minutes later, Jan smiled and waved to a woman of her own age who was leading a small poodle-cross. Neither smile nor wave were returned, instead, the woman made an elaborate swerve around Jan as she passed by, lips pursed, eyes averted.

'Suit yourself,' Jan muttered under her breath, bending to give Paula a reassuring pat.

'Good morning … it's a bit nippy today,' Jan said to a man with an elderly Labrador. Pausing in his stride, the man narrowed her eyes at Jan before looking scornfully at Paula and waiting for them to pass.

'Well that's just rude!' Jan clucked to Paula, who continued to surge ahead like a little pit pony.

On Cabbage Green a mother in a hooded parker stood patiently while her toddler splashed red wellingtons through puddles, shrieking with delight. Jan was reminded of Hayley at three years old doing the same thing on the Rec in Crabton.

'Bless her, I can remember my little one doing just the same thing. They're lovely at that age, aren't they?' Jan said, as she approached the mother and child.

To Jan's amazement, the woman yanked the toddler away. 'Don't touch the dog!' she shrieked, a look of panic on her face.

Jan was stung. 'She won't hurt you … she's a lovely girl.'

'That's not what I've heard … keep that bloody dog away!' the mother said, gripping the child's hand and hauling her away.

The toddler began to wail. 'Want doggeee!'

'Now look what you've done!' the woman called over her shoulder.

•

In the fading light, Jan sat down with a cup of tea and a plate of biscuits but couldn't settle. The morning had left a sour taste in her mouth. All those neighbours – giving her nasty looks or blanking her altogether. She couldn't decide which was worse.

Martin had barely taken his coat off and set down his stash of carrier bags before Jan complained to him.

'Love, are you sure you're not being over-sensitive?' he asked later, warming himself in the kitchen.

'What? Are you saying I *imagined* being ignored

and shouted at? Martin, if you'd been there, you'd be in no doubt. It was horrible … all looking at me like I was dirt.'

'But why? Why on earth would they? It's never happened before, has it?' Martin reasoned.

'I don't usually walk near home, do I? But after the first walk, I couldn't face the woods again – it was just too muddy. It was round here that it happened … up by Cabbage Green.'

Their eyes met. Martin shook his head, as if denying a thought that had just occurred to him.

'You think someone's been talking, don't you?' Jan said, reading Martin's mind.

'I was just thinking about the woman with the tan spaniel. She's not been sticking her ore in and spreading rumours, has she?'

'That's what I was wondering,' Jan said. 'She got very upset when Paula snapped at her dog – and bloody rude with it – especially as it was *her* dog off the lead, not mine.'

'The thing is, Jan, people take umbrage, don't they? They treat their dogs like children … and you in that red anorak with a young Staffie … it's a very distinctive combination.'

Jan got up and paced to the back door. Dusk was falling fast, and the gloom had stripped their modest garden of what little colour stubbornly remained.

'Well that's that then,' Jan said thickly, her back

to Martin. 'Bang goes my chance of making friends or getting any new customers round here. I knew we shouldn't have come. Snotty bitches, the lot of them.'

She brushed past Martin, taking the stairs heavily.

Martin knew Jan was upset, but experience had taught him to let her be – she'd come round. Any mollycoddling from him would only exacerbate the situation.

He felt for his phone and re-read an email from Jeremy Hunter. He had news of his own, but it would keep.

CHAPTER 24

The Wildes

The jostling pack of photographers, police and security staff at Arrivals reminded Lisa of her WAG days. She scanned the crowd, taking in the expensively dressed partners and children who'd come to meet celebrity loved ones from their flight.

Ben had told her not to come, saying there was no need as he was being picked up and chauffeur-driven straight to Eden Hill. But Lisa had wanted to surprise him and had arranged a car to take her to Heathrow, desperate to see Ben at the earliest opportunity.

The minutes ticked by then in a palpable surge of energy, flashbulbs began to pop as a steady procession of denim-clad lanky limbs, glossy hair and dark glasses emerged through the gate.

Ignoring security personnel, Lisa ran forward and threw her arms around Ben – every inch the rock star in a fur-trimmed leather jacket she'd never seen before and aviator shades. Despite an absence of only two weeks Lisa saw at once that Ben had lost weight.

His expression was a mixture of shock and joy. 'Woah! Hey, baby! What are *you* doing here? God I've missed you!'

Ben held Lisa for a moment, before pulling back and studying her upturned face. 'How are you, gorgeous? Bloody hell, it's good to be back.'

Keen to escape the chaos, Ben steered Lisa towards the exit, eyes darting for a sign with his name on it.

'The paps can pick on someone else,' he said, dodging the photographers, 'let's go home.'

•

Dumping his bags in the hallway, Ben gave his wife a lingering kiss.

'I've missed you, Leese,' he said again, adding 'I could murder a cup of tea. It's been booze, fizzy water and coffee since I left.'

In the warmth of the kitchen, with tea and an apple and cinnamon cake that Lisa had baked the day before, they swapped news. They'd skyped most days, but the connection was often fuzzy, and they'd found communicating via a juddering screen clunky.

Ben was ebullient. 'Hey, but listen to this, Leese. We've only gone a couple of notches up the bill. Yeah, can you believe it? The reaction to our set was so good that we've risen up the pecking order.'

Lisa had followed the tour on social media, scrutinising photographs of the band posted on Twitter and Face Book. A live-action shot of Ben singing cheek to cheek with a spiral-haired brunette, his arm draped over her shoulder had made her prickle with jealousy, although she'd tried to dismiss the thought at once.

'That's fantastic! I've been following online. You

look amazing on stage, hon – I can't wait for the London dates, although I'm still thinking of coming out before then. It's not like I'm working, is it?'

'Babe, you should. Let's make it happen. Oh, Rick sends his love, by the way. He's cleaned his act up – a lot. Actually, I think he fancies old Ruby, but she's having none of it,' Ben chuckled.

'Ruby?'

'Ruby Stone, one of the backing singers. We share her with another band. Nice girl, but she'd eat poor Ricky alive. At least he's stopped mooning about that Jessie woman. Anyway, enough about the tour,' Ben said, aware he'd been hogging the conversation, 'what's been going on with you, babe?'

'Oh, you know … same old, same old. I've been going to the gym, walking Nellie, Christmas shopping … oh, and spending a bit more time with Tanya; she and Jason have split up.'

'No! Seriously? I thought they were good together, what happened?'

Lisa explained how in Tanya's view, the age gap had begun to matter and how she'd wanted more.

Ben was philosophical. 'Fair enough. Jason's loss. Is she okay? What's Tan doing for Crimbo? She's welcome here, you know that,' he said kindly. But Lisa had already said as much and knew that Tanya was planning to visit them on Boxing Day.

'Good, well I can't think of anything better than

spending Christmas Day in bed with my missus,' Ben twinkled.

•

Christmas Eve dawned bright and clear. Together, Ben and Lisa walked Nellie on pavements that sparkled with frost. Even in her tiny padded Santa coat, Nellie shivered with cold.

'Ah, bless her, look, she's freezing. We'll have to make it a quick one,' Lisa said, resisting the temptation to carry the poor, quivering dog.

'Leese, she's a dog. She'll soon warm up, won't you girl?' But Nellie turned her pointy little face away and planted her paws.

'Ha! She knows what she wants.' Lisa cajoled Nellie into walking a little further, waiting until she'd squatted a couple of times before the three of them turned towards home.

'Fancy a drink with the neighbours tonight?' Lisa said seeing both Rosemary and Nigel's cars parked outside No. 5.

Ben made a face. 'Not really. I'd like you all to myself.'

Lisa nodded, 'I know, but I'm fond of Rosemary and it would be neighbourly to wish them happy Christmas and give Iris her present. Go on, babe, just for an hour or so … at say, six tonight?'

'Okay then, if you must,' Ben relented, releasing

Nellie from her outdoor coat and heading for the kitchen.

'Great. I'll give Rose a knock … see if they're free.' Lisa stepped outside and rang Rosemary's doorbell.

It threw her when Nigel answered, although there was no reason for him not to.

'Nigel! Merry Christmas. Ben and I were wondering if you'd like to join us for a drink this evening … I mean, all three of you, of course.'

Before Nigel could answer, Rosemary appeared beside him, beaming at Lisa. 'We'd love to,' she said. That's so nice of you.'

Lisa's day passed by in a blur of food preparation, last minute gift wrapping, and decoration tweaking. Ben followed her from room to room, getting in her way and pawing her for attention as she worked.

'Ben, sweetheart, please … just be patient. They'll be here in twenty minutes. We've got Christmas Day all to ourselves.'

Ben pouted. 'Yeah, and we'd have had tonight if you hadn't asked the bloody neighbours round.'

'Love, come on. Where's your Christmas spirit?' Lisa said, lighting cinnamon scented candles.

'It died at the prospect of seeing Nigel's miserable gob … alright, alright,' he said, holding his hands up in submission.

But at six fifteen, Lisa opened the door to find the Bradshaws – minus Nigel.

'I'm so sorry, Lisa – Nigel isn't feeling well. He thinks he might be going down with something so he's going to bed early.'

'Oh no! We're sorry to hear that,' Lisa ushered her guests through to the kitchen, 'aren't we, Ben?' she added, seeing him smirk.

'Yeah, of course – but maybe he can ward it off with an early night. Drinks ladies?'

Ben put on music, opened the champagne and poured Iris a glass of lemonade.

'I think,' Ben said, squatting so that he was eye-level with the little girl, 'that I've seen a present for you on Lisa's beautiful Christmas tree. Shall we have a look?'

Iris nodded and put out her hand for Ben to hold.

'Bless her!' Lisa clutched her heart, moved by Ben's tenderness. She looked meaningfully at Rosemary. 'Is everything okay?'

'Yes, fine … oh, I don't know. I can't tell if Nigel really feels ill or if he's just tired and crabby. His work is very stressful at the moment; he's just made a lot of people redundant.'

Lisa grimaced, 'That's enough to make anyone feel sick.'

They abandoned the subject as Ben and Iris reappeared, her small hands clutching a glittering red parcel.

'Oh, Iris, how lovely! But you can't open it until

tomorrow. What do you say?' Rosemary looked embarrassed. 'Lisa, you shouldn't have … I didn't get you anything.'

Lisa smiled. 'Christmas is for little ones. Adults don't need presents,' she said, accepting a hug from Iris.

By seven-thirty, Ben and Lisa were alone.

'Do you think they've had a row,' Ben said, filling his mouth with cashews.

'That's what I wondered. He seemed well enough when I knocked earlier. I feel for Rose. He's such a cold fish … so difficult to read.'

'Yeah, like me, eh?' Ben said, giving Lisa's bum a pat.

Lisa laughed, 'Nothing like you … I can read you like a book, Ben Wilde. Now are you taking me to bed or what?'

CHAPTER 25

The Mortons

On Christmas Eve Chloe shut the coffee shop at noon and took a cab to the Speckled Hen where Caleb was waiting at the bar. As usual, the mere sight of him made her heart beat faster.

'There she is,' he said, before kissing Chloe's lips. 'Merry Christmas, lovely. Would you like a glass of bubbly?'

Chloe raised her eyebrows. They never drank champagne in each other's company; red wine was their usual tipple. 'Go on then – as this is to be our only shot at Christmas together.' Chloe sat on the vacant bar stool beside Caleb and took his hand.

'I wish … oh never mind.' she smiled into Caleb's brown eyes, feeling suddenly shy.

'I know what you're thinking … I wish we were spending Christmas together, too. But considering we're still in the closet – so to speak …' Caleb handed Chloe a glass of champagne. 'Cheers. Here's to a very happy and peaceful Christmas – in both our houses.'

Chloe smiled. 'Merry Christmas, sweetheart. I hope you and the girls have a really lovely one.'

'So, what does Christmas Day look like in the Morton household?' Caleb asked, the bubbles beginning to take effect.

'Probably much the same as everyone else's,' Chloe

answered, 'except with less bickering as it will only be Jake and me.'

With a pang she remembered past Christmases spent with Jake and William in their Victorian house in Streatham, the table groaning under the weight of turkey roast for seven or eight people as friends and family descended for the day.

'Mum, chill out. It's fine – I'm not a kid anymore,' Jake had assured her when she'd explained that this year Christmas Day would be just the two of them.

And then the inevitable conversation had followed about when Jake should go to his dad's, because to everyone's astonishment, William had booked a week in Lanzarote.

'*Lanzarote?*' Chloe said over the phone. 'Was that Jodie's idea or yours?'

'Er … both,' William answered, sounding sheepish. 'We just fancied a change this year.'

'Well, you got that! Okay, perhaps you could have Jake over for New Year … or … something. Look, I don't care. It's really none of my business.' Chloe had banged the phone down, oddly annoyed by William's new-found spirit of adventure, which she attributed to him having found a younger model. She pictured Jodie on the beach, honey-limbed in a tiny bikini.

But when she'd relayed the whole bad-tempered conversation to Caleb he shook his head. 'Chloe, why do you care *what* he does? You and William have been separated for ages and you're almost divorced. Hey, and now you've got me. What is it *exactly* that's pissing you off?'

It was a fair question and one that Chloe could not answer adequately, so she'd changed the subject. William had ceased to have any real impact on her life the day she and Jake had moved to Eden Hill. As Caleb had so endearingly pointed out, they had each other now – although sex had become the elephant in the room. As single parents of teenagers, it was all a matter of opportunity. There'd been two occasions when things might have got steamy between them; on the first, the timing was all wrong for Chloe's cycle and on the second a minor emergency at home had sent Caleb speeding back to the farm.

A more pressing issue than William's beach jaunt was that Chloe and Caleb were both lying by omission to their children. It had to stop.

•

On Christmas Day, Chloe was awake by seven o'clock, but lay drifting until eight as the house was still and silent.

After pulling on a robe and turning the central heating up a notch, Chloe peeked into Jake's room. Despite the harshly dyed hair, the way his eyelashes curled against flushed cheeks, lips parted emitting gentle snores, Jake looked so young and sweet it made

Chloe catch her breath. As if sensing her presence, he woke up.

'Happy Christmas, Mum,' Jake said, his voice thick with sleep, 'what time is it?'

'Happy Christmas, darling. Just gone eight ... must be the latest we've ever got up on Christmas morning. I remember how you always used to get up before six when you were little, you were so excited.'

'Yeah, what a pain in the butt I must have been,' Jake said, heaving himself upright.

•

Jake devoured their traditional Christmas breakfast of toasted muffins, scrambled eggs and smoked salmon like a fugitive. Then they'd taken cups of tea into the sitting room where Chloe had piled presents under the five-foot pine tree.

'Wow, look at all those! I'll just ...' Jake disappeared and returned carrying two neat packages which he placed carefully under the tree.

Chloe started out playing postman, picking up each parcel, reading the tag aloud and feigning surprise at the two gifts addressed to her.

Jake laughed. 'Well who else? There's only us here, Mum.'

'And there's nobody else I'd rather be with,' Chloe said, pushing Jake's hair from his eyes.

After the presents had been opened and exclaimed

over, Jake followed Chloe into the kitchen and offered to help with Christmas dinner.

'Bless you sweetheart, but there's no need – I prepped half the veg last night. Why don't you road-test one of your new Xbox games?'

Chloe waited until the house was vibrating with explosions coming from Jake's room before texting a smoochy message to Caleb. With a ping, he answered by return. She knew she was acting like a teenager, sneaking around behind her son's back, but every time Chloe pictured the scene where she told Jake, she imagined the shock, anger and pure disappointment on his face as he remembered Caleb's furious outburst when he'd found Jake and Amber together. Chloe shook her head, pushed the thought from her mind and got on with peeling parsnips.

•

On Boxing Day sleet fell from a silver sky.

'Shit,' Chloe said aloud, hoping the adverse weather wouldn't stop Bryony and Paul from making the journey to Eden Hill. She waited until nine and gave her friend a call.

'B, it's me, love. Look, I just wanted to warn you to stick a blanket and a flask of tea in the car … or whatever you're meant to do when it snows.'

'Ooh, how exciting! We haven't got any in London.'

'Neither have we – yet. But it's really cold and

there's sleet coming down, so it could change. Just be careful driving, hon. See you about one o'clock.'

A few hours later, Bryony and Paul arrived, laden with gifts and wine.

It hadn't snowed – if anything the sky had brightened.

'So good to see you,' Chloe said, hugging them both.

Jake leant in the doorway. 'Alright, Paul? Hey Bryony,' he said, affecting nonchalance.

As soon as coats were off and wine had been poured, Jake turned to Paul. 'Would you like to see the games Mum got me? The animation is awesome.' They went upstairs leaving the women alone together.

Bryony looked at Chloe meaningfully. '*Well?*'

'Well what?'

Bryony frowned. 'Chloe, you know what I'm talking about.'

'Haven't a clue.' Chloe topped up her friend's glass.

'Have you shagged the hot farmer yet?' Bryony said.

'Sshhh! No, I haven't. B, it'll happen. We really like each other and–' Chloe stopped abruptly, hearing the boys approach.

'Well, just don't wait too long,' Bryony hissed giving Chloe a gentle shove.

CHAPTER 26

The Wildes

On Christmas Day, Lisa awoke at six-thirty but resisted the urge to rise and busy herself in the kitchen. Instead she snuggled against Ben's musky warmth, listening to his rhythmic breathing.

Nelly sensed her mistress was awake and sat up in her miniature bed, quivering with anticipation. Putting a finger to her lips, Lisa motioned for the little dog to jump up.

Ben did not stir. Studying his handsome face, his hair curled against the pillow, Lisa felt overwhelmed by love. The loneliness and sheer longing while he'd been away had shocked her and the incident in The Gallery had left her feeling vulnerable. But something else bothered her about Ben being part of the Retro Tour, something she was loath to admit: Insecurity about whether Ben would be faithful to her had wormed its way into her head. She'd followed the tour on social media, scrutinising photographs of all seven 90s acts. Three of them were well-preserved girl bands, and most of the women had hung on tight to their looks. To add to her paranoia, most of the backing vocalists were women and then there were the dancers, with their taut young bodies and swishy hair. In Ben's absence, she'd spent hours ruminating on *what ifs* – and despising herself for it.

Ben opened sleepy grey eyes and smiled. 'Morning gorgeous. Merry Christmas.' He yawned. 'What time is it? You should have woken me.'

Lisa smiled. 'Happy Christmas, darling. It's almost eight. You relax and have a cuddle with Nellie, while I make some tea and bring it back to bed.'

'I'd rather have a cuddle with *you*,' Ben said, dragging Lisa back under the covers while Nellie bounced on top of them, enjoying the game.

•

They'd opened presents after breakfast. Lisa had given Ben an absurdly expensive framed print of Mick Jagger, which he adored, and in return he presented her with a be-bowed box of lingerie and some beautiful hand-made leather boots – all of which she knew had cost him an arm and a leg.

'I think you need to try it all on,' Ben winked.

But Lisa had swatted him away. 'Later, baby. They're lovely though. Thank you so much.'

Then despite it being just the two of them, Lisa had cooked an enormous turkey and an obscene amount of vegetables.

'Oh, I get it,' Ben nodded surveying the feast, 'leftovers for tomorrow. Wow, Leese, this all looks fantastic – the food, the table, the decorations. You've worked so hard – thank you, baby, you're amazing.' He began piling his plate. 'I've missed your cooking

… it's all brown rice, beans and pulses on tour, which has its downside as you can imagine, all cooped up in a bloody bus.'

'Is that all you missed?' Lisa pouted, filling Ben's glass with champagne. 'Anyway, cheers sweetheart. Here's to our first Christmas as a married couple and I hope all our wishes come true.'

After making a serious dent in the food, they shared the clearing up, but it still took an age.

'What's the point in having a dishwasher if half our stuff can't go in it?' Ben grumbled, desperate to relax but determined that Lisa would not wash up alone.

Finally, they collapsed onto the sofa.

Barely a minute later, Lisa got up. 'I'll just make us a coffee. We've got some nice mints that Rose brought round …' she left the room, muttering to herself.

Ben sighed and switched the television on; before Lisa could return he was asleep.

•

On Boxing Day morning, sleet filled the sky but by noon, it had brightened considerably. Their guests were due at two-thirty. Ben had been tasked with serving drinks and pouring nibbles into bowls, while Lisa went around lighting scented candles and fluffing the flowers. Once again, the kitchen table groaned with Christmas fare.

'Ooh, I wonder who's first,' Lisa said, jumping at the sound of the door knocker.

'Happy Crimbo, darling.' Towering in four-inch heels, Tanya was resplendent in a teal cat suit, her long dark hair in loose waves. She held out a beautifully wrapped gift, 'for you both,' she said, kissing Lisa and Ben on each cheek.

Ben let out a low whistle. 'Well, how bloody gorgeous do you look?' he said. 'Give us a twirl, Tan.'

Lisa smiled, agreeing with him, although she was secretly irritated by Ben's compliment. The door knocker sounded a second time.

'Mum, Jack, come in,' Lisa said, embracing Rita and offering Jack her cheek. 'Merry Christmas to you both. Go straight through, Ben's on bar duty.'

'What's the matter?' Rita said, studying her daughter, 'you stressed with all the cooking and wot-not?'

'No, of course not. You know me, I love feeding people.'

'Well something's up, I can see it in your face – your left eye's gone all wonky.'

'Oh, thanks for that, Mum. I'm fine – or I *was*.' Lisa, in no mood for Rita's scrutiny, busied herself with coats and scarves.

Ben raised his glass. 'We're just waiting for Rick … he might be a bit late. Has everyone got a drink?

Cheers … Happy Christmas. Anyway, fill your boots, all … Lisa's gone a bit mad with the old nosebag.'

Tanya pulled Lisa to one side. 'I hope you're not trying to fix me up with Rick. He's a nice bloke, but I'm not desperate.'

'The thought never crossed my mind,' Lisa said, taking a sip of champagne. 'Actually Tan, you might be surprised. Now that he's a bona fide rock star on tour, he's looking fit!'

'Oh yeah? Have I got competition then?' Ben's eyes twinkled.

Lisa was embarrassed. 'I just meant … I've seen the photos online and he's looking good compared to when he was squatting here. Poor thing, he was a right mess.'

Upon Rick's arrival, Ben recapped introductions, although everyone had met before.

'I see what you mean!' Tanya said in a loud whisper, taking in Rick's lean frame and long, glossy hair. 'He looks ten years younger!'

Thrusting out her modest chest, she stalked over to Rick. 'Hi, I'm Tanya – Lisa's friend. We've met once before. I hear you're on the 90s Retro Tour … how's that going?'

'Blimey, it's like lunch with the Rolling Stones in 'ere,' Jack remarked, swapping his champagne for a bottle of the pale ale he'd brought.

Ben preened. 'I'll take that as a massive compliment,

Jackie, except that me and the boys are twenty years younger.'

Rita made a face. 'Well you don't look it.'

'Mum, you never miss a trick, do you? You know the Stones are all in their seventies.' Lisa rolled her eyes and turned to Ben. 'Ignore her, darling.'

After an hour or so, and with the light already fading, Rick excused himself for a smoke, sheltering from the cold in the covered side-passage; Ben followed.

Curious as to whether Ben would light up, too, Lisa ducked into the cloakroom where the window was open a notch, letting in their conversation.

She heard Ben's voice. 'Give us a drag mate. I've promised Leese, but ...'

Lisa gasped, picturing Ben as he shared Rick's cigarette.

'So, how's tricks man?' Ben said. 'You and Jules working things out? Or are you still loved up with Jessie?'

Rick groaned. 'What can I say? It's all a fucking mess. The one thing I know is that Jules and me are finished – dead in the water. As for Jessie ...' He sighed. 'I've given up. Her husband won't let go and it's too much like hard work. So, to all intents and purposes, mate, I'm a free agent.'

Lisa pictured them, nodding in agreement.

'Well, good for you,' Ben said eventually. 'There

are worse things to be, especially on tour. Two words, mate: Ruby Stone.'

Another pause followed and some low laughter before Ben added, 'and the old adage is true, you know; what happens on tour stays on tour.'

CHAPTER 27

The Mortons

Jake lay on his bed, trying to decide whether Matthew Garret's party was worth braving the weather for. Matthew fascinated him. He was different to Dylan who lived on the other side of the estate in a house much like his own; come to think of it, Dylan's whole life was a lot like Jake's, except that his dad was around more, and he had an annoying nine-year-old sister. Matt, on the other hand, was kind of posh; not in the way he talked, but because he lived in a wood and glass tree-house thing down a dirt track. Matt called it a Hoff-Hoose or something … anyway, it was cool, compared to living in Eden Hill.

The most interesting thing about Matt's party was that his parents would be away overnight. Girls had been invited (including Amber, who he pretty much avoided these days) and Matt had boasted a stash of beer and cider, garnered with the cooperation of his older brother, Luke, who would also be there, 'to make sure we don't trash the place', Matt had said with a manic snigger.

Jake sent a text to Dylan: 'Are we on?'

Then he went downstairs where his Mum was in the kitchen, singing along to her Ben Wilde album as she removed a side of roast beef from the oven. Jake's stomach rumbled.

'Ready in fifteen minutes,' his mum said, shaking golden roast potatoes in a tin.

He felt bad about leaving her alone on New Year's Eve, but she'd been cool about it, saying it was fine as long as he didn't drink and shared a taxi home with Dylan.

Jake liked that his mum trusted him more lately. They'd even had THE DRUGS conversation, but he'd lied, saying he'd tried weed once and didn't like it. Fuck, he *loved* it – but his mum would only worry, and anyway, he couldn't afford it, except as an occasional treat.

'You are still going to Matthew's party, aren't you, Jakey?' Chloe wiped her hands on a tea towel and faced him. 'I'll run you and Dylan over there at eight thirty. I think I know where his place is.'

'Great, thanks Mum ... if you're sure.' Jake checked his mobile, 'Cool. Dylan's just messaged me that we're on. I'll tell him we'll pick him up, shall I?'

They ate in the kitchen, Chloe forgoing wine, conscious of the short drive through Crabton. It was the least she could do for her only son on New Year's Eve. She piled Jake's plate with his favourite roast potatoes and buttered carrots but was too nervous to do more than pick at her own food.

'Jake, you will be careful, won't you? I don't mind you having one beer, but no more please, darling.

Anyway, I'm sure Matt's parents will be keeping track of things.'

'Of course,' Jake nodded, avoiding Chloe's eyes.

•

By nine-fifteen, Chloe's nerves were in rags. She'd sped back from dropping the boys off, then brushed her teeth and spritzed on her favourite perfume. Then she'd changed into her best matching bra and knickers and pulled on a soft jersey dress before going around lighting tea rose candles and plumping cushions. She was desperate for a glass of wine but wanted her mouth to taste sweet.

At bang on nine-thirty, the doorbell rang.

Caleb held out a bottle of Chablis. 'You smell gorgeous,' he said, his lips grazing hers.

'Thank you, so do you. Do you think we're doing the right thing?'

'What, grabbing an opportunity to be alone, while all three kids are at the same party? Yes, I do. Sweetheart, we said we'd tell them after the holidays anyway, and I think we should stick to that. In the meantime …' Caleb kissed her again, this time it was long and lingering. 'I want you, Chloe,' he said, his voice hoarse.

Chloe caught her breath. 'I do too … want *you*, I mean but–'

'Hey, I'm nervous as well – shall we have a drink?'

They went into the kitchen, which still bore signs of supper.

'Corkscrew?' Caleb said, taking charge of the situation.

Perched nervously on the sofa, drinking wine and attempting to swap holiday news, Chloe felt faintly ridiculous. She'd dreamt of taking Caleb to bed for weeks, now her own inhibitions were getting the better of her.

With resolve, she drained her glass and refilled it.

Caleb laughed softly. 'Hey, steady on!'

'Sorry … okay, let's go upstairs while I'm feeling brave. Look we both want this and we're wasting time. I told Jake to be home by one o'clock … he'll be late as usual but …'

And then all shyness evaporated as Chloe took Caleb's hand and led him to her room where tea rose candles scented the warm air and the bed was made up with crisp new linen.

•

It had been quick and clumsy; a fumble of clothing and a snagging of knees, elbows and noses.

'Blimey. I think that might have been a bit overdue,' Caleb sighed, as they lay panting in each other's arms, 'sorry it was a bit–'

'A bit amazing, actually,' Chloe said, wearing a soppy, blissed-out grin.

'I think we should do that again … just to make sure, don't you?' Caleb began lightly kissing Chloe's throat and shoulders, moving down towards her breasts as she moaned with pleasure.

An arc of light swept the room as a car pulled up.

'Neighbours are home,' Chloe murmured between kisses, 'best thing about a detached house … no one can hear a thing.'

Then her blood froze as a door opened and closed downstairs, followed by heavy footfall.

'Fuck!' Chloe hissed in the semi-darkness. 'Jake's home!'

•

She could track Jake's route by sound. He'd gone straight into the kitchen and was gulping water at the sink. Then he'd looked for her in the sitting room where the lights were still on. She could picture him, dumping his jacket on the newel post at the foot of the stairs, and discarding his shoes with a bump.

They'd left the bedroom door ajar. There was nothing to prevent Jake from walking in and finding Chloe and Caleb together.

Chloe put her finger to her lips. 'Stay here,' she mouthed, sliding out of bed and reaching for her robe. She needed to intercept Jake and get him talking downstairs.

'Hi,' Chloe yawned, feigning sleepiness, 'you're

early, it's only quarter past eleven. Didn't you want to see in the New Year with your friends?'

Jake made a face. 'No, because it was crap. Bloody lemonade and crisps! Matthew's parents had rigged up stupid party games … like we're six years old.'

Chloe tried hard to focus, despite her racing pulse. 'Oh … well … what were you expecting?'

Jake emitted a bark of laughter. 'Not *that*. Matt said his parents were away and that there'd be booze and girls and stuff. I mean, not that I was going to drink or anything,' he added, remembering who he was talking to.

He narrowed his eyes and studied Chloe's face. 'Mum, why have you got all that make up on? You're all red in the face – what's the matter?'

Chloe hesitated before mumbling that she'd gone to bed early with a headache. It sounded unconvincing, even to her.

'I need the loo,' Jake said, moving past her. Then he thumped upstairs, paused outside Chloe's now closed bedroom door, and continued to the bathroom. Chloe stood in the hallway, frozen by indecision. She'd have to style it out; she and Jake would see in the New Year together, with hot chocolate and brownies, then after Jake had gone to bed, Caleb would have to creep out. The irony of the situation had not escaped her.

She heard the bathroom door open and close,

then Jake's footfall on the landing heading towards her room.

'Mum, there's no towel in there,' he called out, bound for Chloe's en-suite.

With leaden limbs, and a creeping nausea, Chloe mounted the stairs as Jake's hand hovered over the door handle.

'Jake, don't go in there!' Her voice was urgent.

'Why not?' Jake said, before throwing the door open and going in. 'Fuck! Who are you?'

Chloe entered her room to find her son and Caleb facing each other.

'Jake, go downstairs, please,' she said, grateful that Caleb had at least managed to scramble into his clothes.

'I know you, don't I? Oh, god – you're Amber's dad! Fuck! What are you doing here ... with my mum?'

'Stop swearing please, Jake. Let's all go downstairs and talk about this calmly, shall we?'

'Talk *calmly*? No one wanted to talk calmly when I was with Amber, did they? What was it *he* called me?' Jake shouted, 'a feral little shit? Jesus Mum. Can't believe you're shagging *him* of all people.'

Then Jake flew down the stairs, slid into his shoes and without even grabbing his jacket went out into the night, slamming the front door behind him.

CHAPTER 28

The Bevans

In the run up to Christmas, Jan's mood became perilously low and Martin feared for her wellbeing.

Jan's chilly reception from other dog walkers had really got to her – so much so that she'd finished work a day early, contacting the dog owners, pretending to be unwell.

'Don't let them upset you,' Martin said, 'you've made a real success of your business and no one's ever complained before. People gossip in a place like this, but it'll soon blow over and things will be back to normal.'

What he really wanted to talk about was his own business venture, but he was picking the right moment for that.

And then the most extraordinary thing happened; something that blew all other news out of the water. On Christmas Day, Hayley and Simon arrived at noon, pink-cheeked with excitement. Martin couldn't remember seeing them look so happy.

In the warmth of the kitchen, Martin popped open the Prosecco but Hayley covered her glass.

'Go on, love, have a little tipple with your dad,' he said, 'your room's all made up, no one's driving home tonight.'

The young couple exchanged shy glances and Hayley's cheeks flushed.

Jan gasped and clapped her hand over her mouth. 'Oh love! You're not, are you?'

Hayley beamed. 'We're pregnant!' she said. 'Baby's due in early-July. You're going to be grandparents.'

After the delighted squeals of congratulations had died down and they were seated before a vast golden turkey with all the trimmings – the joint handiwork of Jan and Martin which had begun on Christmas Eve – Martin proposed a toast. 'A happy Christmas to *all* our family,' he turned to his daughter and Simon, 'and many, many congratulations to you both – you'll make wonderful parents.'

'Aww, thanks Dad – and you and Mum will make brilliant grandparents.'

Looking flustered, Simon cleared his throat. 'Jan, Martin, I know you'll be wondering if we're getting married – and the answer's yes.' He paused as they exclaimed their delight. 'I've asked Hayley and she's said yes, but just so you know, we're waiting until after the baby … there's too much pressure otherwise.'

'Blimey, better start saving up for my daughter's wedding then,' Martin winked, playing to the gallery.

'I thought you were loaded, Dad – what with selling the shop and everything,' Hayley said, spearing a crispy parsnip

'That money's for our retirement, love – we might

be living on that for the rest of our lives,' Jan said, throwing Martin a look.

'Ah ... or we might not be,' Martin said cryptically. 'I've got a little surprise of my own – not quite on par with a new baby, but exciting nonetheless.'

Martin had everyone's attention; he paused for dramatic effect.

'Well go on, Mart, the suspense is killing us,' Jan said.

Martin looked amused. 'I've bought ...' another pause, 'a smashing little starter home, up near the shops – and I'm going to be a landlord,' he said, banging his palm on the table.

Silence.

'Interesting ...' Simon murmured eventually.

Jan was staring at Martin as though he'd gained another head. 'What do you mean, you've *bought* a starter home? Surely you mean you're thinking of buying one?'

'No,' Martin smirked, 'It's a done deal. Thanks to Jeremy Hunter, I've bought a cracking little two-up, two-down newbuild in Cobalt Close for a very nifty price and I've already got tenants lined up.'

'Ooh, that's exciting, Dad,' Hayley managed, ignoring her mother's obvious displeasure.

Jan glowered. 'And you didn't think to mention it to me first, Martin?'

'I thought it would be a lovely surprise,' Martin beamed.

'Oh, it's a surprise alright,' Jan said.

•

When the Bevans had finished ploughing through three courses of Christmas Dinner, Jan banished Hayley and Simon to the sitting room.

'You young people relax. Me and Dad will do the clearing up. Hayley, you put your feet up, love – see what's on the telly and I'll do us all a cuppa soon.'

'Mum, I'm not ill, I'm pregnant. Let me and Si give you a hand.'

But Jan wouldn't hear of it. 'I need to talk to your dad,' she said, before heading for the kitchen where Martin was already at work on the saucepans, looking faintly ridiculous in a reindeer apron and pink rubber gloves, while cheerfully humming *Sleigh Ride*.

Jan gave him a withering look.

'How you can just stand there, singing away without a care in the world is beyond me!' she said, with barely concealed fury. 'Martin, what possessed you to gamble our retirement fund with that wide boy, Hunter?'

Martin looked hurt. 'Now Jan, that's not fair. Firstly, I haven't used the whole lot … about a third of it's mortgaged.'

Jan looked heavenwards and let out a stifled

scream. 'For God's sake, Martin! Please tell me you're joking.'

Martin was exasperated. 'You won't be saying that when we're collecting a thousand pounds a month in rent.'

'But what about when the house is empty, between tenants? What happens when people don't cough up and get behind in their payments? Not to mention all the repairs and maintenance you'll be doing. Have you thought this through at all, Martin?'

Martin was becoming agitated. 'Of course. I'm not daft, Jan. Hunters Estate Agency are going to manage it for me.'

'Ha!' Jan cut in, flinging her tea towel down, 'I might have known! It's win, win, win with that man. Well, I don't trust him. No wonder Jeremy Hunter and his la-de-da missus are millionaires.'

'You're being silly now Jan. Jeremy is a friend and a legitimate business man ... ah yes, and what you *don't* know, is that I'll have an ally on the inside.' He tapped his nose conspiratorially.

Jan groaned. 'I can hardly wait.'

'Trina.'

Jan shrugged.

Martin was becoming impatient. 'I managed to get young Trina a job at Hunters ... she's going to be a trainee on the lettings side.'

'I thought she had a job,' Jan said, temporarily distracted.

'She's miserable in that department store. Jeremy's giving her a three-month trial, and I reckon she'll be marvellous – she's ever so good with people,' Martin said.

'Martin, that money was meant for our retirement and now you've gone and gambled it.'

'Invested Jan, not *gambled*! Love, the expression 'safe as houses' comes to mind. We can't fail – trust me.'

'I'll remind you of that, Martin, when we're living on a pittance, scared to put the heating on in our old age.' Jan rattled tea cups on a tray. 'Right not another word about it while the kids are here. We've got more important things to think about, eh, Grandad?'

CHAPTER 29

The Bradshaws

Christmas Day in the Bradshaw house had been a sombre affair, although Rosemary had done her best to jolly things up for her daughter's sake.

'Love, must you go over that report *now*?' she'd said, when Nigel took to his study at noon. 'Can't you play with Iris for a while – today of all days? Show an interest in her new Christmas stuff.'

But later she'd been mollified to see Nigel and Iris side by side on the sofa, laughing raucously at *Home Alone*. Rosemary was amazed. 'I didn't know you liked this film,' she said, 'have you seen it before?'

Nigel hesitated. 'No, but a colleague recommended it – and it's actually quite funny.'

•

On Boxing Day Rosemary feared the harsh weather would worsen and keep her family away, but by noon the sky had begun to brighten.

'Happy Christmas, sis! Look at you – living it up in the big house, while the rest of us are slumming it. Why haven't I been here before?' Joseph said, with a mischievous glint.

Rosemary rolled her eyes with mock irritation. 'Because you're rubbish at keeping in touch, Joe – it's not like I haven't asked you, is it? Are you going to introduce us then?' she said, smiling at the fine-boned young woman who hung back.

'Everyone, this is Kristal,' Joe said as hugs and introductions were swapped. Abi struggled through the door behind her brother, half-dragging a large bag of presents in one hand and a bottle of champagne in the other.

'Thanks for your help getting stuff out the car, bro,' she said to Joseph, shaking her head.

'No problem, Abs,' Joseph cackled cheekily.

Rosemary beamed with pleasure. Whatever their ages, the relationship was always the same and the three of them became children again, indulging their younger brother.

•

'And what do you do, Kristal?' Nigel asked, raising his voice above the music and topping up the young woman's glass.

'I'm a dental receptionist,' Kristal said, displaying white even teeth. 'I quite like it, but I wanted to be a model.'

Nigel held the young woman's gaze. 'I'm sure there's nothing preventing you,' he said, charmed by Kristal's youthful candour.

'I'm actually a couple of centimetres too short, and even these days, opportunities are limited for black models.'

Nigel raised sandy eyebrows. 'Oh, surely that's not the case …'

Joseph was playing with Iris, putting on a funny falsetto as he moved her dolls around while the little girl shrieked with laughter. Abi was helping Rosemary as the two of them sliced and chopped, filling bowls with snacks.

'They're getting on well, I see,' Abi said in a low voice, inclining her head towards her brother in law and Kristal.

'If you've got something to say …' Rosemary whispered, picking up on her sister's tone.

Abi shook her head, 'Nah, not me Rose. She's pretty though, isn't she?'

Rosemary turned to see Nigel engrossed in animated conversation with Kristal, who was flirting now, tossing her long sleek hair and flashing her almond eyes.

Joseph joined his sisters, a giggling Iris balanced on his shoulders. 'What are you two whispering about?'

'Nothing whatsoever,' Rosemary said, shutting the conversation down.

•

'Well that was a success. Well done, darling,' Nigel said, when Rosemary finally got Iris down, way past her usual bedtime.

'It was. Bless Iris. She loves seeing her auntie and

uncle. They make such a fuss of her, especially Joseph. It's a shame they don't come down more often – they only live an hour away.'

'I don't think they're keen on me, Rose. Too straight, too dull,' he laughed without mirth, 'and too bloody old.'

'I'm sure they don't think that,' Rosemary lied, adding, 'Kristal seems like a nice girl.'

'Yes, god knows what she sees in your brother. She's got ambition, I could tell at once.'

'Hey, that's my little brother you're dissing. He's a good man; kind, good-humoured–'

'And a buffoon. Even at her tender age, Kristal is already a sophisticated young woman. She'd be better off with someone more mature.'

'Like you, you mean?' Rose said, her eyes challenging.

'Don't be ridiculous. I'm old enough to be her father. Christ, Rose, sometimes I feel old enough to be *yours*.' Nigel got up, 'I'm having a G&T – do you want one?'

'No thanks, I've already had wine today. What happens if Iris is ill in the night and we have to drive her to hospital?'

Nigel mumbled something about her being alarmist and went to fix himself a drink.

Rosemary wilted. Was this to be her life now?

Chilly silences, punctuated by snarky, half-uttered conversations?

She'd seen the way that Abi had looked at Nigel, her eyes full of mistrust. If Joseph had picked up on an undercurrent of hostility, he had hidden it well.

She thought of Kristal, with her lithe body, long silky hair extensions and easy banter – and so much more than that. Her dreams.

That was me when I first met Nigel, she thought, suffused by a creeping sadness.

Abi was right; they'd married because she'd been expecting Iris. Joan's words came back to her: *You can't marry him if the love's not there, Rosie.* Why hadn't she listened to her mother? She'd been stubborn then, thinking only of her tiny but growing bump.

Nigel had always been frugal with information about his upbringing in North London, and about the father he never knew; behaviour she'd once thought of as enigmatic now seemed furtive.

She'd read somewhere that divorce applications shot up in January – a result of people being welded together for a fortnight, when they were used to being apart. Soon Nigel would be back at work, commuting to the London office most days as well as driving up to Huddersfield. It should have upset her that his trips had increased from one or two a month to once a week, but instead the nights she slept alone were a blissful relief.

Nigel returned with drinks and nibbles.

'It's alright,' he said, 'it's a mocktail, made with pineapple juice. Thank you for a lovely Christmas, Rose. You do so much for this family and I don't show my appreciation nearly enough.' He sat beside Rose, his hand covering hers. 'I need to figure out a way of spending more time with you and Iris, don't I?'

'We'd both like that, Nigel,' Rosemary said, her voice thick with effort.

CHAPTER 30

The Wildes

Ben could always tell when Lisa was upset. She'd push herself longer and harder in the gym and then come home and attack the already immaculate kitchen floor or the pristine bathroom tiles, unable to relax for a minute.

'Come on, babe. I know something's up – just tell me what it is so I can make it better,' Ben wheedled on New Year's Eve morning.

'Nothing's wrong. I don't know why you keep asking,' Lisa snapped.

'Because you're running around like a Tasmanian Devil. I wish you'd relax, you're making me dizzy. I thought we'd chill out a bit before I go back on tour next week.'

Lisa frowned, opened her mouth to speak then changed her mind.

'I'm going up for a bath,' she announced, before calling Nellie, who scampered up the stairs behind her mistress, giving Ben a haughty look as she passed.

'Even the bloody dog hates me,' Ben muttered, opening his laptop to check for emails.

But when Lisa returned, angelic in an ivory cashmere sweater and jeans, her sour mood had lifted.

'Sorry for being grumpy, babe. I'm just dreading you going away, that's all. I missed you so much at the start of the tour, and this time you'll be gone for months. Being here on my own ... it makes me feel ... oh, I dunno ... vulnerable.' Lisa remembered the thug in The Gallery. It had been a one-off situation, but it had knocked her confidence.

'Sweetheart,' Ben crooned, holding Lisa close and stroking her peach-scented hair, 'I'll be back before you know it, I promise.'

•

It annoyed Ben that the Speckled Hen had sold tickets for New Year's Eve, but Lisa had taken a more pragmatic view.

'Babe, how else can they limit the number of people coming in? It's the best venue for miles around and it's busy enough on a normal night.'

'Yeah, I suppose so.' Ben dithered between two shirts before banishing both to the wardrobe and opting for a Rolling Stones T-Shirt that was decades old. He slid a soft jacket over the top before Lisa could object.

'You look stunning, Leese,' he said, taking in his wife's gym-honed silhouette in a fitted black dress.

Lisa gave her lips a final gloss and grabbed her favourite clutch bag. Then after a brief discussion about whose car to take – and settling for Lisa's due to it being smaller and easier to park – they drove to Crabton.

•

'There they are!' Lisa spotted Tanya standing with a small clique of glamazons whom she knew to varying degrees.

'Blimey,' Ben muttered, 'any blokes coming to this shindig – or am I the token male? Hey, not that I'm complaining.'

Ignoring Ben, Lisa pushed through the throng of people, already three deep at the bar, before hugging Tanya and air-kissing the other women. 'This is my husband, Ben,' she said, giving him a nudge forward and making first name introductions all round.

A couple of men who seemed peripheral to the group exchanged sympathetic looks with Ben.

'Hiya, I'm Kevin. Can I get you a drink, Ben?' said one, a balding, round-faced guy in his forties who looked familiar.

Ben grinned. 'Good luck with that, mate – have you seen the queue? But thank you – I'll have a lime soda, please ... we're not sure yet who's driving. Lisa'll have a–' but when he looked over, he saw that someone had already thrust a glass of champagne into her hand.

Pleased to see Lisa basking in the company of women, Ben began chatting to a second man he recognised from the gym who seemed to know who he was.

'I'm Dave,' the man said, putting his hand out for Ben to shake. 'My missus, Debs – that's her, there –

has got a couple of your albums. I must say though, you look like a normal bloke in the flesh.'

Ben chuckled. 'That's cos I am. Being a musician's not what it's cracked up to be … it's just a job. Anyway, I'm small fry. What's your world, Dave?' Ben said switching the subject as Kevin returned with a round of drinks.

'I'm in IT,' Dave began, before explaining his work in excruciating detail, leaving Ben bamboozled and looking for an escape route. He spotted one in the form of Martin Bevan, who was hanging back from the crush with his wife Jan. The two of them looked deeply uncomfortable.

'Hold that thought, Dave. My best mate's just arrived so I'd better go over,' Ben lied, moving away from the group.

'Hello Martin, Jan. Good to see you both,' he said, surprising the Bevans with his effusive welcome.

'Good evening, Ben,' Martin said, putting out his hand. Jan only nodded, her cheeks flushed from the heat of the room and Ben's attention.

'Lisa's catching up with the girls,' Ben explained. 'Believe it or not, I'd rather be in a quiet boozer … it's all a bit flashy for my liking.'

Martin nodded. 'Indeed. We've never been here before, have we Jan? But we thought we'd make an effort for New Year's Eve,' he laughed wryly. 'I'm wondering why I bothered now. Looks like it'll take me half-an-hour to get served.'

'Allow me, Martin,' Ben said before wedging himself in a good spot near the bar.

After a considerable wait, Ben returned just as a table became free and the three of them sat down gratefully. He indicated Martin's shandy. 'Well aren't *we* a crazy bunch! There's only Jan on the hard stuff … still, someone's got to drive,' he added, catching sight of Lisa, who was laughing hysterically, wiping tears from her eyes.

What am I doing here? Ben thought, *talking to people I hardly know, dodging some other boring git, while Lisa has a blast with her mates?* It was not the evening Ben had planned. He'd hoped to get a little smoochy with his wife; things had been distinctly cool between them all holiday, but he saw now that he'd lost Lisa to the group of women.

'This is Lisa's night,' Ben said decisively, 'and I don't begrudge it, but I think I'm going to shoot off, Martin.'

'Righto, Ben. I think we're right behind you … it's far too packed and noisy for us.' Martin fished in his pocket for his mobile phone. 'What do you think, Jan? Shall I call a cab?'

Jan nodded.

'No need, Martin – I'll give you a lift.'

'Oh, well, if you're sure. But what about …' Martin

looked over at Lisa who was draped over Tanya, her face pink with champagne.

'She's having a great time, bless her – I'll come back for her after midnight. But right now, I fancy a kebab and a bit of telly.'

After kissing a surprised Lisa goodbye and vowing to return, Ben walked Martin and Jan to Lisa's car – via the takeaway – and they set off for Eden Hill.

•

Ben drove at the speed limit, mindful that the police could be lurking. He was conscious of the reeking kebab going cold in the glove box, despite it being well-wrapped. He'd have to spray some air freshener before picking Lisa up; she'd have a fit if she knew what he'd eaten.

'Look at that young lad – he must be freezing in just a shirt,' Ben said as he turned off the bypass and into Eden Hill.

'Young people don't seem to feel the cold. He'll be coming back from a party, half-cut,' Martin said.

'Isn't that Jake?' Jan piped up from the back seat, alarm in her voice. 'What's he–' but the words died in her throat as the boy, wild-eyed, changed direction suddenly and leapt towards the car. Ben swerved and braked sharply but not fast enough to prevent him from hitting the boy with a sickening thud that made all three of them cry out.

'Fuck, I hit him! You saw that, didn't you? He jumped … he just …'

Ben was out of the car, racing to where the young boy lay unmoving on the ground.

'Oh, Jesus Christ. I've hit a kid … I've killed a child,' Ben spluttered. Jan began to cry – only Martin remained calm.

The three of them gathered around Jake's inert form as his eyes fluttered open and he began to keen like an injured animal.

'Jake? Can you hear me?' Martin took the boy's hand. 'Don't worry, son, we'll call an ambulance, don't try to move.'

Ben was bent double, his head in his hands. Then to everyone's astonishment, Jake sat up.

'Get off me! Just leave me alone,' he shouted, getting to his feet but collapsing again.

'It's the adrenaline,' Martin said, 'doesn't mean he's not injured.' He started to dial 999, but Jake knocked the phone from his hand and it went spinning across the tarmac.

No other cars had passed them – the place was deserted. Ben was recovering, realising that he hadn't killed a child after all.

'No ambulance! I'm fine – I'm fucking great,' Jake yelled.

Jan spoke: 'Jake, you're not fine … you could have

been killed. What are you doing out here anyway? Does your Mum know where you are?'

'Like she cares – she hates me!' Jake sank to his knees at the side of the road and sobbed.

Still shaken, Ben said a silent prayer. The lad was a mess, but incredibly, he seemed physically unhurt. Ben moved the car to the side of the road, switched his headlights off and squatted beside the boy.

'Jake, my name's Ben – I was driving. Are you sure you're okay? You gave us a nasty turn there, buddy. I think you should get checked out, but right now, we need to get you home to your family.'

'I don't have a *family*.' Jake winced as he rubbed his left hip.

The adults looked at each other, then at Jake who was in a state of obvious distress.

Martin spoke: 'Well we can't leave him here. I'd take him back to ours, except that he lives next door and clearly there's a problem at home – his Mum'll be beside herself if she doesn't know where he is.'

'Do you think he's on drugs? Should we call the police?' Jan said in a loud whisper that sent the boy into a paroxysm of fresh sobs.

'Come on mate,' Ben said, helping Jake to his feet, 'come back to ours. Everything looks better with a cuppa tea and a biscuit.' He winked. 'I might even give you a bite of cold kebab.'

CHAPTER 31

The Bevans

For the second time in her life, Jan entered the Wildes' home and even in such bizarre circumstances couldn't help noticing the smell of money and the sheer opulence of the place, compared to her own house.

To her immense irritation, Martin offered to walk home, pick up his car and collect Lisa from the Speckled Hen. Well, how like Lisa, Jan thought sourly; the three of them caught up in a crisis, while Lisa batted her eyelashes, drank champagne and saw the New Year in with the rest of her gorgeous skinny mates. The woman was Teflon.

'Cheers, Martin, but I need you here. You've got experience of kids – I haven't,' Ben spoke urgently, before booking a taxi for his wife.

But despite claiming to know nothing about young people, Ben had been brilliant, making them all tea, opening packets of biscuits and making buttered toast; not what Jan had expected from a pop star at all. Still Jake had been morose and silent, clueless about Ben's identity, until in an effort to take his mind off things and get him to open up, Ben had asked Jake if he played guitar.

Jake looked up from under matted hair. 'A bit, why?'

'Yeah, me too,' Ben said, 'have a look at this.'

Then to Jan and Martin's amazement he'd led them all to an upstairs room that housed several guitars – most of them acoustic – a set of keyboards that Ben explained could sound like *any* instrument, and a mixing desk. Jan didn't know what a mixing desk was, but it had hundreds of buttons and looked like an expensive piece of kit.

Jake's eyes grew wide. 'Wow ... you're him, aren't you? You're Ben Wilde. Bloody hell. I heard a rumour that you lived here. I can't believe it! My mum loves you ... I mean, like, *proper loves you.*'

For a moment, Jan saw a flash of the carefree teenager that Jake should have been. She'd seen him around, looking blank-eyed and utterly miserable; the lad reeked of unhappiness. Only now, something had catapulted his angst into another league. Jan knew what she'd seen out there. The lad had jumped – literally leapt – in front of the car. It was a miracle that Ben had reacted so quickly.

It had turned one o'clock when Lisa had arrived home, still looking annoyingly beautiful, and in high spirits, keen to go on celebrating – until she saw Jake hunched over her kitchen table on his second round of Nutella toast.

Ben had taken Lisa aside to explain.

'Oh my god, you poor thing,' she said, putting a

manicured hand on Jake's shoulder and beginning to sober up.

It was Martin who'd shut the situation down by promising Jake that he could stay at the Bevans' overnight, saying that everything else could be sorted in the morning.

Then Ben had dropped them all off at Constance Close, where at Jake's house, the lights blazed.

Jake eyed Ben sheepishly, 'Thank you,' he said, adding 'and I'm sorry … about, you know.'

Then they'd all exchanged the kind of looks normally reserved for people bonded by trauma before Martin and Jan had helped Jake inside and put him to bed in the spare room.

'I'll go,' Jan said, reading Martin's mind, 'it might sound better woman to woman – we're both mothers, after all.'

Then she'd gone next door, where Chloe, wild-eyed, had thrown the door open instantly, as if lying in wait.

'Oh god, Jan! Thank you … thank you so much – I've been beside myself. He just took off before I could stop him. I was about to phone the police – I've already rung round all his friends' parents.' Chloe was babbling with relief. 'Did he say anything?'

'Just that you've had a falling out, love,' Jan said kindly. 'I've been through it all with Hayley – teenagers are bloody hard work. You don't need to explain, but if you fancy a coffee and a natter tomorrow, you know where I am. And don't worry about your boy; I'll send him home after breakfast. He'll probably sleep until noon, you know what teenagers are like. Goodnight.'

Jan lay beside Martin, feeling wide awake.

'Strangest New Year we've ever had,' she said, 'and that Ben was a surprise … I never thought someone like him–'

'Jan, go to sleep, love – we can talk about it tomorrow. Love you, na-night.'

•

On New Year's Day, Jan and Martin rose at nine, padding about the house and speaking in hushed tones.

'Let him sleep, poor kid,' Martin said blowing on his second cup of tea.

Jan pursed her lips. 'We need to tell her, you know. You saw what happened last night, Mart. That boy jumped in front of the car. Now, why would he do a thing like that? His mum's got a right to know. He could have been killed.'

'So you keep saying, Jan, but he wasn't and it's none of our business, is it?'

'Love, wouldn't *you* want to know if our Hayley was in a bad way? We needn't tell Chloe every detail … just that it could have been serious and to have a word with him.'

Martin scoffed. 'I'm sure she'll be doing that anyway, Jan.'

At ten-thirty, Martin woke Jake with a cup of sweet tea.

Jake winced as he attempted to sit up.

'You'll have a nasty bruise today. You really should go to A&E ... just to be on the safe side,' Martin said, backing out of the room as Jake grunted in reply.

Moments later, the doorbell rang, and Chloe stood before him, hollow-eyed and wringing her hands.

'Come through, love,' Martin said. 'Kettle's on – it usually is in this house.'

Then Chloe listened with mounting horror as Martin gave an abridged account of New Year's Eve, leaving out the fact that Jake seemed to have jumped towards Ben's car and that it was Ben Wilde, rockstar and local celebrity, who was driving. It didn't seem necessary to involve Ben any deeper than he already was.

'Did Jake tell you what he was so upset about?' Chloe began, not meeting Jan or Martin's eyes.

'Only that you'd rowed,' Jan said. 'Believe me, we had some right ding-dongs with our Hayley when she was a teenager.'

Chloe's eyes blurred with tears. 'Only, it's my fault ... I feel so awful. I've done a terrible thing.' Hearing Jake on the stairs, she wiped her eyes with the heel of her hand and tried to smile.

Jake hesitated in the kitchen doorway, saying nothing.

Chloe spoke: 'Jake, we need to go home and talk. I'm so sorry about last night – you were right to be upset.' She pulled Jake into her arms.

'Aren't you curious, Martin?' Jan said, after Chloe had thanked them for their kindness and promised to invite them round for dinner the following week.

'Love, you know what they're like at that age. It'll be something and nothing. I'm sure it will all blow over. Anyway, let's give our girl a ring ... wish her and the bump a Happy New Year.'

CHAPTER 32

The Bradshaws

On New Year's Day, Rosemary and Nigel had taken down the Christmas tree, vacuumed up the pine needles and carefully stowed all evidence of the holidays in the loft. Two days later, to Rosemary's relief, Nigel returned to work.

'Rose, I'll need to stay up north for a few days because the shit is about to hit the fan,' Nigel said, folding shirts and underwear into a weekend bag.

Rosemary winced. 'Nigel, is there no other way? All those families, you'll be putting most of them on the breadline. I can't imagine there's much work for them up there.'

'Don't you think we've looked into every possible alternative?' Nigel said, tension registering in his voice. 'Rosemary, I don't own the company and it's not my decision. I'm just one of the poor saps who'll be delivering the bad news.'

'Well, let's hope they don't shoot the messenger,' Rosemary hissed, leaving Nigel to finish his packing.

Half-an-hour later, Rosemary and Iris waved Nigel off at the front door.

'See you both in three days,' he said, pecking his wife and daughter on the cheek 'that's if I survive the lynch mob.'

'Don't even joke about it. Nigel ... just ... just be

careful.' Rosemary said, shutting the front door with a degree of relief.

•

'It was funny having Daddy here over the holidays, wasn't it, Mummy? Has he gone to his other house now?' Iris said, taking an age to put her outdoor shoes on to go shopping.

Rosemary stiffened, 'What do you mean, sweetpea? Daddy hasn't got another house. He lives here with us. But he works hard, too, and when he's away, he stays in a hotel. You know what a hotel is, don't you Iris?'

'Of course I do,' the little girl said, shrugging on her navy puffer coat and tucking her favourite plush Pokémon into her pocket; it had been a Christmas gift from her uncle Joseph and was rarely out of her hands.

'Okay, ready? You hang on tight to Pikachu, and I'll hang on tight to you!' Rosemary said, rubbing noses with Iris as she buckled her into her booster seat.

With the car heater keeping the biting chill at bay, Rosemary drove to the supermarket under an ivory sky. As she trawled the aisles, she kept coming back to her daughter's comment about Nigel's *other house*. What had made her say such a thing? Supposing he had a whole secret life elsewhere?

That night, after putting Iris to bed still gripping her Pikachu, Rosemary telephoned her sister.

'Abi, you read about these people in the papers; bigamists who are married with children, leading a double life. And the poor women never suspect, do they?'

'Now you're being fanciful, Rose,' Abi said. 'I mean, I'm not Nigel's biggest fan or anything and I think your relationship is far from perfect. But honestly? Love, nobody else would have him!' Abi cackled, trying to pass her remark off as a joke.

'Abi, it's not funny – and it could happen.' Rosemary could feel the panic rising.

They talked a while longer, catching up on family news and setting out their new year goals.

'What do you want, Rose?' Abi asked.

'I don't know. More than anything, I want Iris to be happy and–'

'Yeah, darling, but what do *you* want? I see you there, in that big house, behind those gates; it's a gilded cage, Rose – and I don't see it making you happy.'

•

Rosemary had expected Nigel to call – to at least let her know how the staff in Huddersfield were taking news of the redundancies, but she'd heard nothing all day. All her silly fantasising about him leading a double life had made her paranoid, and now all she could think about was whether he'd had a car accident on the motorway.

What is wrong with me? she thought, pulling a woollen throw around her as the wind whistled down the chimney.

It was nine forty-five. Wired and sleepless, Rosemary reached for her mobile phone and sent a text, asking Nigel to get in touch.

A reply arrived immediately: 'Long stressful day, battery low, head pounding. Early night for me. Speak tomorrow. xx'

•

With Iris back at school, Rosemary's routine returned to normal. The long dark days seemed punctuated only by the school run, trips to the supermarket and the weekly visit to Glen Heights.

'I'm coming with you to see Mum,' Nigel announced over breakfast one Wednesday morning, as Rosemary buzzed about cajoling Iris into eating her cereal and coaxing her into her school uniform.

'What about work?' Rosemary said, absently hunting for her daughter's gym shoes.

'I'm taking the day off. They can manage without me for once. I want to see how the old girl is doing and, you know–' Nigel lowered his voice. 'she's not

getting any younger and I don't want to have …
regrets.'

'That's brilliant, Nigel. Mum often asks me when
you're coming. Only, don't be shocked by how she's
changed. Sometimes she's not entirely with it – other
times she's pretty lucid and you never know what
you're going to get.'

•

Nigel wrinkled his nose. 'Whiffs a bit, doesn't it?'
he muttered, noting the sulphurous smell of boiled
vegetables mixed with air freshener.

'I don't notice anymore.' Rosemary smiled at the
plump receptionist she recognised. 'Hi Karen, is it
okay to go up? This is my husband Nigel – Joyce's
son.'

'Of course, she'll be pleased to see you both. Just
phone down if you'd like coffee,' the receptionist said,
making a note on her pad.

Taking the stairs to the first floor, they found Joyce
sitting by the window.

'Hello, Mum. How are you? Look who I've brought,'
Rosemary said.

'Not now, Thelma, I'm watching the birds. They
love those bacon-balls that the gardener puts out for
them … poor little mites must be frozen. You can
bring me a cup of tea though – and a Garibaldi,' Joyce
said, turning back to her view.

'Mum. It's Rose. I've brought Nigel to see you – your son.'

'Who?' the old lady said, narrowing her eyes in Nigel's direction.

Nigel leant forward to embrace his mother, but Joyce shrank back.

'I knew this was a bad idea,' he said under his breath.

'I heard that!' Joyce snapped. 'I'm not deaf you know.'

'Just a bit forgetful these days, eh Mum? I'm Nigel – your son.'

He waited for the penny to drop.

'Oh yes, I know *that*. I think my eyesight's getting worse,' Joyce shrugged defensively. 'Well sit down then – as you're here.'

On the pretext of organising drinks when she could have easily phoned reception, Rosemary left Nigel and Joyce alone together.

A lump came into her throat; it was heartbreaking the way Joyce had failed to recognise her own son. Then again, it had been nine months or so since Nigel's last visit; during that time, his hair had become sparse and his middle had expanded considerably. Perhaps in Joyce's mind Nigel was young and not a man approaching fifty at all.

Ten minutes later, tensions were diffused by the arrival of tea, which Nigel insisted on pouring.

'You've got him well trained,' Joyce winked, her cup rattling in its saucer as she took a loud slurp.

'How is your friend, Mr Baldini?' Rosemary asked, searching for neutral topics.

Joyce snorted. 'Silly old fool's no friend of mine. Thinks he's so superior to the rest of us in here ...'

Nigel and Rosemary listened politely while Joyce complained about her neighbours.

'Mum, you say all that, but I know you're fond of them ... they're your friends,' Rosemary said, catching Nigel's eye.

Back at the car, Nigel looked drained. 'Well, that was hard work. I don't know how you do it, Rose,' he said.

'Because, my love, she's family and I like to think that when my mum gets to that age, someone will show her the same love and consideration – wherever she is in the world.'

'Thank you, Rose; I owe you so much,' Nigel said before starting the engine and pulling away.

CHAPTER 33

The Wildes

It was rare for Lisa to visit Eden Hill's coffee shop. Few cafés could rival the extra-hot frothy cappuccinos and velvety flat whites that she and Ben made at home with their beloved Italian machine. But it wasn't good coffee that Lisa lacked, it was company.

Lonely and stir crazy, two weeks into Ben's tour, she'd begged Tanya to meet her at *Chloe's Coffee*. Her friend had been reluctant at first, reminding Lisa that her midweek day off was strictly reserved for tackling laundry and cleaning.

'Oh, please, Tanya,' Lisa said, 'honestly, I haven't spoken to a soul since Ben left – well except for the odd *hello* at the gym and chatting to Nellie, of course.'

Tanya scoffed. 'Welcome to *my* world. You should try being single. At least you know Ben's coming back in a couple of months.'

They'd arranged to meet at eleven the following morning, but it was already ten minutes past. Lisa stopped fiddling with her phone and looked around. A striking woman of her own age with unruly dark hair escaping its clasp and a red-haired teenager pottered behind the counter.

Only two other tables were occupied; at one, an elderly man sat hunched over a tabloid newspaper, pastry crumbs still clinging to his lips, while at another a harassed young mum was struggling to contain two pre-school children. Lisa winced as a red-cheeked little boy of around two slammed down his plastic beaker for the third time – the final straw for his mother, who removed the cup and scolded the child. Both children began to wail so loudly that Lisa jumped when her friend sat down beside her.

'Hello babe,' Tanya said, grinning, 'you been scaring the kids again?' She acknowledged the young mother: 'Alright Holly? What's up with them?'

A brief exchange about the two toddlers followed while Lisa was on her feet, ordering coffee and granola cakes.

'So, how are you, Leese? Why are you so fed up?' Tanya said, getting straight to the point.

Lisa shook her head. 'Oh, take no notice. I'm just missing Ben, that's all. I don't think I realised quite how much we do together. I mean, apart from the gym every morning, and walking Nellie – I've made everything about him, haven't I?'

'Easily done, hon. You speak every day though, don't you?' Tanya said.

'Of course; we skype most days … but sometimes the connection's terrible, depending on where he is.'

Tanya winked. 'Hey, you could always move Rita in for a bit.'

'Oh god, no! The last thing I need is my mum lecturing me on independence.'

Tanya stirred her flat white. 'Is she still seeing old what's-his-name – Jackie?'

Lisa rolled her eyes. 'Apparently they've fallen out. My mother – in her wisdom – has taken umbrage to Jack playing cards with his friend, Elsie, who lives opposite. Mum says he's cheating on her! I wouldn't mind but the woman's in her eighties.'

Tanya giggled. 'You'd hope by their time of life, all that nonsense would stop, wouldn't you?'

Lisa nodded, and gazed absently outside, where a woman walking an elderly terrier hovered patiently, her right hand gloved by a plastic bag.

Tanya made a gagging sound as the quivering dog squatted. 'Look Leese, what we need is a good night out.'

Lisa frowned. 'Hon, the last time we went out all glammed up, we got into trouble. Don't you remember … that thug in The Gallery? He really scared me.'

Tanya shuddered. 'Good point, perhaps we won't go there then! Let's just go to the Speckled Hen. We'll know a few faces … we can just relax and have a giggle in there.'

An hour later, and with arrangements made for Saturday night, Lisa's mood had lifted. She walked home feeling lighter despite the damp and chill of January's final days.

At home, after turning the heating up a notch and giving Nellie her lunch, Lisa opened her laptop.

No new emails had arrived. She did a quick trawl of Facebook and Twitter, before clicking on the Retro Tour's official website looking for new posts.

Bypassing other bands' photos and comments, Lisa went straight to Ben & The Wilde Ones latest posts. Her heart swelled with desire to see shots of Ben, legs astride, mane blown back, his arm draped loosely round Rick's shoulders.

'Wow, how gorgeous does Daddy look?' Lisa said to Nellie, whose ears swivelled at the mention of Ben. She swirled the mouse, hungry for more images. Click. Ben stage-left, sharing a laugh with Steve. Click. Ben centre-stage, on his knees, face taut with emotion. Click. Ben and Ruby Stone, eye to eye, performing a duet. The next frame was film footage which made Lisa's heartbeat quicken as she watched Ruby, all spray-on black jeans and brunette curls, prowl around Ben, before raking her hands over his torso and jamming her narrow pelvis into his.

Feeling like a rubbernecker at a car crash, Lisa was unable to look away as Ben and Ruby, their bodies grinding together, reached the song's climax as the crowd at the Stockholm arena erupted with deafening delight.

Nauseated, Lisa snapped her laptop shut.

Common sense told her that it was just an act, designed to excite the crowd and ramp up the energy. But her intuition was telling her something entirely different. There was something in Ruby's expression – and more to the point, in Ben's – a kind of nonchalance, a familiarity, as though they actually knew each other intimately.

Lisa opened her laptop again and Googled Ruby Stone – then wished she hadn't. Wikipedia described her as a British session-vocalist and songwriter, born in 1985. '85! That made her thirty-three years old. Lisa would be forty-five in the spring; if Ben was looking for youth and vitality, she couldn't possibly compete with Ruby.

She remembered the night she'd first met Ben at an advertising agency party in London. He'd already turned fifty then, and his girlfriend at the time was a youthful thirty-something blonde called Stacey.

With growing unease, Lisa clicked on 'images'; oh god, another mistake. A mosaic of photographs sprang onto her screen. Ruby in the studio, headphones clamped on, looking the epitome of rock and roll cool. Ruby performing on stage with a whole bunch of house-hold-name stars. Ruby lunching outside a smart London Brasserie in a ladylike designer dress and Louboutin heels. Ruby leaving a nightclub, flanked by two male models.

Shit. Just who the hell *was* Ruby-bloody-Stone?

Lisa zoomed in and scrutinised her face. Her olive skin, full lips and abundant dark hair hinted at a Mediterranean or North African heritage – yet Wiki claimed she was born in Oxfordshire. *Oxford*. What if she'd been educated there ... and was clever, too? Lisa could just about scrape together a handful of GCSEs.

It was obvious that Ruby was fiercely talented; when she sang, she was a powerhouse. Lisa's mind butterflied from one horrific thought to the next. It was a nightmare. A young, beautiful, intelligent and talented woman was on tour with *her* husband; cosied-up on the bus with him, checking into five-star hotels and performing all over Europe, to tens of thousands of adoring fans. Lisa's temple throbbed.

'Oh Nellie,' she whispered, reaching down to pick up the little Chihuahua, and nuzzling her pointy face, 'I think we could lose Daddy.'

CHAPTER 34

The Mortons

After New Year's Eve, Chloe's kneejerk response to being discovered in bed with Caleb Harper was to dump him.

'I'm sorry, Caleb – but this is never going to work, is it? We're parents, and we have to put our kids first. We're living in a dream world if we think that somehow, it'll all be just fine, and we'll become the bloody Brady Bunch.'

Caleb was crushed. 'Don't we deserve to be happy, too? Children are tough. Jesus, the girls survived their Mum dying on them. Jake will come around, I know he will. It was probably the shock more than anything.'

'Yes, and the hypocrisy of it,' Chloe said, 'after you reading Jake the riot act last summer when–'

Caleb cut her off. 'I'm never going to live that down, am I? I've apologised until I'm blue in the face. Chloe, I'm sorry about Jake – but at least it's all out in the open now. Amber and Jade seem fine about us … Jake will accept things over time, he's got to.'

Chloe pursed her lips. 'He hasn't *got to* do anything. He's very upset at the moment – and volatile. I still don't know what happened the night he stormed off. He says he got those awful bruises after he slipped, but I don't believe him. And as for spending the night with the couple next door – it's ludicrous! Apparently, they found him when he fell over.'

Caleb shrugged. 'Well, maybe that's all there is to know.'

They'd gone back and forth until they'd reached a mutual but reluctant decision to put their relationship 'on hold'.

'We can be friends, can't we?' Chloe said.

Caleb groaned. 'That old booby prize. Yeah, we can try ... take care of yourself. I'll see you around.'

•

Chloe wasted no time in sharing her news.

'Jake,' she said that evening, 'you don't need to stress about me seeing Caleb Harper anymore. I ended it. I'm not ready for a new relationship yet, and you're obviously not ready for me to see anyone either.'

Jake grunted. 'Okay. You can do better anyway, Mum.'

Chloe rolled her eyes. 'Yeah, right. But Jake, one day I will want to date someone. Your Dad's got a girlfriend, why should I be on my own forever? It's only fair ... you do see that, don't you?'

Jake had merely nodded, before disappearing to his room.

•

In Jake's opinion, two interesting situations had arisen out of New Year's Eve and his mother's shameful secret. The first was his new friendship with Amber. As soon as he'd calmed down and processed the fact that his Mum was shagging Caleb Harper, Amber's *actual dad*, for Christ's sake, he'd texted her to meet him, saying it was about 'important family stuff'.

The next day, standing outside Crabton's library, shivering despite the warmth of his Christmas puffer coat, Jake watched Amber lope into view. She looked beautiful, amazing – but he was over all that now; a girlfriend was the last thing he needed. For his sanity, what he needed was to talk. Specifically, he needed to know what – if anything – Amber knew about his mum and her dad getting it on.

Jake had braced himself for fireworks, but Amber seemed unruffled.

She wrinkled her delicate nose. 'Gross,' she said, 'although it's nice to think of old people having someone. I hate the thought of my dad being lonely and your mum seems really pretty and nice.'

'*Pretty and nice*? You've never even met her! Amber, did you hear what I just said? I caught them *shagging* at ours on New Year's Eve. Why didn't they tell us they were seeing each other?'

Amber shrugged. 'Adults lie sometimes. Don't you want your mum to be happy?' She began to honk with laughter, her narrow shoulders going up and down.

'Hey, Jakey – if they get married, you'll be my brother. How weird is that?'

'I can't believe you think it's funny! What the fuck is wrong with you, Amber?'

They'd gone for milkshakes then, escaping the bitter sleet that had started falling, and after an hour of sitting by a radiator, sucking on a chocolate-cherry-dream and listening to Amber's girlish banter, Jake calmed down.

'Look, I know that we're not ... you know,' he said, studying his empty glass 'but I've missed you ... can we be friends? I mean, it's cool if you don't want to, or anything, but–'

'That would be brilliant, Jake – I've missed you, too.' Amber smiled and cocked the little finger of her right hand. 'Pinkie promise,' she said, 'friends.'

The second interesting thing was that he'd met Ben Wilde, an actual bona fide rockstar – and had even gone back to the guy's house and seen his studio. The circumstances were a complete cringe of course ... what *had* he been thinking?

Jake hadn't meant to kill himself – he knew that now – he'd just felt so desperate, and everything was jangling, as though his teeth and bones were loose, and he'd wanted it all to stop. Just STOP.

He hadn't told a living soul about that night – nobody would believe him anyway. It would sound freaky and disgusting. He was always reading online about pervy old bastards who'd done stuff to kids – but Ben had been kind, making him tea and toast. The most bizarre thing was that Ben seemed to be friends with the old couple next door. How did they even *know* each other? Old Martin Bevan didn't look the type to have rockstars for mates.

Jake planned to tell Dylan the next time they met; after all it was Dylan who'd told him about Ben living in Eden Hill. And that was the other weird thing. Rockstars were meant to live in mansions and drive Ferraris into swimming pools, but Ben had been so ordinary – and apart from the fact that his house was in the posh bit and behind tall gates, it wasn't much different to where Jake lived with his mum.

He'd wanted to thank Ben – for being kind and not making a big deal of it all, but then he'd Googled him and discovered that Ben was on tour with a load of other old people who were famous in the 90s.

So he'd looked up Regents Square and using his mobile to navigate, had walked round after school one night. He peered through the gates; in the gathering darkness, one house looked much like another and any one of them could have been the Wildes' house.

What did it matter? The whole incident had been an embarrassing freak show. He'd acted like a sulky brat – someone could have been killed; not least himself. Jake was about to walk away when at No. 3, he saw the silhouette of a woman reach up and close the curtains.

He recognised Mrs Wilde at once. She was fit – for an old lady. Jake didn't go in for the whole MILF thing like some of his friends at school, but she'd had great tits and she'd smelled lovely, too, of wine and perfume.

As he stared up at the house, a car approached, pausing in front of the gates before they opened with a judder. Nimble as a cat, Jake passed through, with no plan of what he was going to do or say, until he was outside No. 3, his finger poised on the doorbell. A security light tripped on and he could hear the piercing yap of a small dog.

A woman's voice: 'Who is it please?'

'Um, it's Jake … Jake Morton. I just wanted to … is Ben there, please?' Jake answered, knowing full well that Ben was away.

The door opened a few inches and the woman's face appeared. 'I'm afraid not. Can I help, I'm his … oh! It's you! How are you?' Mrs Wilde scooped up the little dog, who was yapping more urgently now. 'Take no notice of Nellie,' she said opening the door fully.

Jake was sheepish. 'Nellie? Aww, she's sweet. I wish we had a dog,' he said, suddenly feeling like a nine-year-old.

Lisa looked confused. 'What can I do for you, Jake?'

'Um, nothing … I just wanted to say thank you.

Ben was really nice to me on New Year's Eve, when I … fell over.'

'That's okay, Jake. Anyone would have done the same. We were very worried about you – you seemed so upset. How are things at home now? Better?'

'Yeah, a bit … fine, really,' Jake said, his nails digging into his palms from inside his trouser pockets. 'Well, I'd better go. Thanks … um, when will Ben be back?' he said, plunged into darkness as the security timer flipped off.

'Ben's on tour. He won't be back until March. I'll tell him you came though. Take care, Jake, good night.'

Feeling like an idiot, Jake turned and left, wondering what he'd have done if Ben had actually been at home.

CHAPTER 35

The Bevans

In February, on a day when a light dusting of snow arrived, Jan took to her bed. On the third day, Martin rang Hayley.

'Hello, love. How's you and the bump? Oh, good … well you're bound to feel a bit tired, aren't you?' Martin said, biding his time.

'You and Mum alright then?' Hayley asked.

'I'm great, thanks love. But your mum's not too clever. She's been in bed a few days – says she's got the flu.'

'Oh no! Well, there's a lot of it about – has she seen the doctor?'

'No love – she just wants to sleep and watch a bit of telly in the evenings,' Martin said.

'What about her dogs – who's walking them?'

'Presumably their owners, although I've had a couple of them on the phone, and they were pretty annoyed.'

'Well, they can bog off,' Hayley said. 'Anyone can get ill – these things happen.'

Martin paused, then spoke carefully: 'Thing is, love, I'm not sure it's a virus. She's barely got a sniffle. Physically, your mum seems fine to me.'

'What are you saying, Dad?'

'I'm worried that she's depressed. She's been a bit low since she had a run-in with a dog owner round the corner. People haven't exactly welcomed us with open arms around here, and I think it's getting to her.'

Hayley snorted. 'Snotty bitches! Don't know why you're surprised, Dad; it's all *keeping up with the Jones's* round your way.'

'What should I do, love?' Martin said, ignoring Hayley's pronouncement on his neighbours.

'Just talk to her. Tell Mum you're worried that her depression has returned. You can't go through all that again, Dad. You were both trapped in a living hell for years.'

Hayley was right of course; they couldn't go back there – to that dark and terrible time. It would destroy them as a couple, as it almost had before. Martin shuddered at the memory.

He looked at his watch; eleven-fifteen. He had things to do, not least repairs to carry out at Cobalt Close. The tenants seemed nice enough; Mike and Lindsey Hope, a young couple with a baby son. But it was the third time they'd called him out in two weeks.

'Teething troubles,' Jeremy Hunter had said, when Martin mentioned their apparent neediness, 'as soon as they've settled in properly and got their bearings, they'll stand on their own two feet, you'll see.'

With his friend's words ringing in his ears, Martin

drove to Cobalt Close, where he was met by a harassed looking Lindsey, baby Harry clamped to her hip.

'Oh hi, Martin. Come in ... it's the cloakroom,' she said, waving him through, just as Harry began to howl.

Leaving Lindsey to mollify the baby, Martin picked a path between the child's buggy, shoes and wellingtons on the hall floor and coats bulging from pegs, to the brand-new cloakroom. Two rows of tiles had come off the wall and were lying cracked on the laminate floor. Using his mobile phone, Martin took several photographs.

Lindsey appeared in the doorway, jiggling baby Harry against her shoulder.

'That shouldn't happen in a new house, should it, Martin?'

Martin shook his head. 'It most certainly should not. There's a good chance this is covered by the NHBC. Let me make some enquiries and I'll come back to you, Lindsey, love. Oh, and you can tidy up by all means, but keep the tiles for now – just until someone's been out to see what's what. Okay?'

Martin escaped the cramped hallway and drove home to find Jan sitting up in bed gazing in the direction of the muted television.

'Where did you go?' she said without looking at him.

Martin perched on the bed. 'Round to Cobalt

Close. I mentioned it last night, love – don't you remember?'

Jan nodded slowly.

'You should see the state of their downstairs loo; the bloody tiles have popped clean off the wall! Can you believe it? Shocking workmanship. These house builders just fling them up these days.' Martin looked at Jan and waited for a response – none came.

'Are you feeling any better, my love?' he said, chilled by her far away expression.

Jan shrugged. 'Must be a bug. I'm so tired. Perhaps I'll feel better tomorrow.'

'I hope so, love. If not, I think we should pop in and see Doctor Benson … let her have a look at you.'

'There's no need to go bothering the doctor, is there? Please, Martin – don't fuss.'

'Well how about a spot of lunch then? A little ham sandwich … or a bowl of tomato soup?

Jan shook her head, angled her body away from him and closed her eyes; the conversation was over.

Martin sighed and got to his feet. 'Righto … I'll leave you to rest then, love. I'll bring you a cuppa and a few biccies in an hour or so.'

Downstairs in the small bland room he called his study, feeling purposeful, Martin opened his laptop and plucked a ring binder marked 'Cobalt Close' from the shelf. He was a landlord now, and if a job was worth doing, it was worth doing well. He owed it to his tenants. The Hopes deserved a safe and cosy home; any sloppy work by the developers could bloody-well be put right – and without delay. Martin would see to it personally.

•

What time was it? Groping for her mobile phone, Jan almost knocked over a cup of cold tea – how long had that been there? It was almost four o'clock. Jan's bladder throbbed painfully, but her legs were leaden. 'Martin,' she cried out, 'Mart … are you there?'

'Coming, my love.'

Jan heard the stairs creak.

'I was just on my way to–' Martin paused in the doorway. 'Oh dear. This is no good. Let's put some lights on, shall we? No wonder you feel poorly, lying here in the dark.'

'I need the toilet, Martin,' Jan said, trying to sit up, 'but my legs are a bit stiff, give me a hand, will you?'

Martin heaved Jan into a sitting position and helped her out of bed.

'Thank you.' Jan limped towards the en-suite and closed the door. After using the toilet, she ran her tongue over her teeth and tried to remember when she had last brushed. In the dimly-lit mirror, a pale, puffy face framed by limp strands of hair looked back at her. She could hear Martin in the bedroom, vigorously shaking out the duvet and beating pillows.

It was happening again – the fog was coming down. Today was the day. She needed to shake herself; wash, dress and go for a walk. Then she'd eat downstairs with her husband, give her daughter a call … ask about the baby. Yes, *the baby* – that was something to look forward to.

Jan sat down on the edge of the bath, exhausted at the thought of all she had to do.

Oh god – what about all her dogs? She'd neglected them all week. Jan pictured their trusting little faces; the way they wagged their tails and stamped their paws with anticipation while she hunted for collars and leads. She had a job to do; the dogs needed her.

Pulling her three-day-old salty nightdress over her head and discarding it on the bathroom floor, Jan turned on the shower.

CHAPTER 36

The Bradshaws

In late February, rain fell from an anthracite sky every day for a week making Rosemary's mid-week drive to Glen Heights particularly bleak.

Striding past reception with a brisk wave, Rosemary jogged up to the first floor and found Joyce's door wide open.

'I don't want no lunch,' Joyce said as Rosemary bent to kiss her mother-in-law's cheek.

Rosemary poured Joyce a glass of water. 'Good to see you, too, Mum. How are you?'

'Who are you?' Joyce snapped.

'I'm Rosemary – Nigel's wife. I come most Wednesdays, Mum.'

Joyce sat up straight. 'Nigel? Where's my purse?'

'I don't know, Mum, but I can help you look. Anyway, you don't need it right now.'

'Go away! I've nothing worth nicking, you know.'

Rosemary bit her lip. 'Joyce, I'm just popping downstairs – won't be long.'

Then she'd gone in search of Hattie, the senior dementia care nurse, and had found her in her office, tapping away on her laptop.

'Do you have a moment, please, Hattie? It's about Joyce …'

•

'Well can't they increase her medication?' Nigel sounded exasperated above the cacophony of rush hour traffic.

'No, it doesn't work like that, love. Your mum's not eating much, or drinking enough water either, according to the staff. They've checked her bloods and there doesn't seem to be much wrong physically, but her deterioration is plain to see. She was snappy with me today, so I only stayed half-an-hour – she was just too agitated.'

There was a pause before Nigel cursed, and Rosemary heard a car horn flare.

'Oh, this is hopeless. You need to concentrate on the road, but we need to talk – *properly*. Look ... I just wanted you to know, she's *your* mum, Nigel.'

Another pause; Rosemary tried to brighten her voice. 'So, are you finished for the day, or have you got dinner with colleagues tonight?'

'The latter – and I could do without it really, I'm shattered. But Rich and Toby have been trying to catch me all day and I need to sort out a few things before the meeting tomorrow morning. I've got to go, Rose ... so many idiots on the road tonight. Thank you for being so good to Mum ... it's a nightmare for you, isn't it?'

Then Nigel had asked Rosemary to kiss Iris for him and had hung up.

She couldn't remember either of them ending phone calls with 'I love you' like other couples.

•

To the manager's relief, the Bertram Hotel was unusually busy. Earlier in the day, Jacob's team had hosted a psychics' symposium which had attracted clairvoyants and other spiritual practitioners from all over the North of England. All three of the hotel's conference rooms had been packed to the rafters. Now, the guest lounge and bar could barely contain the party atmosphere that had struck up as wine flowed and conversation buzzed at the end of the working day.

'Goodness, it's lively in here tonight, Julie. Still, it's good for business I suppose?' Nigel said, as he pressed his way to the bar and ordered a gin and tonic.

'So long as they tip well; we've all been rushed off our feet today,' the barmaid said, setting a tall glass down on a paper coaster.

Nigel managed to find a seat away from the raucous psychics. He looked at his watch. Six forty-five; he'd arranged to meet Tiffany at seven. They'd dispensed with him going through *the agency* (which Nigel suspected was nothing more than an answering machine in somebody's spare room); instead they'd swapped mobile numbers, so they could make plans by text.

To Nigel's surprise, Tiffany had been coy about their new arrangement. 'Nigel, I am ... you know, fond of you,' she said, 'but I've still got to earn a living.'

'Of course. I merely suggested exchanging numbers so that I don't have to go through the pantomime of hearing who else might be free while your boss tries to sell me a date with someone else. It's very simple. I only want to see you, Tiffany. We get on well, and I like you.'

With their new arrangement established, Nigel had taken a more leisurely approach to evenings spent with Tiffany – to the point where he knew they could be taken for any other couple, or at any rate, one with a large age gap.

He'd become adept at compartmentalising his life in the north, which consisted of meetings and hassle; stress, that to a degree, could be alleviated at the end of a long day with a couple of gin and tonics and a blow-job from an attractive redhead who posed no intellectual challenge and asked for nothing in return except for a modest fee.

Nigel knew men who'd had affairs, colleagues who'd slept with subordinates; but somehow it always got messy when emotions came into play. This way, nobody would get hurt – as long as he continued to be discreet.

The trick was to be a better husband and father

than he was currently being. Nigel had seen the utter disappointment in Rosemary's eyes. She was a bright and instinctive woman – it was the first thing that had attracted him. The fact that she also possessed bucket-loads of kindness, patience and wonderful mothering skills had been a lucky bonus.

He'd begun infrequently seeing escorts when Iris turned three and Rosemary's libido had shown no sign of returning. Their rare (and polite) lovemaking had proved so lacklustre that by the time Iris was five, they'd tacitly dispensed with any further intimacy – an immense relief to both of them.

Nigel's thoughts were pinged back to the present as Tiffany sashayed into the room, bleating apologies for being ten minutes late.

She looked exceptionally pretty this evening in a cream, tight-fitting dress. Nigel said as much.

'Thanks, Nigel,' she touched her freshly curled hair, 'thought I'd make an effort. Hey, who are all these people? It's noisy enough to wake the dead.'

Nigel laughed at her unwitting pun. 'Believe it or not, they're all mediums and psychics. Do you believe in that stuff?'

'Yes, I do – and it gives me the creeps. Talking to people on the other side … it's not natural, is it?' Tiffany shuddered.

A woman sitting nearby, who'd been in earnest

conversation with two others spun around to face them.

'Ah, the dead can't hurt you, dear – it's the living you need to worry about,' she said, patting pearl-grey curls.

Tiffany's cheeks flushed. 'Sorry … I don't mean to be rude … I just find it a bit …' she searched for the right words.

Nigel was exasperated. 'A lot of people are unnerved by the idea of messages from the grave – or predictions for the future,' he gave a little bark of laughter. 'Personally, I think it's utter buncombe!'

The woman studied Nigel for a moment. 'It's interesting that you say that, sir. Because your destiny is *here* – connected to this very place. You will soon experience loss, followed by a great change and–'

Nigel cut her off. 'Fascinating – but I'm afraid we must go.' Standing up, he felt for his room key. The last thing he needed was some bogus medium digging into his private life, pretending to see into his future and his soul. How *dare* she? It was shameful – preying on people's stupidity and desperation. It was appalling to think that some people actually *believed* that kind of nonsense.

Placing his hand in the small of Tiffany's back, Nigel steered her out of the crowded lounge and towards the lifts. In silence, they rode up to the third floor.

Once inside his room, Nigel piped music through the television and opened the mini-bar.

'Drink?' he said, loosening his tie and shrugging off his jacket.

But Tiffany was miles away. 'That lady said your destiny was here, Nigel. Whatever could she mean?'

CHAPTER 37

The Mortons

Jake was sick of bloody winter, and of being cold all the time. It was only four thirty, but it might as well have been midnight it was so dark.

He felt in his pocket for the joint he'd rolled round at Dylan's the day before. His mum would be home soon so if he was having a smoke he'd better get on with it. She had the nose of a spaniel and if she opened the back door for any reason, or went out to the bins, she'd smell weed and go ballistic.

Despite the cold, Jake was just beginning to mellow out nicely when his neighbour's patio light came on and he heard Martin call out to Jan; something about covering the bulbs before tomorrow's frost.

Instinctively, Jake put the thin roll-up behind his back and froze – last thing he needed was old Martin on the war path.

But then to Jake's abject horror, Martin's head appeared above the fence, like a coconut on a stick.

'Is that you, Jake?' Martin said, peering into the shadows where he crouched in the darkness.

Fuck! Surely the old man couldn't see him? Jake held his breath, waiting, hoping that Martin would go away. Jake exhaled only when Martin climbed down, and he heard what sounded like flower pots being dragged followed by a dry rustle as Martin did something or other with plastic bags. He waited until it went quiet before going back inside, careful not to put on lights at the back of the house.

After twenty minutes of gaming on his PlayStation with the volume low, the doorbell rang. Jake rolled his eyes; why did his mum sometimes forget her keys?

Jake opened the front door to find Martin, grinning like someone deranged.

'Good evening, young man. How are you keeping?' Martin said pleasantly.

'Fine thank you.' Jake studied his socks.

'Sorry to bother you, Jake, but I wondered if you could give me a hand with something on my computer – you young people are so tech-savvy compared to us oldies.' Martin rocked on his heels.

'Er … okay. Sure. What, now?' he said, wishing that Martin would leave him to the very pleasant buzz he was enjoying.

Martin nodded. 'You'd be helping me out, son.'

A hot wave rippled in Jake's chest and his stomach fluttered like a moth's wings. He giggled hoarsely before clearing his throat, hoping desperately that Martin wouldn't notice. Then grabbing his keys from the hall table, Jake put on his school shoes, still askew by the front door, and followed Martin down his own path and back up next door's.

Once inside, Martin appeared to lose interest in

his IT problem, walking past his laptop which was open on the kitchen table.

'Cuppa tea?' Martin said, filling the kettle. 'Jan's popped out, so it's just us boys.'

Shit! Had he walked into some pervy trap? Jake studied Martin's rear view. The guy had to be almost sixty, was lightly built and an inch or two shorter than himself; he'd deck him if he tried anything.

Martin was looking at him now, his expression quizzical. 'Did you say something?' Jake said before letting out a bark of manic laughter, which he again turned into a cough.

'I was just asking if you'd like a biscuit.' Martin reached into a cupboard and brought out a tin.

The thought of his teeth snapping into one of the sugary biscuits made Jake salivate.

'Good for the munchies,' Martin added, offering the flowery tin.

Oh god! He'd been rumbled.

Computer issues mysteriously forgotten, Martin put two mugs of tea on the pine table.

'So, how are you, Jake?' he said. 'How's school?'

Why did old people always ask that? It was so fucking lame.

'It's fine,' he mumbled, taking a sip of tea and burning his mouth.

'You can talk to me, Jake. I'm a dad, you know – and

I've seen it all with my daughter, Hayley. Although I'm not sure she ever got into the wacky-baccy.'

A maniacal cackle escaped Jake's lips. Had Martin really said 'wacky-baccy'? He set down the hot mug and tried to compose himself.

'Please don't tell my mum,' he said, avoiding eye contact.

'I won't. But I think *you* should, Jake.' Martin pulled his shoulders back as though he meant business. 'Son, it must be hard for you; your mum and dad splitting up, new school, new area. But getting stoned on your own is a slippery slope. God knows what it'll lead to. Oh, I know you think I'm old fashioned, but that stuff can send you round the bend. I can tell you're a clever lad. Don't go down that road, Jake, please.' Martin paced to the back door. 'What are you into?' he said, peering out into the darkness.

'What?'

'What are your hobbies? Art ... music ... sport?'

'Hate sport,' Jake mumbled, adding, 'I like music ... indie rock mainly – wish I could play guitar as well as my friend, Dylan.'

'You want to book yourself some lessons,' Martin said, sounding pleased with himself, 'who knows where it could lead. Ben Wilde had to start somewhere – him and all the other pop stars.'

'Yeah ... er, about that. I don't mean to be rude – but how do you know him?'

Martin hesitated. 'Oh, that's quite a story, actually. I used to be friends with his wife, Lisa – well I say 'friends' … there was a bit of a misunderstanding … look, I won't go into all that now, but then I met Ben through her and we just hit it off.'

'Oh … right,' Jake said, none the wiser. What was the poor deluded old bastard on about? Jake was about to dig a little deeper when he heard a car pull up outside. Unsure if it was his mother or Martin's wife, he gulped the last of his tea.

'I should go,' he said. 'Cheers, Martin – for the drink. Bye.'

'No need to rush off, son,' Martin said as Jake loped to the front door, 'come again – I'm usually around and it's nice to have the company.'

•

'Everything alright?' Chloe said, surprised to see her son emerging from the Bevans' house.

'Oh, yeah … I was just taking a parcel that came for them earlier.'

'Really? Well, why did you have it? You've been at school all day … or have you? Oh, Jake, don't tell me–'

'Mum, stop! Of *course* I've been at school … the postman left it behind the bins. Maybe they got the wrong house – I dunno.'

Chloe studied her son's face. His eyes looked

glassy and his skin was paler than usual. She hoped he wasn't going down with something.

'Jake, are you alright, darling? You're very white … is your throat sore?'

Jake groaned. 'I feel *fine*. Hey, did you bring any cakes home?'

Chloe produced some leftover rocky road and was mollified by Jake's evident appetite. She mentally ran through options for dinner. 'Have you got much homework, Jakey?' she asked.

'About an hour of chemistry but it's not due until Friday,' Jake said.

'Okay, how about we jump in the car and go for a burger?'

'On a school night? Yeah, cool,' Jake said.

'Great. Give me half an hour to make myself presentable then we'll head off to Lakeview.'

After a brisk shower, Chloe put on black jeans and a navy polo neck. Applying make-up at her dressing table, she heard music and the hiss of a deodorant can coming from Jake's room. Bless him; he seemed so tense. It would do them both good to get outside – it was all too easy to hibernate during the winter.

She thought of Caleb, tending the farm in all weathers, his hands cracked and dry, his lips chapped. Remembering the touch of his long fingers, Chloe felt a pang of longing. Cross with herself, she spritzed on

perfume, grabbed her handbag, and pushed Caleb
Harper firmly from her mind.

CHAPTER 38

The Wildes

Still smarting from the latest crop of photos online, Lisa picked up the phone.

There they were: Ben and Ruby Stone, looking for all the world like a couple, dressed in matching puffer jackets and fly sunglasses, sitting outside a café looking chilled and happy – paparazzi shots posted on a digital-gossip website known for exposing the indiscretions of the rich and famous. Lisa hated herself for logging onto it.

On hearing Ben's voice, she was in no mood for small talk. 'Ben, I've seen the photos ... of you and that- of Ruby. What the fuck is going on?'

There was a pause. 'What photos? Babe, there are paps all over the place – I don't know what you think you've seen, but you've got it wrong,' Ben said, his tone guarded.

'Ben! You're always together. You can't deny that ... what am I supposed to think?' Lisa wailed, trying to keep a hold of herself.

'That we work together and that we get on well. What else? Lisa, sometimes I need a break from the boys ... much as I love old Steve and Ricky, you can have too much of a good thing, you know.'

'So, you don't fancy her then?' Lisa cringed, knowing she sounded like a teenager at a school disco.

'No. Ruby's not my type at all … although she's a cracking girl, obviously. You'd love her, Leese – she's cool, funny.'

'Sorry … it's just … I'm here on my own and every time I see a picture of you and … *her* … it freaks me out.'

'Babe, where is all this coming from? It's not like you. You haven't got a jealous bone in your body – and anyway, there's not a woman alive can hold a candle to you. Look, I fly back in three weeks, then I've got two nights at The O2 and the jobs a good 'un. Money in the bank and a big fat holiday in the sun for me and my girl.'

'Sounds amazing,' Lisa said, unconvinced.

'You are still coming to the London gigs, aren't you, hon?' Ben asked.

Lisa assured him that she and Tanya would be there on both nights, backstage passes in hand and ready to party.

At the start of the tour, they'd talked of Lisa flying out for the Rome or Barcelona dates, but the conversation had dried up and neither of them had pushed for it to happen.

Now Lisa had an increasingly bad feeling about Ben's friendship with Ruby; the woman seemed to be everywhere. She was tempted to get on a plane and surprise them, an idea that Tanya shot down in flames at once.

'Oh no, Leese, you can't do *that*! It looks so desperate and jealous – two words I never thought I'd say about you.'

Tanya had a point; whether Ben was cheating on her or not, a surprise visit could turn out to be a highly humiliating experience. Reluctantly, Lisa agreed with her friend.

'Hon, if Ben says they're just mates, then that's all they are. He's never played away – he loves you to bits and you've only been married ten minutes. You're getting paranoid in your old age,' Tanya finished with a toss of her brunette mane.

'*In my old age*? Yeah, well that's just it, isn't it, Tan?'

'Now I *know* you're being silly,' Tanya said, frustration in her voice, 'you'll always be ten years younger than Ben.'

They'd let the subject drop, but later that day, Lisa had booked a consultation at the cosmetic clinic where she used to work.

•

'Lisa, how lovely to see you. Please tell me you've come to rescue me from Zara my terrible Temp.' Rupert Dale kissed Lisa on both cheeks and asked her to sit.

'Sorry to hear that, Rupert. What happened to your last PA?'

The surgeon explained how Lisa's successor had

left to become a stay at home mum, leaving a hole in the practice that they'd so far been unable to fill.

Lisa made sympathetic noises, impatient to discuss the real reason for her visit. She smoothed down her skirt. 'Rupert, I feel silly saying this to you as we know each other, but well, I'm increasingly worried about my looks.'

Rupert smiled, unscrewed the cap from his fountain pen, then screwed it back on again. 'Lisa … you're as lovely as ever. What's bothering you specifically?'

'I just don't feel very feminine. I look in the mirror some days, and it shocks me how much I've aged.'

'Nonsense! You don't look a day older than when you were my assistant. But the winter can make us feel that way. When was the last time you had a holiday?'

'Last spring, our honeymoon in Portugal. Seems so long ago now.' Lisa felt inexplicably tearful; she puffed out her cheeks, determined not to cry.

'I'm sorry, Rupert. I need to get a grip. Come on – look at this face and tell me what I can do to freshen things up,' she said, leaning forward and sticking out her chin.

'My dear, it's not surgery you need – it's a job … take your mind off things. Come back and work for me. We all miss you … you can go part-time at first and see how it goes.'

'Really? I'll think about it,' Lisa said, 'only for now, can you just give me Botox and a bit of lip plumping?'

'Botox? Of course, we've done it many times, but as for your lips – which in my view are perfectly lovely as they are – I urge you to give it some more thought.'

•

The traffic on the road out of Tunbridge Wells was static as Lisa hit the afternoon school run. Idling in neutral, she checked her reflection in the rearview mirror and was relieved to find that the white hives from the dozen or so needle pricks were already receding.

Ben disapproved of Botox, claiming that Lisa simply didn't need it. It was all very well for him to say; Ben was becoming more handsome with the passage of time, growing into his lines and furrows, rather than disappearing behind them as so many men over fifty seemed to. No wonder he had women flocking around him on the tour.

Perhaps Tanya and Rupert Dale were right. Maybe she was obsessing over nothing. Ben had certainly sounded sincere when she'd confronted him about Ruby on the phone. Maybe part of her problem was that Lisa no longer felt in control of her life; she'd become merely reactive to the wishes of others – to the point where she'd gone for a consultation on cosmetic surgery, and instead ended up with a job offer!

A car horn flared; Lisa realised the traffic had inched forward without her. She waved in the rearview mirror and lurched forward. It was going to be a slow drive home.

CHAPTER 39

The Mortons

The queue that usually straggled outside Burger Meister was absent.

'The joy of eating out on a school night,' Chloe said, triumphantly marching over to a corner table where she could happily survey the whole restaurant.

'I'm starving,' Jake said, relieved that his buzz had abated. There'd been a touch and go moment in the car when a swirl of nausea threatened, and he thought he was going to throw up. Luckily, it had passed just as quickly, and his mum seemed none the wiser.

Only a dozen or so tables were occupied and within a few minutes of arriving, Chloe had ordered for both of them; a full house of bacon and cheese burgers, sweet potato fries and two super-juices.

'Oh my god, these burgers are *so* good,' Chloe said, taking a huge bite of the rare, tender meat. 'Is yours okay, darling?'

But Jake had stopped eating and was staring in the direction of the entrance, where Caleb Harper and his two daughters had paused to pick a table. Amber was first to see them; beaming and waving, she moved easily between the tables.

'Hi Jake!' Amber smiled goofily, waiting to be introduced.

'Hi. Er … this is my …'

'MUM is the word you're searching for, Jake. Hello, you must be Amber. I'm Chloe, lovely to meet you,' Chloe smiled, determined to diffuse the situation.

'Well, this is awks, Mum,' Jake muttered, studying his plate.

Chloe's heart lurched to see Caleb – frozen on the spot, his face unreadable.

'Why don't we all sit together?' Amber hung her teen-handbag on the back of a chair, making it clear she was there for the duration. 'Da-ad … DAD! We're sitting with Jake and his mum.' She beckoned to her father who seemed rooted to the spot.

Amber's sister whispered something to Caleb, who nodded resignedly.

'Hi Chloe,' Caleb said, half-bending to kiss her cheek, before changing his mind so that he was left squatting without reason. He nodded to Jake, who ignored him.

Chairs were scraped and reshuffled on the tiled floor until everyone was seated.

'I'm starving,' Amber declared dramatically, seizing the menu.

'No, you're not. People in Africa are *starving*,' Jade smirked.

Chloe and Caleb locked eyes briefly, before she shrugged and mouthed 'is this okay?'

'How's school Jake?' Caleb ventured.

Jake couldn't quite prevent himself from rolling his eyes. Jesus! Again, the same question – why did adults always ask that?

'Fine,' he said, filling his mouth with sweet potato fries. Jake was spared further probing by the arrival of the waitress, who promptly took orders without the aid of a notepad.

Caleb cleared his throat. 'Er … well … eat up. Don't let your food go cold. I'm sure ours will be here soon – they're usually pretty quick in here.'

Jade turned her gaze on Chloe. 'Are you Dad's girlfriend?' she said, elbows on the table, her chin cupped in her hands.

'Don't be silly, Jade,' Caleb snapped, 'Chloe and I are just friends.' He looked searchingly at Chloe to back him up.

'Your dad's right. We're just mates – like Jake and Amber,' Chloe obliged.

But Jade was on a roll. '*I* want a boyfriend. I'm practically the only girl in my class who hasn't got one. Even Emma Drew's got one and she's *huge*! And her eyes are funny … kind of crossed, like this.' Jade squinted to illustrate her classmate's ocular shortcoming.

'Alright, Jade. Give it a rest – and don't be rude about people. We've all got flaws – like talking too much, for instance,' Caleb said, covering his daughter's mouth. He was relieved when the food arrived.

'So,' Chloe turned to Caleb, 'how are things on the farm?'

'Oh, busy,' he said, 'been getting the ground ready for planting – we'll be sowing during March. Amber and Jade have been helping out at weekends … they love lambing season, don't you girls? It's a scary amount of work; I've had to check and mend all the fences and fertilise the paddocks ready for my ewes to give birth. It's only a small flock but I'm working fifteen hours a day as standard. How about you – what's new at the coffee shop?'

'Nothing really,' Chloe said, 'Lillian's a sweetheart and I've got a young lad helping out on Saturdays – seeing as my son shows no interest in working with his mum,' Chloe gave Jake a meaningful look.

Jake huffed. 'What about my exams? I'm either at school or revising. Jesus, Mother, what more do you want?'

Chloe and Caleb exchanged glances.

Caleb smiled benignly: 'I think your mum just–'

'No!' Jake said, 'you don't get to tell me anything.'

Jade and Amber's eyes widened; Chloe was mortified. 'Jake, that's so rude. If you can't be civil, feel free to keep quiet altogether,' she warned.

The mood had soured, even the Harper girls looked crestfallen – not that it got in the way of them devouring their burgers and fries.

'I don't really fancy any of this,' Amber said, casting

aside the dessert menu. 'Can we go to Krispy Kreme next, Dad?'

Caleb made a face. 'Love, you know I'm not keen on you eating that rubbish. Oh, go on then. I guess once in a blue moon won't hurt. Jake, fancy going with the girls? Me and your mum can catch up over coffee.'

Chloe beamed, 'Brilliant idea. You young people go and have fun together – see you back here in … what, half-an-hour?' She produced her purse, but Caleb was too quick for her, and handed a twenty-pound note to Amber.

'Thanks Daddy,' the girls chorused – even Jake grunted a reluctant 'cheers' – and the three of them exploded from the restaurant, Jade's excited yelps audible as they went.

Chloe turned to Caleb: 'Your girls are lovely – a total credit to you. There's a real sweetness about them.'

Caleb rubbed his stubble. 'Yeah, they're good kids, I'll give them that.'

'I wonder,' Chloe said, 'whether Jake and Amber still like each other.'

Caleb frowned. 'I'm more interested in whether you still like me.'

Chloe bit her lip and avoided his eyes.

'Thing is Chloe, I can't stop thinking about you. We both know the only reason we broke up was because of Jake. You can see how chilled the girls are. You've no idea how much I miss you.'

'Jake's not in a good place. We used to talk so much and now he's ... furtive, and like a stranger half the time. When I got home from work this evening, Jake was leaving our neighbour's house; he said he'd taken a parcel round, but I could tell he was lying. He's got his exams this year, and he's such a clever boy, but I honestly can't tell if he's working hard or not.'

'Chloe, none of what you're saying sounds particularly alarming at Jake's age. What does his dad think?'

Chloe huffed. 'They see less and less of each other – and to be honest, neither of them seems bothered. I'm just waiting for the next instalment ... the one where William tells me that he and Jodie are having a baby together.'

'Wanker,' Caleb said loyally.

Chloe giggled. 'Caleb, of course I miss you, too ... but it is what it is.'

Caleb groaned. 'I hate that expression, it's so apathetic. My wife dying of cancer 'is what it is'; your ex starting a new life with a younger woman 'is what it is'. You and me? Chloe, we've got *choices*.'

Without another word, he leaned forward, taking Chloe's flushed face in his hands, and kissed her long and hard.

'Daddy!' Jade's shocked voice sounded close.

Breaking apart, they found all three teenagers staring at them.

'Gross,' Jake said, stalking towards the door.

Chloe called after him. 'Jake, wait. Come back, please.'

Jake slunk back to the table and took a seat beside her. The girls sat either side of their father, looking bemused.

Chloe studied the girls' expectant faces, and her son's sullen expression. When she spoke, she was matter of fact: 'Jade, earlier on, you asked if I was your dad's girlfriend,' she paused while Jade nodded vigorously. 'Well I wasn't, but I'd like to be … would that be okay with you, love? Amber?' Both girls smiled and nodded.

'Does anyone care what I think?' Jake snarled, not looking at any of them.

'Of course we care, Jake. But it's not fair of you to hold two families to ransom is it? Look, we're both grownups, we're not doing anything wrong and nothing would change. It just means we might all eat together sometimes. We could make this a regular thing if you like?'

'Come on Jakey, don't be an idiot … you're better than that,' Amber said, her eyes pleading.

'Alright … whatever. I suppose it's okay,' Jake said.

SPRING

CHAPTER 40

The Bevans

By March a kaleidoscope of colour had burst through the Bevans' planters and borders as daffodils, hyacinths and crocuses vied for attention in what had previously been a strip of sodden earth.

Jan's spirits stirred. 'Don't you think it's amazing, Martin, that onions buried in November turn into all this beauty by spring? I'd forgotten we'd planted so many bulbs. Aren't they a sight for sore eyes?'

Martin agreed. 'They look an absolute picture. You've done a good job, my love.'

Jan closed the back door; the view had improved, but the early morning temperature less so. She rubbed her arms briskly.

'Seeing the flowers out makes me realise how close the summer is. Just think, it won't be long before there's a baby toddling around out there, Mart.'

Martin filled the kettle. 'Cuppa tea, love? You're right, of course – July will be here before we know it. Aww, I can't wait to meet the little one. I wish I knew what sex it was … not that it matters of course, as long as it's healthy.'

'Perhaps they'll tell us nearer the date. In the meantime, we've just got to respect their privacy.'

Martin studied his wife's face; colour had returned to her cheeks and her eyes sparkled for the first time in weeks. He'd been so fearful of her depression returning; alarms had gone off in Martin's head several times during mid-winter. Nevertheless, Jan had kept on walking the dogs in all weathers and going about her routine.

Martin knew it was a measure of her stoicism, rather than contentment. It broke his heart that she seemed unable to make any friends of her own. The only neighbours that Jan interacted with were Chloe and Jake next door, who were nice enough people, but without a scrap of common ground between them, the friendship was unlikely to flourish.

Mindful of her loneliness, Martin had taken to escorting Jan on her rounds one or two days a week – he could certainly afford the time. He'd seen Alfie-the-spaniel's owner out walking since their altercation; Heather Trinder she was called, according to Roger and Diane who lived opposite and seemed to know everybody; Heather had crossed the road to avoid him.

He'd considered trailing after her and trying to make amends but then he'd remembered the sharpness of her tongue and had thought better of it.

It was Martin's personal belief that Heather Trinder was responsible for Jan getting cold-shouldered by the local dog crowd. He'd seen it with his own eyes; the way the women blanked her on Cabbage Green and the surrounding streets, and it disgusted him that people could be so small minded, spreading vicious rumours after one unfortunate incident.

'Don't you worry, my love,' he told Jan, 'just wait until you're pushing a pram around here … they'll all come flocking then. Everyone loves a new baby, you'll see.'

•

Lindsey Hope answered the door with a red-cheeked Harry clamped to her hip; his little chin shone with drool.

'Thanks for coming at short notice, Martin. I do appreciate it,' she said.

'No problem at all, Lindsey, always pleased to help. What can I do for you?' Martin asked, peering through to the kitchen which seemed to grow more cluttered and untidy every time he called round.

'Up here,' Lindsey said, mounting the stairs as Harry clung on.

In the bathroom, which smelled of toothpaste and urine, Lindsey ran the hot tap. A vibrating sound which soon became a rhythmic knocking, filled the house.

Martin huffed. 'Blast. Now, I'm no plumber, but that, Lindsey love, is called water hammer – and it's notoriously difficult to fix,' he said with some authority.

'Oh no! We can't put up with that racket,' Lindsey wailed, dissolving into tears.

'Hey … what's the matter? It can't be *that* bad,' Martin raised his voice over Harry, who was now bawling in sympathy with his mother.

'I can't take much more,' the young woman snuffled, unspooling toilet roll and blowing her nose.

Martin was embarrassed. 'Come on now, please don't worry. I know a good plumber and I'm sure we can sort it,' he said, his discomfort growing.

'Oh, it's not just that. Harry's teething, and I'm on my own with him, day and night 'cos Mike's doing extra shifts at the hospital … which is a bloody joke, given what porters earn. I feel so trapped … I don't know which way to turn.'

Martin looked at Lindsey's tear-stained face and estimated her to be around his daughter's age.

'Bless you,' he said. 'Tell you what, I'll make us a cuppa while you sort your lad out,' he said, tickling baby Harry under the chin, which only made him scream louder.

Downstairs, Martin cleared a space at the kitchen table which was groaning beneath unopened post, yellow sticky notes, biros and money-off coupons cut from magazines. After finding economy tea bags and milk he set down two steaming mugs.

'Look,' he began kindly, 'I know it seems hard now, but things change so quickly; this little chap will

be at school before you know it. You've just got to
stick with it.'

'Oh, I know … and I love him to bits, he's my world
… but I just get so *tired*. And money's so tight these
days, I can't even go out for a coffee with the girls. If
Mike does any more shifts at the General, he might as
well not bother coming home at all.'

'Right, first things first; let me sort the plumbing in
the next couple of days. Secondly, why don't I reduce
the rent … by say, seventy-five pounds a month? It'll
give you a bit of a breather.'

Lindsey jumped to her feet, wiped her eyes with
the heel of her hand, and thanked Martin profusely.

She seemed so beaten and vulnerable that Martin
wanted to hug her. Instead, he put the empty mugs in
the sink and let himself out.

•

Jan rubbed the small of her back; several hours of
daily dog-walking was taking its toll. 'I'm getting too
old for this, Martin,' she said, searching the fridge for
lunch. 'How are things at Cobalt Close?'

Martin busied himself with buttering bread from
the croc. 'There was a bit of an upset this morning.'

'There's always something with that pair – what
now?'

'That's a bit harsh, Jan. They're a young couple
struggling with a one year old, it can't be easy.

Anyway, *more* plumbing problems. The developers should be ashamed. They throw these starter homes up overnight. Well it's shoddy, Jan – all about government targets and profit.'

Jan nodded. 'I agree with you, Mart, but where's the upset in that?'

'Oh, Lindsey got a bit weepy … the baby's teething and she looked tired out. Mike's doing all the hours god sends at the General just to make ends meet–'

Jan tutted. 'Now don't you go getting involved. They're tenants, not family. I mean it, Martin; promise me you won't start sticking your beak in.'

'As if,' Martin said, making a mental note to say nothing about the reduced rent.

CHAPTER 41

The Wildes

On the last leg of the 90s Retro Tour, both nights at the O2 sold out. In the VIP bay, clutching Tanya's hand as adrenalin coursed through her, Lisa looked out at the capacity crowd and finally understood. *This* was what Ben was all about. Her sweet, domesticated, teddy bear husband took on a whole new persona on stage, becoming a demi-god, a superhero – and ageless, too. Sandwiched between two of the nineties' hottest girl-bands, Lisa felt the excitement soar as Ben and the Wilde Ones hit the stage in the show's final hour, leaving new and old fans screaming for more when their five numbers were up.

Escorted by marshals, the two women raced backstage as fast as their heels would allow, to find, Ben, Ricky, Steve, and a host of musicians, backing singers and crew that Lisa had never seen before.

Fuelled by pride, Lisa leapt into Ben's arms, wrapping her limbs around him without so much as a nod to the others present in the dressing room.

'Oh my god! That was amazing! The best show ever. Baby, you are a genius. I'm so proud of you!' Lisa babbled like a fan.

Beside her, Tanya retained her composure and shook hands with the other band members, except for Rick, whom she kissed on each cheek.

A champagne cork popped; glasses were filled, passed round and gulped gratefully.

Ben extracted himself from Lisa and began to towel his sweat-drenched hair, before peeling off his stage shirt.

'Everyone, this is my gorgeous missus, Lisa,' Ben said, to a chorus of *heys* and *hellos*.

'Hello beautiful – did you enjoy the show?' Rick asked, hugging Lisa. 'Hey, this woman is a goddess. She looked after me for weeks when I was on my uppers ... love you, Leese,' he added.

'Pleasure, Ricky – glad we could help,' Lisa blushed and looked away – straight into the eyes of Ruby Stone.

Ben spoke: 'Sorry, where are my manners? Leese, this is Ruby – best backing vocalist in the business.'

With a look of mock horror, Ruby swatted Ben's compliment and turned to Lisa, putting out her slim hand. She was smaller than Lisa had expected, even in four-inch-heeled boots.

'Good to meet you, Lisa,' Ruby said in a cultured, accent-free voice, 'Ben talks about you so much, I feel I know you already.'

'Oh ... really?' Lisa felt a twinge of guilt mixed with irritation and was lost for words until Tanya came to her rescue. 'Hiya, I'm Tanya. Your voice is amazing, Ruby – have you always been a singer?' she said, enabling Lisa to compose herself.

'Can't believe this is the penultimate gig,' Ben said, switching his empty champagne glass for a bottle of water, 'in two days, all this will be over. Fuck, I'm knackered though. How some dudes tour for years I'll never know. It's been a blast, but I can't wait to get home and chill out.'

Rick joined the conversation: 'That's not very rock and roll, is it mate?' he winked at Lisa. 'Oh, who am I trying to kid? It's been amazing but there's a point where you just fancy a pint and a pie, and to watch the telly.'

Steve agreed: 'One more night. Then we're done … and then I don't want to see any of your ugly mugs for a while.'

'Oi! None taken,' Ben said, enjoying the banter.

An unfeasibly tall man with a headset rammed over dreadlocks put his face around the door. 'Final encore in ten minutes,' he boomed.

Ruby, who'd been topping up her lipstick, caught Lisa's eye in the mirror. 'Are you coming tomorrow night, Lisa?' she asked.

'Of course she is,' Ben answered, 'she wouldn't miss the after-show party for the world – would you babe?'

'Try and stop me,' Lisa said, holding Ruby's gaze.

•

The fact that *Tamara's*, Soho's hottest nightclub, was closed to the public had proved little deterrent to the hundred-odd fans who were being held back by security. Paparazzi jostled outside as limos, SUVs and motorbikes roared up to the red-carpeted entrance as the cream of nineties rock and pop strutted, sashayed and shimmied into the venue in a blaze of flashbulbs.

Standing in line, Lisa's stomach fluttered as she clutched Ben's hand and smiled for photographers; an unwelcome throwback to her WAG days, when she'd trailed behind Justin Dixon, feeling like an accessory.

But Ben was loving the attention, hamming it up for the camera – posing affectionately with Rick and Steve. In a moment of epiphany, Lisa saw that the tour had elevated Ben to full-blown rock star status and that there was no going back. Against all odds and expectations, The Wilde Ones, who'd joined the tour from the subs-bench – *also-rans* from a pre-social media era – had somehow become the darlings of the show, finally claiming third billing behind two uber-nineties bands and creating a giant digital following in the process. It was uncanny.

Inside, the party went from nought to sixty in a heartbeat as people hit the dance floor, competing for who could throw the wildest shapes, while others began drinking in earnest at tables already bedecked with iced bottles of champagne, gin and vodka.

'This could get messy, mate,' Lisa heard Ben say to

Rick as they wove their way through the celeb crowd, en-route to their VIP table.

Lisa had a sudden urge to run home to the sanity of Eden Hill but knew she was probably in for the night.

'You okay, babe?' Ben said, passing her a glass of champagne and kissing her. 'We'll just stay an hour or so ... we can have a dance later if you like. Speaking of which – I haven't seen moves like that since 1995!'

Lisa followed her husband's gaze to where a trio of well-preserved women she recognised but couldn't name were re-enacting a vintage hit.

A dark haired, reed thin woman joined their table. 'Hi, I'm Minty – Jed's wife,' she said, taking rapid sips of champagne.

'Hello, I'm Lisa – I'm married to Ben. I don't know Jed, I'm afraid ... is he a musician?'

'Yeah, a guitarist. He's played with everyone; he toured with Duran Duran a couple of years back ... even missed the birth of our second child,' Minty said with a roll of her kohl-ringed eyes.

'Oh! That was ... unlucky.'

'I'm used to it ... although it was tough at first. I've got my own beauty business, and the kids keep me busy.' Minty laughed and jerked her head towards Jed, who was in earnest conversation with Steve and Ruby, 'I haven't got time for *him* as well!'

Lisa glanced around the table; she and Minty

seemed to be the only partners – everyone else was either in, with, or connected to the band. She leant against Ben, trying to feel close to him, but he was talking across her, and didn't respond. Then, to Lisa's horror, Ruby Stone was on her feet, tugging at Ben's sleeve, and pulling him towards the dance floor. With a grimace and a shrug that said, *'what can you do, eh?'* he was gone, lost in a sea of flailing limbs and flying hair.

CHAPTER 42

The Bradshaws

Rosemary awoke with a start, instantly on high alert. Beside her, Nigel snored softly. She groped for her phone. Why was she awake at three-fifteen? To her relief no sound came from Iris's room, but something had disturbed her.

Padding to the window, Rosemary pulled back the curtain. In the square below, a sleek SUV was parked outside the Wildes' house – engine running, a soft white plume coming from the exhaust. As she watched, her neighbours spilled out, Lisa tottering tipsily on high heels, leaning on Ben for support. He whispered something in her ear that made Lisa throw her head back and laugh raucously, mindless of the hour.

Of course; Rosemary remembered her exchange with Lisa in the street that morning. For the second night running, Lisa had gone into London to see Ben's band play, then afterwards, they'd gone to the wrap party at a club in Soho.

With a stab of envy Rosemary got back into bed, trying to remember the last time she'd gone out in London, but no memory stirred in her.

'What?' Nigel said, half-awake, 'What is it?'

'Nothing, go back to sleep. It's just Ben and Lisa coming home from a party.'

Obediently, Nigel turned away from her and within minutes was breathing deeply.

It irritated Rosemary the way he could sleep on demand, as though nothing troubled him. She sighed into the darkness, knowing that she was unlikely to get back to sleep for an hour or so.

Frustrated, she replayed the intimate scene she'd just witnessed; it was unimaginable to think of her and Nigel ever behaving that way. Had they ever? She could not remember a time of reckless abandon, even in the early days of their affair.

And then a memory came to her; a time when Nigel had taken her for cocktails at the Oxo Tower on the South Bank. It had been their third date and Rosemary had worn a chic black dress and kitten heels. With her hair in a simple twist at the nape of her neck and some fake pearls bought from Top Shop in her lunch hour, she knew she looked stylish, sexy and in control. The effect was not lost on Nigel, who'd made considerable effort with his own appearance and had worn a subtle, classical fragrance that Rosemary had responded to when he kissed her hello.

'You look beautiful,' he'd said, pulling out her chair, 'and so elegant. I've never known anyone like you.'

She'd believed him – enjoying his approval and the power it gave her. She was also a realist; it was clear to Rosemary that Nigel saw in her a degree of exoticism and she'd guessed correctly that not only had he never dated a black woman, but that he'd never had black friends.

That night they'd talked; a conversation that had been like peeling back the layers of an onion. Discovering that neither of them had been blessed with fathers beyond their tender years had been a seminal moment, creating a vein of empathy there and then.

'I don't know which is worse, Rose,' Nigel mused, as they gazed out at the London skyline sipping mojitos, 'the shock of a sudden death which you and your poor family had to endure, or being abandoned as a baby without explanation – at least none my mother has ever shared with me.'

Rosemary tried to remember if she'd fancied Nigel the way he had wanted her that night but although she remembered every other detail of the evening – what they'd eaten, drunk and worn – she could not summon the memory of her emotions.

She felt for her mobile on the nightstand; it had just turned four. In two hours' time, she'd be getting up. It was Wednesday, which meant saying goodbye to Nigel as he left to drive up North, battling to get Iris to school on time, and then driving in the opposite direction to visit Joyce in the care home.

Overwhelmed with sudden self-pity and exhaustion,

tears spilled onto Rosemary's pillow and she cried herself to sleep for the first time in years.

•

'I bet Molly doesn't have to eat all *her* Weetabix,' Iris pouted, pushing her bowl aside.

'I bet she does.' Rosemary was having none of it; her nocturnal ruminations had given her a headache. 'Sweetpea, I can't keep up. Last week you said you loved Weetabix – what do you want instead?'

Iris was decisive: 'Toast and chocolate spread,' she said, folding her arms across her school jumper.

Rosemary put bread into the toaster. 'Hey, what's the magic word?'

'*Please*, Mummy,' Iris said, adding, 'Did I tell you that Molly is my *best* friend?

'Yes, you did – I think it's lovely that you are making new friends. Do you play with her at break time?'

Iris looked offended. 'Mummy, we don't play, we're seven … we talk.'

'Well excuse *me*,' Rosemary said, turning her back to hide her first smile of the day. At least her daughter could be relied upon to make her laugh.

'Okay, hurry up Sweetpea – the traffic is always worse when it rains.'

'And it's always raining, Mummy,' Iris observed.

•

Rosemary's visit to Glen Heights did nothing to lift her mood. When she arrived, she was alarmed to find Joyce blank-eyed, silent and visibly thinner.

'I want to go home,' Joyce whimpered, as Rosemary bent to hug her.

This was new; no 'who are you?' no 'where's my purse?' No bad-tempered accusations about the staff or her neighbours, just a look of resignation.

'Mum, you are home – you've lived here for two years and you've got lots of friends. I think you just forget sometimes.'

'Take me home,' Joyce repeated.

Concerned, Rosemary looked for Hattie who as usual was pleased to make time for her.

'Look, I agree Joyce isn't quite herself, but we can't force her to eat meals she doesn't want, or to socialise when she says she's tired. It's not uncommon for older people with memory loss to get depressed and I suspect that's where we are now with your mother-in-law.'

Rosemary shook her head, 'I hate the thought of Joyce just sitting there … in her own little world, so miserable – she says she wants to go home.'

Hattie's expression was one of patient sympathy; 'She's confused, and again, that's not unusual. You have to accept that Joyce is deteriorating, and her withdrawal is just another stage of dementia. I know it's upsetting, but please try not to worry. I can assure you that her continued care is excellent and we're doing all we can to make her calm and comfortable.'

•

That afternoon, as rain fell steadily, Rosemary ignored the huge pile of ironing in the utility room, as well as swerving the supermarket. Jacket potatoes or fish fingers from the freezer would have to do for dinner. Instead, she lay on the sofa under a fleecy throw, feeling utterly drained of hope.

Was this all her life amounted to? The school run twice a day, endless domestic chores, shopping and cooking; hours spent visiting someone else's sick, elderly mother; evenings passed with only a seven-year-old for company, or worse – nights spent in polite, tolerant conversation with a husband she knew now – and with total clarity – that she could never love.

Could never love. Just forming the words in her head frightened Rosemary and she lay motionless, her breath sharp and ragged in her chest until it was time to collect Iris.

CHAPTER 43

The Wildes

As the spring sunshine peaked through a gap in the drapes, Lisa lay listening to Ben's soft snores. Revelling in her husband's caramel smell and the warmth of his lean body, she was in no hurry to get up; just for once, the gym could wait.

Hearing Nellie snuffle awake, Lisa reached down to the little dog's bed and scooped her onto the duvet, nuzzling Nellie's pointy face. 'Our family is all together again,' she whispered, as the Chihuahua yawned and stretched.

Ben let out a loud snort and opened his eyes. 'Morning, gorgeous. I think I've just snored myself awake,' he reached for Lisa. 'What time is it?'

'Time for you to bring me breakfast in bed,' Lisa giggled. 'You've got a lot of making up to do.'

'Or we can have a quick coffee and go out for brunch?' Ben suggested, sitting up and rubbing Nellie's ears absently.

'Darling, you've only been back a week – are you bored of home already?' It was a joke, but Lisa caught the note of whining in her voice.

'Of course not.' Ben rubbed his eyes. 'Forget that … let's stay at home. There's nowhere else I'd rather be.'

•

Ben considered the possibility of being mobbed in the street – now that he was a bigshot rockstar. He swatted the thought away, smirking at his own self-importance. People were cool in Eden Hill – everyone knew who he was, and nobody cared. He mused on the fickle nature of fame. Only a few years earlier, he'd been considered a has-been, a one-hit wonder – a joke. Then two high profile ad campaigns had used his music as their theme and bingo! He was back in the game. The tour had been crazy, but it was a world away from the gentle suburban life he was used to, and he couldn't see that changing any day soon.

Ben yawned and patted his trim stomach. 'Full English?' he said, baiting Lisa before flat-footing it to the shower.

Ben's 'full English' request earned him an eye-roll from Lisa, but after breakfasting on coffee and berries with yoghurt, they wrapped up warmly against the March wind, and set off for a walk with Nellie, who waddled beside them sniffing every tree, bush and post contentedly.

'Are you pleased to be home, darling?' Lisa asked.

'Yeah, absolutely. I mean, it was great being on the road, and the live shows are what it's all about, but it's not *real* and I'm not that person.'

'What person?'

'The rockstar ... you know, invincible, all that

swagger and energy ... it only comes in short bursts. I needed a nap most afternoons.'

Lisa laughed. 'Bless you. It must have been exhausting. Are you missing the band?'

'Christ, no! I was getting sick of the sight of them – me and Ricky were bickering like old marrieds by the last leg. Oh, good girl, Nellie,' Ben said, producing a plastic bag as the little dog squatted on a grass verge.

'What about Ruby?' Lisa said, in what she hoped was a casual tone.

'What *about* her?'

'Are you missing her?'

Ben frowned. 'No. Why would I? I'm not missing Rob on drums, or Mavis on catering, either.'

'Alright. I only asked.'

'Leese, I don't know what you're driving at ... the things you said on the phone ... I can't believe you're worried about Ruby, just cos she's a woman.'

'A beautiful, talented, single, *young* woman,' Lisa said.

Ben shook his head. 'I've no idea how old Ruby is – but if she isn't talented and decent looking, she's got no place on a European rock tour, has she? Honestly babe, I can't believe you're obsessing about her. It's ridiculous.'

They walked in silence for a few blocks. Ahead, a woman in a scarlet anorak was being dragged towards them by an overweight pug and an excited spaniel.

'Jan! Hi,' Lisa said, grateful of the diversion as the woman drew closer.

'Hello Lisa, Ben – how are you both?' Jan said, holding back the two dogs firmly as they snuffled around Nellie.

'We're great, thanks Jan. How's Martin doing? Blimey, last time I saw you was New Year's Eve – do you remember? That was a weird one. How is young Jake … see much of him about?' Ben was on the ball, brain firing on all cylinders immediately.

'Ooh, he's a mixed-up lad, that one. Martin chats to him sometimes … I think it's just his age.'

'Poor little sod,' Ben said. 'Anyway, you're just the person I wanted to see. Do you think you could have Nellie for a week or two if me and Lisa were to jet off for some sun?'

Lisa's eyes shone. 'Are you serious? Where are we going?' she said after Jan had ambled off with her charges, having agreed to board Nellie.

'Where do you fancy? As long as it's somewhere warm, I'm happy,' Ben grinned, their earlier spat already forgotten.

Back at Regents Square, Ben and Lisa trawled online and found an exquisite Five Star Spa in Crete that ticked all the boxes.

Lisa chewed her lip thoughtfully. 'Can we afford it?'

'Right now, we can afford pretty much anywhere,'

Ben said. 'Leese, the tour was a sell-out – I don't think you realise how flush we are. And you know what? The best thing is, *I* earned it. When we met, you were the one with bunce in the bank – now it's my turn to look after you. So, what do you think; shall we book up?'

Lisa squealed with excitement. 'Yes, as long as we're back for your birthday – I've got plans,' she added.

•

Ben made himself a flat white and contemplated lunch. He opened the fridge to find it stuffed with green and healthy wholefoods; digging through the freezer section, he found a tub of Cookie Dough Ice Cream – even Lisa had moments of weakness.

It was noon; he pictured her, halfway through a punishing Boxercise class, while some hard-bodied instructor in a headset roared at a class of twenty-odd over the thumping dance music. He'd gone to a class with Lisa once, and had barely survived the first half, bowing out backwards, sweat trickling from every pore. Hats off to his missus; she worked hard for that body – no wonder she looked so youthful.

Not that she'd agree with him. Her confidence seemed to be ebbing away at an alarming speed. One of the things he'd loved most about Lisa when they'd first met was her insouciance; it was refreshing to Ben that she'd never fished for compliments or stressed about weight, hair, wrinkles and all the other stuff women tortured themselves over. She'd always trained hard and looked after herself, but had walked tall and with a look that said, *I know I'm gorgeous – deal with it.*

But this new wave of insecurity was painful to watch. Not only did it demean Lisa, but it was a complete turn-off. It was their first wedding anniversary in two weeks' time; how things had changed in only twelve months.

Ben opened his laptop. Sod it. They were fine; they just needed a bit of R&R. He'd book up the Crete Spa to coincide with their anniversary and give Lisa the five-star treatment, make her feel like a princess again. Then when they got back, all bronzed and loved up, he'd get around to telling her about the next leg of the tour; the nine dates in Benelux scheduled for the autumn.

But it could wait.

CHAPTER 44

The Mortons

Jake threw down his guitar in frustration; it slid off his bed with a twang and a thud. Below him, his mum stopped singing.

'You okay, Jakey?'

'Fine,' Jake called back, adding, 'Fucked,' under his breath.

She always did that. Any odd bump or bang in the house and she'd call out to him, making sure he wasn't hurt – just like when he was a toddler and had fallen over.

He reflected on the benefits of being a little kid; when everything was safe and warm, and the only decisions to make involved chocolate or chew-sticks, Spider Man or Transformers, swimming or cinema – and actually, he'd loved all of them as a child. His Mum always said he was an easy baby and a contented toddler; how ironic then that he'd become such a totally fucked-up teen.

Nothing came easily to him these days. Jake remembered how he used to fly through his maths and chemistry homework, anticipating where the questions were going – able to draw down answers as easy as plucking books from a shelf. These days, he often needed to read the question three times – just to be sure he hadn't misinterpreted – before dredging his tired, fuzzy brain for answers.

The idea of taking GCSEs in a few weeks scared him shitless. For one thing, his concentration was awful. Something happened when he tried to revise; his heart would start pounding and his mouth would go dry, however much cola he swilled. A few times, he'd actually fallen asleep – still sitting at his laptop, his chin lolling on his chest. So then he'd end up playing a few riffs on his guitar, which sometimes soothed him – although not today. Today, even his guitar sounded crap. He couldn't even slope off and smoke a joint – not with his mum in the house; she'd go batshit if she found out.

The smell of roast chicken wafted upstairs. There was nothing good about Sundays – when he felt he could literally die of boredom – except for his mum's roast, which always made him feel better. It had always been his favourite dinner, even when he was little. He remembered how his dad would carve the meat, and then do most of the clearing up to give his mum a break after she'd spent half the day in the kitchen. *Two hours to cook, two minutes to eat*, Chloe would often lament.

Jake thought of his father and wondered if Jodie cooked Sunday roast for him and whether he stacked the dishwasher and scoured the pans for her the way he had at home.

Home. Where *was* home? Home had been their house in Streatham, where next door's ginger cat, Tommy, would come in through the back door and pad through the house until he got to Jake's room, then he would curl up on the bed and sleep for hours.

The day he'd left London, kissed the top of Tommy's silky head and thanked him for being a good friend was painful to recall. A tear slid down Jake's left cheek, then another rolled-down his right. He wiped them away with his sleeve, but then more tears came, and he heard himself sobbing, making a choking sound – and couldn't seem to stop.

Jake wept for Tommy, and for his old school friends, and for his dad – who'd promised they'd see each other once a week, but now it was less than once a month. He cried for Amber, who'd once been his girlfriend but was now practically his bloody sister. And he cried for his stupid fucking exams, which he knew he was going to fail.

What the fuck. How had his life derailed so badly?

•

The rawness of the crying had frightened her; Chloe had never seen her son so distressed. On Monday morning, after leaving two brief voicemails – one for Lillian at the coffee shop, and the other for the school's secretary – she'd taken Jake to the health centre and demanded an appointment with their GP there and then.

'Please, it's urgent … it must be today,' Chloe had begged the receptionist, who'd peered over her spectacles, rattled her keyboard and asked them to wait. After almost an hour of flipping through a selection of ancient and dog-eared copies of *Hello!* magazine while her son endlessly scrolled this mobile phone in a state of agitation, Jake was called.

Doctor Benson gestured for them to sit, 'How can I help?' she said, her mouth curved in a slight smile.

'I'm really worried about my son,' Chloe began, looking anxiously between Jake and Doctor Benson. 'He's been very low for months and yesterday, he couldn't stop crying.'

Doctor Benson nodded and addressed Jake directly. 'Why don't *you* tell me about it, Jake?' she said gently.

•

'Depression?' William said, as though trying to figure out the meaning of the word, 'but he's a child … what's he got to be depressed about?'

'Jesus, Will – you really are quite useless sometimes, you know that?' Chloe raged into the handset.

'Whoa – no need for that. Why are you so angry? Just tell me what's going on.'

'Well perhaps if you'd shown a bit more interest

in our son and had spent more time with him in the last year, we wouldn't be at this juncture. Will, this is serious.'

To William's credit, he'd offered to drop everything, drive down to Eden Hill and talk to Jake face-to-face. At first Chloe had declined a visit, saying it would put Jake under too much pressure, but she'd relented by the end of the phone call.

By lunchtime, Jake seemed more positive – as though a weight had been removed just by talking to Chloe and Doctor Benson.

'Dad's coming down,' Chloe said, hoping that Jake wouldn't rail against a visit from his father, but to her amazement he just shrugged.

'Whatever. Is he bringing *her*?' Jake's eyes were wide.

'No of course not. This is about you. Look, you don't need to worry about anything, Jakey. From now on, you come first; not work, not the Harpers, and certainly not bloody Jodie. We're all going to pull together and get you back to ...' Chloe paused, searching for the right word.

'Normal? Mum, I'm not a freak – I'm not some bloody *lunatic*,' Jake spat the word, 'I just feel a bit sad and stressed about stuff.'

'I know, sweetheart, and we're going to sort it.'

•

At three o'clock, William's Audi rolled onto the drive behind Chloe's mini.

'Well, this is … nice. What a lovely bright house.' William said, his smile fixed and his gaze glassy. 'Gosh, it's big, too – I could get my flat in here twice,' he said, following Chloe through to her large, open-plan kitchen/breakfast room.

To the surprise of all three of them, Jake hurled himself at his father, hugging him tighter than he had for years; minutes passed before anyone spoke.

'Tea?' Chloe filled the kettle and busied herself with opening packets of biscuits. It felt weird having her ex-husband in her home. He looked so out of place, shambling and awkward.

Extracting himself from Jake's embrace, William looked out at the garden which was alive with spring flowers that bobbed in the wind.

'Do you get the sun in the mornings?' William's eyes remained fixed on a patch of bright lawn.

'What? Er … yes … later in the year anyway. Look, why don't we all go into the sitting room and talk properly.' Chloe said, trying not to get exasperated and picking up a tray laden with tea, biscuits and some leftover brownies from the café.

'So, what did the doctor say?' William asked, when they were all seated in Chloe's immaculate, tea-rose scented sitting room.

Chloe patiently relayed the conversation with

Doctor Benson, explaining how she'd recommended talking therapies as a starting point.

'She said there are a number of excellent counsellors in the area who specialise in working with young people and who can help Jake to get back on track.'

'Mum, I can't do my exams if I'm bombed out on pills, can I?' Jake said, pulling his knees up and hugging himself.

William nodded in agreement. 'Jake's right. Medication is not the answer and I will not have my son–'

'You don't *know* that, Will. Down the line it might be the best course of action, but the first step is therapy – probably CBT and then … we'll see,' Chloe held up her hands and shrugged. 'Oh, look, I don't know … this is new to all of us. But Jake, you've got to open up a bit … *talk* to us.'

'But that's the point. No one's bothered about me, are they? All you care about is the bloody coffee shop and … and your boyfriend.'

Chloe felt her cheeks redden.

'And you're no better, Dad – in fact you're sooo much worse,' Jake glared at William. 'It's bad enough that you cared so little that you actually *left* us … but well, shit happens and loads of kids at school have got divorced parents. But I never even *see* you. It's like … you just want to forget I even exist, so you can concentrate on *her*. It's been five weeks since I came to yours … it's like you're hiding something.'

William shifted uneasily.

'He's right, Will,' Chloe said. 'We've all moved on, you're in a relationship and so am I, but there's absolutely no excuse for not spending time with Jake on a regular basis. I think we need to formalise arrangements and stick to them.'

'God, Chloe – you'll be suggesting court access next; there's no need to be so rigid about things.' Will sat up straighter. 'Sorry. Look, things have just been a bit … odd recently. I should have mentioned it before but I just …' he splayed his fingers, a gesture Chloe recognised as nervousness.

'What? What's the matter? Just tell us,' Chloe pressed.

William took a gulp of air. 'Jodie's pregnant. Jake, you're going to be a big brother.'

CHAPTER 45

The Bevans

He'd only gone into the guest room for a towel from the linen cupboard, but now Martin watched Jake as he paced the back garden. The way he prowled back and forth, loose-limbed, shoulders hunched, reminded Martin of a caged tiger in a zoo.

While Martin watched, Chloe appeared beside her son; the two of them exchanged a few words before going inside.

It was nine-thirty. The Easter Holidays hadn't started yet, so why wasn't the lad at school? Deciding that one of several grim viruses doing the rounds at Eden Hill must be to blame, Martin grabbed his clean towel and headed for the shower.

Enjoying its hot needles against his back and shoulders, Martin mused on the day ahead. He'd promised to look in on Lindsey mid-morning to check that the plumber had done a decent job of curing her water hammer. Then at noon he'd planned to meet Trina at Chloe's Coffee, which would give him the opportunity to ask about Jake.

Next he'd trot back home and have a sandwich with Jan, who was due to finish her shift by one thirty. After lunch, they'd settle on the sofa for an hour and doze in front of *It's Your Money*, the quiz show they pretended to enjoy, while snoozing from opening to end credits. It was a pleasant routine they'd been perfecting all year.

Martin towelled himself vigorously, checking his reflection and noting that he needed a haircut.

It was incredible to think that only a year ago, he'd been putting in a ten-hour shift as standard, manning the shop with Trina and going out to clients' homes to quote and measure up for new flooring. There'd been stock to order, fitters to book, endless paperwork (although he'd relied heavily on his accountant for that) – even adverts to book from time to time. How had he ever managed all that?

•

Walking briskly round to Cobalt Close, his collar turned up against the shrill March wind, Martin rang Lindsey's doorbell. After waiting a minute or two, unsure if the bell worked, he knocked loudly, but there was still no answer.

Martin fingered the key in his jacket pocket. As landlord, he felt justified in letting himself in – particularly as he'd arranged to visit – but he was loath to intrude. It occurred to him that Lindsey would only be at the shops, or with a neighbour, so he'd wait a few minutes before letting himself in.

Rocking on his heels and whistling tunelessly, Martin waited.

'Doctor's,' said a woman with harshly dyed hair as she emerged from the house next door.

Martin raised sandy brows. 'I'm sorry?'

'Baby's been screaming his head off all night, so Lindsey's gone to get him checked out. I ain't had a wink of sleep myself.' The woman slammed her front door and Martin watched her large rear waddle up the street towards the small parade of shops.

Feeling exasperated, but more concerned for baby Harry, Martin let himself into the house. But before he'd mounted a single stair, he was struck by the appalling stench of the place. A soft keening sound drew him to the kitchen, where two kittens slithered around an overflowing bin, looking for food or amusement. Beside the bin were three empty bowls and a reeking, heavily-soiled litter tray.

'Oh, you poor little souls,' Martin said, bending down to pet the kittens, who rubbed round him, mewling pitifully. He searched for cat food, finding only a handful of kibble in a box.

'Well this is no good, is it?' he said aloud, putting the biscuits in one bowl and filling another with water.

Martin looked around at the nearly new kitchen; at the sink full of dirty dishes, and at the drainer covered in upturned plastic baby bottles. At the stinking pedal bin – so full it wouldn't close – and at the table, strewn with junk mail and unopened post.

This was not a safe and cosy home for a small child.

And when had the kittens arrived? He'd expressly said no pets and the subject had not been broached by either Mike and Lindsey or by Hunters in their capacity as managing agents.

With a leaden heart, Martin went upstairs and turned on the basin taps; the water ran smooth and silent. At least the plumber had done a decent job. But what the hell was going on here? The bathroom was as filthy as the kitchen, with a mound of rolled up disposable nappies in one corner and a pile of dirty laundry in another.

Nobody was expected to be show-home tidy with a baby in the house – but this smacked of desperation, neglect and things spiralling out of control.

Martin peeked into the main bedroom which was untidy but offered less scope for filth.

He opened the wardrobe door, where Lindsey's clothes hung dejectedly. Beside them, a dozen or so empty wire hangers jangled to Martin's touch. Where did Mike keep *his* clothes? Martin crossed the landing into the tiny second bedroom which housed Harry's cot and was strewn with brightly coloured soft toys. Watched by dozens of sparkly eyes, Martin opened the small built in closet – already knowing that he would find only baby clothes.

•

'I feel so sorry for the girl,' Martin said as Trina sipped

her flat white and twiddled her long hair, currently a pearly shade of blonde.

'Thing is, Martin – you're her landlord, not her dad. Sounds like she's wrecked the place and as for the cats, it's in the lease that she's not allowed. You need to get her out, fast – and find some new tenants.'

'Well, there's an estate agent speaking, if ever I heard one,' Martin said. 'Trina, that's all very well, but the girl's in trouble and she's got a one-year old boy. I can't just chuck her out. Talk about kicking someone when they're down. It's obvious her husband's gone AWOL – there's nothing of Mike's in there.'

'But Martin, you can't let things carry on. She must have family she can turn to. And as for those kittens – it's cruel, they need rehoming.'

'I'll talk to her ... find out how bad things really are. You're right – she's not my problem, but I'll deal with this in my own way. No point acting like a bull in a china shop,' Martin said, popping a last piece of lemon muffin into his mouth and dusting his fingers on a paper napkin.

Trina's face softened. 'You're too nice, boss – that's your problem.'

'I'm not your boss anymore, Tee. Speaking of which, how's it going at Hunters? You still enjoying it?'

Trina made a face. 'I preferred working for you. We had our own little world in there. Everybody knew us. You were a pillar of the community in Crabton; I don't think you realise how much you're missed, Martin. Oh, blimey – look at the time! I'd better get back, I only get forty-five minutes for lunch.'

After thanking Martin for the coffee and cake, and pecking him on the cheek, Trina put on her smart work coat and fled, leaving Martin wondering what on earth to do about Lindsey just as Chloe Morton arrived looking harassed.

Acknowledging him with a wave, she walked straight past and took her place beside the pretty red-head who'd been polishing the counter and cleaning equipment between serving customers.

Martin shrugged on his coat and walked up to the counter.

'Hi, Chloe. How's you?' he said, thinking how tired his neighbour looked.

Her smile was weak. 'I'm fine, thanks, Martin.'

'Is Jake alright? Only I saw that he hadn't gone to school this morning … there are so many horrible bugs around. Noro Virus is doing the rounds again, I hear–'

'He's fine,' Chloe snapped, adding, 'he will be, anyway. He's under a lot of strain with his exams and he's a bit under the weather.'

'Bless him,' Martin said. 'Well, if there's anything I can do to help … these poor youngsters work so hard these days …' he trailed off, seeing Chloe's obvious discomfort. 'Righto, I'll be off then. Lunch with the missus – not that I'm hungry after a cheeky muffin – don't tell Jan,' he twinkled, patting his midriff.

At home the comforting smell of warming soup and buttery toast met Martin as soon as he set foot inside; it was a stark contrast to the sour odour he'd found earlier at Cobalt Close.

CHAPTER 46

The Mortons

Andrew Gillham had been Headmaster of Kenilworth long enough to know the difference between mothers given to histrionics and those facing genuine issues. To his mind, the fact that Chloe Morton stood before him for the first time put her in the latter category. He indicated one of the two chairs opposite his desk.

'Please, sit down, Mrs Morton,' he said.

'Thank you for seeing me at short notice, Mr Gillham. What I have to say is urgent.' Chloe crossed her legs and took a breath. 'It's about Jake, obviously. He's not been himself for a while, but things have gone downhill recently ... at home, I mean ... but also with his grades.'

Mr Gillham nodded. 'Yes, I'm aware of a slight deterioration in some subjects. Do go on,' he said, his pen hovering above a notebook.

Palms damp with anxiety and speaking carefully to stop herself sobbing right there in the room, Chloe relayed how she'd taken Jake to see their GP.

'It was such a shock ... but it shouldn't have been ... I just ... didn't see it,' Chloe finished, her voice hoarse.

'Don't be too hard on yourself, Mrs Morton. Jake isn't the only pupil at Kenilworth being treated for mental illness and I like to think the school has a modern and practical approach.' Mr Gillham pressed a few keys on his laptop and cleared his throat: 'I see that Jake is taking nine subjects for his GCSEs – which must seem like an awful lot of pressure. We need to think about how we can manage Jake's exams to minimise stress. I'll speak to his form teacher and department heads so that we can come up with a plan of action. I'm also going to contact the exam boards and request special consideration due to mental illness.'

Chloe exhaled audibly. 'Thank you. So, you think Jake should go ahead and sit his exams?' she asked, reassured by Mr Gillham's pragmatic manner.

'I do, Mrs Morton. Postponing is not ideal. It would mean him dropping back a year and according to previous school reports, Jake's a very bright young man. You may find that he responds well – and quickly, too – to counselling, but if that isn't the case and his results are not as hoped, there are options.'

Chloe raised her eyebrows. 'Such as?'

'Oh, re-sits next summer, here at school – or earlier, with private funding and tuition. I assume that–'

'Oh, yes, we'd pay, of course. All that really matters is Jake not screwing up his future – no thanks to his father and me. We're separated and–'

'Ah, divorce is never easy, Mrs Morton, but young

people are remarkably resilient ... and I speak from experience.'

Mr Gillham laced his fingers and smiled, unwilling to say more about his own circumstances; he pushed back his chair, signalling the end of the meeting. 'Why don't you keep Jake off school now until after Easter – he can use the time to rest, revise, whatever you think is best for him. Kenilworth will support Jake in every way possible, so please, leave things with me and I'll be in touch.'

Chloe shook the Head's hand and left his office feeling significantly lighter than when she'd gone in.

•

The waiting room was no more than a narrow corridor that connected reception with three small consulting rooms. Jake ran his fingertips along a white, wonky wall; the whole building reminded him of one in a Dickens novel he'd read at school.

Jake would have preferred for his mum to drop him off in Crabton High Street and then walk through the labyrinth of passages to the rather grandly named *Mind, Body & Spirit Health Centre*, but Chloe wouldn't hear of it and was now sitting so close that Jake could hear her breathing.

'Mum, you don't have to wait with me ... I'm fine – I'm not about to run off or anything,' Jake said, jiggling his left leg nervously.

'I know, sweetheart – and I won't go in with you, I promise. I'll just wait here until you come out.'

A door opened, and a middle-aged woman emerged, holding a tissue up to her blotchy face. She blew her nose loudly and crept past.

Jake gulped. Fuck. What had happened to her? He wasn't up to some big sob-fest. He'd done that at home, and it had led to a doctor's appointment, followed by an awful meeting with his mum and dad in the same room (which had been freaky); now *this*.

The door opened a second time. 'Jake? I'm Vivian,' a young woman with pale blonde hair smiled, 'sorry to keep you waiting. Please, come in.'

He'd expected his counsellor to look like a teacher and wear a tweed suit and glasses. But the young woman before him was good looking and dressed in a short velvet skirt with woolly tights and long boots – cool street clothes, like the ones Amber wore.

Jake glanced at his mum, who gave him a weird, tight smile, and followed Vivian into a sloping, misshapen room.

•

Jake lay on his bed, replaying the session with Vivian in his mind.

She'd recorded the whole thing, which Jake thought he'd mind about, but he soon forgot about the machine on her desk.

She'd given him a questionnaire – the same one he'd already done on the phone with someone who was either Vivian's assistant or boss, he didn't know which. Jake thought it a pointless exercise. How the hell was some stupid quiz supposed to stop him feeling utterly worthless?

Then she'd asked him what he enjoyed doing; at least she hadn't said 'how's school?' like most adults did.

Jake had struggled with that one. Because the truth was, he didn't *enjoy* doing anything anymore, he was just so tired. But he thought about it for a moment and remembered how he used to love playing and listening to guitar music; he remembered, too, enjoying science at school, and going to gymnastics club, and because he didn't want to sound like a boring twat, he'd listed them to Vivian who nodded and wrote something down. Then to his amazement, she'd asked Jake if he didn't like doing those things anymore; it had blown him away.

Wondering how on earth she knew that, Jake looked at her properly for the first time. Kind blue eyes and nice hands, he thought, wondering if she was married. He liked her voice, too, it was soft and calming. He couldn't imagine Vivian ever being angry about anything.

Shit. He'd obviously missed something because she was looking at him intently.

'Sorry, can you repeat that, please?' Jake said, realising she was expecting an answer to whatever she'd just said.

'Of course, Jake. I asked how you feel about your mum and dad living apart.'

'How long have you got?' Jake snapped before he could stop himself.

'Take your time. Anything you say in this room is totally confidential.'

'It's okay,' Jake lied, 'I mean, my mum works a lot and I see Dad about once a month – and now he's having a baby.' Jake giggled at the mental image of his father with a bulging stomach. 'I meant his girlfriend, Jodie, obviously. Now she's up the – sorry, she's pregnant.'

'And how does that make you feel, Jake … to know that you'll soon have a little brother or sister?' Vivian asked softly, and he'd meant to say it was fine, but before he could get any words out, he'd started to cry like a girl, which was *soo* embarrassing, with tears and snot and everything. But she'd just let him, pushing a box of tissues towards him and saying that it was okay to feel sad sometimes and even angry, too.

So he'd gushed about how his mum had Caleb – who was an arrogant bastard that he didn't like much – and that his dad had Jodie – and soon *they'd* have a bloody baby that would spend its life screaming, shitting and puking – while he, Jake, had nothing and nobody.

The funny thing was, Vivian hadn't tried to give him any advice at all. She'd just listened and every time he told her something new, she asked how he felt about it. He could tell she wasn't judging him, because even when he'd said *fuck* once without meaning to, she didn't flinch.

Jake wondered what it would be like to kiss her lips, which looked soft and pink, even without lipstick; he imagined putting his tongue in the gap between her front teeth. He could already tell that she smelled nice, sort of fresh and lemony.

An alarm vibrated on Vivian's desk. It was the end of their meeting and he was almost disappointed, where had the last hour and a half gone?

'We'll leave it there for now, Jake. Are you happy to proceed with another session? Same time next week? Only it will be an hour from now on.'

'Yeah, sure. Um … thank you.' He thought of the crying and the snot. 'Sorry about the–' he began.

Vivian smiled. 'You never need to apologise in this room, Jake. Good work – see you next week.'

And it was over.

CHAPTER 47

The Bradshaws

Rosemary was shocked when Nigel booked an entire week off work for the Easter holidays.

'Let's make a point of doing something with Iris every day,' he said, before launching into a raft of suggestions.

Rosemary's heart sank. She knew he was trying, which only made her feel guilty.

'Well, if you're sure you can afford to take the time off, Iris will certainly be pleased. Perhaps her new friend, Molly, can tag along on one or two outings … maybe to the safari park or the cinema.'

'Good idea, Rose. I must squeeze in a visit to Mum as well – give you a break from her.'

'She'd like that,' Rosemary said, astonished by Nigel's sudden interest in his family, although it irritated her that he felt he was somehow doing her a favour.

True to his word, when Easter arrived, Nigel stayed at home, rising later than usual and wearing casual clothes fit for car journeys and sightseeing.

'Why is Daddy here?' Iris said, holding tight to Rosemary's hand as the three of them wandered around a small petting zoo on the first day of the holidays.

'Don't you think it's nice to have Daddy here? He works so hard, sweetpea, daddies need holidays, too.'

'Yes, I suppose so,' Iris said, 'oh, look at the baby goats, Mummy – so cute!' she squealed, not quite daring to touch them.

Nigel stood back, his hands in his pockets, a tight smile on his face.

Further round the route, in a barn pungent with the stench of urine on straw, new born lambs and their mothers had attracted a bigger crowd, including older children who gathered in front of Iris, blocking her view.

'Bless you, little one,' said the mother of twin redhaired boys, who grinned at Iris and made space for her. 'Perhaps Grandad will lift you up so you can see better,' the woman added.

Iris was indignant. 'That's my *daddy*,' she said, haughtily.

'Oh! Sorry ... I thought ... you can never tell these days,' the woman said, catching Rosemary's eye and digging herself in deeper.

'Take no notice,' Rosemary said, when the three of them where back in the car, sharing ham sandwiches from a Tupperware box, and one of Iris's chocolate Easter eggs.

Nigel's laugh was dry and mirthless. 'What do you expect? I look my age ... unlike my youthful wife.'

'Nonsense,' Rosemary said, cringing inwardly. Why was Nigel flirting with her?

The day after Good Friday a light drizzle fell all day. Unperturbed, the Bradshaws arranged an afternoon cinema visit that included seven-year-old Molly, Iris's new best friend.

'Impressive,' Nigel said when the SatNav led them to an elegant stucco-fronted house two miles from Eden Hill. 'How the other half lives, eh? Wonder what Molly's father does.'

'Sshh. Not in front of little ears,' Rosemary said. 'Right, you and Iris stay here – no point in all of us getting wet.'

Smoothing down her trench coat, Rosemary crunched across the gravel drive and pressed the bell. The door was opened at once by a lean blonde woman in a taupe cashmere sweater and jeans, whom Rosemary recognised from the school gates.

'I'm Davina,' the woman said, 'glad to put a face to the voice. Please, come in.'

With a grimace, Davina angled her head towards the grand staircase. 'I'm afraid we're upstairs having a shoe crisis.' She raised her voice: 'Come on Molly, just pick a pair … Iris's Mummy is here – and you don't want to miss the film, do you?'

'We've plenty of time,' Rosemary said evenly, hoping she was not about to meet a spoilt and wayward brat, but after a few minutes, Molly – who was as blonde as her mother – appeared, in jeans and suede purple ankle boots.

Rosemary beamed at the little girl. 'Hello Molly; they're fab, good choice,' she said, before turning back to Davina. 'We'll take the girls for a snack afterwards. Any food allergies I should know about?'

To Rosemary's relief there were none and after she'd buckled Molly into the backseat, Nigel drove them all in the direction of the cinema complex near Tunbridge Wells.

'Well?' he said, once the girls were gabbing animatedly.

Rosemary looked across at her husband. 'Well what?'

'What are the parents like?'

'I only met Molly's mum … she's lovely,' Rosemary said.

'That house must be worth well over–'

'Nigel, stop. Please,' Rosemary hissed, then louder, 'shall I put some music on girls? What do you fancy?'

•

The film – a big budget number which was heavy on CGI effects and light on plot – passed pleasantly enough and the girls giggled hysterically on cue.

'Well there's two hours we'll never get back. What a load of absolute twaddle,' Nigel said under his breath as they left the cinema and started towards the restaurant zone.

Rosemary rolled her eyes, 'It wasn't *for* you – the girls liked it. It was lovely to hear Iris laughing so much.'

'Thank you, Iris's mummy,' Molly said, her face upturned. 'It was sooo funny. I loved the bit where the dog had to fly the plane.'

'Oh yes! That was brilliant … sooo funny,' echoed Iris as they burst into fresh peals of laughter and linked arms.

'Girls, what do you fancy? Pasta, burgers … pizza?' Rosemary asked.

They'd eaten delicious stone-baked pizzas, although neither of the girls had touched the salad Rosemary plied them with.

'Okay, I suppose it won't hurt just for once. But extra greens for you tomorrow, young lady,' Rosemary said, tickling Iris's soft midriff.

'My mum's a vegetarian,' Molly announced, 'but me and Daddy eat *everything*.'

Iris was aghast. 'What, even liver?' she made a gagging sound.

'Hey, stop that, silly. Anyway, when have you *ever* eaten liver?' Rosemary said.

'At school,' the girls replied in unison, with such tortured expressions that both Nigel and Rosemary laughed aloud.

Replete with pizza, the children grew sleepy on the journey home.

'So, early nights all round is it?' Nigel said, watching his daughter stifle a yawn in his rearview mirror.

Iris was having none of it: 'But it's the holidays – can't I stay up late, Daddy?'

'Sweetheart, you're already tired … we'll see after we've dropped Molly home,' Rosemary said.

'My mum and dad let me stay up until ten o'clock during the holidays,' Molly said, folding her arms across her chest.

Rosemary and Nigel exchanged looks and smiled.

'Well, here we are,' Nigel said, pulling up outside Molly's parents' home, 'let's all go and say goodnight, shall we?'

Before Rosemary could object, Nigel had helped the girls from the back seat and was walking across the gravel, leaving Rosemary to scuttle after them.

Beaming, Molly's parents opened the door together. This time Davina was wearing a short black dress, her fine blonde hair in a messy bun.

'Crispin Taylor,' said Molly's father, shaking hands with first Nigel and then Rosemary.

'Did you have a lovely time, Moll?' Davina squealed, pulling her daughter into her arms.

Molly nodded. 'It was brilliant, wasn't it, Iris? And then we had pizza, which was yummy,'

Crispin waved them inside. 'That's great. Look,

come in, all of you. Stay for a drink ... Dee's just opened a bottle of wine.'

Rosemary longed to go home but Nigel was halfway through the door, his eyes hungry and alive.

'That's very kind ... if you're sure,' she said, following Nigel and the girls through to the kitchen.

'What a wonderful room,' Nigel gushed, accepting a glass of red wine, 'Smallbone?' he added.

Crispin nodded. 'Correct. Well, cheers. Thanks for taking Molly out for the day – we'll organise something with Iris next time.'

Mindful of driving home, Rosemary declined the offer of wine and accepted a glass of fizzy water.

'How long have you lived here, Crispin?' Nigel asked.

'Oh, about five years. It needed a bit doing when we first arrived, but we're settled now, aren't we, Dee?'

Davina nodded 'Yes. I can't imagine living anywhere else. Where are you based?'

Rosemary opened her mouth to speak but Nigel jumped in: 'Just outside Crabton,' he said.

'Oh, great – such a charming market town. Don't you get fed up with the estate dwellers though? Eden Hill caused a riot when they started building twenty years ago. People were furious with the hike in population.' Crispin was on a roll. 'And I don't blame them. I mean, you can't just dump thousands of people in the middle of the countryside without improving the infrastructure, can you?'

Rosemary shifted uncomfortably; she looked at Nigel, who remained tight-lipped.

'So how do you both keep in such terrific shape?' he said changing the subject and directing the question to Davina.

'Oh, I do a bit of pilates ... when I remember,' she said, 'and we both play tennis at the weekends.'

'That explains it,' Nigel smarmed, his eyes drifting over Davina's svelte body, while Crispin topped up glasses.

'The girls are quiet up there ... is that a good or bad sign?' Rosemary asked.

'Oh, I expect they're on the iPad – so hard to limit screen time, don't you find?' Davina said.

The two women began talking about the pitfalls of social media, but even through her own conversation, Rosemary could hear Nigel pumping Crispin for information; about his work, where they'd recently holidayed, and even where they shopped.

'Thank you so much for the drinks, but we really must go,' Rosemary said, 'Iris will be so crabby tomorrow if we don't get her to bed soon.'

'Of course. Well, thank you for having Molly today – see you another time, I hope,' Davina said, before calling upstairs for Molly and Iris to come down.

•

'I knew it,' Nigel said, perching stiffly in the passenger seat as Rosemary drove and Iris gazed into the darkness. 'He's a fund manager. That's where the real money is these days.'

'I can't believe you lied about where we live,' Rosemary whispered, her head beginning to throb.

'What? I didn't … Crispin made certain assumptions and I just didn't get around to correcting him.'

Rosemary kept her eyes on the road and said nothing. Nigel's sycophancy at the Taylors' had made her feel queasy. All day, she had looked for redeeming features – anything that might provide a ray of hope, but she'd seen nothing to endear her husband.

It was eight-thirty, which meant at least another two hours spent in Nigel's company after putting Iris to bed, a prospect which filled Rosemary with dread.

CHAPTER 48

The Wildes

On the Wednesday before Easter, Ben and Lisa walked Nellie in the woods at the back of Regents Square, then Lisa packed the dog's bowls, blankets and coats and drove her round to the Bevans' house.

Martin opened the door before Lisa had even rung the bell. 'Lisa! Come in. Aww look, she's a little smasher this one,' he said, attempting to tickle Nellie, who snapped her tiny teeth and let out a piercing yap.

Lisa was embarrassed. 'Sorry, Martin. She's not quite herself today – she knows something's going on.'

'Don't you worry about that, we'll soon get her settled. Have you got time for a cuppa? Jan should be back any minute.'

'Go on then, just a quick one. This is lovely, Martin,' Lisa said politely, taking in the bland décor, and the ceramic knick-knacks dotted about. 'Looks like you're really settled here.'

'Work in progress, as they say,' Martin answered. 'You look well, Lisa. How's Ben? You looking forward to your holiday? Alright for some,' he said, dropping tea-bags into mugs.

'We are; it's just what the doctor ordered,' Lisa said, realising they were both talking in clichés.

After ten more minutes of excruciating small talk,

Jan arrived, flushed and breathless and smelling of outside.

'Hi, Lisa. Aww, here she is,' Jan crooned, bending to stroke Nellie, who, still in the crook of Lisa's arm, repaid Jan's affection by baring her teeth.

'I'm so sorry … it's 'cos she's guarding me,' Lisa apologised, setting the dog down on the tiled floor.

'Lisa, it's not a problem. Nellie will be fine here with us – in fact she'll be spoilt rotten, won't she, Mart?' Jan said.

Martin nodded. 'Yes, indeed. Now, you and Ben enjoy your holiday, and if you're worried, just give us a ring.'

Then with a lump in her throat the size of a plum, Lisa handed over Nellie's possessions and instructions about her diet and daily routine and left before the tears that threatened spilled over.

Back at Regents Square, she found Ben flinging clothes into a bag.

'How did that go, babe?' he asked.

'I don't think Nellie was impressed – she was a bit growly. I hate leaving her,' Lisa said, her voice catching, 'What if–'

'*What if* nothing. Jan looks after dogs all the time; I'm sure Nellie be completely indulged and won't want to come home.'

'D'you think?' Lisa said, her lip trembling. What on earth was wrong with her? She'd left Nellie before, and it wasn't usually a big deal. The least little thing seemed to upset her these days, she thought, double checking her own packing and squeezing in an extra bikini and a pair of gold sandals.

Ben watched as Lisa struggled with the zipper on her designer holdall.

'You do know we're only going for ten days, not six months,' he teased.

'So? I can take what I like!' Lisa snapped.

'Alright babe, just saying. Are you okay, only you seem a bit …' Ben searched for the right word.

Lisa was defensive: 'A bit what?' She took a deep breath and exhaled slowly. 'Oh, darling, I'm sorry. I just hate leaving my baby behind. I'll be fine when we get there … hey, I can't wait to get in that infinity pool,' she said, forcing a smile.

•

Ben's aversion to getting up at silly-o'clock had prompted them to check into an airport hotel overnight, which should have made their seven A.M. flight relatively civilised. Instead the Easter crush at Gatwick combined with their packed budget flight rendered Ben and Lisa short-tempered and stressy.

'You see? This is what happens when you fly EasyJet,' Lisa hissed as they slunk down in their seats at the rear of the aircraft, Ben's trademark curls jammed under a baseball cap in an attempt at disguising himself after clocking up several knowing stares.

'Babe, don't have a go. This was the only direct flight available. Let them look; it's not as though anyone's bothering us, is it?' Ben pulled his cap down further and opened the GQ Magazine he'd bought in WHSmith.

Nevertheless, an hour into the flight, a diminutive, round-eyed brunette with fake, fuchsia nails hovered in the aisle for a moment before passing Ben her boarding card to sign.

'I've got all your albums, Ben. Mind if I do a selfie?' Without acknowledging Lisa or waiting for an answer, the pouting woman put her cheek to Ben's and snapped away with her smartphone.

'Thanks! You've made my day,' she said, her eyes sparkling as she returned to her seat.

Moments later, two more forty-something women made an elaborate business of dropping some sunglasses in the aisle before they too asked for photographs.

'Er … sure, why not?' Ben said hoping he wasn't about to become the in-flight entertainment.

Lisa bristled. 'I hope this doesn't happen all holiday,' she said, appalled at the thought of sharing her husband with anyone, let alone female fans.

'Yeah, me too. But what can I do? The tour's put

me back in the public eye ... I can't complain, can I? It goes with the turf.'

The rest of the flight passed slowly as Ben read and Lisa seethed in silence. But as they stepped down from the plane at Heraklion, Lisa's heart soared as she felt the warm breeze on her face and caught the unmistakable holiday scent of jet fuel mixed with cologne; a bud of happiness unfurled in her.

She looked at Ben, who in addition to the cap was now hidden behind aviator shades and was grinning broadly. They were here now – on a beautiful sun-kissed island, about to check into a five-star spa hotel; so what if the occasional gushing fan wanted a selfie or an autograph? She smiled graciously and took Ben's hand.

•

Lisa gasped. Either Ben had secretly upgraded their room or there'd been a mix up by the reservations staff.

'Wow! Darling, it's stunning, is this the honeymoon suite?' Lisa said, drinking in the opulent room before passing through filmy drapes out onto the balcony with its view of the lagoon.

Ben beamed. 'Not quite – it was already taken, although I did try to book it. Not too shabby though, Leese. I wanted to surprise you ... I thought it would make a nice anniversary present,' he said, looking pleased with himself.

'Sweetheart, thank you, I love it ... and I love you,' Lisa said, putting her arms around Ben and kissing him.

Ben was encouraged. 'Mmm ... now that's more like it. Why don't we shower together and road test this magnificent Super King bed?' He wiggled his eyebrows suggestively.

'Sounds perfect, babe,' Lisa extracted herself, 'but I'm starving, aren't you? Let's check out the restaurants first and grab a bite to eat in the sunshine.'

'Okay ... must admit I'm a bit peckish myself, and anyway, we need to keep our strength up, Leese. I've been dreaming about having you all to myself since we booked,' he growled softly.

After freshening up and a brisk change of clothes, Ben and Lisa set out to explore the resort's handful of restaurants and bars, settling on the relaxed pool-side brasserie; it was three-thirty and only a few stragglers remained from the lunchtime sitting.

'This is the life,' Ben said, after they'd ordered club sandwiches and were sipping ice cold white wine.

Lisa raised her glass in a toast. 'It sure is, babe. To us!'

•

Lisa awoke with a start and a whoosh of nausea.

Only two hours earlier, suffused with tenderness after making love, Ben and Lisa had fallen asleep tangled in fine linen and each other's arms.

Now, convinced she was about to be sick, Lisa pushed Ben away, staggered to the bathroom and leant against the cool marble, sweat tricking from every pore, heart racing. Crouched over the lavatory, Lisa waited to throw up, but nothing happened.

Eventually she stood up, catching sight of her wild-eyed expression and flushed cheeks in the mirror.

Shocked, Lisa ran a mental check of what they'd eaten and drunk at dinner, deciding that the crab salad had to be the culprit. On the other hand, Ben had eaten it too, and was sleeping soundly. Had she developed a sudden allergy to seafood? Now, that would be a pain ... but surely if that was the case, she'd have eliminated the offending substance, one way or another. Grimacing at the thought, Lisa washed her face and crept back to bed, mortified by her damp sheets. As the nausea continued to abate, she settled back against the pillows and closed her eyes, but it was almost dawn before she fell asleep.

•

'Morning gorgeous,' Ben was leaning up on one elbow, with the first stirrings of an erection. He rolled closer. 'Sleep well?'

'Morning. What time is it?' Lisa spoke thickly,

momentarily confused before remembering where they were and that she'd felt ill during the night. She fought to sit up.

'Hey, someone's sleepy this morning, it's normally me that's crap at getting up,' Ben said.

'Sorry, weird night,' Lisa admitted, before telling Ben about her bizarre nocturnal malaise.

'Bloody hell, Leese – why didn't you wake me? How do you feel now?'

Lisa shrugged. 'Okay, I think … just tired. I'll be fine … give me a minute to wake up properly while you take a shower,' Lisa yawned.

But when Ben returned from the bathroom, Lisa had dozed off.

'Bless you, babe – you must be knackered,' Ben whispered, pushing a lock of blonde hair from his wife's face before going in search of coffee.

CHAPTER 49

The Bevans

By the tone of Trina's voice Martin could tell at once that her message was urgent; he called back.

'Trina, it's me. Sorry I missed your call. Is everything okay ... you sounded a bit–'

Trina cut him short: 'Martin, they've gone.'

'What? Who's gone?'

'Your tenants. The keys to Cobalt Close and a note addressed to you were put through Hunters' letterbox sometime last night.'

The words began to sink in. So, Lindsey had done a moonlight flit, thought Martin, wondering what state the house would be in.

'Don't suppose there was a cheque for last month's rent as well,' Martin said, knowing the answer.

''Course not. They've dropped you right in it, Martin. They never paid last month's, and the current month is due next week.'

'Well, perhaps I should have a word with the managing agents,' Martin said, knowing his dig would go straight over Trina's head. 'I'd better get round there and take a look. I'll pop in for the keys first and see what's in the note.'

Martin hung up. *Why does everything have to be such a bloody drama?* he thought, pouring his mug of tea away and scribbling a note for Jan on the kitchen jotter. He was dreading telling her the latest in what she called *'the Cobalt Close saga'* and hoped she'd resist gloating.

•

Parking outside Hunters Estate Agency, Martin found Trina at her desk.

'Martin, I'm sorry this has happened. Wish I could get my hands on the silly–'

Martin shushed Trina before her colleagues could overhear her being unprofessional.

'Tee, at the end of the day, it's only money,' he said, 'I'm more concerned about what's happened to Lindsey and the baby … where on earth have they gone? Have you got the note, please?'

Tearing open the sealed envelope, Martin read Lindsey's childish scrawl.

Dear Martin

Mike has left and I can't cope anymore. I've gone to my mum's in Sidcup – she loves Harry and we can stay as long as we like.

Thank you for being so nice to us. Sorry about the rent – I'll pay you back one day, but for now, here's my last £20.

Lindsey X

p.s. please take the kittens to a safe place – sorry, don't hate me.

Martin re-read the last line with mounting horror. 'Oh my god,' he groaned, 'the cats are still in the house.'

Trina, who had just taken a call, mouthed for Martin to wait a moment; instead he marched out of the office, got into his car and drove home. There seemed no point in going to Cobalt Close empty handed. What he needed now was a box or carry-case to remove the cats. Then before he embarked on a clean-up operation, he'd find the nearest animal rescue centre and convince them to take the poor creatures in.

'What a bloody mess,' Martin said aloud. Unsmiling, he waved to Jake who was just leaving the house, his hair damp and fluffy, his cheeks pink.

An idea struck him.

'How's you, young man?' Martin called out, 'No school today?'

'Easter holidays,' Jake said, 'I go back on Monday.'

'Of course. Jake, I could use a hand if you've got an hour or so.'

'Well I was just, er … my mum's expecting me at the coffee shop. I'm supposed to be helping her out, but it's more so she can keep an eye on me,' Jake said, with disarming honesty.

'Oh, well if that's the case, why don't we pop in and see your mum on the way? I'll explain everything, but first we need a nice sturdy box,' Martin said, heading for the garage.

After rooting through half a dozen plastic crates, and shelves groaning with tools and DIY appliances, Martin found a suitable receptacle for the kittens. Jake stood by, hands in pockets, eyeing Martin uneasily.

'Eureka!' Martin said, pulling out an old lidded picnic basket and dusting it down with a rag.

Jake cleared his throat: 'Do you think you'll be long? Only I told Mum–'

'We're ready, Jake. This,' Martin held the basket aloft, 'is just the job.'

Then he unhooked a dustpan and brush, shoved them in a plastic bucket and shooed Jake out of the garage before pulling down the hatch.

Only twenty minutes earlier the situation had seemed sad and desperate; now Martin had to admit that bizarrely, he was enjoying himself.

Jan had once called him a natural rescuer. Perhaps she had a point. He liked solving problems and helping people. Poor Lindsey had been beyond help, but at least the kittens could be rehomed to a happier place and maybe Jake would get something out of helping them, too. Martin gave Jake the bones of the story during the few minutes it took to drive to the village square.

Jake was outraged. 'Oh my god. That's so awful. How could anyone *do* that? To just move without taking their pets with them. It's disgusting. We should report them to the RSPCA.'

Martin shook his head. 'I think my tenants were in a very bad place – Lindsey didn't strike me as the kind of person who'd be deliberately unkind to animals. People do funny things when they're desperate. Stress has a lot to answer for.'

''Spose,' Jake said, unconvinced.

'Right, let's ask your mum if it's alright for you to come with me – see if we can sort this pickle out,' Martin said, marching towards the coffee-shop as Jake slouched in his wake.

It was almost noon and the café was buzzing. Inhaling the scent of freshly ground coffee, Martin was tempted to order one; instead he went up to the counter where Chloe and her assistant were working through the queue with alacrity.

'Morning, Chloe – how's you, my love?' Without waiting for an answer, Martin pushed on, 'I wonder if I could borrow Jake for an hour or so. My tenant's done a runner, leaving the house in a right state, but worse than that, two cats have been left on the premises. I was hoping that Jake could give me a hand,' Martin paused, wondering why on earth he was involving his teenage neighbour.

'Oh, how awful,' Chloe said, 'Yes, of course – it will give him something to do; he'd only have been washing up for me,' she added, much to Martin's surprise.

•

The stench of rotting rubbish and cat urine hit them. Jake hesitated. 'Urgh, gross,' he said, putting his hand over his nose and mouth.

'Don't you worry, son, we'll soon sort this lot out,' Martin said, sounding more confident than he felt.

A mewling sound was coming from behind the closed kitchen door – soft at first but growing louder as the kittens became aware of someone in the house.

'Oh god!' Martin said, pushing the door open and releasing the fetid stink of cat faeces.

'Jesus! You poor little things,' Jake said, squatting beside the cats, mindless of the smell now.

'No food, no water and by the look of this,' Martin pointed to their litter tray, 'nobody's cleaned up after these two for a week.' He shook his head, 'What a sorry state. Come on Jake, let's get them out of here … place is a bloody disgrace. To think that a baby was living here until yesterday, Lindsey must have been in a right state.'

Dehydrated and weak with hunger, the kittens were limp as Martin and Jake lifted them into the basket.

'How could anyone be so mean?' Jake said, his voice breaking, then to the kittens: 'Come on, I'll look after you.'

'I was going to drop them off at the RSPCA, but perhaps we should call in at the vet's first – get them checked out,' Martin said, handing the basket to Jake to hold while he drove towards Crabton.

He'd been so concerned with rescuing the cats from their filthy prison that Martin hadn't even looked at the state of the house, although it was apparent that Lindsey's meagre furniture had gone.

'She must have had help – she'd have needed a man with a van. It just shows, Jake, you can never tell. I thought they were such a nice young couple; bonny baby, him a hospital porter at the General. They seemed so respectable.'

Jake didn't answer.

'It's okay,' Martin said, realising that the boy was close to tears, 'there's no real harm done. A bit of TLC and this pair will be right as rain. Come on, let's get them to the surgery.'

CHAPTER 50

The Bradshaws

Standing in the supermarket aisles vacillating between salmon or chicken, Rosemary felt her mobile phone vibrate in her pocket; *School* said the display.

'Mrs Bradshaw? Hello, this is Wendy Cooper, secretary at South View,' said a nasal voice. 'Sorry to be the bearer of bad news, but Iris is vomiting, I'm afraid – twice in the last half-an-hour.'

'Oh god, how awful. She seemed fine this morning … has she got a temperature?'

'She's a bit warm, but I suspect it's only a forty-eight-hour thing; three others in Iris's class have had something similar in the last week. We're keeping her in the sickbay, but she wants her Mum of course.'

'I'm on my way,' Rosemary said, dumping her basket and running out into the carpark, all thoughts of dinner shelved.

On arrival at the school, Rosemary went straight to the main office where Mrs Cooper was waiting anxiously.

'Thank goodness you're here. Iris is still throwing up, and these things are very contagious,' the older woman said, leading Rosemary to a small monastic room that housed two narrow bunks, a couple of plastic chairs and a sink in the corner. The sour smell of vomit mixed with disinfectant was unmistakeable.

'Oh darling, you poor thing. Let's get you home,' Rosemary said, alarmed by her daughter's pallor and helping her to sit up.

Mrs Cooper handed Rosemary a cardboard bowl, mouthing 'for the car' over Iris's head, and they set off for Eden Hill.

Grateful that the bowl had not been necessary, Rosemary made her daughter a bed on the sofa and sat beside her, willing her to recover. The way Iris seemed to shrink and fade before her eyes when she was ill always frightened her.

Iris sat up sharply. 'Mummy, I feel sick,' she moaned.

'Okay, sweetpea – don't worry about getting to the loo,' Rosemary held the bowl as Iris retched.

'You'll be better soon, darling, I promise,' Rosemary said, settling Iris back under the fleecy throw.

The landline chirruped; Rosemary cursed. 'If this is bloody PPI …' She snatched up the handset.

There was a pause before a hesitant voice came on the line: 'Rosemary? This is Hattie – Nurse Dobson from Glen Heights. Look, I'm so sorry to tell you this, but it's about Joyce. I'm afraid she died a few minutes ago.'

'What … Joyce?' Rosemary was confused. 'Joyce has died?'

'Yes, I'm sorry, it's only just happened, the doctor was with her. We sent for him as she was complaining of chest pain … we think it may have been a heart attack. It all happened so fast. Rosemary, I'm very sorry for your loss. You were lovely to her – I know she meant a lot to you.'

Rosemary sucked air into her lungs; *had* Joyce meant a lot to her? Visiting Glen Heights had always seemed like a duty and a chore. Now Rosemary didn't know what to feel.

'Thank you for telling me, I need to contact my husband at once – tell him about his mum. What do I need to do?'

'Even though Joyce was old and not very well, it was a sudden death, so we've informed the Coroner and it's likely there'll be a post-mortem. As next of kin, your husband will need to identify his mother's body. You'll need to appoint a funeral director and start making arrangements … I know this must be a terrible shock.'

It took Rosemary a moment to process the information. 'Thank you, Hattie,' she said after a pause, 'we'll take your recommendation regards an undertaker … but I need to get hold of my husband, he's away overnight and he'll have to come home.'

Promising to call later, Rosemary hung up, swapped to her mobile, and dialled Nigel's number, grateful that Iris had not stirred.

As was often the case, her call went straight to voicemail. It was six-thirty; by now he would have left

the Huddersfield office, and would either be on his
way to the Holiday Inn nearby or having dinner with
colleagues in the town centre.

Rosemary dialled the Holiday Inn and asked to be
put through to Mr Bradshaw's room.

'We have nobody here by that name,' the heavily
accented receptionist said after a lengthy pause.

'Well, can you check, please? It's Nigel Bradshaw;
my husband stays with you every week … he'll probably
be on his way now. Can you at least put a note by his
room number to call me when he arrives – it's very
urgent.'

'One moment please,' the line clicked, and
Rosemary was left listening to the William Tell
Overture.

'Sorry to keep you waiting, Madam, but we have no
bookings past or present for a Mr Nigel Bradshaw,'
came a new voice – male, clipped, English.

Rosemary's heart began to pound: 'Okay … my
mistake,' she said, hanging up.

Now what? She trawled her contacts for Nigel's PA;
they'd never met but he spoke highly of her and had
given Rosemary Joanne's mobile number, 'in case of
emergency'. Well this situation surely qualified.

To her immense relief, Joanne picked up at once.

'Oh, thank goodness. Joanne, it's Rosemary,
Nigel's wife. I need to contact him urgently. I've tried
his mobile and left a message, and I also phoned the

Holiday Inn, but they say they don't know him ... which is weird. Can you help me, please?'

'Ah, well,' Joanne said, 'that's because he just *pretends* to stay there ... he actually stays an hour away so that people can't spring meetings on him. He says they take enough liberties during working hours.'

'Can you *please* just give me the number?' Rosemary said, irritated by Joanne's chatty and plodding manner.

•

'What a pig of a day,' Nigel said, laying back on the bed.

Indulging him, Tiffany took off Nigel's shoes, loosened his tie and undid his top button. 'You just tell me all about it,' she said, hoping that a quick fuck was all he wanted, rather than having to spend the night with him as she'd done several times already.

'I'm starving actually,' Nigel said, sitting up. 'Shall we phone room service, get them to bring something up?'

After ordering from the limited menu, he settled back on the bed, and began idly stroking Tiffany's breasts through her lacy top.

'Hey, you've just ordered food, but I can be for dessert,' she giggled, picking up the TV remote and surfing the channels.

'You're such a tease,' Nigel said, going to the

bathroom just as the phone rang. 'Get that, will you? It'll be reception telling us what they've run out of – as usual,' he grumbled, closing the bathroom door behind him.

'Hello, the Bradshaw residence,' Tiffany said, in a silly, faux-posh accent.

'Hello?' A woman's voice. 'Who is that?'

Tiffany hesitated, less certain now that it was the receptionist.

'Can I speak to Nigel?' The voice was unmistakeably that of a black woman. Tiffany froze.

'Put him on the phone – it's urgent,' came the voice again, insistent now.

'Nigel … it's for you,' the young woman said as Nigel appeared, drying his hands.

Tiffany's haunted expression and a sickening sixth sense told him at once that his wife was on the phone.

'It's me,' Rosemary said, 'and I don't know who that was, but it will have to wait. Nigel, you need to come home – Joyce is dead.'

•

Rosemary dropped the phone as if scalded. Nausea bubbled behind her sternum. The voice had sounded young, breathy and playful. Who did it belong to – and why on earth had the girl been in Nigel's hotel room?

She shuddered as a queasiness washed over her. It

had been, she decided, some strange quirk of fate – a peculiar coincidence that a chamber maid, or some other female staff member had answered Nigel's phone in his absence.

What mattered was that she had managed to reach him and had let him know that Joyce had passed away.

She hadn't meant to blurt out the news in that way and afterwards Nigel had said little, other than promising to leave right away.

She'd wanted to ask about the young woman – but compared to Joyce's passing, anything else seemed trifling and grilling Nigel about it tonight would be wholly inappropriate. But what if … what if Nigel had a lover, a girlfriend – *a wife* – in the north?

She remembered the conversation with her sister about men who spent time away from home, leading secret lives – it seemed preposterous. And yet. Possible.

Outside, it had grown dark. How long had she been sitting alone with her thoughts, while Iris slept soundly on the sofa? Thankful that at least the bug seemed to be abating and knowing that Nigel would not be home for several hours, Rosemary rang Abi. 'Sis, it's me,' she said.

Abi's voice was low: 'Telepathy, Rose. I was just thinking about you and I had a funny feeling …'

Rosemary took a deep breath. 'Really? Well, it's been a funny day.'

CHAPTER 51

The Wildes

So much for ten days in Crete, Lisa thought, slathering on fake tan. Thanks to an even split of sunshine and showers – and more pointedly, a consistent lack of sleep, Lisa had returned from holiday looking and feeling more exhausted than when she'd left.

Well it was one thing to feel awful, but she was damned if she'd look it.

'Babe, you look amazing as always,' Ben had reassured her before heading out to catch the London train for a meeting with his record label and a potential new producer.

'You're just saying that,' Lisa had snapped, desperate for some space. But after a morning which began with a punishing boxercise class and continued with a top to toe home-pamper session, Lisa began to feel more human and was looking forward to a good catch up with Tanya over coffee.

'So, how was it – apart from being a total shag-fest?' Tanya said, kissing Lisa on each cheek and scrutinising her now glowing appearance.

'Lovely, thanks. The resort was … nice,' Lisa said.

'*Nice?*' Tanya narrowed her eyes. 'That's not saying much is it? What's up? Is Ben okay?'

Lisa emitted a bark of bitter laughter. 'Oh, Ben's great, never better. He loved the hotel, the beach, the food, the fans who kept wanting selfies, the staff who would burst into spontaneous applause every night when he walked into the bar – not to mention the fact that he's looking ten-fucking-years-younger.'

Tanya looked shocked by Lisa's outburst. 'And breathe. Look, screw coffee, let's go over the road for a proper drink.'

Outside the Garden Gate Inn, pretty hanging baskets bobbed in the April breeze and sunshine lit up the women's faces.

'Sorry,' Lisa said, tucking her arm into Tanya's so that they entered the pub in step, 'I don't know what's wrong with me recently. I'll get these, what do you fancy?'

Lunchtime customers were clustered in small groups; men in work clothes leant on the bar, while office workers sat at the dozen or so tables.

'Over there … that one has our name on it,' Tanya said, stalking towards a table away from the bar and the slot machines that kept whooping into life despite an absence of players.

Returning with two vodka and tonics, Lisa sat down and gulped hers gratefully.

'Thirsty much?' Tanya said, her eyes wide. 'Come on hon, what's up? I'm sensing there's trouble in paradise.'

It was the last thing she'd planned to do, but Lisa found herself unloading to her friend.

'Sorry Tanya, a complete whinge fest is the last thing you need on your day off, but I just feel out of sorts all the time and *so* bad tempered … about everything and nothing. I was excited about going away, but honestly, I could hardly wait to get back; what with broken sleep every night and Ben's rampant demands,' Lisa finished, swallowing the last of her drink.

Tanya's face was a picture of concern. 'Leese, I think you should call in at the Doc's. I'll come with you if you like.'

Lisa rolled her eyes: 'And say what? That I've turned into a moody bitch and I've gone off sex?'

Tanya chewed her thumbnail. 'Lisa, this time last year, you were all over Ben like a rash, and you've been really down for months – not your usual self at all. Anyway, hold that thought while I get us some drinks.'

Tanya's walk to the bar caused a drop in the volume as most males in the room eyed her pneumatic form in spray-tight jeans and butter-soft leather jacket. Lisa felt a stab of jealousy. This was ridiculous! Even her best friend was making her feel lousy.

'Diet Coke; we drove here, remember?' Tanya set down two glasses, adding, 'Babe, I'm wondering … and I know you're a bit young, but it could be early menopause.'

Lisa's throat tightened. 'But I've just turned forty-five – I've got years yet … haven't I? Christ, Tan, what if you're right? Oh god … it would explain so much,' Lisa said, her face flushing at the mere idea.

•

Ben had travelled off-peak to avoid the commuter crush into London. His meeting with Electra was for eleven-thirty and seemed totally unnecessary; what was wrong with Skype? But the team had wanted him to meet some new faces, including a hot young producer earmarked for the next Wilde Ones album.

Ben had expected a hiatus after the tour, but apart from his sunshine holiday with the missus, there seemed to be no let up.

There was a distinct possibility that he'd be recording through June and July, and then he'd be back on tour for the Benelux dates during September. Weird to think how only a year earlier he'd been convinced his career was washed up and had been fearful of turning fifty-five.

Picking up a fuggy odour as the train slowed into Victoria, Ben buttoned his navy pea coat and jammed his hair under a baker-boy cap. Sometimes it pleased him to be recognised, but it slowed him down, too, and covering his curls usually did the job.

The station was rammed with smacked-arse faces, barely missing each other, and the taxi line was long.

The underground would have to do, Ben thought, with grim determination.

He'd asked Lisa if she wanted to travel up with him, to do a bit of shopping in Bond Street or the Kings Road, but she'd looked at him as though he'd grown another head and muttered something about 'me time' and catching up with Tanya. Ben was all for that. Tanya was a good mate and was bound to lift Lisa's spirits, which had been in the gutter for months.

He hated to see her so low, jumpy and frazzled all the time. She'd been weird on holiday … sleeping poorly at night and exhausted all day. They'd both put it down to a bug, but Ben wasn't convinced – it had simply gone on too long. But when he suggested looking in at the Doctors' surgery, she'd bitten his head off and told him to stop fussing. *Suffocating her* was the expression she'd used.

Even worse, in Crete, she'd knocked him back in bed, which was the last thing he'd expected and was unheard of before the tour. No wonder he'd chickened out of telling her about the autumn dates – it was just another thing to piss her off.

The tube rattled into Oxford Circus. Swept along on a tide of tourists, Ben switched to the Central line and boarded for Tottenham Court Road where a busker was making a decent fist of *Seagull*. He paused to listen, fished a twenty from his wallet and flashed the youth a dazzling smile: 'I couldn't have played that better myself,' he said with a wink, tossing the cash into the guy's guitar case before striding off, leaving the young musician to gape in his wake.

•

After forcing down an indifferent Caesar salad, courtesy of the Garden Gate's Lite-Bites menu, Lisa hugged Tanya goodbye and drove home to Eden Hill.

After walking Nellie and giving the little dog a tasty chew stick, Lisa removed her makeup and ran a deep scented bath, despite already showering that morning.

'I will *not* cry,' she said aloud, sliding into the steamy warmth. But despite her determination, tears began to course down Lisa's face.

The menopause: How could it be happening to her? She was too young, yet all the symptoms were there in text book form; the mood-swings, the insomnia, the lack of confidence, even the tell-tale erratic cycle, which Lisa had vehemently ignored – or denied.

She pictured herself in years to come; pot-bellied and red-faced, with heavy jowls sprouting chin hair. It was happening already – her favourite jeans were growing tighter and her beautiful blonde hair was losing its lustre as every day more greys stubbornly squiggled through.

In the last year she'd become an angst-ridden

wreck. No wonder Ben had looked elsewhere. She thought of Ruby Stone; strong, sassy, beautiful – and in her thirties. How could she possibly compete? Supposing Ben was with Ruby right now? Lying in her toned arms and kissing those pillowy lips?

She had to stop this indulgent self-pity. Ben had been loving and sweet on holiday; it was *she* who had been ill-tempered and distant, to the point where Ben had asked Lisa why she'd gone off him.

Well, menopause be damned. Lisa simply wasn't at home to it. In three weeks' time it would be Ben's fifty-fifth birthday and she hadn't spent the last couple of months organising his surprise party for it to flop; she *had* to be on form for it, no matter what.

CHAPTER 52

The Mortons

When May arrived, the warmer temperature caught Chloe off-guard as if summer had arrived by stealth.

The coffee shop seemed to buzz with new life and became the favourite haunt of Eden Hill's yummy-mummies who rewarded themselves with soya lattes after their morning gym and pilates sessions. Chloe tentatively introduced a modest savoury menu of flatbreads, soup and toasties and, voilà, the office crowd ramped up between noon and two every afternoon.

Out of necessity, Chloe took on new staff; Dominic, a watchful forty-something underemployed copywriter, who did three afternoons a week, as well as making Jake her Saturday boy as soon as he turned sixteen.

Jake had categorically refused a birthday party and had begged for two foundling kittens for his sixteenth. Chloe had to hand it to him; he'd made a good case on both counts.

'Mum, I'm in therapy; that's not the kind of thing you can hide for long. Everyone at school knows I'm fucked up and having counselling. It would really suck if I just had some random party and pretended everything was okay,' he'd explained a week before his birthday.

But Chloe's heart swelled with hope when he'd added, 'But a family dinner would be nice – all of us … the Harpers, too – and Dad if he can make it … although that might be a bit weird.'

She'd smiled at Jake's attempt to include everyone. There was no doubt that the weekly sessions with Vivian were calming him down and giving Jake a new perspective.

The cats had been a bizarre and fluke thing, and Chloe couldn't argue with fate. Jake had helped Martin Bevan to clear the rental house he owned, and they'd found two dumped kittens.

'How could anyone *do* that?' Jake said, shaking his head. 'I think we should keep them. Martin's already had them checked out at the vet's and they're both healthy, just a bit thin. Mum, if they go to a shelter, it could be months before they get a proper home. They've been through enough already … and look how *cute* they are,' Jake said, snuggling the tabbies against him.

So Chloe had laid ground rules; about how it was Jake's responsibility to clean the litter tray daily and to feed and regularly de-flea them.

'Of course – I love them. I'm calling the boy Raffles – after Tim Raffles, Baby Dogs' guitarist – and the girl is Scarlet, because of the red patch on her head.'

True to his word, Jake began caring for the kittens with a devotion that melted Chloe's heart.

Her son's friendship with Martin Bevan was a weird one. To her shame, Chloe had been suspicious of Martin's motives, sifting his acts of kindness for some hidden agenda. But for reasons she could not fathom, Martin got through to Jake in a way that neither his father, nor Caleb had managed to do. She'd hear them chatting over the garden fence sometimes, when Jake could be heard rattling with laughter – at, or with Martin, Chloe could not be sure.

'He's cool, Mum – he knows all sorts of things – *and* interesting people. Not all wrinklies are boring, you know?' Jake said.

Chloe gave him a playful shove. 'Really? Well, thanks for that.'

'Yeah,' Jake continued, immune to Chloe's irony, 'Martin's invited both of us to a party up the other end of Eden Hill. Mum, this is a big deal. I can't say anymore – it would ruin the surprise – but trust me, you'll love it!'

•

'You're amazing, you know that?' Caleb said, refilling Chloe's glass with red wine.

She raised her eyebrows quizzically. 'Well, thanks … but how do you work that one out?'

'Because, my darling, you just take everything in

your stride. Look at what you've been through in the last couple of years ... a separation, a move, starting a new business – and now your son has been diagnosed with depression, and you're handling that, too.'

'What else can I do? And anyway, back at you,' Chloe said, taking Caleb's hand. 'Look what a fine Dad you are to the girls – they are an absolute credit to you.'

'Thanks, but they're far from perfect. Jade seems to be getting cheekier every day – and her language would make a sailor blush.'

'Bless her ... it's just her age,' Chloe said, taking a sip of Merlot before snuggling against Caleb's chest and enjoying the steady rhythm of his heart.

Between three teenage kids, the coffee shop and the farm, evenings spent alone together were rare and precious, yet neither of them seemed to want or need more.

Chloe smiled, remembering a recent conversation with Jake.

'Mum, are you and Caleb having a baby, like Dad and Jodie?' he'd asked in a matter of fact tone following a session with Vivian.

Chloe scrutinised her son's face, trying to read his expression. 'Good grief, no. Life is quite complicated enough. Why on earth would you think that?'

'Dunno really. But women always want babies, don't they?'

'Not *all* women – Bryony hasn't got any … she and Paul chose not to. Anyway,' she said, closing in for a cuddle, '*you're* my baby.'

'Gross! Mum, please – get off me,' Jake said, making no attempt to escape.

'I'm proud of you, Jakey,' Chloe said, 'you're doing really well. I think your work with Vivian has made a big difference already.'

'Yeah … maybe,' Jake said, nodding earnestly, before returning to his English Language revision.

'Hey, this'll make you laugh,' Chloe said, before relaying the entire baby conversation to Caleb.

'Blimey! Is that what you want?' he asked, looking so shocked that Chloe burst out laughing.

'No. No, really! It isn't. Things are good as they are … feels like everything has settled down a bit. I'm happy taking things slowly … aren't you?' Chloe searched Caleb's dark eyes.

'Yes,' he said, 'very.'

•

Jake was beginning to view his recent history as Before Vivian and After Vivian, which he'd abbreviated in his head to BV and AV, and there was no doubt – AV was better. For a start, thinking about his exams didn't make him want to puke anymore, and when he revised the words on the page made sense – like they used to, before leaving London.

It was funny how, AV, good things had started to happen. Like the kittens – which wasn't so great for them, given that they'd been dumped in a filthy, empty house. But they seemed blissed-out now, devouring their food, batting their toy mice around the house and sleeping on Jake's bed at night. Raffles could be a bully sometimes, eating Scarlet's food as well as his own, and hiding her favourite toys, but other than that – they were perfect. He smiled to himself; purrrfect – ha! Jake had dreaded telling Dylan about Vivian, expecting him to freak out and take the piss. Instead he nodded his approval: 'Cool. You've been stressed for too long, Jakey – life doesn't have to be that hard.' And then they'd played guitar like they always did, only without the weed and Jake felt lighter, and his fingers were more nimble.

'Whoa! Incredible … where did *that* come from?' Dylan said after Jake had ripped through a particularly complex riff from Babydogs' new album.

Jake laughed, 'Dunno,' he said, 'something just clicked.'

Even Caleb seemed bearable these days. His mum was more cheerful when he was around – which wasn't often – and he liked it when they all got together for Sunday lunch or went out for burgers as they had on his sixteenth birthday. Jake had almost cried when Jade gave him a hug and a glittery card she'd made herself, addressed to *The World's Best Big Brother*.

'Take no notice of her, she just couldn't spell *World's Biggest Loser*,' Amber quipped seeing Jake's eyes begin to well.

Then they'd all bombarded him with cool stuff, like games for his PlayStation and accessories for his phone – except Jade, who'd bought him a book of funny cat photos. She really was a sweetheart, he decided.

Now, when he thought of Amber – all legs, swishy hair and flicky eye-liner – he knew he loved her, but not like before. It embarrassed him to think that they'd seen each other nearly naked and had *done stuff* to each other. What Jake felt now was something else … more substantial and grounded … as well as knowing he'd want to kick the crap out of anyone who tried to hurt her.

As for his dad and Jodie. Well, they were trying – yeah, bloody trying, actually – but at least his dad was sticking to the schedule his Mum had organised. It wasn't their fault they were acting all 'icky. Babies did that to people, didn't they?

CHAPTER 53

The Bradshaws

Determined that her mother-in-law would be despatched into the next world with dignity and decorum, Rosemary steered Nigel through the funeral arrangements with grace, putting aside her own feelings and postponing the inevitable undoing of her marriage.

The Coroner had ruled heart attack as the cause of death, which seemed ironic, considering it was Joyce's mental state that had confined her to a care home for the last two years.

On the day of the funeral, the sun climbed high into a cloudless sky and Rosemary walked Nigel to the front of the crematorium where he sat, head bowed, clutching an Order of Service from which a photograph of Joyce smiled out, resplendent in a lavender jacket and pearl earrings.

Among the twenty-odd mourners who had come to pay their respects to Joyce and to offer comfort and condolence to her only son, were friends and family whom Rosemary had not known existed.

Joyce had never been a church-goer, so a Humanist Ceremony had been the natural choice. Not that Nigel had expressed an opinion. He seemed to be in shock; eating little and sleeping less, yet dry-eyed and distant.

'Ah, bless him, poor Nigel. I didn't realise they were that close,' Lisa said, when Rosemary walked Iris round on the morning of the funeral, grateful for her neighbour's offer to babysit.

'They weren't. People deal with death in different ways, don't they?' Rosemary said.

'Are you alright, Nigel?' she whispered, noticing her husband's pallor and shaking hands, as the last few mourners shuffled into pews.

'Yes. I'll be relieved when it's all over,' he said without looking at her.

•

After the service, which thanks to the deft skills of the Celebrant had been gentle and even uplifting in parts, Rosemary and Nigel were driven to the wake in a gleaming black Mercedes. They'd booked a small and traditional hotel near Glen Heights that came highly recommended by the care home's manager.

In a private function room bedecked with green and gold wallpaper, Rosemary was touched to find Mr Baldini and two elderly women sitting by French windows that led onto a pretty courtyard.

'Nigel, look – some of Joyce's friends from Glen Heights are here. Come and say hello.'

'Why? I've never seen them before,' Nigel said. 'It's bad enough that I have to speak to relatives that I haven't seen for decades.'

'Because, Nigel, they were her friends – and because at their ripe old age, they've made a huge effort to come today.'

'Sorry,' Nigel said, shame registering on his face.

Somehow the day passed without incident and Rosemary endured Nigel's estranged family. One man, introduced to her as 'Uncle Frank', bore such an uncanny resemblance to Nigel that Rosemary wondered if he was really her husband's father.

Nigel had never been forthcoming about his family, and she'd attributed *cultural differences*. But if any of Nigel's relatives were surprised to discover he had married a black woman, they did not show it and by the end of the day, Rosemary had garnered several invitations to introduce 'little Iris' to the clan.

She looked out at the sea of black nylon suits and polyester frocks, cheap shoes, and home-dyed hair. Suddenly it all fell into place: She had never met these people before because Nigel simply didn't care for them. It's not me he's ashamed of, she thought, observing her husband's ham-fisted attempts to mingle; it's them.

She remembered his eager, sycophantic small talk with Molly's parents and the way he'd been vague about where he lived. And yet, in comparison to this crowd, Nigel had hit the jackpot and was enjoying a life of leafy suburban luxury.

For three weeks, Rosemary had put aside the issue

of whomever had answered the phone in Nigel's hotel room. A part of her already knew, but for Joyce's sake she had vowed to tell nobody – not even her sister – until after the funeral.

Well today would come to an end. And then she would have her say.

•

After the funeral, Nigel had taken the rest of the week off work. 'Compassionate leave' was the term he'd used when he'd telephoned first the London office and then Huddersfield HQ.

Rosemary got up at six-thirty as usual, determined that Iris would go to school.

'But you let me stay at home yesterday, for Grandma Joyce's funeral,' Iris whined.

'Yes, because I didn't want to involve Lisa with the school run. We've already put her to enough trouble. You're going, madam – now go upstairs and brush your teeth.'

Then Rosemary had driven Iris to South View, her stomach knotted with anticipation as she thought about the conversation ahead. Arriving home, she found Nigel sitting at the kitchen table, unshaven, wearing shapeless clothes and drinking tea. There was no evidence of his phone or laptop, and no radio or television playing in the background.

'It's a gorgeous day,' Rosemary said, opening the

back door and regarding the sparse lawn and empty
flowerbeds with sadness. 'How come we've never done
anything with the garden?' she said, not expecting an
answer, adding, 'Nigel, we need to talk.'

His tone was resigned: 'I know.'

'I mean, properly ... *honestly*. Nothing matters now
except that Iris is okay ... I think you feel the same.'

For a moment, silence hung in the air like smoke,
then Nigel put his head in his hands. When he spoke
his voice was almost a whisper: 'Jesus Rose, I'm so
ashamed.'

•

Rosemary had expected drama and raised voices;
accusations by her, denials from him – not this
pathetic, beaten confession.

'I can't bear the lies anymore, Rose. I've done
things ... awful things that I'm not proud of. There's
a woman ... we have sex sometimes, I pay her ... and
it's only that, but it's disgusting ... *I'm* disgusting –
and I hate myself for the way I've treated you.' Nigel
twisted his wedding ring absently, then wiped his eyes
and sniffed loudly.

'The woman on the phone ...' Rosemary sat down
heavily and waited to feel something – a visceral pain
or shock-induced nausea, but neither came.

'I'm so sorry, Rose ... after everything you've done
for this family. You look after our daughter single-

handedly, you showed my mother more love and kindness than I ever did. And ... the weird thing is ... you never complain. You never get on my case about all the time I spend away or–'

'Would it have made any difference?' Rosemary interjected, 'If I'd asked you to spend less time at work – or to visit Joyce more often? Nigel, you've been living your own life and doing your own thing since the day Iris was born. It mattered less when we lived in London, at least there I had my family and friends around me, but when we moved, life got much harder for me. To this day, I can't imagine why you wanted this big house, on this god-forsaken estate. Why Nigel?'

'Because it's what we all do, isn't it? Get married, have children, move to the suburbs, get a bigger house. But it's all bollocks, isn't it? Neither of us are happy. At least you have Iris – she pays no attention to me. I only irritate and embarrass her since she's been at that fancy fucking school.'

'The *fancy-fucking school* that *you* insisted on sending her to. she'd have been fine in Eden Hill Primary – and *I* might have made local friends at the school gates.'

His confession heard, Nigel had stopped snivelling and was now staring ahead, unblinking, unseeing.

'Look, all these justifications ... smoke and mirrors!

You were using *prostitutes*, Nigel – that trumps everything.'

Nigel was peevish. 'Not prostitutes – I used an escort agency, and always the same girl.'

'Oh, that's alright then,' Rosemary snapped. 'Do you have feelings for her?'

'What? No, of course not. That's the whole point of paying for sex – it's just a transaction … a release. You made it quite clear years ago that you wouldn't tolerate me in bed.'

'*Tolerate*? My god, Nigel – can you hear yourself? Are you actually blaming me because I wouldn't have sex with you after Iris was born?'

'Of course not. There are no excuses … but there are reasons,' Nigel hung his head.

'Well, right now, I can't think of a single one for us to stay married – can you?' Rosemary said.

'I'm sorry, Rose. I really am. You deserve better.'

'I do,' Rosemary squared her shoulders. 'Nigel, I want you to move out – today. I'll tell Iris that you're working away for a while.' She laughed bitterly. 'She won't notice the difference. Longer term … well, the house will have to be sold and then we can go our separate ways. It's for the best, we both know that.'

'You're right. I won't make things difficult – you're a wonderful wife and mother, Rose – it was me who screwed up.'

'No shit,' Rosemary said. 'Look, we've both been

unhappy, Nigel. But you need to change – not for me, it's way too late for that, but for your health and sanity.'

Nigel paused, nodded, and left the room to pack.

CHAPTER 54

The Bevans

To Martin's relief and gratitude, Jan had resisted saying 'I told you so' after the Hopes had left Cobalt Close owing two months' rent and a confetti of unpaid bills.

'You bent over backwards for that family,' Jan said, 'You're a good man, Martin.'

'Mug might be a better word,' he said, wondering how much a professional top to bottom clean would set him back.

'You're too soft, that's always been your trouble, but I love you for it,' Jan said, planting a kiss on Martin's cheek.

'I just hope the little one's alright.' Martin finished his tea. 'Any more toast going?'

Jan put white bread into the toaster. 'Bless that poor child – I hope his nanna will be a steady influence. Ooh Martin, sometimes I forget … *I'm* going to be a grandma in a couple of months. We'll have our own baby soon,' she said, her eyes shining.

'I know, my love. It's a shame they work so far away – I'd happily give them that house for nothing if it meant Hayley and the tot being around the corner.'

'Their lives are in Brighton, Mart. We can't expect them to up sticks … they've both got good jobs and all their friends are there. Never mind – at least we've got plenty of space and they can stay whenever they like.'

The toaster popped. ''Scuse fingers,' Jan said, handing Martin two golden slices. 'Right, you'll have to butter these, my dogs won't walk themselves,' she said, going upstairs to finish getting ready.

•

Jan checked her list; a handful of dogs needed to be exercised by lunchtime, starting with Mavis, an elderly Shih Tzu recovering from minor surgery and as such booked in for a twenty-minute walk, rather than Jan's standard hour. The little dog lived barely three minutes away, so Jan went on foot, basking in sunshine and the scent of the wisteria that climbed several neighbours' houses.

As she approached Cabbage Green, Jan spotted a familiar silhouette. At once, something about the way the woman moved signalled trouble.

The figure turned to Jan, her matronly form breaking into an ungainly trot.

'Have you seen my Alfie?' she called, her tone desperate.

'No, I haven't. What's happened?'

'Some stupid workman left our side gate open and Alfie got out when I let him into the garden this morning. He's a golden spaniel and about–'

'Yes, I know what Alfie looks like. We've met before

– we had a run-in when I was walking a customer's staffie once,' Jan said, her voice even.

'Oh! I didn't recognise you … well, I … ,' the woman blushed; she began calling the dog again.

'Where do you walk him?' Jan called out.

'I'm sorry?'

'Where do you normally walk Alfie? In the woods, or on the streets? Jan said, trying to anticipate the dog's route.

'Mostly around here. He likes to play ball on the green, you see.'

Jan hesitated. Not only had the woman's cruel words cut her to the bone months earlier, but her loose and vicious tongue had shredded Jan's reputation locally, rendering her a pariah on her own doorstep. Then Jan pictured Alfie, running scared and confused. What if he completely lost his bearings and went skittering out of Eden Hill and onto the by-pass?

'Alright. You stay here in case he comes home, and I'll look around Coopers Close via Winton Avenue where I'm dog walking shortly,' Jan said, realising there was only one course of action.

'Oh, thank you! That's so kind of you,' the woman said, adding 'I'm Heather – Heather Trinder. I live there … at number seventeen,' she pointed to a neat redbrick house where hanging baskets framed a green door. 'Alfie's my baby, you see, I couldn't bear it if–'

'We'll soon find him. I'm Jan, by the way,' Jan said, quickening her pace and rustling the packet of pungent dog-treats she always carried in her pocket.

On high alert now, Jan scanned driveways and front gardens during the short walk to Mavis's house. With the Shih Tzu attached to collar and lead, Jan dove back into the morning sun, pausing to speed-dial Martin.

'Love, it's me,' Jan said, before Martin had chance to speak. 'Remember that miserable old cow with the spaniel? The one we fell out with over Paula-the-staffie?'

'Yes, of course,' Martin waited for the punchline.

'Well, her dog got out – Alfie's done a runner,' Jan said, gently chivvying Mavis who was more interested in sniffing posts and hedges than putting one paw in front of the other.

'Righto, shall I come now then? See if we can find the little poppet,' Martin said.

Jan felt a sudden whoosh of love for her husband. 'I knew you'd say that, Mart. Meet me in Coopers Close in fifteen minutes. Bye love.'

'Good girl, Mavis,' Jan crooned as she changed the dog's water and filled her bowl with kibble, 'your mum will be back at lunchtime and I'll see you tomorrow.'

When Jan emerged into the light, Martin was waiting on the drive.

'You do look lovely,' Jan said, thinking how trim he looked in dark blue jeans and a lemon polo shirt.

Martin's eyebrows shot up. 'Do I?' he said, not used to compliments from his wife. 'Anyway, never mind that,' he said, smoothing short sandy hair, 'where's little Alfie gone?'

After debating whether to split up or stick together – and deciding on the latter – the Bevans went home for their car and drove to the next two dogs on Jan's list.

'Do you think we should call the local vet's … or even the dog warden?' Martin said, as Jan loaded two more furry charges into the back of the estate car.

'Not yet, Martin, let's just keep our eyes and ears open. He's probably enjoying himself – leading Heather-bloody-Trinder a dance. Let's swerve the woods today and take this pair back to Cabbage Green,' Jan said determined to find Alfie but wondering why it seemed quite so important to her.

Sun visor down against the glare, Martin drove while Jan attempted to quieten the two dogs in the back as they snuffled and whinnied, impatient for freedom and their morning ablutions.

'Bloody idiot … he never even looked!' Martin said, as a navy van pulled out of a side road, causing Martin to break sharply.

The van slowed to a crawl in front of them.

Martin huffed. 'He's looking for an address, isn't he? Half of these roads aren't on the SatNav.'

'Martin, look! There's Alfie,' Jan cried as a toffee-hued dog burst through a hedge and ran alongside the car before overtaking them, the whites of his eyes showing in fear and confusion. Suddenly the van turned left into a close, but Alfie kept running until a piercing yelp followed by a pathetic whimper told them that the spaniel had been hit.

The van stopped at once and the driver got out, his colour draining beneath his suntan as he started towards Alfie's inert body.

'I didn't see him, I wasn't going fast, honest … I was just looking for …' he trailed off, realising he was talking to himself.

Jan, who'd barely waited for Martin to stop before she was out of the car and running to the dog's aid, crouched beside Alfie as he whined softly.

'Where there's life, there's hope,' Jan said, ignoring the van driver. 'Martin, get the rug from the back of the car; we'll take him straight to the vets'.'

•

'It looks as though Alfie's leg is broken and he could be left with a permanent kink in his tail. But other than that, he should be fine,' Patrick the senior vet said, discarding latex gloves with a snap. 'Anyway, we've called his owner and she'll be here in a moment; thank goodness for microchips, eh?'

Just then, Heather Trinder's voice could be heard from reception: 'Oh, where's my baby,' she boomed.

The vet narrowed his eyes at Martin: 'Didn't I see you recently, with two abandoned kittens?'

'Yes,' Martin said, 'my neighbours have taken them in – dear little things they are.'

In the reception area, Mrs Trinder looked fit to collapse.

'I can't thank you enough, both of you. You saved my boy … if you hadn't been there …' she snuffled into a flowered handkerchief as tears sprang into her eyes and ran down plump, ruddy cheeks.

Jan smiled. 'Anybody would have done the same. He'll be fine after his op,' she said.

Heather lowered her voice to a whisper. 'But that's the thing … not everybody would have put themselves out, especially after the way I treated you. I'm terribly sorry; when Alfie's recovered, would you like to come for a walk … meet some of the girls?'

'I'd like that a lot,' Jan said.

CHAPTER FIFTY-FUCKING-FIVE

The Wildes

Lisa paced the kitchen reciting her To-Do list under her breath.

Tanya sighed. 'For god's sake, Leese; you'll wear the floorboards out. Honestly, I don't know why you're so stressed. It's just a birthday party and it's only a few years since you organised a festival for hundreds of people, so this should be a breeze.'

Lisa pursed her lips. 'That was different. I had loads of help … remember that event company I used?'

Tanya snorted; 'Yes, and you fired them because they were useless *and* expensive – not a good combination.'

'I just want everything to be perfect, you know? Fifty-five is a big deal and Ben's been dreading it – although I don't know why, he gets better with age,' Lisa pouted.

'Well, so do you. Babe, did you see the doctor? After … you know … what we talked about?'

'No, not yet. Anyway, I feel great now,' Lisa lied, scrolling through her phone for the catering company's number, 'I'll go next week, when all this is over.'

'Well make sure you do – there's a lot they can do for the meno–'

'Uh-uh! We are not talking about the 'M' word today … I've got too much else to think about.' Lisa shut down her friend abruptly and missed the look of hurt on Tanya's face.

Tanya shrugged. 'Okay. Well, as I seem to be in the way I'll get out of your hair.'

'Okay, hon – see you tomorrow,' Lisa said, barely looking up as Tanya let herself out.

•

Weeks of hardcore planning were finally coming together. The caterers had been booked and briefed in the minutest of detail; the cake company had created a twelve-inch sponge, iced to look like a vinyl version of Ben's latest album; the decorations had been squirrelled away in the garage all week, and next-door Rosemary's utility room bulged with beer, wine, champagne, and a choice of specialist gins – all ready to chill in vast rubber buckets courtesy of the caterers.

The sixty or so guests were under strict instructions to arrive at seven o'clock sharp; any earlier and they'd be under Lisa's feet, any later and it would be tough keeping Ben out of the house. He was already suspicious.

'Oh, go on, babe – tell me what's going on,' he'd wheedled, 'I hate bloody surprises.'

'Ben, I told you, I've invited the neighbours round

for drinks – oh, and Tanya. I didn't think you'd want a fuss at your age,' Lisa joked, dodging a playful slap.

Ben made a face. 'Oh, a-ha-*ha*! You're hilarious. Just wait until it's your turn, Leese – we're all going in the same direction.'

Ignoring Ben's comment Lisa continued to throw him off the scent: 'I just hope the forecast's right for a change, be nice to sit in the garden with a glass of bubbly.'

'Yeah … smashing – can't wait,' Ben said.

Rick had proved a worthy ally, commandeering Ben for twenty-four hours prior to the party.

Lisa had feigned surprise and annoyance when Ben, treading carefully, had pitched the plan.

'So, Rick's only gone and put an offer on a house … in bloody Glastonbury of all places,' he paused, 'should suit him down to the ground … he's always been an old hippy … joint in one hand, guitar in the other. Thing is babe, he needs a wingman. He's never had that sort of cash before and he's scared to commit. Anyway, the daft sod's booked a viewing at noon on my birthday, and it's a bugger of a drive so I'll be away overnight. Don't worry though, gorgeous – I'll be back early evening.'

'Well that was thoughtless of your so-called best mate,' Lisa said, her back to Ben as she appeared to be concentrating hard on chopping salad for lunch.

Ben nodded, 'Yeah, well, sensitivity has never been Ricky's strong point.'

•

'I'll drive, mate – give the DB7 a blast,' Ben said, taking the keys down from their hook.

Rick grinned. 'I was hoping you'd say that … don't fancy slumming it in mine when the beast is at our disposal.'

Ben unlocked the car with a satisfying *voomp* and paused before entering, enjoying the pleasurable fizz in his gut. Money was a funny thing; it came, and it went. The trick was to enjoy it while it lasted. The Aston Martin had lost none of its lustre for being a teenager and had been a present to Ben from Ben after the tour.

He'd dared to hope that Lisa would find it a turn-on and had imagined them getting hot and heavy down some deserted country lane, but his hopes of that ever happening were fading faster than a tan in January; they barely even fucked in the bedroom these days. Lisa was too antsy about everything; about being too fat, too hot, too tired – it was becoming a drag.

Rick pushed his seat back and stretched his legs with a sigh. 'Is the missus alright about us heading west?' he said, as if reading Ben's mind.

'I don't think she's too impressed with your timing,

mate. Don't know if you realise, but it's my birthday tomorrow. I'll be fifty-fucking-five. She's having the neighbours round in the evening, not that I give a shit; boring gits, the lot of them. Hey, you should come.'

Rick snorted. 'Thanks! You sold that really well. Anyway, don't be like that … let Lisa have her little 'do'. You know the saying, Benny; happy wife, happy life.' He paused, 'I hear Jules has got a new bloke in tow – a mechanic. I hope he makes her happy … I never did.'

'Oh, don't get all wistful on me,' Ben said, joining the M20 and manoeuvring into the fast lane. 'Look, there's no shame in being single and it's not like you've had no action, is it?'

Ben could feel Rick studying his profile. 'You mean to tell me that you'd swap life with the lovely Lisa for a bit of freedom?' Rick said, incredulous.

'No, of course not. I love her to bits. It's just … you know … things can get a bit … stale.'

'*Stale*? Well how does that work then? We've been on tour for months and we're back on the road in September,' Rick said.

Ben took his left hand from the wheel and rubbed his stubble. 'Yeah … about that; I haven't told her. I'm waiting for the right moment. Lisa was so weird about the last tour … clingy … you know? Here, this'll make you laugh; she thinks there's something between me and Ruby.'

Rick grimaced. 'Well is there?'

'Do you have to ask? Course not! We're mates, end of. I thought you fancied her anyway.'

'She knocked me back – and it wasn't subtle,' Rick shuddered at the memory.

Ben grinned. 'Maybe you're getting old … losing your touch. Or perhaps Ruby's complicated – and there's stuff you don't know.' He changed the subject: 'Anyway, never mind that – tell me more about this house we're seeing tomorrow …'

•

The Saturday of Ben's birthday dawned with a weak yellow haze. It had rained during the night and mist hovered above Lisa's lawn.

Deciding it was too early to call Ben and wish him a Happy Birthday, Lisa put on sweats and trainers then walked Nellie around the streets of Eden Hill, enjoying the solitude and the honeyed scent of the hedgerows.

At Ben's insistence, Saturdays were often gym-free but after walking Nellie, Lisa drove to their club intent on a gruelling workout, mindful of the sleek dress she'd be wearing that evening.

Tanya was already there, lifting hand-weights in

front of a wall of mirrors, her coltish limbs encased in black lycra, her long mane diminished by a tight bun.

Lisa felt a pang of guilt, remembering how she'd all but dismissed her friend the day before.

The women's eyes met in the mirror. 'Hello gorgeous,' Lisa said.

Tanya's smile was tight.

Lisa tried again: 'Tan, I'm sorry I was so stressed yesterday … you're right – it's just a party and what will be, will be.' She put out her arms to hug her friend.

Tanya wrinkled her nose. 'Ooh, I'm all sweaty. Hon, it's fine, honestly. Fancy training together now you're here?' she said, relenting to Lisa's embrace.

•

Ben came to a stop outside the gates of Regents Square, his route blocked by myriad parked cars.

'What's going on? Is this what I think it is?' he asked Rick, who was miming innocence.

A tanned twenty-something man in skinny black jeans and a crisp polo shirt strode over to the car. 'Welcome home, Mr Wilde,' he said as Ben lowered his window, 'allow me to park for you, Mrs Wilde is waiting in the garden.'

'Well don't look at me,' Rick said, trying not to laugh at Ben's obvious discomfort as he checked his reflection in the rear-view mirror.

'You sly git! You knew about this, didn't you? Have I just driven hundreds of miles for a ruse? What about the house we looked at?'

Rick raised his hands in submission. 'Okay, you got me … but the house is for real, only … I already bought it. Come on, be a good boy and make your missus happy,' Rick said, putting an affectionate arm round his friend's shoulders.

•

'You bad girl, Lisa Wilde,' Ben said, a huge grin lighting up his handsome face, 'you know I hate surprises.'

'Happy Birthday, darling,' Lisa hugged Ben before handing him a glass of champagne.

Ben scanned the rows of eager faces; a sea of suntans, white teeth and shining eyes – all turned upon him. For a moment, Ben felt humble, moved, as people surged forward to congratulate him.

'Thank you, babe,' Ben mouthed to Lisa as he accepted hugs, kisses, fist bumps and be-bowed gifts from a seemingly unending line of friends and family.

•

Unable to stand another minute of listening to Rita complaining about her bunions, Rosemary gratefully escaped to the loo, taking Iris with her.

'But I don't need to go, Mummy,' Iris said in her

high, clear voice as Rosemary dragged her into the house.

Once inside Lisa's fragrant cloakroom, Rosemary took a deep breath. 'You can do this,' she whispered to her reflection, 'for Lisa.'

'Are any children coming?' Iris asked as they walked back to the party, 'or is it just old people?'

Rosemary stifled a giggle, 'Hey, don't say that – you mean adults, sweetpea.'

'Is Daddy coming later?' Iris said, her eyes wide.

'Darling, I've already told you, Daddy's working away for a while, he's very busy.'

'My friend Nancy's mum said that, but her daddy never came back and now they're divorced.'

'Ssshh ... don't say that either, for goodness' sake. Come on, let's get something to eat, the food looks lovely.' *Out of the mouths of babes*, thought Rosemary, desperate to change the subject.

She wanted to tell Lisa that Nigel had left – that she'd thrown him out – but it would have to keep. An extravagant birthday party was not the time or place. Then Lisa was beside her, offering a plate of cheese straws.

'You alright, Rose?' Lisa said, 'Well done for dodging Mum. I was just about to rescue you when you went inside.'

'Oh, I just needed the loo – your mum's lovely,' Rosemary said.

Lisa rolled her eyes. 'Ha! A ray of sunshine my mother is not. Hey, where's Nigel? Is he coming later?'

Rosemary hesitated; faced with a direct question she was reluctant to lie. 'Sweetpea, can you please get Mummy a napkin ... look, over there,' Rosemary said, despatching Iris out of earshot before telling Lisa that Nigel had left and would not be coming back.

'Jesus, Rose – that's awful, I'm so sorry. Are you okay? Look, I'll pop round tomorrow when this is all over and we can have a proper chat,' Lisa promised.

The two women locked eyes for a moment, before Ben stole up on them with Steve and a man he introduced as 'Gibbo'.

'Lads; have I got a gorgeous wife, or what?' Ben said, putting an arm around Lisa, and absently grazing her right breast.

'Stunning,' Gibbo said, 'and even more gorgeous in the flesh. Oh, yeah. I remember ... I was a County fan. Tragic the way your husband died,' he droned, oblivious to Lisa's discomfort.

'Hey,' Steve said, pointing to two new arrivals, 'There's Ruby. Ruby Stone!' he bellowed, 'get your pert little arse over here.'

Lisa's face froze. Who had invited Ruby? She'd deliberately left her off the guest list.

'Ruby, great to see you,' Ben was all smiles as he

hugged her, before letting out a playful growl in appreciation of her close-fitting black jumpsuit.

Lisa, who'd been happy enough with her scarlet dress, now felt safe and suburban beside the younger woman.

Ruby smiled. 'Hi Lisa, this is Dominique,' she indicated the woman beside her whose white-blonde urchin-cut hair, deep tan and short canary yellow sundress had already caught the attention of most men present.

Rick joined the group; he kissed Ruby. 'Talent's arrived,' he grinned, adding, 'glad you could make it, girls. Did my directions help?'

Lisa scowled. So, Rick was the culprit. Then again, he wasn't to know. Her issue with Ruby was her own private hell.

Lisa walked to the bar, plucked a glass of champagne and drained it in three swallows. 'Another, please,' she asked the startled barman, who obliged at once. No way would she let Ruby and her stylish friend ruin Ben's big day.

By now, the sun had dipped behind the poplar trees beyond Lisa's garden and the light was a soft rose gold. DJ Jeff (who came highly recommended by Tanya) was playing a blend of Ibiza chillout and old school dance music, and the buzz of laughter and conversation swelled as loosened by alcohol, guests chatted and flirted with people they'd never met before.

Lisa spotted Martin and Jan sitting with a teenage boy she recognised. A woman – dark haired, lean and watchful – hovered beside them. Narrowing her eyes, she saw that it was Chloe from the local coffee shop. Why had *she* come? Not that it mattered, Lisa knew hardly anyone; a penalty of meeting Ben so late in life, she thought wistfully. She'd snaffled Ben's address book and had secretly sent out dozens of invitations by text, email and post. Ruby Stone had been deliberately omitted and yet here she was, drinking Lisa's champagne and nuzzling up to her husband.

To Lisa's dismay, she saw that an exclusive club had formed as Ben, Rick and Steve and now Ruby and Dominique seemed to communicate in some muso, Bohemian shorthand that only they knew. People were openly staring at them now and the air around them quivered with expectation.

Lisa felt something rotten twist within her. She walked unsteadily to the bar. 'Fill me up, please,' she said before drinking deeply.

•

'Mum, this is so cool – can you believe we're here? I mean, at Ben Wilde's actual birthday party?' Jake enthused.

Chloe laughed and shook her head. 'Not really, no. Weird to think I've got all his albums. Anyway, I thought you didn't like my music ... you never used to.' She smoothed Jake's hair with sudden affection; it was soft and clean, back to its natural colour.

'Yeah, it was something Dylan said that made me realise *all* musicians are amazing – and the thing about Ben,' Jake said, quoting his friend, 'is that he writes all his own material – and he can play keyboards *and* guitar, as well as sing. The guy's a genius!'

'Praise indeed, Jake,' Martin said, beaming. 'Why don't we go and say hello – you too, Chloe – Ben's very down to earth ... completely normal actually.'

Chloe was unconvinced. 'Won't he mind? We've kind of gate-crashed, haven't we?'

'Not at all. I invited you and he'll remember Jake from–' Martin stopped talking and shot Jake a look.

'What? Have I missed something?' Chloe said.

Jake's cheeks flushed. 'Mum ... it's nothing. I'll tell you another time ...'

'You can tell me now, please,' Chloe put her hands on her hips and waited.

Jake chewed his lip. 'Mum, you remember on New Year's Eve, when you ... when I was upset about Caleb? Well, I slipped and fell ... on the road ... and Ben and Martin were there ...'

Martin nodded in support.

'Anyway, we ended up at Ben's house – and he

made us all tea and toast. Mum, he's really kind and his wife's nice, too.'

Chloe gaped. 'Bloody hell, Jake. And you didn't think to mention any of this?'

'The lad was a bit embarrassed, I expect,' Jan said, patting Chloe's arm.

Chloe gave Jake a warning look. 'We'll talk about this later,' she said.

•

Clicking his fingers and walking in time to the music – a 70s funk standard that everyone seemed to know – Martin edged his way into the clique that had formed, altering its dynamic.

'Ben, someone wants to say hello. Do you remember Jake?' he asked.

'Yes, of course. How are you son? You're looking well … taller, too.' Ben said.

Jake blushed. 'I'm good thanks … doing my GCSEs at the moment – it's going okay. This is my mum by the way.'

Chloe put out her hand. 'Hi, I'm Chloe. Lovely to meet you, Ben. The last album was brilliant … they all are actually.'

'Yeah? Cool,' Ben said, 'Hey, do you want to meet the band?' he introduced Rick and Steve. 'Jake plays guitar as well,' Ben added to Jake's horror.

'He's a good-looking lad,' Rick said, 'should I be worried about my job, Benny?'

Jake knew that they were playing with him now, massaging his teenage ego, but it felt good – quite possibly the best moment of his life so far. He couldn't wait to tell Dylan.

'Tell you what … hold up,' Ben disappeared into the house and returned moments later, a guitar held aloft in each hand. He thrust the smaller one into Jake's arms. 'Fancy a jam?'

Jake beamed, wondering if he was in a parallel universe.

•

Feeling frumpy in her dress – despite its vibrant colour – Lisa changed into skinny black jeans and a shimmering halter neck that showcased her cleavage. *She* could do rock-chick style, too; perhaps Ben needed reminding. After a spritz of perfume and a dab of lip-gloss, Lisa returned to the party. To her annoyance, nobody noticed her entrance.

DJ Jeff was on a break, drinking Bud from a bottle and sorting his twelve-inch collection. Now the party had a different soundtrack – that of acoustic guitars, as all eyes were on Ben and the serious-faced teenager that Lisa now recognised as Jake; pink with pleasure, the tip of his tongue protruded with concentration.

'What have I missed?' Lisa said in Martin's ear.

'Hello lovely. Oh, you've changed,' Martin said, copping an eyeful of Lisa's breasts and looking away in case Jan noticed. 'Young Jake's quite a fan of your husband's, bless him.'

'Great,' Lisa pouted, 'yes, everybody loves Ben.' She walked away and got herself another drink, wobbling slightly on her heels.

'Right. Give me that,' Rick said, taking Ben's guitar from him; he turned to Jake. 'Do you know Happy Birthday, mate?'

The delighted onlookers giggled as Jake admitted he'd never played it before, but he'd join in regardless. Then Lisa watched in horror as everyone sang Happy Birthday, accompanied by a beaming Rick and a hesitant Jake.

Lisa swallowed the bile rising in her throat. This was all wrong! She'd planned to say a few words, then lead the singing as one of the catering team carried out Ben's beautiful cake, its fifty-five candles flickering in the dusk.

Above the tuneless tipsy warbling, Ruby's voice was clear and strong, holding each phrase. How *dare* she draw attention to herself like that, Lisa thought, fury building.

As Happy Birthday neared its crescendo, Lisa signalled for one of the serving staff to present the cake, then taking a deep breath, she marched up to Ruby. 'Can I have a word?'

Ruby's smile vanished.

'I'm only going to say this once,' Lisa's eyes blazed, 'leave my husband alone.'

Ruby's nostrils flared. 'You've got that wrong, Lisa. I've no designs on Ben.'

The singing had finished and there was a lull in the conversation as people began to eavesdrop.

'I mean it – you stay away from him. I know all about your cosy set up on tour. I've seen enough bloody photos to prove it,' Lisa said quietly.

Ben was beside Lisa now, his face dark. 'What's going on, Leese?'

'Ask your girlfriend. I've had enough,' Lisa hissed.

'Babe, you've got it wrong, I promise you … it's not–' Ben started.

'Not what I think? No, it never is … do I *look* like I was born yesterday? She's been all over you like a rash since she arrived.'

Ruby flashed Ben a desperate look. 'Don't go there, Lisa. As Ben said, you've made a mistake. Why don't you sober up and speak to him about it – *in private*,' Ruby said, with emphasis.

'Liars!' Lisa shouted.

Dominique put a protective arm in front of Ruby. 'Rubes, are you going to tell the silly cow, or am I?' she said.

'Be my guest, babe,' Ruby said, giving Lisa a look of contempt.

'You see, Lisa,' Dominique began, 'Ben's not really Ruby's type. I am. Yeah, that's right. We're a couple. Thanks for outing us, though. Bitch.'

Lisa said nothing, her mouth a silent 'O'.

'Happy Birthday, Ben. Sorry for the scene – *very* un-cool,' Ruby said over her shoulder as the two women stalked away, heels clacking, heads held high.

In the silence that followed, Lisa watched the cake being borne towards the huddle of stunned guests, her cheeks blazing as hotly as its candles.

'Nice,' Ben said, sticking his index finger into the frosting and licking it, 'now who's for a piece of cake?'

CHAPTER 56

The Wildes

Lisa swallowed two paracetamol and prayed for the hammering in her head to stop. It was hard to say which had sickened her more; the copious amount of alcohol she'd guzzled or her own reckless behaviour.

Ben fumed. 'I never thought I'd say this, Leese, but having women fight over me was not pretty. Acting like a mad woman – Jesus! You know, what gets me is that you're the only woman I've ever been totally faithful to. I may be your knight in tarnished armour – but it's me, Sir Laugh-a-lot. I can't believe you thought I'd risk everything we've got for a fling.'

'Darling, I'm so sorry,' Lisa said, trying to ignore the spin cycle in her stomach.

Ben snorted. 'Yeah, so you said. Look, I don't want to row with you, so I'll be at Steve's for a couple of days until we both cool off.'

'Ben, please don't go,' Lisa said, panic rising in her voice. 'I made a terrible, embarrassing mistake – and you could have stopped me. Did you know that Ruby's gay?'

Ben paused. 'I did, as it goes. But she's not out yet and it wasn't my secret to tell, was it?' He sighed heavily. 'So thanks for that – now the whole world will know, whether she's ready or not.'

'Ben, darling, I'm so sorry,' Lisa repeated, 'please forgive me.'

'I need some space,' Ben said, moving past her.

Then Lisa watched from an upstairs window as Ben, weekend bag in hand, got into his car and drove away.

'Oh, Nellie … what have I done,' Lisa lay on the bed and sobbed into the little dog's fur.

After what could have been three minutes or three hours according to Lisa's perception, the doorbell rang.

Loath to see anyone with her eyes and nose red from weeping, but in dire need of a friendly face, Lisa was surprised to see Rosemary.

'Oh! Rose – it's you. I thought it might be Tanya.'

'I wanted to check you were okay … I saw Ben leaving and I just thought … after yesterday … Lisa are you alright?'

Lisa's chin wobbled. 'No …' she whispered, waving her neighbour in.

In the kitchen, party debris remained; glasses to be hand-washed, plates of savoury snacks still covered in clingfilm – and the ruins of the cake that Lisa had so lovingly planned and designed. In the garden furniture was strewn about, and a handful of helium balloons mocked from the trees.

Lisa blew her nose. 'Sorry, Rose' she sniffed, 'you've got problems of your own. I don't want to dump on you ... I just can't believe the way I wrecked everything.'

'Lisa, listen to me. Ben will get over this – he loves you ... any fool can see you're mad about each other. He's just a bit embarrassed that's all.'

'*He's* embarrassed – my god, Rose, I acted like a crazy woman. It's early menopause ... at least I think it is, I'm having blood tests done next week to confirm it.'

'Bless you; we've all got that coming, girl,' Rosemary said.

Lisa composed herself. 'I'm sorry, I need to pull myself together. I was going to knock for you today anyway. Please, tell me what happened with you and Nigel.'

SEPTEMBER

Ben gulped the last of his coffee and placed his cup in the sink beside a modest pile of washing up. He looked around; the kitchen shone less brightly these days, but it was better this way.

In the hallway, he re-counted the number of bags by the front door, checking the side pocket of the smallest for his passport and boarding card.

Ben paced. The house was eerily silent now, except for the squeak of his trainers as he waited for his car to arrive.

It felt weird leaving an empty house – but he'd get used to it.

His mobile shuddered in his jeans pocket. 'Hello … yeah, I'm just waiting to be picked up. What are you up to?'

'I'm about to book Rupert Dale's London trip for the annual BAAPS conference next month,' Lisa said.

Ben sniggered. He knew it stood for the British Association of Aesthetic Plastic Surgeons, but it still made him laugh. Maybe all those boob jobs had rubbed off on the regulator when they'd tried to come up with a name.

'Child!' Lisa admonished. 'Darling, you're okay with me not waving you off, aren't you? Even Nellie's at auntie Jan's while I'm at work.'

'Yeah, I'm fine with it, babe. You've got a job to do. Besides, it's only Benelux this time … nine dates, and I'll be back before you know it. Leese, you're happier when you're working. It's great that you're busy and back to your old self again.'

'You're right, I missed this place. Hey, I've got to go, I can hear Rupert calling me. Safe flight, darling. Call me when you land. Love you.'

'Love you too, Leese.' Ben ended the call, just as a blacked-out SUV pulled onto the drive.

'Give me a hand with these, mate,' he asked the suited driver.

'Sure,' the driver said, easily managing three of Ben's bags at once and loading them into the boot. He hesitated. 'You're Ben Wilde, aren't you? My wife's got all your albums.'

THE END

ACKNOWLEDGEMENTS

Much love and sincere thanks go to my wonderful partner Mark Payton; to Ali and Rob Gooderham, David Harvey and Lyn Beer; to cousins Helen Crookes, Carol Bage and Linda Millard: I hit the jackpot when families were being handed out. Thanks to Sam and Phil Rice; to Jo, Sue, Lucy, Terri, Jane, Jo, Mandy and Priya; to Marika Cooke and all the Kings Hill Super-Women and dog-walkers for their support and encouragement. Many thanks to Matthew Smith at Urbane for allowing me to continue the Eden saga – and to several fellow Urbaneites for their kind support; Kelly Florentia, you rock – thank you. Thank you to the Romney Marsh teaching community for advice and guidance concerning Jake's delayed exams.

Finally, I dedicate this book to my wonderful and much missed parents, David and Gwen, whose regular admonishments of 'calm down and read a book' turned out to be brilliant advice.

For almost thirty years Beverley Harvey worked in the communications industry, initially in advertising and later in PR, before becoming a freelance consultant in 2001.

Beverley (Bev to her friends) then swapped PR campaigns for plot lines and completed her first novel Seeking Eden in 2017, also published by Urbane Publications Limited.

Beverley lives in Sussex.

Before **Eden Interrupted** there was …

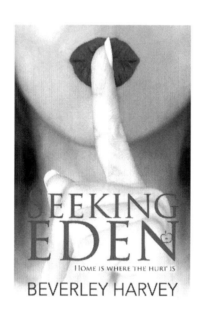

SEEKING EDEN

HOME IS WHERE THE HURT IS

BEVERLEY HARVEY

'50 is the new 30 – haven't you heard?' Or so says Ben Wilde's record producer on the eve of his comeback. If only Ben could win back ex-girlfriend, Kate, he'd be a happy man. But married Kate has moved on, and moved out – to Eden Hill, a quiet housing estate in the suburbs. Lonely and homesick for London, can Kate resist ego-maniac Ben's advances and save her own flagging marriage? Streets away, Kate's new friend Lisa, a Chihuahua toting ex-WAG, is primed for a fresh start – until her footballer ex-husband is found dead and she is vilified in the gutter press. But Kate, Lisa and Ben aren't the only ones having a midlife crisis; local shop owner Martin dreams of escaping his dutiful marriage and develops an unhealthy obsession with Lisa and her friends in Eden Hill. Alongside a colourful cast of friends and family, Kate, Lisa, Ben and Martin are living proof that older does not always mean wiser because in Eden Hill, there's temptation around every corner.

AVAILABLE NOW ON AMAZON AND FROM ALL GOOD BOOKSHOPS.

Urbane
PUBLICATIONS

Urbane Publications is dedicated to
developing new author voices, and publishing
books that challenge, thrill and fascinate.

From page-turning thrillers to literary debuts,
our goal is to publish what YOU want to read.

Find out more at
urbanepublications.com